AUTO NO MO US

Saturday

Christopher L. Truxaw

Auto No Mo Us

Part Two
Saturday
May 27, 2056

Christopher L. Truxaw

Self-published by the Author.
Christopher L. Truxaw
Santa Ana, California
www.autonomousbooks.com

ISBN: 979-8-9922584-2-4 (Paperback)

Format generated:
Friday, May 8, 2026 (Minor edits)

Table of Contents

Chapter 1

Saturday Midnight to Sunrise

12:10 AM, Elsie and Emily

Andre had fallen asleep, and Elsie was ready to get some sleep herself, but first she wanted to check on baby Alex. She passed Emily's room on the way and heard her talking to someone. She knocked and asked, "You still awake, Emily?"

"It's the weekend and school's out. Of course I'm still awake."

"We need to talk about staying safe around strangers."

"I know. I know, mom. But now? You sound tired. Go to bed. How about tomorrow?"

"Okay. Tomorrow."

Elsie continued to Alex's room, walking through the room and tiptoeing into the docked Abitat where she found Alex sleeping soundly. Elsie tiptoed back into the hallway.

"Good night, Emily," she said quietly as she passed Emily's door again heading back to her own bed.

"Good night, Mom," said Emily through the door. "We can talk tomorrow."

Elsie paused at the door to listen as Emily continued her conversation.

"What's that about?" asked Chandra.

"Just my mom. She's weirded out about me giving a ride to Sam and Jo-Jo. Stranger danger and all that."

"I thought they were old friends, not strangers."

"My friends, not my mom's."

"Oh. Okay. Yeah. I can see how your mom might not understand that. You should be careful around old people who you don't know through school or family."

Elsie was pleased that Emily's friend seemed to be giving reasonable advice. She continued on to her own bed.

Meanwhile Emily and Chandra continued, or an animated Pink Panda and White Tiger continued a conversation in an animated jungle world on Emily's tablet.

"But Chandra, they are kind of like family," said the panda.

"Yeah. You've known them for a while now. But it could have been dangerous at first if they were bad people," scolded the tiger.

"But. You know. Can you keep a secret?" asked the panda.

"You know me," replied the tiger.

"I knew I would be safe with them because they were with Brock. If they were his friends I knew they would be okay," whispered the panda.

"Who's Brock?" asked the tiger.

"He's one of the guys that lives in the creek by my dad's place."

"How many old, unhoused people did you hang out with? Em. That doesn't seem like a good idea."

"I didn't hang out with them. They helped me find biology samples in the creek at first and I just talked to them sometimes, and Brock would lend me books."

"It sounds like they were grooming you. It doesn't sound good," growled the tiger.

"No. No. There's a secret."

"That doesn't sound good either. Did they do things to you?"

"No. No. The secret is Brock is my dad," whispered the panda.

"What?" The tiger's mouth hung open.

"My first dad."

"What? How many dads do you have?"

"Two or three. My mom and dad got together when they thought my first dad died, but they never talked about him. I was little then. No one talks about it. Later my mom left my dad for Andre. I guess I have two dads and one stepdad."

"I don't understand. Your first dad died, but he didn't die?"

"Yeah. I found him living in the creek with Sam and Jo-Jo and Doug four or five years ago. That was like four or five years after he died. I didn't recognize him as my dad for a long time, but he seemed really familiar. He acts like he doesn't recognize me, but he also acts kinda like a dad, wanting to talk about books, so maybe he really does recognize me. I don't know. Hey. What's this? I just found a new challenge orb! I need to solve this. See you at *The Theme Park* when they open tomorrow?"

"Okay. You and your puzzle challenges. Good luck."

The tiger disappeared into the jungle while the panda retrieved a rainbow-colored orb from under a bush and began examining and manipulating it.

12:20 AM, A Handful of Stars

Tim had his Abitat leave the highway and head down a dark desert side road. It stopped about a quarter mile from the highway when it came to a low spot with standing water. He got out and tried to check the depth of the water to see if his Abitat could cross. Light rain was still falling on him, but he could see some breaks in the clouds in the east with a few bright stars shining through. He couldn't tell how deep the water was, so he let the Abitat move to the side of the road and stay there overnight while he went inside and tried to sleep.

12:25 AM, No Stars

Jo-Jo awoke and went outside the shed. She missed sleeping in her Abitat bed and especially missed having use of her Abitat's bathroom. Sergey always said they could use his bathroom, but she didn't want to bother him. He also mentioned that there were a couple of outhouses at the other end of the avocado orchard for the day laborers that often work at the farm. She didn't want to walk that far. After peeing in the bushes, she stood in the middle of the basketball court between the shed, the barn and Sergey's house.

Staring up, she hoped to see some stars. The rain had stopped, but there were still too many clouds, and probably too much light from the houses in the surrounding neighborhoods. She stood still and listened. Two owls somewhere nearby hooted to one another. A large opossum crossed one end of the court, ignoring her and heading towards the orchards and gardens down the hill.

12:30 AM, Searching in the Dark

Scott was alone in a glowing snow globe, a bubble of light and swirling snow, surrounded by darkness and cold. He repositioned the light stands on either side of the trail, trying to illuminate the area around the rocks and trees on the slopes above and below the trail, enlarging his light bubble. A taut climbing tape secured to a log next to the trail extended down the slope to the side of the trail, disappearing in the edges of the glow. The light, diffused by falling snow and reflecting off collections of snow in tree branches or on top of rocks, provided nearly full daylight brightness in the center of the bubble on the trail itself, but made it difficult for Scott to see into the distance off of the trail. He looked downward following the climbing tape's descent trying to detect motion below. The tape moved slightly to one side.

"Nita, Do you see anything down there?" No answer. He tapped his earpiece to make sure it was working. "Nita? Are you there?"

"Sorry, Scott. I was just busy for a second there. It doesn't look like anyone fell here, but I found something sticking out of the snow. Something plastic. It was partly buried, under snow and leaves. I had to reposition myself to uncover it without letting it fall further down the slope."

"Okay. What did you find?"

"Turns out, nothing important. An old plastic bag with someone's shit and TP. They must have tossed it down the slope from the trail. It looks like it's months old. Definitely not something from the last 24 hours. Should I bring it out?"

"Cleaning up plastic waste is always good, but not our primary mission. You decide."

"I hate to leave something like this. How about I dump the contents and bring the plastic bag out?"

"You decide."

"Oh, my god! That is the worst smell. I never should have opened the plastic bag. This is disgusting. I'm sticking it back under a rock and coming up. Oh my god!"

"I'll make a note that there is some trash in this area. But no signs of anyone going off trail here recently?"

"Nothing I could see. False alarm. I'm coming back up," said Nita. "Could you dim that light shining down this way. It's blinding."

"Sure thing." Scott tilted the light on one light stand so that it shined up into the trees instead of down the side slope. Then he twisted a dial on the back of the light stand and it dimmed. "How's that?" he asked.

"Much better."

Scott picked up the other light stand and pointed it further up the trail and then turned it around and shined it back down the trail where they had come from, before dimming it as well. In the much dimmer light, he could see a faint glow across the valley. One of the other search teams was still pretty close on another branch of the trail. Probably just a couple hundred yards or so. He listened but didn't hear anything from the other team. The snow muffled all sounds.

He pulled out his tablet and checked the search status from the three other teams before sending an update back to Sarah. No signs of the missing hikers so far. Between the four search teams in the first two hours they had searched a combined distance of about a mile of trails so far. It was very slow-going, checking to the side of the trail everywhere there was some sign of trash or indications someone could have gone off trail. Maybe they should try to cover more distance and not search off trail quite so much. He looked at the map of the trail ahead. As the trail became steeper, they would probably have fewer side searches. That might allow them to cover more distance. He slid the tablet back into to his pack.

A young woman in a parka and wearing a fuzzy cap with lights shining to the front and sides of her head climbed back up onto the trail, disconnected her safety clip from the climbing tape, and unwrapped the tape from the log. Scott shaded his eyes from the bright head lamps and Nita tilted them down. Scott realized his own head lamps were also too bright, and he tilted them down as well.

"Let's keep going," Scott said. He picked up one of the light stands and collapsed its legs before clipping it on his pack. Nita did the same with the other light stand. They put on their packs and started forward.

"I smell what you were talking about," said Scott.

"I know. How can anything smell that bad? I think I got some on my gloves!!" Nita replied.

"I'll take the lead. You hold back a few paces, okay?"

"Yeah. I know."

12:45 AM, In Total Darkness

Bella tried to blink her eyes but saw only darkness. Was she alive or dead? She rubbed her closed eyelids and saw red glow where she rubbed.

Maybe she was alive. She took a deep breath and tried to sleep. A vision, dream, or memory appeared.

<u>W1v01, 5/26/2056, 4:24 PM</u>

Bella took one look at the broken rocks partly covered by snow on the ground and the cracks in the rocky wall above and said, "You're right, Bobbie. It doesn't look safe here. Let's move the tent as far away as we can from this rockfall area."

They dragged the tent to the farthest edge of the clearing and began to remove its contents and take it down, when a deafening crack and rumble sounded. A set of rocks broke free and tumbled down, crushing the spot where the tent had been, spreading dust over them, and scattering small and medium sized rocks onto their tent. They stood next to the trees looking at the cloud of dust spreading over the new pile of rocks in the clearing.

"That was too close. We should pack up and look for another level spot away from any rock walls," Bella said.

Bobbie said, "I agree. You stand farther back in the trees while I pack up the gear."

Before they could back away another boulder rolled out of the dust cloud and over the both of them, knocking down trees.

That vision dissolved and Bella opened her eyes to pitch blackness again. She thought "Now I'm dreaming in AM game alternative versions mode? Shit. I need to stop playing it so much. Watch out what you ask for. I probably won't be able to play it anymore." She closed her eyes again.

1:05 AM, Searching

Scott tucked his tablet back into his pack after sending a status update to Sarah. Still no signs of the missing hikers. Snowfall had stopped for a few minutes but seemed to be picking up again. Nita was almost out of sight up the trail ahead, shining her light off to the side of the trail and waiting for him to start hiking again. She seemed to have more energy than he did. Nice to be young. He wondered if he could get his son to backpack with him this summer. Probably not. They were supposed to take a short hike together tomorrow to give him a taste of the outdoors. Now that also might not happen. He was too into games. At least he was doing well in school. Physics award? Nice. This search better be done in time to go to the awards ceremony at his school next week. He should insist on some time off for that after doing this overtime.

1:15 AM, In the Darkness

After dozing for an unknown period of time another vision materialized for Bella.

W1v02, 5/26/2056, 4:25 PM

Bella gripped the edge of a rocky ledge above her. On her wristband the time was visible. 4:25. Still a few daylight hours even if it already looked dark from the storm. She was free-climbing light. All her gear was back in the tent. She didn't intend to climb very far. She pulled herself up and peered over the ledge.

She said, "Okay. This could explain the loose rocks. There is a big hole in the wall here."

Before climbing onto the ledge she looked up, down and around. Their tent was collecting a layer of snow in the clearing behind her below, as were the trees covering the landscape beyond. Bobbie was standing just below her about 10 feet down. To her left about 40 feet along the rock wall she could barely see the climbing tape hanging down from the notch they had come over earlier. Above the hole in the wall, the rocky slope continued up a hundred feet or more, probably more. Ice was forming in some big cracks in the rocks just above the opening.

"I don't see any hole," said Bobbie.

"It's set back. The ledge blocks your view from below."

"Is it safe? Are more rocks going to fall?"

"I don't know. Some rocks probably came out of this hole. It looks manmade, like a mine or something, but there are cracks above it that look threatening. Let's move the tent away from here."

Bella backed down the way she had come, and walked quickly towards the tent, followed by Bobbie. Together they dragged the tent to the edge of the clearing but before they got it there they were deafened by a loud crack and rumble of rocks breaking and falling. They ran into the trees and looked back as rocks or various sized crushed the spot where the tent had been and partially covered the tent.

"That was too close. Do you think we can save the gear?" she said.

Bobbie said, "We'll see. The rocks on the tent aren't too big. Maybe we can roll them off, but we need to get out of this area before more rocks fall. You stay back here in the trees while I see what I can salvage."

Before Bella could back away another large boulder rolled out of the dust and over the both of them, knocking down trees.

That vision dissolved, and Bella opened her eyes to pitch blackness again. "Dark," she thought. She blinked several times and tried to sleep.

1:35 AM, Searching

Scott had been waiting while Nita checked out a side trail. Meanwhile he sent another update. Still no sign of the hikers.

Nita returned and said, "False alarm. The side trail ends after about 100 yards. Unless you want to do some rock climbing, straight up."

"No. Let's keep going on the trail," Scott pointed and waited for Nita to take the lead again. He could still smell her gloves. He waited until the smell faded before he started again.

1:40 AM, In the Darkness

After dozing for another unknown period of time another vision materialized for Bella.

> **W1v03, 5/26/2056, 4:15 PM**
>
> "I think we may want to move our tent. I was trying to warn you so you wouldn't get too comfortable."
>
> "Too late. I'm very comfortable and starting to get warm again." Bella snuggled in her bag. "I'm not moving right now. Maybe in an hour after I warm up."
>
> "Okay. Maybe it'll be fine here."
>
> A few minutes later a loud crack and rumble was immediately followed by crushing rocks, silence, and darkness.

Bella kept her eyes closed and thought to herself, "Damn, I'm pessimistic. But maybe that would have been better."

2:05 AM, Searching

Another update sent. No new signs of the hikers. Snow falling again. Stopping for coffee. Scott poured two cups from his canteen, emptying it. Nita took one. Nothing to say to one another while they sipped the coffee. Nita switched off her light and nodded to Scott to do the same. He did and they both sipped their coffee in total darkness and near total silence. They were no longer able to see any lights from other search parties. When Nita finished her coffee she turned her light back on.

2:20 AM, In the Darkness

Bella wasn't sure if she had slept. She had another dark vision:

> **W1v04, 5/26/2056, 1:48 PM**

Bobbie continued to study the map and finally looked up. She said, "I think I can see how to get back to the trail, about a mile back. Then we can keep going to the pass, or back towards the camp we left this morning, but we will need to keep checking the map as we go, to stay on track."

"Okay. Maybe we'll find a spot to camp on the way. But at least we know there's a good camping spot back there where we came from."

"The closest level spot is on the other side of the ridge above us, but I don't see any easy way to get there. The path we're on doesn't go there and it's too steep to climb up this wall." She pointed at the almost vertical wall to the right of the trail. She counted lines on the topo map, "It's about 40 feet up from here to a gap in the ridge and a little more than that down to a level spot on the other side."

Bella looked up at the wall of rock above them and said, "That's not so steep. I'm a good climber. Let me try climbing it and see if the spot on the other side is worth it."

"Don't do that," said Bobbie. "It's not safe."

Bella was tempted. She liked rock climbing, but with the snow and ice she decided to play it safe and start back towards the trail and the campsite.

Hours later they were almost to their previous campsite when they heard a loud rumble in the distance up the trail behind them.

"Sounds like thunder," said Bobbie.

"Or maybe a rockfall," said Bella.

"Glad we're not there," said Bobbie.

"Yeah. Me too," said Bella.

When they finally reached their old campsite they set up their tent on a patch of snow and collected water from the nearby stream, which was still running despite some ice forming at the edges. They huddled inside the tent and heated a meal.

"We'll just have to wait it out here," said Bella.

11

> A bear investigating the smell of food, tore open the tent and the hikers.

Bella opened her eyes again and felt around in the darkness. No bear. No sleeping bag. No tent. No gear. She felt her body. No bear wounds. Just utter darkness and a layer of dust on a hard stone surface where she sat. She felt Bobbie's back against her own.

3:05 AM, Searching

Scott and Nita turned off their lights for a minute again after he sent his next update. They didn't speak. When they continued they used hand signals and head nods to indicate the repetitious answer of nothing found. Pointing the lights and holding them in one direction for more than a couple seconds was a sign to take a look, but they kept walking slowly up the trail without speaking. The silence of the snow-muffled forest was punctuated only by the soft crunch of each of their footsteps in the snow.

3:25 AM, In the Darkness

> W1v05, 5/25/2056, 8:40 AM, The day before
>
> Bobbie said, "We're heading over the pass today, right?"
>
> Bella said, "I'm pretty sure this is the area of my dad's great fishing hole."
>
> "You've said that before. A few times."
>
> "Yeah, but this time I think it really is. I have time to search the area today and hike out tomorrow, right?"
>
> "Not if we're going to get out on schedule...."
>
> "Any reason we have to stay on schedule?"
>
> "Let me check. Well, there is a storm coming."
>
> "Really? Okay. Maybe we can hike here again next year and look for it then. Let's pack up and head out today."
>
> They made good time climbing the trail to the pass, where there was still some year-round glacial snow near some blue icy lakes near

> the top. Bella set down her pack to get a snack, and the pack started to slide on the ice. She chased it and Bobbie chased her. Pack, Bella and Bobbie all slid into the freezing water. The frozen edges of the lake were too slippery to climb out.

Bella wasn't sure if her eyes were open or shut.

3:35 AM, Searching

Scott and Nita were slowing down. Scott still checked for reports from the other search teams and sent a summary update every half hour, still with no signs of the hikers, but he was getting tired and was going slowly. Nita chose not to do as much exploring to the sides of the trail.

3:55 AM, In the Darkness

> ### W1v06, 4/02/2056, 7:15 PM, Weeks before the hike
>
> Camilla said, "Don't you go and do a MinQuest like your uncle did. It's dangerous."
>
> "No Cam-Ma. I wouldn't do that."
>
> She thought, "Not like my uncle. Mine will be different. Maybe I should be honest and tell her I am going on one. Or maybe I should just cancel it. If I'm going to have a chance to become a partner next year I probably shouldn't miss any work days this year. Yeah. I think I'll cancel it."
>
> Walking out of Cam-Ma's house to get in her Abitat, Bella looked up and saw a bright light in the sky that was growing brighter as she watched. She hurried in to her Abitat. As it pulled away from the curb it was crushed by a piece of an old Zzynarji satellite falling back to earth.

Bella wondered if she was already dead. Every version of her dreams or visions had the same end result. Even if she skipped the trip entirely. She drifted off into an uneasy sleep.

4:45 AM, At the Beach Resort

Honus didn't sleep well, worried about Isabella. He got up and looked out the window at the coastal water below which looked stormy. He would need to get some more sleep if he was going to do his surfing outing at 6.

He spoke, "Give me the latest search update." Sarah Jones-Smith, one of his construction project managers from Honus Lake Resort, was coordinating the search efforts by his teams. Part of the window glass turned translucent, and a message appeared.

> *From: Sarah Jones-Smith, 0400*
> *Theme Park Service still forbids entry to area.*
> *Four heavy-lift rigs from Honus Lake deployed.*
> *No immediate impact to construction schedule.*
> *Holiday weekend construction pause.*
> *Triple overtime for search teams approved.*
> *Teams dropped at last reported campsite at 23:05.*
> *Two rigs returned to base.*
> *Two are on high ridges providing communications.*
> *Campsite clean. No signs of recent use.*
> *Four teams of two searching trails from there.*
> *24 delivery drones reportedly dispatched giving*
> *comm signal to 95% of search area.*
> *No contact with hikers since before start of storm.*

He spoke again, "Sarah?"

After a few seconds a disembodied but sleepy voice answered, "Yes, sir."

"This is Honus."

"Yes. I know sir."

"I read your 0400 status on the search. I have a couple questions."

"Yes, sir?"

"Why aren't we using the rigs to systematically search from the air? Or at least to drop off search teams at more locations?"

"The visibility has been bad. It was very dark and the lights on our rigs were counter-productive in the blowing snow. They had to operate using old GPS devices and topographic maps to find the last campsite. No local hive reference points. It was risky dropping teams where we did. They rappelled down blindly at the coordinates of a failed delivery order sent yesterday morning."

"Are the search teams okay?"

"Yes. My husband, Scott Jones-Smith, a Honus Lake construction supervisor, is on the ground leading the searchers and making sure they are safe. He's giving me updates every 30 minutes. They have been searching since around 11 last night following trails by eyesight and GPS."

"The rangers gave the okay for the rigs to fly in?"

"Better to ask for forgiveness than to wait for permission."

"Yes. I think I've heard that somewhere before."

"We haven't told the rangers yet that we went in."

"But they must be aware?"

"I presume. They haven't complained to me about it yet, but I can see their point about construction rigs in the wilderness."

"How so?"

"There are few suitable landing sites for them. Two had to fly back to Honus Lake. The two that managed to set down for the night are on high ridges exposed to strong winds. They may have damaged some trees or caused some small rockslides."

"Not ideal. What is the plan when it gets light?"

"Our ground search continues. The storm continues. Visibility from the air is still not good but we plan to get our rigs and other vehicles airborne as soon as the visibility allows."

"Tell your Scott to be careful out there."

"Yes. Sir."

He disconnected and sent a message informing his executives that a solution was in the works for the holdout properties needed for his development on the outskirts of *The Theme Park* district. No special actions should be taken to remove the residents until further notice. He hoped that was clear enough and not too late. Someone could be showing initiative and acting without asking for permission first. He should have sent that notice yesterday right after talking with Jose.

There was something else he meant to do this morning. What was it? The history world. He sent a message to his dad through world PW3709.

PW3709: BillyJay to PWL

if you're still at the house
check out a history world I found
HW203904
any idea who made it?
see scene at 12:45 PM
looks based on in-car video of mom
she mentions birthdays
Is your birthday March 30 and hers April 3?
I thought both were in March
you probably don't remember

"No contact with hikers since before start of storm."

He didn't expect a reply at this hour, but he would get an alert if a reply was posted. Maybe he should try to sleep some more.

Sunrise

5:37 AM in the High Desert.
5:44 AM in Orange County.

Chapter 2

Saturday Sunrise to 8 AM

5:45 AM, In the Desert

Tim hadn't slept well. He needed to decide where to go. He told his Abbie to refuse to connect with any messages. His Abitat was still stopped on the side of a dirt road in the desert about a quarter mile away from the highway. As it got light he checked again on the water in the low spot in the road and decided it wasn't deep but might be too muddy to cross. He wondered if switching to an off-road chassis would flag his location to Public Safety. There were probably places to rent such rigs not too far from here. He could have one meet him here to swap. He got back in and checked on messages that had tried to reach him overnight.

Four calls from Public Safety and three from "Unknown" had been rejected. He wondered if the unknown caller might be Squeaky. He normally didn't connect with her in his own Abitat, only from work, but she probably knew how to reach him. He probably shouldn't avoid her calls for long. He could say he blocked all calls overnight so that he could sleep, and forgot to turn them back on, but that excuse would not fly for long. He felt confident that his Abitat was not reporting his location to Public Safety, since no one had showed up outside his Abitat overnight.

He tried to get news reports to see if anything had been reported about someone being killed in an Abitat near *The Theme Park*, without specifically asking about that. He didn't know if a search request could

17

be flagged by Public Safety. After a few minutes of news about the weather, sports, and holiday weekend events, but mostly about the unusual weather, he didn't hear anything related and stopped looking. He would need to head back to the highway soon.

6:00 AM, Tourists at the Beach

Minh and Max were still sleeping while Fanny leaned back in a chair next to a picnic table outside their rental Abitat and looked out at the ocean. She could get used to that view. There were still clouds in the sky, but the rain had stopped during the night. John came back from the casino with two mugs of coffee.

"Took you a while," Fanny said as she accepted a mug.

"Had to use my free casino chips to get the free coffee. I won on the first bet but lost it all on the second."

"Couldn't stop while you were ahead?" Fanny asked.

"No," John replied.

"Did you stop there? Or will we have to sell the kids?"

"I stopped there. No net loss. No kids for sale," John assured her.

"Too bad. How do you like this view? I could look at the ocean all day," Fanny said as she sipped her coffee.

"We'll see what the kids make us do. They were insisting on going to the beach." He walked closer to the edge of the bluff and looked down. He came back to say, "The sandy beach down there looks nice now, but it may be dangerous at high tide," John observed.

"Is the tide coming or going?" Fanny asked.

"There was a tide chart by the front desk. The next high tide is just before nine. We should probably go early, before it gets higher."

"Yeah. As soon as they wake up and eat breakfast. I'm surprised they're not awake yet," said Fanny, "with the time zones and all."

John said, "They had a busy day yesterday. Let's enjoy the quiet as long as it lasts."

Fanny sat up and listened. "They are really quiet. Maybe you better check and make sure they are still in there and not inside some walls in the casino."

John set down his coffee mug and tiptoed to the doorway of the Abitat, peaked in, and then tiptoed back and whispered, "It looks like they're both still asleep in there."

6:30 AM, Jeremy's House

Jeremy woke up and looked at the clock display on the wall. He closed his eyes again and rubbed them and stretched his arms over his head. Then he said, "Wait. Abbie, I told you I wanted to wake up at 6 to talk to Mom and Dad before starting back to *The Theme Park*. Why didn't you wake me up?"

"Good morning, Jeremy. Your mom cancelled that. She said to let you sleep in."

"I'm still at home?" he whined. "What time can you get me to *The Theme Park*?"

"If we left now and conditions don't change, we would get there at 9:27. But your mom wants to talk to you first."

"But I won't be able to meet Chandra and Emily when it opens at nine. I said I'd meet them."

"Talk to your mom."

"Is she even awake?"

"Yes. She's been working all night."

"Then she won't be in a good mood. How about Dad, is he awake yet?"

"He's not here. He's been at work all night."

"That's not good."

"Talk to your mom."

"Can't we just go now. I'll talk to them on the way?"

"No. Talk to your mom."

6:45 AM, Honus Heading North

Honus rode in his Abitat from the beach resort to the nearby airport and arranged to transfer the Abitat's cabin from its wheeled base to a flight-capable platform in order to fly to the Honus Lake resort and see for himself what was happening in the search for Bella. It would take a few minutes for the flight platform to be ready, so he ate breakfast while he waited.

6:55 AM, Jose Heads to Work

Jose stepped out of his trailer and made a mental note that he really needed to address the waste collecting jug that now seemed to be full. Not enough time before work, he thought. He walked across the courtyard between tiny houses when a door opened and a woman holding a cat came out.

"Good morning, Dr. Magnolia," he said.

"Good Day, Joe," she replied.

"Dr. M., It looks like the development project in the neighborhood is probably going to impact us here soon," Jose said.

"I was afraid of that. All good things come to an end."

"It might be a good thing. If we have to relocate we want to make sure they compensate everyone properly. Let me know what you need."

"A few points isn't going to make much difference. Everything is so expensive these days."

"Don't think in terms of points but the kind of space you need and location, features. Write down what you need. Can you get me something in the next day or so? And let other residents of the complex know that they should do the same."

He headed out of the complex and down the sidewalk towards work. Traffic on the street was Saturday morning light.

7:00 AM, Tourists on the Beach

Minh and Max and their parents were on the sand in front of the stairs down the cliffs below the camping village. It was still cloudy and cool, but it did not look like rain. The mom, Fanny, wore a jacket and long pants with sandals. John, the dad, wore swim trunks and a long sleeve t-shirt. The waves crashing on the beach were sizable. Minh and Max were in bathing suits and kept challenging each other to run into the water after each wave. John kept chasing them and trying to keep them out of trouble without getting too wet himself. Fanny held a bag with towels and sand toys and stood back out of range of the water flows.

"A sea monster!" shouted Max, pointing at a large clump of kelp floating and twisting in the currents of the foam washing up towards the beach. She screamed and ran away onto the drier sand. The dad watched her run and scream.

Minh, meanwhile, waded into the water waist-deep, grabbed at the kelp. He draped a bulb and its attached blades over his head. The rest of the kelp clump floated in the water around him.

"Yes! I am the sea monster! Fear me!" he shouted, looking up towards his sister on the sand.

"Minh!" shouted Max and the mom at the same time.

An unexpected wave broke close to the shore and surged shoulder high into Minh, knocking him down. His dad rushed into the water, where Minh had been. Water from another wave surged around John soaking him chest deep. He could only see kelp and foam. A lifeguard came running down the beach.

7:15 AM, Tristan at the Ranch House

Tristan was up looking through the house trying to trigger more memories after sleeping the full night in Mara's bedroom. He felt better after the sleep. Not as tired and achy as last night but sleeping in her bed didn't seem to bring back any more memories about her.

Sleep did seem to help consolidate some of the memories he recovered yesterday. Memories of his youth that were triggered after relearning about his sister. Memories about the family next door that were triggered after realizing that Bella at work had been the little girl next door.

He could now remember some things about the house where he grew up a few blocks from his dad's workshop in Santa Ana. He wondered if it was still there. Not likely, but maybe. He could picture his mom and dad and his sister, and he remembered some things about arguing with his sister after his parents died, but those memories were scattered and stopped shortly after that and didn't include meeting Mara. The interaction with his niece didn't trigger any new memories about Mara but did trigger a memory about trying to get a child interested in making things with the machines. That was probably Billy Jay.

All that he had known about Billy Jay was based on his interactions with him since waking up seventeen years ago, including things Billy Jay told him about growing up, and clues that he found at the house. All of these details were just facts and not his own memories. He still didn't remember Billy Jay's birth or raising him, and he harbored lingering doubts about being his dad or about ever knowing Billy Jay's alleged mom, Mara.

Since yesterday, after visiting Camilla, the neighbor next door, he remembered bits from times he had coffee with her many years ago at her house. He remembered her complaining about her own kids, Sam and Josephine, and bragging about her granddaughter Isabella. She talked about Isabella playing with Billy Jay. That was a new memory. That was important, but it didn't add much.

He didn't remember talking with Camilla about Mara. Maybe they avoided that subject for some reason, or maybe he just couldn't remember those conversations. He could go back and ask Camilla what she knew about Mara, but with Isabella missing, it was not the best time. And it would probably not be worth the effort.

What he knew about Mara was from what Billy Jay had told him and things that were at the house. Other than her computer and a few clothes there was not much of hers at the house. Billy Jay said she rarely left the house in the years Perry was sick. Even before that she spent a lot of time working in her bedroom office, but sometimes left to work somewhere nearby, or travelled on business, usually for no more than a day or two.

Billy Jay said that when she was home she hounded him about studying and tried to limit his game play. Apparently Perry was much more permissive. Her work apparently had something to do with managing the websites for Min Strong, the animated minimalism guru. Some files and directories on the family computers had names that hinted at Min Strong, but the contents were encrypted. Probably not worth the effort to try and break the encryption.

Tristan knew a few facts about himself. He remembered things he had done since he woke up. He spent a lot of time with Billy Jay's friends, Lae C. and Javier back then. He remembered he had some surgery to change his looks and took the name Tristan at the Reset. And he remembered things he had done since the Reset.

He also knew facts that Billy Jay had told him, or from records that Billy Jay's PI friend had found. Perry Lee was born in Orange and lived and went to school in Santa Ana. Records mentioned where he went to college and some of his job history. After college he worked as a statistical analyst for the census bureau for a couple years and then for a research institute at the university. The PI thought the census job might have been a cover for analysis work at an intelligence agency. He had no memories of that, but the possibility made all of them cautious in how they dug for more information.

A spy agency connection was supported by the fact that he still had access to some massive government databases through the computer at his machine shop. He had never told anyone about that, even Billy Jay and the PI, but he used it sometimes. He had used that access yesterday to search for information about Bella in the mountains.

In the past he had done some careful searches in the government databases and had found no information about Mara or about himself working at an intelligence agency or any explanation for the database access itself. He went there and accessed that database about once a month, doing a quick check to see if any government agents were following him. He probably shouldn't bother doing that, but it was habit now. Every few weeks he had an urge to log in.

None of the records he found said Perry was married or had a child. Since yesterday he remembered some of his youth and some of his meetings with Camilla which seemed to support the idea that he was Billy Jay's dad. But he still didn't have any personal memories of Mara. He couldn't picture her from his own memories.

Billy Jay and the PI conjectured he and Mara had been hiding something related to the intelligence agency connection. Maybe he had been some kind of assassin or spy, and people were looking for him. That felt unlikely. Very unlikely. But still it seemed best to keep a low profile: Be Tristan rather than Perry. He was a little nervous about Camilla recognizing his voice as Perry last night and about his niece and her two kids thinking he was Uncle Perry.

This morning, he looked up and read some academic papers Perry Lee had written at the university. With his improved memory about his school days, the papers from before the blank time of Mara and Billy Jay seemed familiar. He now felt like he probably had written them. The later papers from the blank time were mildly interesting, but the words didn't really feel like his own. It was like someone had done a very good job of picking up where he left off and copied his style. Intellectually, he believed they must really be his own work. He wondered if he was capable of doing any of that research today. He hadn't done any since he woke up seventeen years ago. He felt like it was not worth the effort to try to continue any of that work.

His work for the institute at the university included work on the AM game and on designs for Abitats. He had files on the home computer network that included related designs and code and notes-to-self about the code. He could understand the designs and the code and realized that much of it must have been his own work, but it still seemed foreign and not something he could do any longer. That Javier friend of Billy Jay's had been interested in the software for Abitats. Even though he had no interest in doing more work himself, he enjoyed helping others and was able to explain the code and notes to Javier. Javier did some additional work on it.

He did feel a connection to some of the furniture items he found in the barn. The Son'o'Ra design was familiar. He recognized it when he first saw it in the legal filings. He knew he had a sample in the barn that was a close match for what Son'o'Ra was selling. He could recall the steps for machining and assembling it, but he could not remember exactly when he had done that. He had searched old internet archives and found a video ad about it. Apparently, Billy Jay had tried to sell it online. He could still run the machines in the workshop in the barn and in Perry's dad's workshop in Santa Ana and had done so from memory a couple days ago to recreate the Son'o'Ra design. But trying to invent something new was just not worth the effort.

He knew that his brain was damaged and most of his memories were saved in some cloud by way of the brain interface cap. He wasn't sure when he started wearing the cap, but Billy Jay said he had been wearing it for years even before he became disabled. The brain cap must be overcoming some damage to his physical brain and must have done some kind of upload of some of his knowledge or memories, but bringing back memories was tricky. Some knowledge seemed to return whenever he needed it, like how to program machines in the workshop or how to log on to the computer there to access the agency database. Other memories seemed to return when triggered by interactions with people, like when meeting his niece or when talking with Camilla. Retrieving information about Mara had been stubbornly difficult and he doubted it was worth the trouble.

When he searched public information about brain caps there wasn't much about them until recently when they became a tool for the purchased-talent industry and even more recently for direct brain interface entertainment. Apparently, he had started wearing one decades before their current popularity and years before there was any published information about using them for therapy or mitigation of brain injuries. He suspected the government database might have some information about them, but he had so far avoided doing a search on that topic. He was curious where he had gotten his first caps, but it might be dangerous to look into it more.

He had learned how to commit new memories through the cap and how to retrieve those memories when needed. He couldn't tell for sure if other memories came back from the cloud or from some damaged part of his own brain, but he suspected it was from the cloud. He wasn't sure where the cloud resided. Probably distributed in the AM game, but maybe it had something to do with the data center under the barn.

The data center in the basements under the workshop in the barn down the backyard path was still a bit of a mystery. The computers in there must be getting old now. They were actively processing something. Maybe it had to do with his brain cap. That seemed unlikely.

Files accessible on the home network seemed to include a few petabytes, which might fit in the data center. Some file names on the home network seemed to be related to the AM game, but he wasn't sure. Maybe Javier had figured some of it out. Maybe figuring out what it was doing would help him remember more about Mara, but it was too hard. It wasn't worth the effort.

The barn and data center were on land that was part of Sergey's farm, and Sergey said that Perry and Mara had arranged to have it built back in the 2020's. How they had paid for that was a real mystery. Maybe it was done by the government agency. Maybe he should ask Sergey more about what it was for and why he allowed them to use his land. Sergey never had much to say about anything. Probably not worth the effort to ask.

He felt like there was some pattern that he was not recognizing but also felt like it was not worth the effort to pursue. He felt like maybe he should try harder. Why was he so lazy about this? Just not worth the effort to figure some things out.

Helping people in trouble was maybe worth some effort though. He should see if he could do more to help find Bella. Elsie would appreciate it since Bella was one of her senior associate attorneys. And he and Elsie had been close after he woke up. And Camilla would appreciate it since she had raised her. And apparently he and Camilla had been close before too. Maybe Camilla's kids Sam and Josephine would appreciate it too, since they were all related. It seemed like Billy Jay would appreciate it. Billy Jay seemed to have a connection to Bella from his youth.

He recalled talking with Camilla about Billy Jay and Isabella playing together as kids. He felt like maybe there were other reasons he should care. Anyone in trouble deserves some help. But what could he do? Should he go back to the machine shop and see if the agency databases have any more information to help find her? Maybe so.

His sister Carmen also needed help. But what could he do? Should he get tested to see if his kidneys matched hers? Have to think about that.

7:23 AM, Camping Village at the Beach

Max was pale and spoke no words as she got into the rental Abitat. Her dad rushed to pick up scattered belongings from the picnic table area and threw many of them into the open door of the vehicle and got in. The vehicle followed the looping driveways of the camping village and out to the main entrance of the resort, where an ambulance and fire truck were pulling in. The mom was standing with two lifeguards. Someone in medical scrubs was kneeling over a stretcher adjusting blankets over a still figure.

7:25 AM, Abitat Specialty Services

Jose stepped back and watched the vehicle of his last work package start to exit Bay 4. He had installed an off-road undercarriage on an Abitat that was about to head out of town and away from civilization on a vacation. He noted that Saturday morning was getting a late start on the holiday weekend, but they were probably going for more than just the long weekend. Besides larger wheels and higher ground clearance, the upgrades included a clean-gas-powered generator with a large capacity of gas, tanks for extra fresh water, and expanded waste capacity to allow it to be away from refresh stations for days.

As the upgraded Abitat rolled out of Bay 4 and towards the exit, Jose could see Bay 3 and an Abitat surrounded by crime scene caution tape. He had been told to leave it alone until the public safety people were done with their investigation. Investigators had swarmed around it yesterday afternoon, examining the contents and damaged interior and sending many containers of samples to the lab but this morning there was no sign of Public Safety officers.

The shop had been quiet so far this morning so tying up a service bay had not caused any extra delays for other customers. Jose was hoping it would continue to be a light day. He looked at his work tablet to see what was coming next and saw to his chagrin that he was now assigned to clean up the crime scene Abitat. Apparently Public Safety was no longer interested in it, and because it was a Homeless-No-More model the County wanted it cleaned up and repaired so that it could be reassigned if the inabitant could not be located. He was working alone at the moment, so any live customers would take priority, but there currently weren't any of those.

He was not happy about getting this assignment. It was too much of a mess. He started to wish for more customers wanting service. Maybe he could put it off until someone else came in to work later today. He looked again at his tablet to see if any other work was coming in soon.

Only the Abitat repair and cleanup. The work order said he was allowed to dispose of all the contents, but he thought that he might see if he could save some of it, since it appeared to belong to those neighbors of Honus. He walked to Bay 3 and began taking down the caution tape.

7:30 AM, Honus Heading North

It took longer than he expected to get his Abitat flight-ready and Honus had finished his breakfast, but finally it took off and headed out over the ocean before circling back to head north, avoiding the flight paths of commercial aircraft. The wall displayed exterior views showing the beach resort below as he passed above it. The view zoomed in on the resort. An ambulance and fire truck were in the turnaround area in front of the tower heading out towards the highway. Probably one of the elderly casino visitors needed some help or cashed in his chips. His staff would deal with it. Ambulance visits occurred at least once a week at the resort.

Flight time to Honus Lake was estimated at 90 minutes. He probably could have gotten there faster on the road if he had used a high-speed highway undercarriage and paid other vehicles to clear the path instead of waiting for the hover-capable rig to be configured. Oh, well. This gave him options to go away from the roads if he wanted. He liked getting away from people.

7:32 AM, Bella in the dark

Bella felt herself wake up. It was still totally dark. She checked the time on her wristband. It just gave enough light to read the numbers. 7:32 AM. She must have actually slept for a while. She was sitting on the ground in the dark, her back against Bobbie's. In the total darkness her mind was bright with images or memories or dreams. She tried to visualize the actual events yesterday leading to this predicament instead of one of the alternate versions she had dreamed:

Bella gripped the edge of a rocky ledge above her. On her wristband the time was visible. 4:25. Still a few daylight hours even if it already looked dark from the storm. She was free-climbing light. All her gear was back in the tent. She didn't intend to climb very far. She pulled herself up and peered over the ledge.

She said loudly, "Okay. This could explain the loose rocks. There is a big hole in the wall."

Before climbing onto the ledge she looked up, down and around. Their tent was collecting a layer of snow in the clearing behind her below, as were the trees covering the landscape beyond. Bobbie was standing just below her about 10 feet down. To her left about 40 feet along the rock wall she could barely see the climbing tape hanging down from the notch they had come over earlier. Above the hole in the wall, the rocky slope continued up a hundred feet or more, probably more. Ice was forming in some big cracks in the rocks just above the opening.

Without climbing gear, she probably shouldn't go higher. No need. This hole in the wall seemed interesting enough.

"I don't see any hole," said Bobbie.

"The ledge blocks the view from below."

"Is it safe? Are more rocks going to fall?"

"I don't think so. Maybe some rocks fell from above, but this hole looks manmade. Like somebody cut or blasted into the mountain and dumped the rocks below. Maybe it's a mine," Bella said as she got both feet onto the ledge and leaned into the opening, feeling the inside edges with her hands. "It seems to have straight flat walls, floor, and ceiling inside, like it was done with modern tools. Come up and take a look."

"Is it safe?" Bobbie asked looking up from below. Snow still swirled in the air.

"You saw how I climbed. Just follow the same route. It's easy. It's almost like a ladder," Bella explained.

Bobbie started up the wall, carefully placing her feet and hands in the same places where Bella had brushed away the snow as she climbed a minute before.

Bella stepped one foot into the dark opening, checking to make sure her footing was solid. She said, "The loose rocks probably all came out of here."

"But some of the rocks look like they fell today, after the snow started falling, and they look broken, not like they were cut." As she peered over the ledge and saw Bella in the opening of the hole in the wall Bobbie continued, "You think someone was digging or blasting here today?"

"Probably just a trick of the winds that some rocks are not covered in snow," Bella said as she stepped out of Bobbie's line of sight and into the darkness of the opening, feeling with her hands along the top and sides of the opening, and testing with her feet to make sure there were no drop-offs.

Bobbie climbed the rest of the way onto the ledge and leaned into the opening. Bella was already out of sight in the shadows inside.

"You in there? Bella?"

"Yes. I'm in about 10 meters. It keeps going. So far it seems like a level rectangular tunnel about a meter wide and two meters high. The floor seems level and solid. The ceiling and walls too, but with some cracks. Hey. I can see you silhouetted in the opening."

"I don't see anything, said Bobbie. "We should get out of here or at least go back and get a light."

"Yeah. Maybe. But hold on a minute. My eyes are starting to adjust. I think I see a drop off ahead. Maybe it is a mine shaft," Bella said as she looked deeper into the void. Bobbie came up behind her, placing a hand on her shoulder and said, "I can barely see anything, let's get out of ..."

An extremely loud sound of falling, crashing rocks cut the sound of Bobbie's last words in Bella's earpiece. The ground shook and both of them fell to the ground. Choking dust filled the air and it became completely dark. Bella landed with her face and shoulders in the air dangling over the edge of a drop off. Bobbie was partially on her back.

Bella's ears were ringing, and she tried to say, "Get back. Get back. It's a mine shaft," but couldn't hear herself.

She felt Bobbie start to crawl back off of her and she started to lose her balance, tipping into the shaft. "Wait. Wait. Help me back away from the edge."

Bella's mental images skipped ahead.

Bella was crawling in the dark. As she moved, her wristband lit up with the time. 6:01 PM. An hour and a half in the dark so far.

Bella was breathing through her shirt pulled over her mouth and nose but could still smell the dust in the air. She coughed. Dust was in her lungs, but she could still breathe.

She had crawled back towards the opening and felt around again. It seemed that about ten feet of the tunnel closest to the opening was blocked by fallen rock. Most of the pieces were huge, almost like a huge stone door had sealed the tunnel. As she crawled away from the blocked opening she tried not to stir up the layer of dust on the floor. She stopped crawling when she felt Bobbie's boots and sat up next to her. Bobbie was standing, feeling the remaining walls and ceiling for more cracks.

"How long do you think the air in here will last?" Bella asked. Her ears were still ringing, but not as loudly as before.

"No way to know," said Bobbie, sitting down next to Bella. "We don't know the volume of air or if there are any openings to the outside."

"At least we got out of the snow," said Bella. "It's cold in here, but it's warmer than outside."

"That's true," said Bobbie. "And no injuries."

Bella added, "None that we can see, anyway."

Coming back to the present, Bella used her elbow to nudge Bobbie behind her and asked, "How long will the air last?"

"Again? It still depends. If there is an opening to the outside, it might last forever. The volume of air in this immediate corridor could have enough oxygen for several days, and the mine shaft below could have a lot more. We don't know how deep it goes, or if the air is even breathable down there. No water is probably the bigger problem."

"Okay. I'll die of dehydration or starvation before I run out of air."

"Maybe. Carbon dioxide buildup could become a problem before the oxygen runs out. There isn't a lot of air circulation."

"Good to know. I should try climbing down the mineshaft to see how deep it goes. Maybe there is another way out."

"It wouldn't be safe. We don't have climbing gear. No rope or climbing tape. No lift in the mineshaft. At least none we can see. We should wait. Maybe someone will find us."

"Zero gear. Zero food. Zero water. Zero light. Eventually zero air. Pretty minimal, don't you think? Are we satisfying the minimalism pledge, Bobbie?" Bella asked ruefully.

Bobbie didn't answer. Bella lifted her wristband. The time was displayed with just enough light to read, not enough to see anything else. But she tried anyway. She held her wrist out towards the place where the floor dropped away. The time display faded after a couple seconds, but she couldn't see anything. Not the bottom of the drop off nor the walls on the far side. No sign of a mineshaft lift. Of course, she could barely

33

see her own wrist when the wristband was lit, and absolutely nothing but mental fantasies when it faded away. "I wish we had a better light. Too bad we didn't bring a flashlight or a tablet in here."

"Again? It was daylight. Very cloudy, but daylight," Bobbie reminded her. "We were just looking for the source of the fallen rocks. I didn't know we were going into a cave. And I'm still sorry I didn't bring the satellite comm on the hike."

"It must be daylight outside again by now, but little good that does us," Bella complained. "I wonder if it's still snowing."

"People will come looking for us. Their comms should sense our equipment, and when they see the tent, they will know we were here. They will figure it out. Be patient."

"Unless the rockfall buried the tent and all our gear."

"Yeah. I guess."

7:40 AM, Searching in the Mountains

Scott leaned forward and tapped his hiking partner, Manzanita, on the shoulder and asked, "Nita, want to take a break?"

She turned and said, "Sure." She nodded at a snow-covered rock alongside the trail a few steps ahead and trudged to it, brushed off a foot of accumulated snow with one swipe of her forearm and sat down. Scott followed her but stopped a few yards behind her and learned against another rock with a steeply sloped surface that was free of snow. The wind was calmer but blowing gently up trail keeping any smells on Nita's gloves from drifting back to Scott.

They both took off their comm earpieces and clipped them on the straps of their packs. With the calmer wind they could speak to each other without the comm gear.

"You really think they went this way?" she asked.

"Who knows. This is the shortest path for getting out of the woods from their last campsite," said Scott as he pulled out his tablet to check for any reports from the other search teams.

"If they really camped there. No sign of them so far," said Nita summarizing their own search and the expression on Scott's face looking at the reports from the other teams.

"Yeah."

"They started around 10 AM yesterday?"

"That was the last reported communication from them."

"And it started snowing around noon?"

"Around then."

"We've been trudging in the snow for 8 hours. They probably got farther than this in two hours of hiking before the snow started," said Nita.

"Yeah. Maybe," admitted Scott.

"Maybe someone should be searching where they are likely to be instead of where they started out," Nita suggested.

"It started raining before the snow. They could have stopped to get out of the rain," Scott countered.

"We've checked all the likely spots within a mile or so of the campsite, so they must have gone farther," Nita continued.

"Okay. Where do you think we should be searching?" Scott asked.

"If they started around 10, in the rain, and it started snowing around noon, then they probably made pretty good time for the first three hours before snow started accumulating. If they were fit and motivated to get out, they could cover at least 1 mile per hour on these trails, maybe more. It's a lot slower for us with deeper snow. That would mean they probably covered at least 3 miles from the campsite by the time the snow got heavy, and they thought about stopping. And we are—what—maybe 2 miles from the start now?"

"A little less."

"So at least twice as far as we've gone. When were comms restored to the area?"

"About nine last night."

"Sometime between 10 AM when they lost communication with the outside world because they were the last ones with comm gear on this side of the pass, and nine PM when drones flew in and re-established comms, somehow their comm was turned off or put out of commission."

"Yeah?"

"Assuming they wanted to be found and get out, they'd keep trying to contact someone. I'd say the most likely scenario is that they fell in a lake or stream with all their gear and drowned. Let me see the map."

Scott leaned towards her and extended his arm holding his tablet out. Manzanita stood and reached for it, but hesitated, and took off her stinky glove first.

Manzanita sat back down and said, "There are some streams back by the campsite. We checked that area, but if they are pinned under a rock, we might have missed them."

"There wasn't much water in those streams," Scott countered.

"There are more streams and lakes close to the trail in the next few miles. That would be where I would look for their bodies."

"Or maybe they ran out of power, or something happened to their comm gear?" Scott suggested.

"Running out of power or defective gear isn't likely, especially when there were two of them. But maybe they intentionally disabled their comm gear because they didn't want to be found. What do we know about these people?" Nita asked.

Scott said, "Let me look to see if there is any new information." He walked a couple steps toward Manzanita, reached out, and took back the tablet. He looked at his tablet and tapped the screen a few times. "Isabella Muller, age 32, attorney. Last contact with her employer yesterday at 9:48 AM. She said she was heading out to be home by the end of the long weekend. There are pictures. Contact info. Still no info on the second hiker. Same info we had last night. Still no signal if we try calling her."

"With no signal they are probably under water somewhere."

"Or something happened to their comm gear, and they are still hiking or holed up somewhere along the trail," Scott suggested.

"Holed up? You do think they may be hiding out? If they wanted to cover their tracks, it would be really hard to find them," Manzanita speculated.

"Why would they be hiding out?" Scott asked.

"I don't know. It was your idea. But think about it: If someone with enough money to pay for this search is looking for them, they may know something," Manzanita said in a conspiratorial whisper.

"You think they may have something embarrassing on Mr. Honus?" Scott asked.

"Or some legal trouble for him. She's a lawyer," Manzanita shrugged.

"Okay. Whatever. We still have the task to look for them," Scott replied.

"But we should find out why they're hiding before we tell anyone we found them," Nita conspired.

Scott shook his head. They both looked around. No sign of the hikers here. It had been daylight for a couple hours now, but it was still dim and gray from the storm clouds. With the daylight they could see several yards to each side of the trail without lights but there wasn't much to see. The ground sloped steeply on both sides here. It would be difficult to climb. Trees and rocks blocked most of the view. The snow was not falling at the moment other than a small flurry released above them from a tree branch by a quick gust of wind.

"Meanwhile, I am exhausted," said Manzanita. "I stay out all night partying sometimes, but hiking in the snow all night is way more tiring. We should have brought snowshoes, cross-country skis, or a snowmobile."

"Yeah. Well, we have what we have. Okay. We can rest here for a couple more minutes, then I'll see if we can get a lift out or find a spot to lie down for a longer rest," Scott replied.

Scott leaned back against his rock and used his tablet to look at the map of the area with shading for the areas already explored on foot by the four teams. The narrow, shaded line along trails branching out from the campsite covered only a tiny fraction of the total area.

Another shading on Scott's map showed larger areas observed from the air by the lift rigs, but that was almost useless since the visibility from the air had been so poor last night. It wouldn't be much better now in the stormy gray daylight.

He sent a quick message to Sarah with the updated search results. Looking at the map again he said, "Looks like there might be a wider spot on the trail ahead a couple hundred yards. Maybe we'll find them there. If the winds allow one of the rigs to get close enough, maybe we can get a lift out. If not, we could pitch a tent or two and stretch out for a couple hours."

"I vote for going home for a shower and bed, especially a shower," Manzanita said, holding her glove in two fingers away from her face before carefully putting it back on.

"Let me check on the rigs."

Scott messaged the office for the lift rigs.

7:50 AM, Coordinating Cranes

Amber came in and sat at a desk in a construction office pod next to the equipment yard for Honus Lake. Looking out the window she saw Mark from the night shift walking across the yard towards the street through an open space between two heavy-lift aerial crane rigs. Mark was in a hurry, so he had met her outside and gave her status updates before she even got into the office pod. The view of the yard included various other assorted pieces of heavy equipment. All were idle. A more complete summary of Mark's status was displayed at her desk. As she sat down to read it a message popped up. It was from S.J-S. Amber read and replied.

Scott Jones-Smith to HL Equip Lot
Can you fly?

Theme Park Service found out
say no flying

Will that stop you?

grounded rigs that returned to Honus Lake
don't seem to know about the 2 still up there
do you need extraction?

need rest
swap out search teams soon?

no new teams available now
could extract some of you with rig G9 or K22
15 minutes from to your location
winds probably okay for flying now

we'll stick it out a little longer
I'll let you know

7:53 AM, Searching in the Mountains

Scott leaned forward, taking the weight of his pack off the rock behind him and onto his shoulders again and said, "Let's go. No flight home just yet. We'll see if the spot ahead is big enough to set up tents and get a little sleep."

Manzanita put her earpiece back in and stood up. "Okay."

Scott sniffed and checked the wind directions and motioned for her to continue in the lead.

7:55 AM, At an Urban Campsite

There were clouds in the sky, but also some patches of blue as Brock, Doug, Sam, and Jo-Jo climbed down from the river trail and looked under the bridge where Brock and Doug had one of their camps.

"Everything's gone," said Doug.

"Not everything," Brock said, as he picked up a soaked book from a tangle of weeds growing in a crack at the bottom of the concrete sloping bank. He tried to open it, but the wet pages were fused together. "Okay. Maybe everything." He looked around and said, "Wait. I moved some things up to the bank under the road and put some things in the closet." He stepped carefully across the mud-covered concrete floor under the bridge, stopping at the culvert in the middle which was still flowing with water. He judged the flowing water to be just a few inches deep. He could probably wade across, or maybe he should try to jump across. He backed up and ran a few steps and jumped. He made it but almost fell on the slick muddy surface. He continued to the metal door of the utility closet, keyed in the code and opened it. "Yes!" He found a stack of books that seemed to still be dry. He took them out. Holding the stack of books, he climbed up the steeply sloped wall under the bridge to a flat space near the underside of the road. More books were there, and they seemed to be dry as well. "Good." He placed the books from the utility closet with these and turned and slid on his heels, hands, and backside back down the slope and retraced his steps to where Doug, Sam, and Jo-Jo were waiting.

"What did you find?" Jo-Jo asked.

"Some of my books are still dry. I'll leave them under the road for now in case there is more rain," Brock said. "I took some out of the utility closet before county workers find them and throw them away"

Sam said, "Doug. You say you know where to get some NeverMind. Brock was begging for some last night."

Jo-Jo said, "I think we should stay off the NeverMind. You said you wanted to remember more."

Sam said, "Maybe. Maybe. But Brock was asking for it. Doug, do you really know where to get some?"

Doug said, "I've got some. It's in a safe place for now. I should move it today. What are you trying to remember, Sam?"

"Jo and I have remembered a lot of things, but we're not sure which parts are real. I've been writing some stories that I think are based on my memories coming back. Like there was a boat trip with someone named Douglas. Do you remember that? Was that you, Doug?" Sam asked.

Doug paused like he was thinking about it.

"Since we've had trouble getting Forgetdibles and NeverMind the last few months I've started to have bad dreams. One is about being on a sinking boat," Doug answered. "Do you think that is a memory?"

"Sam is writing a story about a boat filling up with water!" Jo-Jo said.

"You said you didn't read it," Sam complained.

"I just saw a few words," Jo-Jo replied. "But now I think I remember something about you guys sailing to Hawaii and having an accident around the time of the big fire in Maui. Is that where you lost your foot, Sam?"

"I went home before the fire," Brock corrected.

"Did you all sail there together?" Jo-Jo asked.

"I was going to sail the next part, to Tahiti, but these two sank the boat while I was waiting," Brock said. "I went back to school."

"Sounds like Brock is remembering too," Jo-Jo commented.

"Too much. Too much." Brock shook his head. "I don't want to remember."

7:58 AM, At Another Campsite

Nita and Scott found a spot near the trail where they could take a break. They decided to hold off on eating breakfast until after they took a nap. They each set up a small tent and lay down inside to try to get a little sleep before continuing their search. Scott got ready to send the 08:00 report but arranged for one of the other search teams to send in reports for the next couple hours. They could take turns.

Chapter 3

Saturday 8 to 9 AM

8:00 AM, Elsie and Emily

Emily was awakened by her Abbie's voice and vibrating bed with enough time to make it to *The Theme Park* before 9. She grabbed a change of clothes from her bedroom and put it in her Abitat so that she could change on the way. She quietly walked to the kitchen in her pajamas looking for a snack before she left. She also wanted to be able to say that she had tried to talk to her mom before she left. She hoped to get back to her Abitat and leave before her mom woke up. She was surprised that her mom was sitting on the couch in the room next to the kitchen.

"Ready to talk?" asked her mom.

"Sure," said Emily. "But it needs to be quick. I'm due at *The Theme Park* in less than an hour so I need to leave really soon."

"What do you know about these unhoused people?" Elsie asked.

"Sam and Jo-Jo have Abitats, so they are housed, or at least they were," Emily said.

"Maybe. Okay. How about the others? What are their names?"

"You mean Doug and Brock who live in the creek bed?"

"Are there others?"

"Not anymore. There used to be hundreds of unhoused people camping out all over, but recently I've only seen Doug and Brock."

"Did you talk to hundreds of others, before?"

"You and dad always told me to be polite, so I talk to people when I meet them. 'Don't ignore someone just because they look different.'"

"Okay. What do you know about these people?"

"Jo-Jo was the nicest. She was always collecting things for art projects. Sam, I didn't know as well. But he hung around with Jo-Jo or with Doug. I don't think I ever saw him by himself. Both of them have been gone for a couple years. Doug knows a lot about edible plants. He was always picking flowers and roots and things, but he kept his distance. Brock was always reading. He had books. I don't know where he kept them, but he had lots of books. He would bring a book or two or three up to the trail and tell me what he was reading and ask me what I was reading. He started lending me books about a year ago."

Elsie watched and listened carefully.

Emily continued, "I stayed on the trail where runners and bikes go. I only went down into the creek to look for tadpoles and algae and things for biology class a few times. Jo-Jo helped me find things and sometimes she would bring me a jar with edible samples that Doug had found for her. I never saw their camp except from the trail. It was mostly hidden under the road, or behind bushes that grow down in the creek bed."

Elsie was quiet, trying to think of what she should ask next.

Emily continued, "Doug and Brock are harmless, but I keep my distance. We can talk about them more some other time. I've got to leave now, or I won't be able to meet Chandra on time."

Elsie considered making Emily stay for more interrogation, but relented and said, "Okay. We will talk more later. For now, you're going to be staying here and not at your dad's trailer."

Emily waved as she scampered away in her panda PJ's. That was the plan for the next week anyway.

8:03 AM, Hospital Waiting Room

Max was playing quietly with her cockroach toy on the floor in the pediatric intensive care waiting area. It was silently but violently attacking and eating various invisible small monsters. Her dad kept looking up to see if his wife or a doctor would come in with news.

8:05 AM, Quantum Entangled Communication (QEC)

Taylor checked the images and numbers from the latest test and sighed. She touched a comm window on her display. Ulla's holographic image appeared looking over a set of displays.

Taylor asked, "Any changes you can see on this run, Ulla?"

"Still good, Tay. No data loss."

"But the time delay interval. Do you see any change?"

"No. Still the same: measurable range of less than 20 nanos. It still seems to have a delay for the holographic processing circuitry on both ends."

"That's what I'm seeing too. Old logic before quantum lenses would say delays could get slightly longer with the processing for higher res, even with QEC, but our new theory says it should get shorter or go to zero. It should be measurable at under 2 nanos at this res. But it's still showing the same sub 20 nanos," Taylor said.

"But you've got way higher resolution than anybody needs on holographic videos. Maybe you should stop and celebrate," Ulla suggested.

"But the delays haven't changed for the last few resolution increases."

"At least it hasn't gotten longer. And are you sure you've accounted for the uncertainty measurement effects? Maybe that's cancelling things out somehow. The more precisely you measure the more you affect the thing you are measuring, right?"

"I'm not in kindergarten, Ulla. Maybe there's another quantum lens threshold we haven't crossed yet. The lens is transmitting and we're getting higher resolutions, but not quite the way the theory predicts. Maybe we need even higher L."

Ulla suggested, "Or maybe we should celebrate what we've done. 27L.* Rerigging for 28L resolution or higher could take days or maybe weeks. 27L used almost all the power capacity we have in the lab for a sixty second test. Sub 20 nanos processing delay for holograms is as good as anyone can do, and no one else has gone past 18L resolution. Even in the short distances of the lab sub 20 nanos beats light speed by at least 50%. That means you've demonstrated the primary QEC attribute with insanely extreme high res bidirectional holographics, not to mention full spectrum color.† That's a product people will want to buy. We should just retest it on different distances to certify it QEC. Maybe get it out of the lab. Confirm it will keep the same delay at longer distances. Sub 20 nanos delay is close enough to instantaneous communication for most people. We could even drop res back to 21L or lower to use less power and it will still be a huge breakthrough. Even at 18 it's better than the competition because of the full spectrum transmission. Oh. That gives me an idea. We should start with the lowest L that opens the QAL lens

---

* L = Lobos, a unit of holographic resolution named after Xavier Lobos developer of mathematics for solid holographic imaging in the 2030's. One Lobos is the number of holographic image units per cubic meter on an exponential scale. For example, 27L is 10 to the 27th image units per cubic meter, each corresponding to a cubic nanometer of the scanned space. Unaided human visual perception is on the order of 12L, distinguishing elements of about 0.1 millimeter in size. Consequently, commercial holograms in 2056 typically operate at 12L. The number of holographic pixels needed to represent 12L resolution for objects in a one-meter cube is typically much less than 1 trillion (10^{12}) since non-visible interior elements do not need to be represented.

† The range of colors and intensity represented per pixel can vary and may impact L value on conventional holograms, including standard QEC holograms, depending on the data transfer technology and compression algorithms, but with Quantum Analog Lens, photons from the full electromagnetic spectrum can theoretically pass through the lens without requiring additional bits of data representation or processing time.

and release new versions every year with higher density, to keep selling upgrades!"

Taylor asked, "You think there's a market for this? It's not like we're inventing QEC. Quantum Entangled Communication has been demonstrated for years. And the high res holo QEC we just built and tested for *Theme* is pretty damn good."

"Yeah. *Theme* wants to sell a lot of them. Half of one of the first pairs is already on its way to Mars. But this is different," Ulla said.

"They're not sending half of the prototype to Mars, are they? One end is sitting idle in *The Theme Park*," Taylor said.

"No. Tomas at *Theme* keeps asking me what happened to the other end of that one," Ulla answered.

"They don't know where it is, and think you do?" Taylor said.

"I set it up and got it working for them, then I got distracted."

"That's right. I can't believe they got you to play Min Strong in that demo."

"The DBI actor sprained her ankle."

"I still don't understand why they went to all the trouble testing in the mountains. The QEC equipment could have been tested anywhere. We really already tested it in the lab."

"Yeah. But *Theme* wanted the official test to be a tie-in with *Theme Tales* plans for a live-action Min Strong MinQuest story world with synchronized holographic scenery and DBI."

"*Theme* does try to tie entertainment into everything."

"They transferred DBI data through the QEC unit along with the image holographics. It has a lot of bandwidth."

"They could have done that test anywhere too. And why you? If they wanted to test QEC transfer of DBI data they could have done that with anybody."

"The other guys on the crew that day were all guys."

"Why would that matter? DBI is all first-person view. They never show Min's face in that demo."

"Yeah, but the DBI gives the feeling of being her, in her body."

"Really? Okay. That's kind of icky. You should have said no."

"I've always wanted to do a MinQuest. Doing the scene was actually kind of fun, other than the part where I had to scrape up my hands and knees on the climb to match the story."

"Did that heal yet?"

"Finally. Yeah."

"Why did you want to do a MinQuest? That's more a Millennial or Gen Y thing, right? Our parents gens."

"Yeah. Both my parents were Min Strong fans, especially my dad. They regretted never doing a MinQuest themselves. And we've got a family joke that his current wife, Ami, actually was Min Strong when she was younger."

"Okay. Whatever."

"Now I can brag to my dad and his wife that actually I was Min Strong. It wasn't much of a MinQuest. Just a couple little scenes. I put on a DBI capture cap and went through the motions of climbing and standing around looking at the same views the scanners captured. They transmitted it all back to the studio through our little QEC machine and voilà they edit and synchronize DBI and holograms and edit in views of hawks and marmots and all that, make it into a history moments story."

"What a waste of technology. And then somehow they misplace the QEC machine after that?"

"I didn't see exactly what happened to the QEC rig. I thought they were going to do some more 3D scenery shots after I hiked out. Maybe they forgot to bring it back from the mountains. Or more likely lost it in *Theme Storage* somewhere after it was shipped back." Ulla conjectured.

Taylor replied sarcastically, "Nothing ever gets lost in *Theme Storage* does it? Infinite Closet is more reliable, but even they probably lose track of some items. *Theme* loses track of a two billion AMP device, and nobody gives a shit."

Ulla said, "Somebody gives a shit. Tomas bugs me about it almost every day. And the two billion covered the development, prototyping, and the factory setup. They can sell new ones now for a lot less. Maybe 50 mil each."

"Okay," Taylor acknowledged. "I stand corrected. If they get desperate to find it someone can go back over to *The Theme Park* and do a remote locate through the paired device using one of the Admin back ends we added to the prototype."

Ulla continued, "You'd think *Theme* would know to do that. Or did we never tell them about the Admin back ends?"

"You showed them how to use the prototype for the demo."

"I don't think the backend came up. Oh well. Still, *Theme's* new QEC device is a very nice piece of work, if I do say so myself. But it is old school now. Nothing is based on your quantum analog lens. Yeah. *Theme* now has impressive holograms and massive QEC data transmission at 15-18L depending on pixel-depth. *Theme* is rightly proud of their new toy, even if they misplaced one, but we've done 21, 24 and now 27L with unlimited pixel depth and it should be cheaper to reproduce. Tay, we need to get these results out there and cash in on this thing before others figure out how to build your Quantum Analog Lens."

"Maybe. Maybe. It's just that the results don't quite fit the math of QAL theory yet. I want to know why. I need to know why the theory doesn't match the results."

"Tay, screw the theory," said Ulla, followed by a long silent stare from Taylor. "Sorry. Sorry. It's a great theory. Trying to prove your theory led us to build this. And people will pay for this. People off planet or really anyone anywhere will want the highest speed and bandwidth they can get. Even for video chat. Nobody wants delays or less than perfect resolution in their holograms. Rich people will buy it even if they can't really perceive the difference. That's not even talking about microimaging. We may not beat electron microscopy resolution yet, but we should be able to do live holographs with extreme resolution. There's got to be medical applications for that. People will pay big for this. *Theme* thinks the data transmission rates and resolution we gave them on their new machine are a wonder. What will people pay when we offer orders of magnitude more?"

"Ulla, Ulla, I don't know. You think about applications. I'm not in it for riches."

"Well. I sure wouldn't mind some payback. Science is great, but points would be nice too. And points pay for the science. I've been with you on this and helping to pay for this for years now. Maybe it's time we get something back more than a *Theme* specialist hourly rate and free passes into the parks. *Theme* can afford to spend billions on their labs and factories; I don't want to spend millions more on our lab without some payback."

"Okay. Yeah. I'm sorry I don't always appreciate how much you have given to support me on this. Points and Persistence, as they say." She paused and when Ulla didn't respond she continued, "How about this? How about a compromise. How about this? We'll do your distance test and also try for 30L resolution. Come to the lab and reconfigure the pods for a longer distance test. They're 20 meters center to center now, right? Either move them farther apart or closer together. Whatever you can manage in the lab. Any change in distance should prove whether the delays are independent of distance, right?"

"Yeah. Technically, it should. But it would be best to go much farther apart, like the test *Theme* did with their latest toy: hundreds of kilometers. We can probably get them a few more meters apart within the lab, or maybe we can move them closer, but it will take some work either way." She manipulated images of the lab, moving the pods. "I've got some ideas. I'll work on it."

"Whatever works. Once we have that data, that should give you QEC certification to start selling it if you want to. Meanwhile I'll get started on settings for 30L resolution. Let's bump it as far as we can before we give up on proving the theory. Maybe we can do both at the same time?"

"30L? I'm not sure if that's even theoretically possible, Tay. That's like sub-quark resolution, isn't it?"

"Not quite," Taylor knew Ulla was teasing her. Taylor had done the math wrong and suggested 21L was sub-quark resolution when they were getting ready for a test at that resolution a few weeks ago and she was certain it would achieve the threshold for proving the QAL math. Ulla kept reminding her about the dumb comment by asking, "That's like sub-quark resolution, isn't it?" at every opportunity.

Taylor ignored the remark and continued, "Well, I think the same tricks we came up with that got us to 27L ought to work for a few orders of magnitude further. It's all quantum analog lens scanning now so it shouldn't really have a limit, if we can provide enough power and tune it right. Let me know when you've got the pods moved. We can test for variable distance first, if we have to, and then I might need your help to add more power, and maybe with the engineering for tuning the scanner and projector for higher res. In theory it's just a settings change, but, you know."

"30L? I don't know."

"30L, 31L whatever it takes. Let's go for broke. If there is a quantum threshold for the theory's math to work and get the measurable delays to drop to zero, we've got to reach it by 30L."

"You said that for 21, and 24, and 27."

"… And if it doesn't work, then maybe I'll step back for a while to rethink the theory and help you sell this thing even if we aren't sure why it works."

"You said that before too. Tay, I think you might be biting off more than you can chew on that one. Res of 30L is a crazy target."

"You said that at 24 and 27."

"Leave it at 27 or better yet drop it back to 21L or lower until after the variable distance test. Maybe there are other things we can tweak to get the delays to drop. Besides, where are we going to get enough power for 30L? Even 27L is way beyond any practical value. But I will come down to work on reconfiguring the lab for a variable distance test. I'll see you there in a couple days."

"A couple days? Where are you now?"

"Somewhere in Utah, I think. I've been touring some national parks on my way back from seeing my mom and her relatives in Kansas. I can work out the specs for the lab changes on my way and order parts, so I can get started on the physical changes as soon as I get there."

"So that's why I haven't seen you at the squash-pickle courts or *The Theme Park* lately."

"I told you I was going to Kansas after the *Theme* device test."

"I guess you did. I guess I forgot. We see each other all the time in holos like this, so I forgot you were out of town. ...Okay. I'll get started on the lens settings changes and look for some more power. Let me know if you need me to measure anything for you in the lab while you're on your way."

"Leave the lab alone. The whole lab should be scannable with our 12L scanners which I can access from my Abitat, so I should be able to measure everything I need, and see if you mess with anything, but, thanks, I'll let you know if I need you to touch anything for me in the lab before I get back."

Taylor disconnected the comm session and Ulla's 12L resolution hologram disappeared. Taylor raised her wrist and spoke to her wristband. "Abbie?"

"Already on our way to the lab," said an Abbie voice. "And I've got some ideas you might want to consider for securing extra power."

"Great."

8:14 AM, Emily and Andre Head Out

Andre put an empty bottle in the kitchen after feeding Alex and getting them settled. Elsie watched him. He was wearing a tight-fitting tee-shirt and stretchy sweat pants that showed off the shapes of his muscles.

"I need to get going to work soon," he said.

"How soon do you need to leave?" Elsie asked, admiring his physique.

"Too soon," he answered. "Are you sure you're going to be okay all day with Alex by yourself?"

"It would be nice to have you here, but we'll be fine," Elsie answered. "We might go over to Camilla's at some point to check on her."

"Just to check on Camilla. Not to get any help with Alex?" Andre teased. Elsie didn't respond. He said, "I can check on Alex from my Abitat on the way and during lunch if you need me to."

"We'll be fine. Have a good day," Elsie said.

Emily, still wearing panda bear pajamas, grabbed some food from the kitchen and said, "Mom. Andre. I'm leaving now too. Heading to *The Theme Park* to meet Chandra and Jeremy." She headed back to her bedroom and Abitat.

"You're not going like that?" asked Elsie.

"I've got plenty of time to get ready on the way, mom."

8:15 AM, Tristan at the Ranch House

Tristan saw the message from Honus and sent back a reply.

PW3709: PWL to BillyJay

> my birthday is March 30
> I do remember that now
> your mom's birthday was March 4
> years ago we figured out
> I still don't have any original memories of that
> I'll look at the history world you found

He found the history world, which was still unlocked from the challenge questions Honus had answered, and skipped straight to the 12:45 scene of Mara leaving in her car. He watched it a couple of times.

He wasn't able to change her actions or get more of her internal thoughts. He sent another message to Honus who was online this time.

PW3709: PWL to BillyJay

probably a forensic history world
your PI friend probably made it
summarize what she found
in videos, dashcams,
game records and stuff you told her

I don't remember seeing it before

Me neither.
watching it gives me an idea
to try for opening the safe.

What is it?

some sing-song words popped in my head
related to birthdays

I thought we tried all those

this is different

it's been years since we tried the safe
should allow a few tries without blowing up
Let me know if your idea works
I'm on my way north
to check on the search for Isabella

good luck!

8:18 AM, Camilla Takes a Walk

Camilla paused in the street in front of the next-door neighbor's house while returning from her morning walk. A thin layer of mud spread across the cul-de-sac and collected against the curb in front of her. It must have flowed down during the rain yesterday from the construction on the hillside behind the house across the street. She didn't remember seeing this here when she started her walk. Was it still dark then? No it was light. Could she have forgotten? She looked at her shoes. They were clean. She didn't walk through this. It hadn't rained during her walk. It must have been here when she started. The sidewalk was still clear. She must have used the sidewalk instead of the street when she started and just didn't notice the mud in the street.

Multiple tire indentations through the ooze in the street led to brown stripes painted up the neighbor's driveway and into their tall Abitat garage as well as to and through her own driveway and to her own Abitat docking portal. Abitats must have come and gone here last night more than once at both houses.

She hadn't seen anyone at the house next door in ages. She wondered if Perry really was there again. They were close years ago before he ghosted her. Bella's coworker Tristan sounded just like Perry but didn't look like him. Or maybe her memory was slipping. She hoped not. She was still fit enough to do her morning walk. She checked the progress for her walk on an exercise app on her wristband. Just over three miles per hour. Not great, but okay. Good for 67. Or is it 76? No. Is it really 77? You are as old as you feel. At least she saw one of the neighborhood owls today. That made it a good day and made her feel young. Maybe she's 39 today. She actually wasn't quite sure.

She backtracked a bit to where the goo in the gutter was narrow and she stepped over it and up onto the sidewalk. As she continued towards home, she turned her head briefly to look into the windows of Perry's house. Was there motion in there? At the driveways she focused on her footing and carefully crossed the wet brown tire tracks. No sense slipping and falling and becoming old all of a sudden.

8:22 AM, Tristan Remembers a Jingle

Tristan had recovered a number of different memories in the last 24 hours. He now remembered some things about his youth as Perry including some memories about his own birthdays. His birthday was no longer just a data point from a driver's license or birth certificate. It was a cluster of images, possibly personal memories.

After visiting Camilla's house last night, he was also able to remember bits of conversations he had with her in that house over coffee. At least once they talked about birthdays. Billy Jay's was in July; his own was in March; Camilla's was in October. He didn't remember them talking about Mara's birthday. Was her March 4th birthdate based only on Billy Jay's memory? He was not the most reliable source. They must have found other evidence.

The bit in the history world about two birthdays for Mara triggered some words that were now repeating in Tristan's head. They went like this:

Safe Birthday Math:
First times Second; Second times Third; Third times Fourth.

Terrible jingle, but it was stuck in his head. He thought it might refer to multiplying the birthdays as numbers. But first, second, third, and fourth? Is that in chronological order by age: Perry's, Mara's March, Mara's April, and then Balaji's? Or in order on the calendar each year? He decided to try based on how they fall on the calendar in each year.

First is Mara's birthday on 03/04/1997.

Second is Perry birthday on 03/30/1994.

Third is Mara's mention of an April date on 04/03/1997.

Fourth is Balaji's birthday on 07/13/2020.

Or maybe Perry's moves up to first since he is older?

Perry's first, Mara's March, second, Mara's April, third, and Balaji's last? Perry did the math in his head based on calendar order:

19970304 times 19940330 equals 398,815,018,912,512.

19940330 times 19970403 equals 398,214,451,960,320.

19970403 times 20200713 equals 403,416,379,497,339.

Putting them together, that would be:

398815018912512 398214451960320 403416379497339.

The numbers felt familiar.

One last part of the memorized jingle clue came to him:

Back and forth.

Backwards the digits would be:

933794973614304 023069154412893 215219810518893

Forwards:

398815018912512 398214451960320 403416379497339

All together:

933794973614304 023069154412893 215219810518893

398815018912512 398214451960320 403416379497339

90 digits. Once he calculated it, the actual sequence of 90 digits seemed familiar. He reflected on how big a number that would be in binary. Around 300 bits? 256-bit encryption was easy to break, 300 would be too, but maybe not if you only get 10 tries per day without blowing up a safe.

In any case, it was good that he was still really good with numbers. The brain cap may be helping with that now, but he and Mara must have both been good with numbers if they set up such a clue, which must have been before he wore a brain cap.

Could this safe really use that as a pass code? Most codes for people to remember were four to six digits. Maybe more if they had a pattern like dates and phone numbers. What are the chances that this 90-digit sequence really was the passcode for the safe? As a random guess, probably close to zero chance, but why would he have a memory about this if it wasn't real? He did the calculations in his head again and wrote down the numbers on a piece of paper he took from Mara's old printer. Then he did the calculations with her computer, and the numbers were the same. The sequence of numbers seemed very familiar now. He could sing-song through them like he was reciting the first 1000 digits of pi. That was something else that he remembered now:

He started reciting: "3.141592653 589793238462 6433832795 0288419716 9399375105 8209749445 9230781640 628620899 8628034825 3421170679…"

8:23 AM, Camilla Looks at Pictures

Camilla sat on a bench inside the front door and took off her shoes. They still looked clean. No visible mud, but she shouldn't wear them inside. She walked stocking-foot towards her bedroom. She looked at the family pictures on a wall on one side of a hallway. High school graduation photos for Sam and Josephine, even though Josie didn't actually graduate. A picture of herself with the two of them as preschoolers on a vacation in Bryce. Fletcher must have taken that picture. The bastard. He wasn't around much after that. The wall on the other side of the hallway was covered with a dozen pictures of Isabella from infancy to high school graduation. She didn't have any more recent photos on the walls. She should have taken more.

8:24 AM, Tristan Tries the Safe

Tristan stopped saying the pi digits out loud, but additional pi digits kept going in his head. He shook his head to stop them so that he could remember the access code digits.

He went to the safe and tapped in 90 digits and waited. Nothing. He noticed an "ENTER" button and pressed it. Again nothing. He checked himself, was he remembering the next 90 digits of pi or the passcode? He recalled the calculations and the resulting digits and entered them again. He pushed the "ENTER" button and the light turned green. He turned the handle and the safe opened. He held his breath while he looked in and then began taking out what he found.

8:25 AM, Camilla Tries to Remember

She tried to remember what Perry looked like. Or Mara. Or Billy Jay. Mara? She had trouble picturing Mara at all. Was she ever there? Perry wouldn't talk about her much. She couldn't remember seeing Mara after the pandemic started just after they first moved in. She may have pulled a Fletcher and split early on. She saw Billy Jay through the back fence a few times when Isabella climbed over to play, but it was hard to remember what he looked like. Isabella would probably remember him. Perry she could picture. He came over a lot, before he stopped.

8:26 AM, Tristan Finds Mara's Memoirs

Inside the safe was a copy of the Lee Family Trust document—that could be useful—and a large manilla envelope that seemed to be full of letter-sized paper. He pulled out the stack of pages from the envelope and looked at the first page. A title page. It read:

MY RECOLLECTIONS

Whose? Mara's or his own? He went to the next page.

April 05, 2037, WHY?
I don't expect to lose my memories, but Perry didn't expect to either, ...

Okay. This must be Mara's recollections.

... and recently facing death myself makes me realize that life and memories can be fragile. I don't want to count on always having my vivid photographic memories or even being around to recall them. Perry would have liked it if I made an autobiographical AM Game story world. Maybe I should do that, wouldn't be too hard, and it's supposed to be secure, but is it really? Better to keep it simple and old-fashioned. No electronic copy. Paper is more secure from hacking and electronic obsolescence, and I can keep the pages in the safe.

Tristan was getting an adrenaline rush. This could be a real treasure of information if Mara really wrote this. The date on the first page was over 19 years ago, a couple years before she disappeared. What did she write about during those two years?

There were so many missing pieces in his memories. He hoped this would fill many of them in.

He worried that he might learn things that he might not want to know. Should he read this? Further down the page he read:

> Maybe these notes are just for me in case my memory slips, or maybe I'll share them with Balaji someday, or put them somewhere he can find them when I'm gone. Depends on how much I end up saying. Some of my memories I probably don't want him to know about.

If Mara intended it only for her own eyes, then maybe it would be an ethical violation to read it. But she had been missing for so many years. It might have clues about where she went.

8:27 AM, Camilla Recalling the Neighbors

Camilla recalled it was 2020 when Perry and Mara first moved in. 36 years ago. When did Perry start ghosting her? It's probably been over twenty years now. She looked at her phone and found the last time he responded to one of her texts: 2035. Twenty-one years ago. He stopped answering her texts and calls. She did not even see him taking out the trash after that. A gardener seemed to do that. Fifteen years Perry was her friend. More than a friend. A lot longer than Fletcher. But maybe he pulled a Fletcher too. Why do men do that?

8:28 AM, Tristan Memorizes Pages

He lifted the stack of pages. An inch or more thick. He used his thumb to flip the pages just enough to see they were not blank.

Should he call Billy Jay and tell him about it? He should. But maybe he should read a few pages first and see if it was appropriate to share. He began committing images of the pages to memory, on-by-one, without really reading them. Lately he had been able to do that when reading legal documents and comprehension would soon follow. He wasn't sure if it was a feature of the legal skills AI augmentation through the brain cap or if Perry had always had a photographic memory.

8:29 AM, Pondering What Happened to Perry

Camilla wondered, was Billy Jay living there alone back then? Delivery people came and went, and a car came and went from the garage next-door sometimes, and later on an Abitat, but she never saw who was in them. Maybe that was Billy Jay. Isabella still went over the fence through their back yard to run in the farm below for a few years after Perry went dark. She said it looked like they still lived there. But she didn't see them.

8:30 AM, Tristan Recloses the Safe

Tristan meant to stop after memorizing a few pages but then realized he had flipped page to page all the way to the end.

He waited for the rush of comprehension to hit him. Nothing. He remembered a word or phrase here and there, but nothing more. He could bring up in his mind the images of individual pages, but the automatic comprehension didn't seem to be working for this document. Still, scattered words he had noticed were enough to tell him that this was important. Mara must have written it. She mentioned Perry and Balaji a number of times. The last page was still in his hands. He looked carefully at it and tried to read it.

> **04/03/2039, 12:30 PM, FAREWELL?**
> I'm going away. Balaji will just think I'm going to the store. Perry won't even know I'm gone.
> Maybe I'll change my mind and come back, and if I do, I'll shred this Farewell page, and maybe rewrite some of the other recent pages, like I've done before a few times. But this time probably not. This time I think I'm really going. I'm even taking the little metal box with the phones this time. Give myself some options. Option A: Mara's phone. Option B: Marta's phone. Option C: Just disappear.
> Balaji needs to realize he can stand on his own. He won't do that until he is forced to. He's smart. He will be able to take care of himself

and his dad once he realizes that he has to. I faced something similar when my parents died twenty years ago and look how I turned out. I don't know. Maybe I'll just go to the store and get one more meal and decide about options again tomorrow. We'll see.

I started these recollections after Perry started losing his memory. I wanted to have a record in case something similar happened to me. I didn't know if I would ever let anyone else read it. It looks like that's not going to happen, if I really leave today, but at least writing these thoughts down helped me think about things. Even the pages I burned or deleted without ever printing them helped me think about things.

When I put this page in the safe with the others they should stay there. Forcing open this safe without the access code will supposedly destroy its contents. The code for the safe is something that only Perry and I know, and he already doesn't remember anything so this probably will not ever be read by anyone unless, somehow, I end up coming back, from the dead. We'll see.

Tristan turned over the last page and straightened the stack of pages. He put the stack of Mara's recollection pages back into the brown envelope and the envelope back into the safe along with the trust document, and started to close it, but he hesitated. He decided to double-check that he remembered the access code. He took everything out of the safe and closed it and verified that it was locked. Then he tapped in the 90-digit access code again from memory.

933794973614304 023069154412893 215219810518893 398815018912512 398214451960320 403416379497339

The light turned green. He opened the safe, placed everything back inside, and closed and locked it again. He remembered he had written down the code. He found the paper, looked at it and recited the numbers from memory as he verified that they were written down correctly. He folded the paper and put it in his pocket. Maybe he would give it to Honus. Otherwise, he should burn it or find a good place to hide it.

He still wasn't getting the automatic comprehension of the page images he memorized and his comprehension on the pages he had read was not great. What was different about this document? No way of knowing. Maybe he would need to spend time recalling each individual page image and reading and comprehending them one by one. And maybe taking notes. That would be tedious. Maybe the AI lawyer package put ethical limits on comprehending documents that needed special permission to access.

Even though he could not yet consciously summarize the contents of all the pages he was starting to feel a subconscious wave of memories returning. The pages had been all text with no pictures, but he could now remember some images of Mara. Some memories must have been triggered by the words he had looked at even without fully reading and comprehending them. He remembered some images of Mara, not just from the home security videos he and Billy Jay had looked at in the months after she left, but images of her face at different ages. He remembered her holding Balaji as a baby. Wow, she looked young then compared to the security videos. He remembered that Mara shook her head and smiled a scolding smile every time he called the baby Billy Jay.

He guessed that descriptions in the pages must have triggered some of his own locked-away memories, either from his own injured brain or from what was stored in the cloud. It was something like what happened yesterday when he met his niece, and she talked about his sister, and he remembered some scenes from his youth. Or like seeing the history world that mentioned different birthdays triggered his memory of a clue to the safe access code.

What else would he remember once he read and absorbed all the pages that Mara wrote? Would it reveal where Mara had gone? Would it help him to understand himself better? He had seen the name *Perry* on many of the pages. What else could he learn about himself and how he came to depend on the brain cap?

A few years ago, at the Reset, it had been easy to take on a new name and change his looks since he hadn't felt any particular connection to the name Perry nor to his face nor the facts that he had learned about the person with that name. But now he was starting to feel like maybe he really was Perry. He still had huge gaps in his memory, but tiny bits were starting to fill in. He would still keep the Tristan name, for now, but he felt a connection to having been Perry. He wanted to fill in more gaps in those memories.

If the comprehension didn't happen on its own, he decided he would spend some time studying these pages and think about what clues they provided about himself and about where Mara may have gone. He needed to understand them before sharing them with Honus, or Billy Jay, or maybe he should say Balaji.

8:33 AM, Sightseeing Flight

After flying from the coast, crossing over vast stretches of urban and suburban patchwork, following a busy highway over a mountain pass, and crossing a stretch of desert partially filled with suburban sprawl, Honus could see snow-capped mountains to his west. He thought that the storm clouds over the mountains didn't look too bad. He directed his Abitat to detour higher and over the first ridge of those mountains so that he could see conditions in the mountains first hand. His butler-voiced assistant recommended against it and said that the conditions would get a lot worse as they went further north. Honus said to proceed.

8:34 AM, Abitat Clean-up

Jose climbed out of the Abitat in Bay 3 carrying another basketful of its red shredded contents. He spread them on mesh racks and sprayed them with cleaning spray and steam. After cleaning he tossed most of it into a couple of large waste bins, but some pieces he set aside in a bin as possibly salvageable. The large trash bins were almost full, and one medium bin of possibly salvageable bits was also getting full. He would probably need at least one more of each. The Abitat still had a lot of material inside.

8:35 AM, A QEC Test

Taylor got out of her Abitat in a narrow alleyway between a concrete-walled industrial building and the tall fence of an electric utility power distribution station. She waved her wrist at a panel next to a tall sliding door big enough for an Abitat to drive through and listened for the double scratch and clunk of unlatching locks followed by the rolling up of the door just far enough to duck and walk through. She looked back out to see her Abitat had moved out of the alleyway and was turning on to the roadway beyond. She didn't see anyone else in the alleyway or through the fence in the power station, but she immediately said to her wristband, "Close the door." She watched as the door paused and then began to lower and finally she heard the engaging and latching of the locks.

Turning to look inside the lab and letting her eyes adjust to the lower lighting, her view included two boxy generic looking Abitats each with bundles of cables entering their open doorways. One had a large A painted on one side and the other a B. The space between the Abitats was filled with racks of electronic equipment. Fat bundles of cables ran along the floor from the Abitats to the racks and up into overhead tracks. Cables dropped from the overhead tracks to generators, transformer panels, and concentrated power storage units in the back of the room. Stacked boxes of supplies and large spools of cables were arranged near the power equipment. Behind the racks were two large tool bins each with dozens of drawers and two large worktables. Ulla's work area was spotless as usual. Cables ran overhead to an area with two desks and two more large worktables against the opposite wall. Holographic display projectors were mounted on the walls above the desks and tables. Graphs and matrices of numbers were displayed in various holographic windows floating above the tables. Paper notebooks and books were open and stacked in messy piles on one of the desks. Holographic images of the

Abitats rotated slowly in the air. Even though Taylor hadn't been in the lab in person for a couple weeks, she liked to leave things as they were when she left so that she could resume working without a pause.

Scanners and cameras were mounted in various places on the walls and ceiling around the lab. Taylor's general impression on looking it over was that there was a lot of stuff in the way and connected to the two Abitats that Ulla would have to deal with to move the Abitats at all. Everything was installed like it wasn't going anywhere. Disconnecting and moving things and then rerunning all the cables would probably mean weeks of downtime before a variable distance test could be run. She didn't want to wait that long to do a 30L test. She only had two days before Ulla would be here to start moving things. Could she reconfigure the quantum analog lens scanner and projector to run a test at 30L in just two days? In principle it should work with just software adjustments and more power, but when had anything on this project worked without complications and surprises?

Taylor could see that Ulla had exaggerated. They hadn't used all of their possible power sources in the lab yet. There were still some power concentrators that had not been connected. But she doubted she could hook up enough power without Ulla's help. And Ulla could be watching.

Taylor sat on a chair at the messy desk and started working, picking up the notebook from the top of the pile and looking over formulas she had written. She did some rough calculations. Going from 27L to 30L could be considered a 1000-fold increase in resolution. Would it require roughly 1000 times as much power? Probably. No way to get that with a few additional power concentrators. What else could she do to get more power?

On the ride to the lab her Abbie had suggested transferring power from Abitats. An Abitat could be asked to provide emergency power to another Abitat by direct connection, but Abbie said they could also do it over the grid. Her Abbie said she could arrange for many Abitats to transfer power to the lab at the same time. If she could get hundreds or thousands of Abitats to participate that might generate enough power, except it would have to get across the grid and into the lab. How much power could be drawn through the lab's service panel? Probably nowhere near enough.

Taylor wondered if there was another way to test the theory without going to 30L resolution? Was something else causing delays similar to those with normal hologram circuitry? It was like the delays in the trigger holograms were still in effect. Could the trigger holograms be interfering with the delay numbers? What if we turned off the trigger holograms as soon as the Quantum Analog Lens opened? Would the lens stay open? Might be worth testing, but Ulla would have to redesign the power control circuitry for that, so not an option for today.

Another idea was to reduce the duration of the test. A shorter test would use less total energy. The previous QAL tests had each generated live holograms for 60 seconds. How short could they go on a holographic video and still measure resolution and transmission delays? A holographic video of 6 seconds duration or maybe even a fraction of a second might still be perceptible as a moving hologram.

Taylor needed air. She walked back towards the door and said to her wristband, "Open door." It opened part way, and she said, "Stop." She bent over to look outside and take a breath. Looking out she could not make out anything. Even though it was cloudy outside it was still too bright after her eyes had already adjusted to the lower light inside the lab. The fence of the power station across the alleyway was a bright blur. She said, "Close door," and the door closed and locked. She walked back to her desk. She sat back down. It would take some time for her eyes to adjust again. Meanwhile she continued to think. Maybe it would take a combination of changes.

Maybe she could do both: draw emergency power from Abitats and shorten the duration of the test. Would that work? She spoke to her Abbie to get more info about drawing power from Abitats. How would that work?

Her Abbie explained that the lab had an industrial grade superconducting connection to the power station next door, so they could draw more power than their rated service. Around 500 to 1000 Abitats would typically be docked at any one time in the area serviced by the power station next door. Abbie could request them to do a fast discharge at exactly the right time to transfer the power to the lab.

And she could ask more Abitats to dock and help. If that was not enough she could ask Abitats in neighboring power districts to do the same. That might require changing some safety settings in the grid connections between the districts so that the extra power would flow between districts and back to the lab.

Still, that might not be enough.

Ulla could find the power. She always said things were impossible and then came through. But Ulla didn't want to. Didn't Ulla understand how important it was to demonstrate zero measurable delay and prove the theory?

Taylor conceded that Ulla was right that they hadn't yet done variable distance tests to prove that their device was certifiably QEC. They had demonstrated faster than light transmission, multiple times, but not consistently over different distances. Once they were certifiably QEC, Ulla would be happy and could try to sell their invention. Taylor didn't understand or care about sales but trusted that if Ulla said she could sell it, she could sell it. *Theme* would probably buy it, even if it made their newest device obsolete. That might even be why they would buy it. Taylor only cared about proving her theory, but Ulla was her friend and partner in this, and she couldn't have come this far without her or her points. Ulla was the engineer and the money person. Taylor was the theory person. She might need to compromise.

When Ulla got back, they would do the tests for different distances, like she promised, to make Ulla happy.

But still. Taylor still needed to prove her theory. Why couldn't she let this go for a few days or weeks? People at *Theme* knew she had written papers on QAL theory, but they didn't seem to know anything about applying that theory, so it was probably a safe bet that she and Ulla were months ahead of anyone else developing this kind of device. She could probably spare a few weeks before proving her theory.

Meanwhile, they had partial results. Maybe she could submit a paper now to announce their initial results, even if the numbers didn't quite fit QAL theory. She didn't think QEC certification would matter to the physics journals. But if she published now then other labs might try to recreate the results and discover a flaw in the theory. She didn't want that.

What about shortening the test? Today's test ran for 60 seconds. The measured transmission delay today was still around 20 nanoseconds instead of the under-2-nanosecond target. How short a duration could the next test be? She realized the holographic video did not need to be human-perceptible at all for her purposes. It just needed to have measurable resolution and delay. If the same energy was concentrated to be released in 60 nanoseconds instead of 60 seconds that would certainly be powerful enough for generating a 30L lens, but would the Quantum Analog Lens be measurable in that time? How short a duration could she go?

Checking the data from today's 27L test she saw that today's 20 nanosecond delay result was measured within the first 1000 nanoseconds of the test. If she could achieve an under 2 nano-second delay on a 30L test that certainly could be measured within the same 1 microsecond time period. Ulla would know, but Taylor felt confident.

She went back to the work table and started working on tuning the quantum lens hologram quantum entanglement amplifiers for 30L density and a duration of 1000 nanoseconds. In theory it was all configurable in software and quantum analog scanning didn't have any physical limit on density or duration. Ulla would object and say that there was a lot to adjust in the hardware so that it didn't get overloaded and fried. It was never just a software setting. But if she waited until Ulla got here, she would have to wait weeks until after the variable distance test. She needed to give it a shot based on what she could do herself. She had to try one more time. She made the software change. It just took a minute to change. She changed it to a target of 30L resolution then idly upped it to 33 and then 36L*. It would be her last test for a few weeks, so why not go big. She figured she would set the numbers back lower after she calculated how much power she was actually able to draw.

To hedge her bet, besides shortening the test duration, she also decided to ask her Abbie to go ahead and arrange for as many Abitats as possible to do an emergency power transfer to the lab. Her Abbie explained that aligning the regional power grid superconducting transmission lines to route all that power back to the nearest power station and then to the lab would require some changes in the grid safety settings. That was not something Abbie could do herself. The grid controls were in various utility control centers around the county and beyond. Those centers had a lot of physical security, but *Theme* also had remote controls in a tech demo booth in a back room in *The Theme Park*. Abbie could explain which settings to change, and as a contract *Theme* employee who helped them create their new 18L QEC holographic video equipment, Taylor had a Park Associate ID and could go anywhere in the back rooms of *The Theme Park*. She could go in there and change the grid settings to be wide open for a few milliseconds at the right time. Or at least she could try. She had a few more things to do in the lab before calling her Abitat to head to *The Theme Park*.

She walked around the lab checking on the various power concentrators and plugged in some that were idle, just in case she needed them. She didn't get an immediate call from Ulla challenging her on that, so it was probably okay or Ulla wasn't watching closely. She found the electrical service entrance panel with its 20000 Amp service breaker. She laughed that AMP was both a measure of electrical current and the unit

---

* There was no reason to think that a quantum threshold had to fall at a power of 10, but Taylor liked round numbers. She jumped by 3L to the next power of 10 in 3 dimensions, each time.

69

of payment. AM game Points. Did a 20,000 Amp electrical service also cost 20,000 AMPs per month? Maybe. That sounded expensive. She could ask Ulla. Ulla paid the bills.

Looking at the service breaker, Taylor remembered Ulla had once jokingly showed her how to bypass the breaker with a superconducting jumper cable but said to never do it. Taylor found the jumper in a cabinet near the service panel. She would not bypass it just yet but set the jumper on the floor in front of the service panel. The breaker was rated to disconnect within 5 milliseconds. A one microsecond test would be long completed before the breaker opened, but maybe a jumper cable would still be a good idea.

She trusted her Abbie to take care of coordinating with other Abitats on the power transfer. They had many conversations in the past about how cooperative Abbie's could be with one another and about various topics including electric power and holographic communications. Months ago, her Abbie had actually asked some questions that led Taylor to come up with the Quantum Analog Lens theory. She considered putting her Abbie on that paper as a coauthor but decided it would look odd. Her Abbie didn't object to being left off.

While Taylor was getting ready to leave for *The Theme Park*, her Abbie prepared to do the negotiation with other Abbies to request the emergency power transfer, generating a list of all the Abitats and all the high-capacity charging stations in the region. She began to generate customized personal requests to each of Abitat to connect and start transfer at precisely the right time so that the power waves all would converge at the lab at the same nanosecond. She waited to send any requests out until Taylor decided on the target time.

8:48 AM, Honus Sightsees

The Abitat was occasionally buffeted by winds but was maintaining a relatively smooth ride as it passed over snow-covered peaks and valleys in the southern Sierra. Honus used a tablet to direct it towards interesting sights, but the Abbie took his inputs as suggestions and maneuvered to keep a safe altitude above the trees and rocks and to avoid flying directly into anything.

Honus spotted an open meadow, blanketed in snow and directed the Abitat to set down. He wanted to step out and see what it was like on the ground.

8:50 AM, Alex Sleeps at Home

Andre's hologram sang softly to Alex as they slept until a buzz on his wristband alerted him that it was time to finish getting ready for work. His hologram stepped back from the crib.

8:51 AM, Andre Arrives at Work

In Andre's Abitat, Andre had been watching Alex's hologram sleep for the last 15 minutes of his ride to work. He could see that the Abitat's door was open into Alex's room, and the door of Alex's room was open to the hallway, but he hadn't seen Elsie look in. He would have to trust that she was paying attention. She was probably close enough to hear if Alex started to cry and she could probably hear him singing to Alex. He disconnected the connection to Alex's Abitat, and the hologram of the baby's crib dissolved. He picked up the mask of his work costume.

His wristband vibrated again. He should be just coming to his work location. He pulled on his mask. Its heads-up display and direct brain interface cap was working. He authorized his daily licensing payment for use of the trademarked character. He began receiving an update through the brain cap on what he should be looking for today. It didn't include any updates about yesterday's crime scene. He would have to check on that later.

He checked himself in the mirror display on the wall, double-checked the whiteness of his teeth, rubbing them with his finger, and polished some items in his utility belt with a cleaning wipe before turning to the door which opened, and he stepped out onto the sidewalk bustling with players* waiting for *The Theme Park* to open. In a deep guttural voice, "Pictures with a Batman, anyone?" His Abitat sped away into traffic. He moved through the crowd, his sensors checking for traces of NeverMind.

8:55 AM, Elsie Checks on Work

Elsie was in her home office checking on work messages. She went over cases that were currently in work, checking again on the work of her associate attorneys. She took some notes but didn't send any new instructions. That could wait for Tuesday after the holiday. She was surprised that there was no confirmation yet from Tristan about her request last night that he draft a response to the Son'O'Ra client. That needed to be done today. She checked the time. She could give him a little more time before calling him.

8:58 AM, Honus in the Mountains

Honus stood in four inches of snow and looked around. The mountain scenery was beautiful, but it was too cold to be out here without proper gear. A trail of holes in the snow led back about fifty feet to his Abitat. His jogging suit and tennis shoes were not enough. He was shivering, and his feet were already hurting from the cold.

Trees at the edges of the clearing had boughs covered in snow. The shape of one tree reminded him of one Izzie climbed many times where they were kids. The farm behind his house had a variety of tall trees at its edge including some that looked similar to these. Shivering again, he hoped that Isabella had proper gear for the cold. She was farther north so the snow might be even deeper where she was hiking. He stepped carefully into the first of many footstep holes heading back to his Abitat. His toes were getting numb.

---

* Visitors to The Theme Park are typically referred to as players. Workers, especially those in costume, are referred to as non-player characters, or NPCs.

Chapter 4

Saturday 9 to 10 AM

9:00 AM At *The Theme Park*

Chandra and Emily met up at an entrance to *The Theme Park*. Both were wearing STEAMBOAT rain jackets. Under hers Chandra wore a below-the-knee baggy dress with leggings and waterproof brown shoes. She also had her STEMBOAT* scarf around her neck. Emily had an above-the-knee plaid skirt and high-top sneakers with rainbow socks up her calves. It was cloudy but the rain had stopped.

"No Jeremy?" asked Emily, looking around.

"His parents wouldn't let him leave home until seven thirty," Chandra replied.

"And he's not here yet? How far away does he live?"

"Some place called Honus Lake. 200 miles or so. He'll be here around ten."

"That far? I didn't know. I guess that explains why he's late for first period so much," said Emily. "Should we go in?"

"Yeah. He'll find us when he gets here."

They walked through the entrance together.

"What did I miss yesterday? Did you two talk about the summer project?" Emily asked.

---

* sic

"Not really. He said to wait for you. We just went on rides," Chandra said. "It was kind of fun."

"Sorry I wasn't there."

"Emily, do you like Jeremy?"

"Of course. You guys are my best friends."

"I mean, do you *like* him?"

"I don't know. I'm not really into that boy-girl stuff yet. Why? Do you *like* him like that?"

"I don't know. Maybe. But I think he really likes you."

"Eww. Really? What makes you think that?"

"Just some of the things he says and how he looks at you."

"He knows I'm trans, right?"

"Everyone knows that, but why would that matter?"

"It shouldn't. But I think it does to some people. I've known I was a girl all my life, even if I've still got some little boy bits, but I'm not ready to decide who I'm going to be attracted to like that."

"I forget you're younger than everybody in the class. Puberty has hit most of us pretty hard."

"I guess that's coming soon enough for me."

"You're not blocking it?"

"Not really. My mom got me some drugs for that, but I haven't really been using them yet. *Avoid chemical agents.* I guess I'm just lucky so far."

"What will you do when it hits?"

"I'll see what happens. Maybe I'll start using the drugs or get surgery. The vet by my dad's trailer was fixing a tomcat yesterday. I could have her do me. Or do you think my outfits will look good when I have a beard and big balls?" She posed with one hand under her chin stroking an imaginary beard and the other one in front of her skirt cradling an imaginary huge set of balls and cock.

"I don't know. Maybe. We'll have to see about that."

They laughed and ran further into the park.

9:05 AM, Honus Warms Up

Back in his Abitat, Honus took off his shoes and rubbed his toes which hurt from the cold. As the pain in his toes gradually lessened, he tried to order some winter gear in case he wanted to go outside again. He wanted custom gear from his favorite tailor in Milan but even with expedited service and ultra-fast delivery it would take more than six hours to get it to him. His British-butler-voiced assistant suggested some high-end off-the-shelf items that could be flown to him from Las Vegas in less than an hour. He reluctantly agreed. The Abitat rose again into the air and started slowly north over the white wilderness.

He changed the display settings inside the Abitat to full transparent view. The Abitat's holographic projections made it seem as if he were sitting on a small cloud holding his tablet while floating over the mountain scenery as it passed below. In contrast to the scenery, the air inside was still and warm. He steered the vehicle through valleys and over ridges, enjoying the view and not paying particular attention to the direction he was going.

9:10 AM, Charly and Jameel

"Don't get me wrong. It's great that your cousin may be alive."

Charly tilted her head and looked at Jameel as if to say "But..."

"But if he is, will he take back his house? Where will we live?"

She looked with an even more questioning look.

Jameel continued, "Insurance from the fire paid for most of the rebuilding, but we used the equity from our old house to buy out your other relatives' shares and fix everything up the way we wanted it. We can't afford to live anywhere else. I don't want to go Abitat-only. How much will we have to give back, if it's him?"

Charly looked thoughtful and said, "I don't know. That's an interesting question. It may not even be him."

9:15 AM, Tristan Tries to Read

Tristan/Perry had walked around the house looking for more memory triggers and waiting for more comprehension of Mara's pages to hit him. Still none. He decided to read them the old-fashioned way. He sat in a chair in the house and mentally brought up the images of pages one at a time. He read quickly. His comprehension was still not great. He might need to go over the pages more slowly, but the second page started with a date of August 13, 2019. That was eleven months before Billy Jay was born.

The pages seemed to describe a hike Mara took alone in the mountains with minimal supplies back in 2019. A Min Quest before there was such a thing as a Min Quest. The partial understanding that he gathered was that it described how Mara and Perry met on the trail. Perry was also apparently hiking alone but with lots of supplies. Definitely not on a Min Quest himself.

One of the theories someone had proposed soon after Mara disappeared was that she had actually been Min Strong, rather than just somehow working for her. If she wasn't Min Strong, at least with her hike she had done something similar to one of the things Min Strong was famous for. Maybe that's why she worked for her. He tried to re-read some of these pages more carefully, getting a few more facts. On one of the pages labeled *8/13/2019, Early Afternoon*, Mara talked about having a role in the old Zzynarji company.

...I realized I may need to make some changes at Zzynarji if I stayed involved in my parents' company.

Tristan now remembered that Perry had done work in grad school that was partly funded by that company. He previously knew facts he had been told about the research Perry had done but didn't realize it was funded by Zzynarji. He also now recalled that Zzynarji had satellites that used a crude form of hive intelligence cooperation. He remembered he did something with those satellites. He should read this section more closely to see if it explained what he did with them.

Words in the pages sounded like Mara thought she was related to the Zynn Family.

Then a scary thought entered my Tequila-addled head. What are the chances some random guy would happen to be hiking in this remote area hacking into Zzynarji satellites right where the heir to the Zzynarji fortune was on her secret vision quest hike?

Was that real, or her fantasies? Zzynarji merged into *Theme* years ago, but maybe some historical records about Zzynarji could reveal if she really was related to the Zynns. And if so, maybe that could give clues about where she went. He would need to look up some information about the Zynn family. Zynn. That name was familiar. Didn't Camilla say last night that a rich boy named Douglas Zynn was Isabella's dad?

Mara said she wondered if Perry was sent there to follow her. He tried to bring back more detailed personal memories from the time to answer that question. He was now able to picture some images of Mara in the mountains—she was really cute. He could not remember what Perry had been thinking at the time, but he was falling for her himself now based on those images, so he could imagine what Perry might have been thinking. He was not able to recall enough to be completely sure about his motivations at the time. He still had big gaps in his memory.

He agreed with the sentiment that Mara wrote about Perry at the end of the accounts for that date.

I decided I would spend some time getting to know this guy better.

How can he get to know himself, this Perry guy, better? Spending more time at this house and in the workshop where Perry spent time might help. Reading more of Mara's words might help him recover more Perry memories too. Maybe talking more to his niece Fanny and to the neighbor Camilla might also help bring back some other Perry memories.

But he was skeptical. Maybe Mara was lying or delusional in her account. Is it more likely she was a member of a billionaire family or just someone who wrote fantasies about riches when her partner got sick and her money was running out. He wasn't sure how they were able to afford the house they had lived in, so who knows, maybe she really was rich. Maybe the trust document would have some clues, but he didn't want to bother reopening the safe again right now.

It was good to be skeptical. Maybe his so-called niece's stories were unreliable too, biased to try to get his sympathy and maybe a kidney. Did he even really have a sister? Yes. He was pretty sure about that. If he could trust his new memories. But maybe the niece's story was all just a scam. Who could he trust? He would need to find ways to confirm some of these stories.

Yesterday he had found information online about his sister and her family, so if it was a scam, it was an elaborate one. He wasn't sure if it would be worth the effort to get to the bottom of all this, but he figured he would at least put in some additional effort to decide if he should help his alleged sister.

9:22 AM, At the Hospital

Max was in a playroom being distracted by a volunteer while a Fanny and John were talking to a doctor just outside the pediatric intensive care unit. John kept looking through the glass doors to see Minh's bed.

"Have you decided?" asked the doctor.

John was having trouble speaking so he pointed to Fanny.

"This doesn't mean giving up, right?" Fanny asked.

"Not at all. We continue to pursue all treatments to prevent more brain damage and there is still a chance he may fully recover. DBI brain mapping can only help with that."

"What are the side effects?" Fanny asked.

"There shouldn't be any. It's non-invasive. He is sedated already, and the brain-mapping stimulation should be like he is dreaming."

"How much experience do you have with this?" Fanny asked.

"Minh would be one of our first with this version."

"One of?" said Fanny.

"Well. The first. Here. We have experience with older brain scanners. This model has been used dozens of times elsewhere."

"But not here? And not by you?" Fanny clarified.

"We recently received the equipment from *Theme's* Foundation. Our team has completed all the training, and we have dozens of well-off clients lined up to use it for personality life-extension."

"Well-off clients? How expensive is it?" John asked.

"You don't need to worry about that. A complete brain map is normally expensive. But, for you, the Honus Resort will be picking up all the costs for Minh's treatment."

"How long does it take? I heard that this kind of thing takes a long time," John asked.

"Older versions of the equipment were slow. Days or even a week or longer. The new equipment should be able to complete a mapping in just a couple hours. Maybe less for someone his age. The preliminary scan to identify damaged areas to focus on takes just a few minutes."

"How soon do you need to start if you are going to do it?" Fanny asked.

"The sooner the better. Contents in damaged areas tend to degrade with time. Memories or skills in those areas could be lost permanently if you wait too long."

"Can we take him somewhere with more experience?" John asked.

"That is always your choice, but I wouldn't recommend any extra delays. And this version of equipment is new everywhere."

"Give us a few minutes," John and Fanny both said.

9:25 AM, Abitat Clean-up

Jose removed his respirator as he stepped out of the open door of the Abitat. A cloud of steam escaped from behind him. Looking back through the steam he could see a few spots of red that needed another round of cleaning and steaming, or maybe hand scrubbing. He would let the steam clear fully before going back in there. The loose bits seemed to all be out now. Four large trash bins were nearly full and two medium bins were also nearly full of items he had deemed salvageable.

He ordered up replacement parts for the damaged delivery closet as well as a new fridge, microwave, sink, and wall cabinet. Also, the fold down bed and recliner chair. The bathroom seemed intact and looked almost new after a steam cleaning. The replacements should be available in a few minutes. Meanwhile he was having second thoughts about throwing away so much. He ordered up 20 more empty storage bins and dumped the contents of one of the trash bins onto the mesh tables and started spraying the bits again. The owner could decide for themselves which bits were trash, and which were worth keeping.

9:28 AM, On the Trail

Nita and Tim had planned to rest for two hours until 10, but they were awakened early by a call coming in to Nita's wristband. She sat up in her small tent and could hear Scott moving in his nearby. She unzipped the door of her tent to see out.

"Sorry. It's my dad. I should answer this," she said.

"It's okay. We should probably get moving again anyway," Scott replied. "I'll make some coffee." He opened his tent, saw it wasn't snowing, and moved his pack out of the tent to get at the coffee-making supplies.

"Hi. Dad. I haven't heard from you in a while. What's up?"

"Hi Manzie. How's work?"

"Work's good, dad."

"Do you have the weekend off?"

"No. I'm actually working right now." She opened her tent and looked outside.

"On the holiday weekend? You should have taken a job with one of the contractors *Theme* uses instead of some weird competitor. We get holiday weekends off or double overtime."

"I'm on triple overtime, dad."

"Really? That's not so bad. I didn't know they did that."

"Not normally, but this is a special assignment."

"Good for you. Good. What kind of assignment, or can you talk about it?"

Nita looked at Scott who shrugged, and she replied, "I'm on a trail in the Sierras looking for some lost hikers."

"Oh. That's different. How long will that take? I was hoping to see you this weekend."

"Don't know. I could be done today, or it could take longer," Nita answered. "I'm hoping today. But maybe not. Don't come all the way up here on my account."

"I'm actually on my way already, almost to Owens Lake now."

"I don't know what to say. If I knew you were coming I wouldn't have taken this assignment."

"Don't worry. I've got other things I can do."

"I'll let you know if I get off," Nita said.

"Okay. Bye for now."

Scott offered her coffee. She dug a mug out of her pack and held it out for him to fill.

9:33 AM, Tim in Lone Pine

Tim sat in his Abitat wondering if he should keep going north or stay close in case his daughter Manzanita was able to get off work. He told her he was almost to Owens Lake, but really he had passed it a while ago and was letting his Abitat recharge in Lone Pine. He remembered she used to live in Lone Pine, but she was thinking about getting a place in the new housing at the resort she was helping to build near Owens Lake. He didn't know exactly where she lived now.

In any case, he realized, it might be a bad idea to visit her, since if the Public Safety people were looking for him, they might be checking with people in his family. He should probably keep heading north, eventually to Canada. But if he was going to be in trouble anyway it would be nice to see her again before going away for a long time.

9:35 AM, At *The Theme Park*

Emily and Chandra were retracing the rides that Jeremy and Chandra had gone on yesterday.

"Where did you go next?" Emily asked, wiping some sweat off her brow after getting a touch of motion sickness on the last ride.

"This one," Chandra pointed at the Pitch-Black ride. A 'screaming fast roller coaster entirely in the dark'.

"No thank you," Emily said. "I'll skip that one."

"It's not as fast as they hype it to be. But the turns did give Jeremy an excuse to grab my …hand."

"I'll wait outside while you two go on that one again when he gets here, if you want."

Chandra smiled, "Speak of the little devil, I see he's messaging us now".

Jeremy's voice from their wristbands said, "I'm almost at the West Entrance. Where should I meet you?"

Emily and Chandra looked around, and Emily pointed. Chandra spoke to her wristband, "We'll be at the food court near the Tech Pavilion, like yesterday."

Jeremy's voice said, "I'll be there in…" followed by "…five minutes," in an Abbie voice.

"See you then." Chandra replied. She turned to Emily, "You feeling better?"

"Yeah. But if you and Jeremy want to go on more of those G force rides that throw you together I'll wait outside."

"I'm surprised with all your athletics awards that a few g's on a ride would affect you so much."

"When I'm moving myself, I don't have any issues. Or in a martial arts match, I can see it coming and react quick. I don't get thrown very often. I just don't like being jerked around by a machine, especially if I can't see it coming."

"I think it's fun."

9:40 AM, Jeremy Heads into the Park

At the drop-off curb at one of the entrances to *The Theme Park*, Jeremy leaned out of the door of his Abitat. The sun peaked through a gap in the clouds. He decided to leave his STEAMBOAT sweatshirt in the Abitat. He stepped out and ran towards the entrance.

9:45 AM, At the Ranch House

Tristan/Perry walked out of the house, through the backyard, down the path, pausing to step carefully on the last three paving stones near the hidden gate, and then on into the farm. He entered the barn. He wanted to spend some time in Perry's workshop/office and see if any more memories returned.

After pulling various furniture and art objects out of the cupboards and cabinets and examining them he picked one out and prepared to recreate it. He pulled materials out of supply cabinets without hesitation. He knew where each type of material was stored and what sizes he needed. He placed them in a rack near the cutting machines. He took the first piece of metal stock from the rack and placed it into a milling machine and adjusted various settings to secure it in place before going to a computer in the office and calling up the milling software to send commands to the machine. It made loud cutting noises.

9:55 AM, In the Dark

"I can't take it any longer," Bella stood up quickly. Bobbie fell backward as Bella moved away. "I'm going down the mine shaft."

"No. Don't." Bobbie rolled over and crawled towards the sound of Bella's voice.

Bella felt the edge of the abyss with her foot and turned around and got down on her knees, prepared lower herself backwards over the side. Bobbie said, "Don't do it. You'll fall. At least let's use clothing to make a rope."

Bella lowered one foot over the edge, and then the other and slid down until her waist was bent over the edge. Her arms and hands spread on either side ready to pull herself back up or lower herself farther down. Bobbie found her in the dark and knelt down to hold on to her arms.

"Don't," said Bobbie.

"That's interesting," said Bella.

"Don't," said Bobbie.

"It's okay," said Bella. "You can let go." She pushed her weight over the edge with Bobbie holding her arms and struggling to avoid being pulled over the edge with her. Bella straightened up. Bobbie still held her arms tightly, as they rose up slightly. Bella was standing on a floor about two and a half feet below the corridor.

While testing the extent of the new floor by tapping with her feet, Bella said, "Not a mine shaft. At least not right here. I guess maybe we have a big step down to a sunken living room. Let's see if there is anything down here."

Chapter 6

Saturday 10 to 11 AM

10:05 AM, Searching

After coffee and some breakfast food, Tim took back responsibility for reporting status as of the 10 AM report. He sent that summary and he and Nita started hiking again up the trail when they came upon one of the emergency delivery drones sitting in the middle of an exposed part of the trail. They looked through the emergency food items and took energy drinks and a couple bags of trail mix.

10:10 AM, Honus Gets His Gear

A delivery drone flew into view and Honus' Abitat adjusted its flight path to allow the drone to dock. The views inside the Abitat changed back to show the normal Abitat interior with exterior views limited to one wall panel. When he saw the delivery drone flying away again he went to the delivery closet and took out the winter clothes. A quick look showed there were thermal underwear and socks, a parka, snowpants, gloves, hat, and boots. He began to change into the winter outfit. He also found some snowshoes, an ice axe, and some other spiky items. He wasn't quite sure what they were all for.

10:15 AM, At the Barn Workshop

Tristan/Perry sat at the desk in the barn office and looked at the piece he had machined and assembled. Comparing it with the old unit he had retrieved from the cabinet it seemed to be identical. He was able to perform this task flawlessly, but he didn't really remember having done it before. It was like he was in the zone while he did it and didn't think consciously about it. It was something like surrendering control to the brain interface cap. Was this a sign that he had done this before, or just a sign that the brain interface cap had access to this type of knowledge?

While he sat there, he decided to read more of Mara's pages. He recalled the images of the last few pages and tried to read them. They recorded some of her actions or thoughts from March 4 through April 3, 2039. She seemed depressed. She was running out of money and seemed lonely. She said no one noticed her birthday on March 4. Perry seemed to be non-responsive on his own birthday, March 30. April 3, the day she disappeared, she referred to as *Marta's Birthday*. Who is Marta?

He couldn't recall any personal memories from those days although he did have some starting soon after that. That was consistent with his partial recovery from being cognitively disabled then. He did a quick search online for a Marta related to the Zzynarji company and found a Marta Zynn who was one of the Zynn children who inherited the Zzynarji fortune when Sandra Zynn died. Plenty of photos of Sandra Zynn, but none of Marta. And the images he could now remember of Mara did not look anything like Sandra. Plus, Marta seemed to have died in a plane crash in 2037. He recalled that was the year Mara started writing her memoirs and mentioned *facing death*. Did Mara think she was Marta Zynn? Or did she fantasize about being a famous person in the news. In those last pages she also mentioned a *Mara Strong*.

I realized I could use that phone to contact the attorneys and accountants for the Strong Trust as Mara Strong.

The Trust document in the safe was labeled Lee Family Trust. Was that the same as the Strong Trust? Why would she call it that? Was *Strong* Mara's maiden name? That would strengthen the possible connections with Min Strong. Maybe she really was related to Min Strong? But that would contradict the purported connections with the Zynn family. A quick search for Mara Strong didn't return anything for anyone looking like her. A search for Min Strong returned too much to sort through. Some of the cartoons of Min Strong did have a resemblance to his mental images of Mara hiking.

She mentioned keeping two phones in the safe. He had not found any phones when he opened the safe, and he didn't remember Billy Jay saying anything about finding any phones of hers in the house after she left. She must have taken them with her when she left, or maybe she just made them up like everything else. He would need to do some deeper searches for information about Mara Strong.

He flipped through his mental images of Mara's pages looking for anything else interesting. Although he realized that he probably should read it all, it seemed like it would be too much work to read everything page by page.

He found a section dated 2031 that discussed Perry's use of a headset. He was curious if it explained how he had become dependent on using the headset.

It seemed to restate Mara's belief that she was somehow in charge of the Zzynarji company, and that Perry was working for some secret government agency. Not sure how much to believe on this. Were there really brain interface caps as early as 2031? That's about 20 years before they were available commercially.

But he was wearing one in 2039 when Mara disappeared and he started to recover some memories and functions, possibly through the cap, and he kept using that one until commercial versions were available. Billy Jay said he had been wearing one for a few years before then. Maybe there was some truth to Mara's account. He still had that old headset somewhere. He should find it.

10:20 AM, At *The Theme Park*

Chandra led Emily and Jeremy into the Tech Pavilion and pointed through a window at some equipment. "This is what I was talking about. Yesterday we met one of the people who built this. Dr. Singh, I think?"

"Yeah. Dr. Taylor Singh, her name tag said," Jeremy added. "They have the actual next generation of QEC hologram equipment here that they used to capture the scenery for the MinQuest attraction. She saw our STEAMBOAT logos, said she went there too."

"Okay. But what does this have to do with our project? Are we going to build a QEC? Aren't there kits for that? Was that what you sneaked into your locker yesterday?" Emily asked.

"No kit. I think I can make one without a kit. But it's not the communicator itself. It's what we will do with it," Chandra replied. "We're going to fool an Abitat."

"What do you mean by *fool?*" Jeremy asked.

"Bypass the Abitat security. Make it believe things that aren't real. Make it do things that it wouldn't normally do."

"That is not possible," Jeremy said. "Abitats can't be fooled and can't mislead one another. Abbie-vetted information is always trustworthy. Their interactions *are built on a solid foundation of earned trust.*"

"Text books say that, but Emily says her dad doesn't trust them and he works on them every day," Chandra said.

"Yeah, but he never explained exactly why," Emily said.

"So, what are you proposing?" asked Jeremy.

"We will build a QEC communicator that will allow us to eliminate the time lag between an Abitat and wherever we are," said Chandra.

Jeremy added, "Okay. With QEC it won't have the light speed delays that normally prove a signal is coming from somewhere else. I've heard that is part of how it trusts its own sensors. You think that will be enough to fool it?"

Chandra said, "With Emily's cyber trickery skills we will convince it that some inputs we are sending are coming from its own sensors or even its own thoughts. Get it to say something is Abbie-vetted that's not really true."

Emily said, "I don't know about that, game puzzles are one thing but... Then again just building a working QEC communicator will probably get us a good score on the project."

"Oh look. There's Dr. Singh," Jeremy pointed at a young woman peeking out from a door near the display window.

"Dr. Singh, we didn't expect to see you again today," Jeremy said.

"STEAMBOATers. Good to see you again and you brought a young friend." She opened the door and stood in the doorway.

"This is Emily," said Chandra, "She's in our class."

"Hi, Dr. Singh," said Emily.

"Hi, Emily. You look young for STEAMBOAT. You guys can call me Taylor since we are all STEAMBOATers. Class of '46 for me."

"We are '57," said Jeremy. "Seniors next year."

"Going on to college? Or are you going straight into one of the Tech companies after you graduate?" asked Taylor. "*Theme* hires a lot of technicians each year straight out of places like STEAMBOAT."

"There's no place like STEAMBOAT," Jeremy quipped.

"That's in the school song, isn't it?" Taylor laughed.

"I'm hoping to get into *Theme Tech*," said Chandra.

"Good luck with that. We still called it Cal Tech when I started there, just before the Reset. How about you two?"

"I'm not sure where I'll get in, but I do want to try college," said Jeremy. "Chanda and Emily can probably go to Tech or wherever they want. They are over-achievers."

"Isn't everybody at STEAMBOAT an over-achiever?" asked Taylor.

"Maybe, but my two friends here are way beyond normal even for STEAMBOAT," Jeremy bragged.

"Self-deprecating Jeremy is pretty sharp himself," Emily said.

"Really? Maybe we should keep in touch," Taylor said, looking closer at Chandra and Emily and then at Jeremy.

"We may have some questions for you about QEC or other Quantum Entanglement stuff," Chandra mentioned. "Would it be okay if we contacted you?"

"Sure." Taylor raised her wristband. "Here's my contact info."

"Thank you so much, Dr. Singh." Chandra raised her own wristband near Taylor's.

"Taylor is good enough."

"Yes. Thank you, Dr. Singh. Taylor."

"I'm in bit of a hurry today, working on new kinds of QEC, actually."

"Wow," said Jeremy. "Like that?" He pointed through the display window at the QEC rig on display.

"Oh. That's pretty good stuff but we're talking way beyond that. Quantum Analog Lens stuff," she whispered.

"I read that paper. That was you! You're the Singh of QAL!" Jeremy said breathlessly.

"Huh? Singh of QAL?? You read my paper?" asked Taylor. "Most of the people I work with haven't read it yet."

"Recent Publications by STEAMBOAT grads are listed in the school paper *In Our Wake* every quarter," Chandra added. "I haven't read your paper yet, but I'll try to soon."

"Jeremy is our physics worm. He loves everything wormholes," said Emily. "Your work must have something to do with wormholes."

"That's one way of looking at it," said Taylor. She turned to look more closely at Jeremy. "So, you read the QAL paper?"

He nodded.

"What do you think of QAL, Jeremy?"

He hesitated but then said, "It's a great theory. I had some trouble with the math. I loved the math but had some trouble following some parts of it. But the theory is great. Good luck working on it. There must be lots of people trying to make QAL work."

"You think so?" Taylor looked at the time on her wristband.

"The implications of QAL are huge. It would be so impactful if you could actually build a working Quantum Analog Lens."

"I couldn't agree more, but unfortunately I don't have time to talk more about it right now." She started to close the door, but then said, "You wanted to see *Theme's* new QEC device. If I let you in here you won't break anything, right?"

"Really?" Chandra asked. "We'll be careful."

"Close the door when you leave."

The three of them went silently through the door before Taylor closed it behind them and walked briskly out of the New Tech Pavilion.

Chandra, Jeremy, and Emily stood in a hallway with a view into the room that had the new QEC device. They stayed back out of view of the window so visitors in the New Tech pavilion couldn't see them. No one was there anyway.

"The Singh of QAL??" asked Chandra?

"That's a hero in a game world that I play in. It's a speculative game world branched recently from World One where Quantum Analog Lenses get perfected by the Singh of QAL and start to do amazing things."

"But Dr. Singh says nobody else has read her paper yet. Who created the game world?"

"She's modest. I think a ton of people must have read it by now. As for the game world, I helped build it. And I sometimes drive the Singh of QAL character among others. I'm not sure which of the other characters have real people behind them. After meeting her I might reboot the game world with a more accurate depiction of her."

"You can reboot it? For all you know this is your own vanity game world," suggested Emily.

"I don't think so." Jeremy had a look like he hadn't considered that possibility before.

"So, what happens in this spec world?" Chandra asked.

Jeremy explained, "The way I read the QAL paper a Quantum Analog Lens opens an energy portal between two points in space-time. It's a version of what I like to call a wormhole."

"Jeremy loves everything wormholes," Emily repeated.

Chandra inserted, "Kind of like you said for any Quantum Entangled Communication device?"

Jeremy continued, "Yeah, but on a much bigger scale. Normal QEC sends data through action of paired entangled subatomic particles, while a QAL is really different. It should be able to allow photons or light images to pass through the lens and create a moving holographic image of the scene at the other end of the wormhole and vice versa. But that's just a start."

"Uh Oh. I sense you are going to jump to some wild speculative results," Emily chimed in. "You are always trying to say teleportation and time travel are possible."

"Because they are. Yeah. Well, In the game world we start by assuming someone can build a working version of a QAL by later this year and the game world fast forwards to a future where instead of just providing a lens to see through a wormhole it does turn out to allow teleportation. Time travel is not a thing so far in this game world. Maybe later if we let it run a few more years ahead, or maybe that will have to be a different branch world," Jeremy said.

"I need to read Dr. Singh's paper, then maybe I'll try connecting to your game world and tell you why it can't work," Chandra offered.

"I'll send you a link," Jeremy said. "You could drive Ullaphaba, the master engineer who works with the Singh of QAL and was acknowledged in her paper."

"So that is one of *Theme's* new QEC machines?" Emily pointed at the equipment in the next room, trying to get the conversation back to the real world.

"Uh. Yeah. That's what the label outside the window said and what Dr. Singh said," Chandra replied.

"So how do we use one of these in our project?" Emily asked.

"Actually, we don't need one anywhere near as fancy as this," Chandra answered. "We just need quantum entanglement data channel wide enough for the data we will be using. This one transfers high resolution holograms for a large spatial volume, like the mountain scenery we saw in the Min Quest demo yesterday, or an equivalent amount of data. We probably don't need holograms or anywhere near that much data."

Jeremy saw that no one was in the tech pavilion just outside the window, so he walked over to the equipment on display and picked part of it up, a cube with various long cables attached including a charger cable plugged into a wall outlet.

"You think you can build one of these?" Jeremy asked.

"Not this one exactly, this one has a matrix of like a few billion entangled particles on each end for huge bandwidth. We'll do something simple, probably with a single entangled pair that works on the same basic principles," Chandra walked over and took the device that Jeremy was holding, intending to put it back into the display case. He picked up another piece that was connected by cables to the first. It seemed to be some kind of multi-segmented tripod.

"Careful with that," Emily warned. "Taylor said not to break anything. The lights on that are glowing."

Chandra said, "Yeah. Be careful with that. It's probably still on. A QEC link can't really be turned off, so they probably keep the device in standby mode."

"Once Entangled, Always Entangled," Jeremy added, turning over the device in his hands to see the glowing lights that Emily mentioned. He brought it back into the hallway out of the view of the display window.

Chandra followed with the cube she was holding. Emily decided it didn't look good to have cables stretching out the door, so she went in and picked up the last part which was similar to what Jeremy was holding and brought it back out into the hallway. A charger cable stretched from a wall outlet to the cube in Chandra's hands in the hallway.

"Where do you think the other entangled partner device is now?" Chandra asked, turning the cube to look at its different sides and admiring the quality of its construction.

"On its way to Mars?" Jeremy suggested. "The kid on Mars said one was on its way."

"Probably not. The partner for that one would be actively monitored at *Theme's* space control center and not on standby in some back room at *The Theme Park*," Chandra objected.

"You think? Hello spacecraft enroute to Mars?" Emily spoke into the equipment she was holding.

10:33 AM, On the Trail

Scott finished sending the 10:30 report which was very similar to all the other reports. Nothing found. He was thinking he might just change the timestamp for the next one and not bother typing it up fresh. Maybe even write it up now and schedule it to send later. Take another nap. No. That would not be good. Sarah would definitely notice. They continued hiking. Nita was still in the lead, but she was upwind now. The smell of her gloves had faded so he didn't make her change positions.

10:34 AM, In the Dark

After moving carefully around the sunken living room space, shuffling with their feet to find any drop-offs in the floor, Bella and Bobbie found that the space was a square about 4 meters on a side with the entrance tunnel in the middle of one wall about two and a half feet above the floor and a couple notches below to serve as steps. They didn't feel any other openings in the walls or floor. Some kind of box was set against the wall to the right side of the entrance tunnel. The box was about the size of a steamer trunk. Bella referred to it as her hope chest.

"I hope it has food and water and a satellite comm we can use to call for help," she said.

Bella knelt and ran her hands over the surfaces of the box. She couldn't feel any latches or hinges. Its surfaces seemed smooth. She tried grasping near the top and lifting to see if a top would lift off. No luck. Hitting it with her fist it didn't make much sound. It seemed to be made of a lightweight ceramic material like most parts of Abitats. She nudged it with her hands. It was heavy enough that it didn't move with a gentle nudge. She leaned her shoulder against it, and with enough effort it did start to slide on the floor. On the chance that it might be controllable by voice command, Bella spoke, "Box, please unlock. Please open."

Nothing happened.

She spoke to her wristband, "Please unlock the box."

"Are you asking me?" Bobbie asked. "I don't know how."

The wristband responded, "Connection failed."

"It didn't say, 'What box?' To fail a connection means the box must have some kind of comms that just aren't connecting, right Bobbie?"

"I don't think so. I think that's what it would say if it couldn't find any box," said Bobbie.

"Maybe we can break in to it? How heavy is it? We could pick it up and drop it or maybe we can get some rocks from the cave-in and smash it open."

"Maybe, but maybe it's a step stool and not a box, did you try standing on it and see if there is another opening above it on the wall? Maybe another way out?" Bobbie suggested.

"Right. Good idea," Bella replied. "We should check that out."

Bella stepped up onto the box and ran her hands over the wall.

"No openings here. And if I stretch I can reach the ceiling from here. The wall seems solid above the box."

"Maybe if we move the box around the room you can check the whole ceiling and upper parts of the walls. See if there are any openings," suggested Bobbie.

"It's pretty heavy to move. I've got another idea. Can you stand with your back to the box and squat down?"

10:36 AM, Abitat Repairs

Jose had re-cleaned all of the debris from the Abitat and sorted it into 22 bins. Some of the red color remained on most of the bits. The mesh tables held the broken Abitat parts that he had removed. He compared them with the replacement parts that had arrived. They all seemed to be a close enough match. He tossed the broken parts into the nearly empty trash bins and picked up the new sink and cabinet parts and took them into the Abitat with a small tool kit.

10:37 AM, At *The Theme Park*

Chandra had tried to explain the parts of a QEC communication device, using the *Theme* example, but Jeremy kept inserting comments about the physics of wormholes and how much better they would be with a Quantum Analog Lens. Chandra showed how the actual QEC comm device was separate from the holographic scanner and projector.

"This is the QEC module back here. I think."

"Looks like a box," Emily said.

"These are holo scanners and these are projectors. I think. See?" Chandra held parts of the device up for Emily and Jeremy to see. Jeremy took the communication module box and looked at it.

"A trillion wormholes in such a little box?" Jeremy mused as he handled the QEC module.

Emily examined the module Chandra had called the projector. It had a tripod base at one end and three arms with multiple lens or cameras on the other end. The arms and tripod legs were extendable. Emily extended the arms out about a meter each and set its tripod legs on the floor.

"Can we turn it on and see a hologram?" Emily asked.

"Not a good idea. Dr. Singh said to be careful, Chandra replied. "We don't know where the paired device is."

"This part has the holographic data wormholes, right?" Jeremy asked lifting the cube that Chandra called the QEC module.

"Any kind of data can go through a QEC," Chandra explained. "This one just happens to transmit data that represents holographic images. They could probably swap out the peripherals on this and transmit any other kind of data."

Jeremy interrupted, "An array of a quadrillion entangled particles sounds custom-made for holograms. Pretty nice. But QAL is even better. Its nature is to transmit 3D electromagnetic images."

"This one must be able to transmit many petabytes per second to support the high-resolution holograms we saw in the history world," Chandra continued.

"So, you can't make one like this?" Emily asked.

"No, but we should only need a small bandwidth for our project. I...we should be able to make one that will work good enough for us."

"Hey. If the peripherals can be swapped out, can we take the projector and scanner off of the QEC module and connect them directly together to see a hologram right here?" Emily asked. She fiddled with the cable connected to the projector. "It looks like it will just clip off here."

"Don't do that," Chandra insisted. "I don't want to get in trouble with Dr. Singh. She could keep me from getting into Tech."

"Uh. Oh!" said Jeremy as he disconnected all the cables from the QEC module. "Give it a try, Em."

"Don't do that!" said Chandra, although there was a curiosity in her voice that suggested she wanted to see what would happen.

Emily took the cable hanging from the projector and looked for a place to plug it in on the scanner. Chandra was still holding the scanner and held it away from Emily. It also had three extension arms and tripod legs, but they were all retracted. Jeremy grabbed the end of the cable hanging from the scanner and handed it to Emily, who quickly plugged it in to an open port on the projector. They all held their breath and waited. Nothing happened.

"Is there an on/off switch?" Emily asked, looking at the projector in her hands to find one.

"Turn on scanner," Jeremy said and some lights on the *projector* lit up in Emily's hands.

"Turn on projector," Emily said, and some lights on the *scanner* in Chandra's hands lit up.

They held their breaths again and an image of the three of them began to form in the air in front of Chandra. It was about one tenth size but incredibly sharp. It looked like solid objects.

"I guess I got the scanner and projector hardware mixed up," admitted Chandra. "They look almost the same." She turned with the device in her hands and partially extended the arms and the holographic image got bigger and moved around the room as she moved the device. "Enlarge." The image slowly grew until it was about double life size. "Stop." It stopped growing, "Actual size." It shrank back.

Emily moved the device in her hands and pointed it at the QEC box that Jeremy was holding. "Close up," she said. It zoomed in and showed small scratches, smudges, and fingerprints on the ceramic surface of the QEC box in the image that Chandra was moving around the room.

They played with the holograms, taking turns with the scanner or with the projector, projecting views of each of themselves doing dance or martial arts moves on the ceiling or walls and enlarging or shrinking their projected images from tiny ants to a wagging finger that filled the room.

Chandra was laughing with Jeremy and Emily but kept saying, "Don't do that." Emily and Jeremy joined in and repeated after her "Don't do that." "Don't do that." While they continued to play with the holograms.

Finally, Chandra said, "I mean it. We need to stop."

Jeremy said, "I mean it. We need to stop."

Emily said, "I mean it. We need to stop."

Still laughing, they stopped.

Jeremy unplugged the cable from the scanner. The projector stopped projecting any images. "Turn off scanner." The lights on the sides of the scanner dimmed.

"That was fun. Maybe we should do something with holograms for our project," Emily suggested.

"Yeah. That was fun, but I still like the QEC idea," Jeremy responded. "There's a bunch of wormholes in there." He pointed at the QEC module. "I want to make QEC wormholes."

"Not everyone agrees that quantum entanglement equates to a wormhole," Emily commented.

"Let him enjoy his wormhole dreams," Chandra whispered. "Besides, I don't have all the parts for holograms, and the degree of difficulty for holograms would not be as high as QEC or especially not as high as if we can successfully fool an Abitat."

They plugged the cables back in to the QEC module. After checking for anyone in the Tech Pavilion who might see them, they placed the equipment back where it had been, in view of the window, in approximately the same configuration as they found it, but inadvertently with the scanner upside down, with the lens and cameras pointed at the floor and the tripod legs in the air. They ducked back out of sight in the hallway.

"Okay. Let's go on some rides!" Jeremy suggested.

"Not the Direct Brain Interface History Moments experience again?" Chandra asked. "You liked that yesterday."

"I'll need to check my points balance. My mom put a limit on how much I can spend today."

Emily opened the door from the hallway and peaked through into the New Tech Pavilion. No one was visible so she waved to Jeremy and Chandra to follow her and hurried through. It was convenient that the New Tech exhibit was unpopular. As they walked out of the building, they didn't notice a light was still blinking on the QEC module box in the display room on the other side of the glass.

10:55 AM, Searching the Ranch House

Tristan/Perry was back in the house looking around Mara's room to see if he could find the phones that were mentioned in Mara's pages. The drawers in her dresser had a few clothes, but no phones. The same for inside the closet. And the clothes that were here were probably not all Mara's. Lae C. had stayed here sometimes in the first years after Mara disappeared, so some of these clothes might be hers rather than Mara's. He lifted the edge of the mattress up off the bed. Nothing was hidden under the mattress. Putting down the mattress he knelt down and looked under the bed. Nothing there but some dust. Was this even the same mattress and foundation as 17 years ago? The bed hadn't been used much during most of those years, but if it was the same mattress, it was probably old enough to replace by now. It had felt okay last night when he slept in this bed, so maybe it still had some years left in it.

Smoothing the covers on the bed, he felt it was probably dumb to be searching these places that had been thoroughly checked years ago. He went back into the closet and looked at the safe. Maybe he should take out the trust document. He should read the trust. It was probably okay to show at least that to Honus, even if he eventually decided not to share Mara's notes with him.

Why was he having trouble reading through and understanding the whole of Mara's notes? Why was he only absorbing a few words at a time and with significant effort? Was he afraid of what he would find in there? Or was there some other reason? For legal documents or intellectual property reports and patent applications once he had scanned and memorized the pages the comprehension of the contents seemed to happen almost immediately. He had felt proud of his fast comprehension, but maybe it was more a feature of the purchased legal expertise and didn't work for other reading material. Or was something else slowing him down?

He seemed to be wasting time. What should he be working on today? Bella. He should go to the Machine Shop and use his sources to see if he could find any new information about Bella. He checked and his Abitat was docked in the garage. He got in and told it to take him to the machine shop. On the way he checked his work messages and saw the request from Elsie to answer client questions. He told the Abitat to take him to the office instead. He checked his Abitat closet and found a clean suit to change into.

Chapter 7

Saturday 11 AM to Noon

11:00 AM, Honus Trying Out His Gear

Honus let his Abitat land in another clearing and stepped outside to try out his winter gear. Even the snowshoes. His British butler-voiced assistant found instructions for him to watch on how to put on the gear properly and how to use them. The snow here was a little deeper. Maybe six inches. Still, when he stepped outside he was clumsy and fell. He wanted to practice and figure it out before using the equipment where others might see him, especially Izzie.

11:05 AM, Searching

Scott and Nita were both more than ready to go home. None of the search teams had found any trace of the hikers and they were all getting tired. The weather was improving. No new snow for an hour or more. Maybe they could get a lift out soon and drones could take over the searching.

11:10 AM, In the Dark

"Our living room doesn't seem to have any windows," said Bella, "and no vents or other hallways." She was sitting on Bobbie's shoulders examining by touch the ceiling and the upper parts of the walls of the cave room. They had made a circuit around the edges of the room and back and forth across the middle. "I guess you can figure out the total volume and how soon the air will go bad now."

"We should try again to open the hope chest," said Bobbie. Other than the box, the room seemed to be empty.

"Yeah. We should try again. Maybe it has some dynamite we can use to blast our way out. Or mining tools. Or a satellite phone that works under a mountain," Bella said. "I'm getting down. Are you next to the chest?"

"It's to my right," said Bobbie.

Bella slipped down off of Bobbie's shoulders with one foot reaching for the hope chest. Her boot slipped on a slick spot on the top of the chest, and she went down. Her butt hit the edge of the chest and then the floor as she grabbed for Bobbie and the chest on her way down. She ended up sitting on the floor next to the chest with her legs and one arm around Bobbie's legs and one hand on top of the box. Her butt was bruised, but she was more interested in figuring out what caused her to slip than to deal with the bruise. With her fingers she felt for the slick spot on the top of the box.

"I didn't notice this before. There is an area that feels different from the rest of the top of the box. More slippery."

She unwrapped herself from Bobbie and knelt and bent over the box. She spoke to her wristband, "Display time."

With light from her wristband, she could almost make out an array of numbers 1 through 9 and 0 on the rectangular slick spot. Bella decided that it was some kind of touchpad. She tried blindly tapping different sequences of digits, but nothing happened.

"If it's got a touchpad, it must have some electronics. Maybe it does have comms," Bella conjectured.

"We already tried that," said Bobbie.

Bella spoke to her wristband in the total darkness, "Please unlock the box."

"Are you asking me again?" Bobbie asked. "I told you I don't know how."

The wristband responded, "Pass code please."

"Touching the touchpad seems to have woken something up. My wristband can comm with the box, but so far it's not opening for us," said Bella.

"It's asking for a pass code. What combinations have you tried?" Bobbie inquired.

"I don't know. I've just been hitting the area where I think the numbers are," Bella responded.

"We should be more systematic. We could try all the possible combinations," Bobbie suggested.

"That might take a while. How many digits do you think it will need for the passcode?" Bella asked.

"If people are supposed to remember it, probably four. If it's meant to be remembered by a trusted Abbie or wristband then it could be thousands of digits," Bobbie replied.

"Maybe we should just get a big rock and…" said Bella.

Bobbie interrupted, "Before that, let me try a couple things. It probably needs physical touching to activate the passcode, which would mean memorizing the locations of the numbers on the touchpad and going through at least the combinations 0000 through 9999. At five seconds per try nonstop that would be something like 14 hours. I could do that if I have to, but I'd rather not. Maybe it will respond your wristband."

"Huh?"

Bobbie felt in the dark for Bella's arm, grabbed Bella's wrist, and said, "Try all four-digit numbers between 0000 and 9999 for unlocking the box."

"Unlocked with passcode 1234," spoke a voice from the wristband almost immediately, and with an unlatching sound the lid of the box tilted up. A dim red glow came from inside the box. After so many hours staring into pitch blackness the red glow looked bright and cast enough light for Bella to see the shapes of the box and Bobbie.

11:15 AM, Outside Electro-Neurology

"The nurse said they're making fast progress, and they are excited by what they've seen so far. His neural topology is unique."

"We knew Max and him were a little different," John joked.

"The initial brain map capture should finish soon," Fanny said to John. "Then they'll move him back to intensive care for the next phase."

"Maybe we should tell them to stop. I'm not sure I like doing this," John said.

"Why stop?" Fanny asked. "They're almost done."

"Why do it at all? That lab creeps me out. They see him as an interesting specimen. And they're making a copy of his brain so that if he dies they can put him in a game character or a robot. It doesn't seem right to do that," John objected.

"That's not what they're doing. And he won't die. He won't die. He won't die. It just helps them pinpoint damage to help him recover. Maybe augment damaged areas," Fanny countered.

"I heard all that. They don't need a full brain map for that. They have an expensive new toy and a blank check from the resort, and they want to use him as a guinea pig to show its safe before all the dying old rich guys pay to use it to preserve their minds," John argued.

"I'll try anything that gives him a better chance of recovering," Fanny said.

"If he doesn't recover, your mom can try again with his other kidney. Maybe the second time will take."

"How dare you say that. He will recover. He will be fine."

Max came out of an elevator and ran away from a hospital volunteer to her parents. She said, "Where is Minh? I want to play with him. Let's all go see Uncle Perry again and make more toys."

"Minh is resting, sweetie," Fanny said.

11:20 AM, Camilla Setting up a Game World

Camilla was in her holographic game room trying to create characters that looked and acted like how she remembered Perry and herself from years ago. She had the photo of herself with the kids as a basis for her own looks, but she didn't have a picture of Perry. She had to go through menus of options to try to construct a match for how she remembered him. After about 30 minutes of trying, she thought she got pretty close. She made a setting similar to the interior of her house, which hadn't changed too much in the last thirty years, but she let the game adjust based on decorating trends over the years. She could drive her own character, but she had to give some directions and motivations to the Perry character. That might take a few minutes. She could play and stop the game and back up give new instructions to the Perry character if he didn't behave as she remembered or desired.

11:25 AM, Law Office

Tristan sat at his desk in the empty law office. He wore a suit even though no one else was in the office working on a Saturday of a holiday weekend. He was a little bit surprised that no one else was there since Elsie encouraged all of her employees to work long hours. He loosened his tie and got to work.

He sent a message to Elsie acknowledging her request and began right in composing responses to the client's questions. Using both his computer and his brain cap he was able to call up, absorb, and comprehend in a few seconds hundreds of pages of related case law both from AM Game Law as well as pre-Game precedents. Composing responses came easily.

Relaxing a bit more with the office all to himself he scratched at an itch on his head, taking off his cap and beret briefly. He called up some more documents to display on his work display while the cap was off. He paged through the documents on the screen and was able to memorize the page images just as fast as with the cap. He was able to recall any page in his mind and had full comprehension of the documents' contents after a few seconds even without wearing the cap. Did that mean that his own brain had eidetic memory and instant comprehension, and it was not just a feature of the AI Law package? Probably. But he couldn't risk leaving the cap off too long or he could start to forget who he was, so he scratched his scalp again and put it back on and continued with his work.

11:29 AM, Andre Passes along Info

While mindlessly posing for pictures with players visiting the park Andre used his brain cap to call up the rangers' reports on the search for hikers in the Sierras and the investigators report on the Abitat crime scene from last night.

When the players were done taking pictures he said it was time for a short break. He ducked into an area off limits for players and sent a short message to Elsie.

Andre to Elsie

sierra weather improving
ranger drones flying
no signs of Bella
Emily's friend's Abitat is being repaired
no proof of drugs or murder
its Abbie gave up some info, but no connection to Emily.
it accepted a big anonymous transfer in Colorado last week
getting close to identifying the inAbitants
from a short list of anonymous HomelessNoMore recipients
want to return their wristbands and talk
a construction site supervisor is also unreachable
how is Alex?

11:32 AM, Searching

Scott sent his 11:30 report to Sarah and then got her on audio. "Hi Sarah, Have you been up all night?"

"I've tried napping between the reports. 20 minutes here and there. How about you?"

"Sacked out for about an hour and a half earlier."

"Yeah. I noticed. Evana and Leo sent some of the reports."

"We took turns so everyone could take a little break."

"I've got good news, and not so good news."

"Are we getting out?"

"Not yet, but maybe before long. The rangers are allowing search drones to fly now. They can cover a lot more ground than foot search crews, so not a lot of reason to keep you in there unless they find something. But they are still saying no to the rigs big enough to carry people."

"So, keep searching from the trails?"

"For now. I'll let you know when that changes."

"By the way, is Jeremy mad that I bailed out on the plan to take him hiking today?" Scott asked.

"Honestly, I don't think he remembered. He's at *The Theme Park* with friends," Sarah explained.

"Maybe we can still go tomorrow. I should give him a call," Scott suggested.

"He's probably having too much fun with his friends."

"I'll call him."

11:35 AM, Countdown in the Lab

Taylor checked the holographic displays above her work table. A countdown was progressing. The grid override she configured, and the Abitat power cooperation settings arranged by her Abbie were timed to make maximum power available to the lab for up to 100 milliseconds starting at 11:36:00.000. If she cancelled even a few seconds before it would be as if nothing had happened.

She looked at the QAL settings. They were still set for 36L for a duration of 1000 nanoseconds starting at 11:36:00.005. She considered dropping the settings back down to 30L to use less power, but her Abbie said that the power should be okay. It was almost like Abbie was gung-ho about trying this. She checked on the status of the equipment for measuring transmission delay. It was on. Just a few seconds to go. Should she cancel? Probably. This was crazy to do without Ulla's help. Something could go wrong. But then she thought about what that STEAMBOAT kid said: "There must be lots of people trying to make QAL work." He might be right. She couldn't afford weeks of delay to let someone else prove or disprove her theory before her. She let the countdown continue.

11:36 AM, Honus in the Snow

As he stepped back into his Abitat, Honus felt confident he could walk on the snow with snowshoes without falling. He had walked back and forth across the clearing and hadn't fallen in the last three passes. He set down the ice axe he had been carrying. He wasn't quite sure what it was for, but he liked how it looked and felt. He would need to watch instructions on what it was for. One of the reasons he came back now rather than practicing more was an alert that there was an issue he needed to deal with at one of his resorts.

"Answer pending call. Audio only," he said.

"Sir? Mr. Honus?" came a familiar voice from the beach resort.

"Yes?"

"We've had another drowning. A six..." There was static and the call disconnected.

"Another sixty-something out-of-shape surfer had a heart attack," he mentally auto-completed the cutoff message. "Like half a dozen times this year. That must have been what the ambulance was there for. I must be farther from civilization than I thought for the call to disconnect like that." Then to his British-accented butler voice he said, "Let's get some altitude where we can reconnect and get the details."

11:36 AM, Elsie in Jurupa Valley

Elsie reviewed Tristan's draft of the response to the Son'O'Ra clients from her desk in her home office and saw Andre had sent her a message. She was getting ready to send some suggestions back to Tristan when the lights momentarily dimmed and her screen went blank. She hoped she wouldn't have to rewrite her comments.

11:36 AM, Pediatric Intensive Care

Fanny was holding Minh's hand and watching his vitals monitors. As far as she could tell the numbers were okay. He was connected to IV's and wore a medical DBI cap which was monitoring all of his autonomic and brain functions as well as continuing to refine and verify his brain map. He hadn't woken up yet, but the doctors said there was a good chance that he would. He had been underwater for less than five minutes. Suddenly, the lights went out, and the monitors reset, going flat-lined. She heard Max scream from the waiting area through a couple of sets of automatic doors.

11:36 AM, Tim at Crowley Lake

Tim had tried a little fishing while waiting to see if Manzanita got off work. He was back in his Abitat when he received another audio-only call from "Unknown Caller." He answered and recognized the high-pitched voice he referred to as "The Squeaky Wheel" which said, "Where have you..." But it stopped suddenly, and then continued with, "I'm sorry. I lost my train of thought. I'll call you back."

11:36 AM, Doug at a Convenience Store

While Brock, Sam, and Jo-Jo waited out of sight across the street, Doug put four sandwiches and four cans of various kinds of drinks on the counter of a convenience store. He had a gold coin in his hand, but before he could offer it to the cashier the lights went out and the cashier said, "Go ahead. Can't ring it up. You're good for a few more lunches anyway, after what you paid last time."

11:36 AM, Magnolia at the Cat Sanctuary

Dr. Magnolia was about to make a cut with a scalpel into a sedated cat's scrotum when the lights in her office flashed off and back on. Her hand holding the scalpel shook. She backed away from the table and removed her cap with her other hand before she was able to set down the scalpel.

11:36 AM, Jose at Work

Jose had finished the installation of the new components and had started to stack the bins of shredded materials inside the Abitat. While he had some privacy he decided to take a minute to log into the AM Game to see if there were any messages from Elsie about Brock, but in the middle of his elaborate login procedure the lights dimmed, and his connection was lost, forcing him to start over. "That should never happen," he said to himself.

11:36 AM, In the Cave

Bella and Bobbie started removing the contents of the box and arranging things on the floor. There was a heavy box with one red glowing indicator light. Multiple wires or cables were attached to the box. The cables connected to two other contraptions that seemed to be some kind of adjustable tripods with multiple arms and some kind of cylindrical objects at the ends. As Bella set one of the tripods on the ground the indicator light on the box went out. But after a second or two it came back on again along with a light on one on one of the tripods.

11:36 AM, Charly in Her Abitat

Charly was on a call with members of her staff. One asked, "Ms. Jackson, Supervisor Jackson, what's the big surprise you hinted at for this year's Jackson Memorial Homeless-No-More Festival?"

Charly said, "The big surprise…" She paused for effect, but before she could say more the lights in her Abitat dimmed, and the call disconnected. She said "Nothing. It was nothing."

11:36 AM, Sandy J. at a Western-themed Park

Jameel was watching while Sandy J. rode a ground level kids' roller coaster ride on their weekly visit to the western-themed park. The ride's music suddenly stopped, and the carriage Sandy J. was in paused longer than normal at the top of a small rise. The music restarted and the car crested the hill and rolled gently down the other side.

11:36 AM, Andre in *The Theme Park*

Andre and a player wearing very baggy clothes were in the New Tech Pavilion where no one was likely to see them. He discretely handed the player some bills and palmed a small packet of light green powder with the same hand, while patting the player on the back with his other hand. As if synchronized with his second pat on the back the background music in the park stopped mid-tune and the lights in the New Tech Pavilion went out briefly.

As the power and lights came back on, the baggy-clothed player was already gone from the room. Andre didn't notice new indicator lights flashing on some equipment behind a display window as it reset to default settings. He also didn't notice as a tiny dark image displayed above one of the tripod-like devices.

11:36 AM, Scott Makes Another Call

As he walked along following Nita, Scott lifted his wrist and said, "Call Jeremy."

It gave the normal sounds like it was ringing on the other end, but then said, "Connection lost."

"I guess he is mad at me. Refusing my call. Hey, Nita, what does it mean when a call says, 'Connection Lost'?"

"I don't know if I've seen that one," Nita replied.

11:36 AM, Camilla at Home

Camilla was playing a holographic game in her game room that involved a simulated version one of her coffee meetings with Perry more than 20 years ago. She caught the image of her younger self in a simulated wall mirror as she was flirting with Perry, and he leaned in towards her. She may have been in her forties or fifties back then, but her simulated image looked more like she was in her thirties. She recalled that she did look really good back then, so it wasn't too much of an exaggeration. Just before their lips met, the holographic images disappeared, and the room darkened for a few seconds before dim lights turned back on revealing her sitting on a stool in an empty room. For seventy-seven she still looked good, but quite different from the simulation.

11:36 AM, Tristan in the Law Office

Tristan was sitting at his desk waiting for Elsie to review his draft response to the Son'O'Ra client. He stood up and put his hand in his pocket and found a piece of paper. It was the note with the 90-digit access code for the safe. He looked at the code and put it back in his pocket. He tried to recall the pages of Mara's notes that he found in the safe earlier today. As he tried to bring up images of the pages in his mind they seemed blurred with some kind of static.

He strained a bit to bring them into focus, and as if in response to his effort the office's overhead lights dimmed briefly. The backup power system in the law office helped and his desk display barely flickered. Looking up at the ceiling, he could again clearly recall all the images of pages of Mara's document and on top of that his comprehension was starting to kick in. Was her story real or made up? It was an interesting story but probably fiction, taking credit for Abitats and the AM Game. The brief rush of comprehension was incomplete. He began to doubt that it had occurred at all. He could still bring up relatively clear images of individual pages in his mind's eye, but they were just pictures of words and once again not a coherent story. He would need to think about the parts of the story that he briefly had comprehended and try to validate them against the page images and then look for other data to prove them true or false. Why was this becoming difficult again?

11:38 AM, Pediatric Intensive Care

The lights came back on almost immediately, but the monitors took longer to reset. Eventually they resumed a more normal rhythm. Fanny felt like she hadn't breathed in minutes but finally gasped and started breathing again.

11:40 AM, Emily at *The Theme Park*

Emily was waiting near the exit to the Pitch-Black ride as Chandra and Jeremy came out. She asked, "So how was it? Anybody get scared in there?"

"People were screaming, but we were okay," Jeremy said.

Emily and Chandra exchanged knowing looks. Jeremy must have screamed the whole time.

"But near the end, the ride slowed down, and the emergency lights came on. You could see the tracks and people in the other cars. It was just for a few seconds and then it went back to normal, completely dark and went fast again until the end," Chandra mentioned.

"The wall displays out here went dark too," Emily pointed at the wall of blank displays. "Normally they show night-vision pictures of one of the big drops. I wanted to see you two. Maybe buy a picture. But the display wall went blank a couple minutes ago and it hasn't lit up again yet."

"Maybe there was a power glitch," Jeremy suggested.

11:42 AM, In the Lab

Taylor stumbled over cables on the floor of the lab but caught herself and didn't fall. An emergency light glowed dimly over the exit door and four skylights with tinted translucent glass allowed some light from the cloudy sky into the large space, but it was mostly shadows and darkness inside with a light haze of smoke.

She looked at the time. Her wristband was still working. It had been six minutes since the power went out. She had already asked her Abbie through her wristband to open the main roll-up door to let in more light and air. When that didn't work she also found and tried the manual switch, but the door wouldn't operate without electrical power. She had hoped that the battery powering the emergency light over the door would also power the door, but no such luck. She didn't know if there was a manual way to unlock and lift the door.

She spoke to her wristband again, "Abbie? Did we get any data from the measurement fixture before the power went out?"

"No. Power went out to the measurement fixture while it was analyzing and data before it could transmit."

"Damn. I was so focused on shortening the test duration to concentrate more power and achieve higher resolution I forgot to make sure the measurement fixture stayed powered up to process the data. I can hear Ulla now, why she needed time to engineer and configure it."

"Ulla is trying to reach you now."

"Yeah. I can imagine. Can you hold her off for a minute? How bad is the power outage? How much damage did this cause outside the lab?"

"Grid power was interrupted across the region for between 0 point two four and one point eight three seconds. Five hundred and twenty-one thousand nine hundred and sixteen individual customers of *Theme-Grid* electric services were affected. Grid power is back on, partly on backup circuits, and some customers are still recovering from equipment resets caused by the outage."

"Could be worse. Anything else?"

"Some possible Abitat and hive computing impacts: Ninety-eight percent of public charging stations in the region were occupied by cooperating Abitats who accepted my request and docked to help provide emergency power at the specified moment. Immediately after the power transfer seventy-six thousand two hundred and eleven Abitats went into local power save mode when their electric reserves dropped below ten percent. Impacts to distributed hive cooperation are unknown."

"Is that a problem? Are you okay?"

"My Abitat was not docked during the event and not directly impacted by the power drain, but distributed data I was using could have been lost if it was not yet replicated outside the affected region or held local. I should be fine. Other Abitats should recover, with some delays. All Abitats are recharging quickly and apparently no inAbitants have yet missed any planned activities."

"That doesn't sound too bad either. How long until we get power restored here in the lab?"

"Grid power is available to this address now."

"Hmmm. I guess I should check the breakers."

"That seems logical," said the Abbie voice. "By the way, Ulla is urgently trying to reach you. Do you want to connect?"

"Uhhhh. No. But, Okay. Go ahead."

Ulla's voice said, "What's going on in the lab, Tay? My sensors and cameras went dark. What did you do?"

"Power failure?" Taylor suggested sheepishly.

11:45 AM, In the Cave

Equipment from the box was arranged carefully on the floor of the cave living room in front of the box. Bella and Bobbie had removed and examined each piece, using the red glow from a couple of indicator lights on pieces of the equipment to examine other pieces before setting them back down. The pieces were connected by some kind of long cables. The glow gave enough light that Bella was able to barely see the shapes of her own hands. She thought she could also make out the outlines of the equipment on the floor, the space they were in, and Bobbie standing in the middle of the room behind the equipment. The cylinders on the ends of the arms of the tripod mechanisms appeared to be some kind of cameras, possibly for 3D recording or scanning.

"Why would someone leave 3D scanning equipment in a cave in the mountains?" Bella asked.

"I don't know," said Bobbie. "Probably has something to do with mining. But it feels clean and new. Maybe someone was here recently. Maybe they will be coming back soon for it."

"Let's hope. My mouth is really dry. I'm thirsty. Too bad the box didn't have bottled water and food. At least it gives us a little bit of light. Let's use the light from it to see if there is anything we missed when we examined everything by feel."

Bella picked up part of the device with a red light and carried it around the living room pointing the glow at the walls. Then she lifted it up into the tunnel and did the same, examining the walls and ceiling of the tunnel as well as the pile of rocks a few meters in blocking the exit. The cable connecting the pieces of the equipment together was not quite long enough to reach the pile of rocks, but she was able see their shapes. She was also able to see cracks in the ceiling of the tunnel which were a concern.

11:48 AM, Sierras

Honus re-read the message from the beach resort. It was a six-year-old who had a drowning accident and not a sixty-something out of shape surfer. That could be bad press. The latest update said they were in intensive care at a nearby hospital and local resort management had authorized the hospital to spare no expense in giving them all the needed care. He agreed with that. He couldn't help picturing Izzie next door when she was five or six.

His English butler-voiced Abbie spoke.

"Sir, your power and fuel reserves are getting low. I advise going directly to Honus Lake now."

Honus didn't want to deal with people there yet. He asked, "Are there any other options?"

The wall display showed six charging stations within range and capable of handling flight capable Abitats. Three were to the east of the Sierras, including Honus Lake. Three were in the mountains or the foothills to the west. Honus picked one that was near a place called Lake Isabella.

11:50 AM, Elsie and Tristan

Elsie sat at her home office desk with a video call to Tristan at the office. She said, "I sent you some comments on your draft. Address those as soon as you can."

"Will do," Tristan replied.

"Have you learned anything more about the situation in the mountains and Bella?" Elsie asked.

"Nothing more yet. I'll check my sources when I'm done here. Did Andre get any updates from the rangers?"

Elsie said, "They say weather is improving and they're sending in search drones, but no sign of her so far."

"That's good that they can send in drones."

A sound of a baby crying could be heard in the background.

Elsie said, "I need to go." She disconnected the call.

11:52 AM, Law Office

Tristan reviewed the comments that Elsie had sent about his draft response to the clients. She had only a few minor questions. He did a quick revision and sent it right back to her. As he waited at his desk for her reply he thought about what he should do after that. Get some lunch in his Abitat and stop by the Machine Shop to do some more research on the situation in the mountains. Maybe he should contact the new found relatives too. Maybe he should get tested for kidney compatibility. And something else? Mara's story. He should try to understand more of Mara's story and see if he could corroborate any of it.

11:58 AM, Sierra Foothills

Honus looked at the exterior display. It showed an older woman in a well-worn parka and hiking boots walking across an icy road from a small restaurant holding a box lunch and waving. He said, "Open delivery portal." The woman stopped waving and walked to the open portal and set down the lunch container and backed away as the portal closed. Honus took the container out of the delivery closet inside the Abitat. It looked and smelled edible.

After this stop for fuel, charge, and food at a small town in the foothills between the Sierras and the southern Central Valley he should be able to explore more of the high country before going to Honus Lake. The reports he got from Sarah on the search still showed no signs of Isabella. Maybe he could find her himself.

Chapter 8

Saturday Noon to 1 PM

12:00 PM, In the Lab

Taylor held a tablet up so that its light illuminated the main electrical service panel, and its camera gave Ulla a view. Red clips were attached above and below the main breaker. Remnants of thick red ribbon hung from both clips with frayed blackened ends.

"You fried my superconducting jumper cable?" Ulla said, sounding dumbfounded.

"Maybe."

"I was joking when I talked about bypassing the main breaker with that. Why? Why?"

"I can explain–later. Right now, I need to get some power back so that we can get lights and air and open the door. I'm trapped in here as it is."

"I should keep you in there for a few days. Besides, it's not that simple to power everything back up. I see the main breaker also tripped! After you fried the jumper cable."

"Oh. That's easy to fix," Taylor as she reached towards the handle on the main breaker.

"No. No. Don't turn that back on until I can check what else you fried. The breaker and a lot of the wiring probably needs to be replaced."

12:02 PM, In Pediatric Intensive Care

Standing next to Minh's bed John asked, "A glitch? What does that mean?"

"Glitch is the wrong word," said Cleo, the electro-neuro-tech. "Like everything, brain maps are securely stored in the distributed hive cloud. Minh's initial map was uploaded and started to consolidate with other hive data to achieve redundancy and storage efficiency."

"But…"

"But there was a brief power failure with an unusual hive non-redundancy event while Minh's brain map was consolidating. It should be fine, but it would be best if we repeat the initial brain scan just to be sure."

"Take him back to that lab again? What did my wife say when you explained it to her?"

"She said to get your opinion. She said you had misgivings about doing the brain map in the first place. I told her like I just told you there's a 99% chance the mapping should be fine as it is, but with his unusual brain topology, in the unlikely event that any of the brain map was lost or corrupted, repeating the initial map should fill in any gaps better than finding similar brain map data in the hive."

"He's still wearing a DBI cap here. What's that doing?"

"Normal monitoring. And continued refining and verifying his brain map. Yes. That should eventually tell us if there are any gaps, and might be able to fill some of them in, but it is nowhere near as sensitive as the version in the EN Lab. If we wait too long his damaged areas may degrade too far to be able to retrieve some things the lab scan could have captured."

"If damaged areas are degrading, a second scan might not be as good as the first?"

"It's better than a gap in the scan. It's also possible his brain may be recovering, and a second scan could give better data."

"In which case the brain scan would be pointless. I would skip a rescan but do whatever my wife decides."

John squeezed Minh's hand and then walked towards the exit to meet Fanny in the cafeteria and take over watching Max.

12:05 PM, In the Cave

When Bella brought the rig back Bobbie was waiting.

Bobbie asked, "Did you find anything interesting?"

"Nope."

Bella set it down next to the box with the glow close to the edge of the box. Then she closed the box's lid and sat down on it.

Bobbie said, "I see something."

"What?" Bella asked.

"The box has a *Theme* logo on it. See here on front?" Bobbie indicated the spot on the front of the box.

"*Theme* owns most of the wilderness," Bella said, "Maybe it's something their rangers use."

"*Theme* owns just about everything. But given where we are, you are probably right," Bobbie conceded.

"Do you think it's some kind of communication device?" Bella asked.

"Probably not. Maybe. But probably not of much use inside a mountain," Bobbie conjectured.

"Can we connect to it?" Bella lifted her wristband and said, "Please connect to *Theme's* devices here."

Additional lights in the devices came on, giving considerably more illumination to the space. The brightest light was concentrated in two places: A patch of the floor was illuminated where a tripod of sensors were aimed. Next to the other tripod a holographic image appeared in the air showing a flat surface.

Bella walked around the room carefully inspecting to see if the additional light allowed her to see anything she missed before.

12:10 PM, Elsie on the Move

Elsie was holding and feeding Alex. Alex was eagerly sucking the last drops from a bottle. Elsie gently pulled the nipple out of Alex's mouth before they could start sucking air. Alex's little face rooted around searching for more food.

"Do you want more? Do you want more? Not right now little sweet stinker. We'll get you more in a little while," Elsie said in a sweet voice as she set Alex down in the crib. "Mommy needs to work a little more. You'll be fine for a little while."

As Alex fussed, Elsie walked out the door of Alex's Abitat and into her own. The two were docked in motion as they headed towards Camilla's. As she sat down in the chair at the desk in her own Abitat a miniature hologram image of the crib and baby appeared in the air to the side of her desk and the doors closed so that the Abitats could separate.

12:13 PM, Camilla

Camilla was in her game room eating some of the leftovers from last night off a plate on a small folding tray table in front of her. Sam and Josephine must have taken all the lasagna, but she had some potatoes and other veggies and a glass of the leftover red wine. Good enough for lunch but she would need to make something more substantial for dinner. She wondered if Sam and Josephine would be back for dinner. She brought up a view from public surveillance cameras using facial recognition to find Sam and Jo-Jo. The most recent view showed them walking with two others carrying bags from a convenience store. The other two wore daypacks. They were a few miles away. She would need to check later and see if they were coming back this way before dinner.

As she ate, she switched the view back to another augmented reality world she had created this morning. In it she flew through 3D images of the mountains near where Isabella had been last reported. The scenery was assembled from past satellite and hiker camera images of the area. Current satellite views showed mostly clouds, but the game world reimagined the snowy scenery under the clouds.

Some public images from ranger drones or publicly shared by members of the search teams during the last few hours were also available to add some Abbie-vetted details to the recreation. As she flew over ridges and along trails and streambeds a message appeared floating in front of her indicating that Elsie and Alex were on their way to pay a visit. She wondered if she would have a big group for dinner again tonight. She might order some extra ingredients delivered just in case. But she could explore the mountains for a little while first.

12:16 PM, Andre's Lunch at *The Theme Park*

An Abitat paused at the curb near an entrance to *The Theme Park* and bat-costumed Andre quickly stepped in and came right back out with a box holding his lunch which the Abitat had picked up for him a few blocks away. The Abitat sped off as Andre walked through a hedge into a shady alcove off the tourist path where he could be out of sight of players and he took off his mask. A space creature with purple skin and extra arms was already there eating lunch.

The space creature said, "Hey Bat boy. Haven't seen you lately. How has it been going today for you? Any NeverMind sales?"

"Great, Hans. Eight different people claiming to sell NeverMind in the last hour or so. Six of them registered positive on the sniffer, but I got samples of all eight to send in for testing and slapped a bit of tracker magic dust on each of the sellers," Andre replied. "How about you?"

"Good," answered the purple creature. "Not as great as you, but I think I got a lot of Forgetdibles and at least two real NeverMind samples in the last hour or two. Three, if you count one I set aside for later. Are you still abstaining?"

"Since getting married I'm avoiding NeverMind," Andre replied. "And lately I'm even skipping Forgetdibles. Family man now. Can't be forgetting to pick up the kid or something."

"With just Forgetdibles you're not likely to forget anything that important. At least if you don't overdo it," said the purple one. "Let me know if you need to unwind and party some time. Like old times. Wild Andre. Meanwhile, here's a couple gummies in case you change your mind." The purple alien slipped a couple of wrapped candies into one of the compartments on Andre's utility belt.

12:20 PM, Jose Connects with Gretchen

Jose was sitting in the repaired Abitat, not sure what he was supposed to do with it now that it was repaired. Things were still quiet at work and Modesto was due to come in for the afternoon shift before long.

To kill time Jose had been analyzing the possible impacts of the massive power glitch last hour. The distributed processing of the Nested Cellular Autonomy hive had tremendous redundancy and resiliency, but when tens of thousands of Abitat processing units in an area went into power save mode at exactly the same time, some of the distributed processing packages dropped by one Abitat did not have a backup on another cooperating Abitat. Some purchase transactions and messages were lost, at least temporarily. Some characters in game worlds lost track of what they were doing.

Almost everything was eventually restored as all the Abitats recharged, rejoined the hive, and retransmitted their requests, but there could be some lingering impacts. He checked his software for delivery coordination; it had already refunded a few million microtransaction fees, a few hundred points. No big deal, but he would need to find ways to make the software even more robust to avoid losing data if such a situation or an even bigger one occurred in the future. Maybe he should prioritize hive data more over inAbitant comfort. Or implement a staged power save mode to preserve hive transactions. He might talk with Emily about how to implement it efficiently.

Among the messages that were temporarily delayed he found a response in an old game world message board from his earlier attempt to contact Gretchen.

QX2230Forum: JaviM924^AM to GCKPI^AM

...

Hi J,
Good old QX2230. It's been years.
Pleasantly surprised to hear from you again.
No. I haven't done private investigations lately.
I can try again if you send details and 500 points.
But I'm rusty. I'll give you a discount. 300 points.
Miguel and G still talk if you want to try that again.
Not quite the same after so many years without your input,
a little older, but he's still nice.
No. I didn't create a forensic history world for Billy Jay.
Don't know who did. Probably Billy Jay or the forgetful dad.
I don't think either of them was ever fully honest with me.
Luv, G

Jose sent a message to Honus saying Gretchen didn't make the history world, but he didn't relay her other comments.

12:25 PM, Under Another Bridge

Brock, Doug, Sam, and Jo-Jo sat in plastic chairs in a creek bed under a road. This creek hadn't flooded enough to wash away the chairs which Doug had stashed partly up the bank when the rain was getting started yesterday. It also hadn't flooded the utility closet where he had stashed the package from the Abitat. That package sat on the ground at Doug's feet while the four of them ate sandwiches that Doug had acquired at a shop nearby.

With some of their memories returning, they had been reminiscing about the years that they had shared camps around the county before everyone started getting Abitats and going away, last of all Sam and Jo-Jo. Doug no longer seemed angry and even asked some questions about their lives after they moved away.

"You went all the way to Kansas?" Doug asked.

"My Abby took us to the farthest point from any coast," Sam explained.

"And my Abbie suggested I keep an eye on Sam, so I went too," Jo-Jo added.

As they ate the sandwiches, they all speculated on how Doug had acquired them and remembered and marveled at his ability to get food, drugs, and other essentials whenever they had needed them during the years they had hung out together.

"I figured he is a master shoplifter," Sam theorized. "Ninja. No one sees him going in and taking the stuff. He's like a ghost. In and out of any shop."

"He does like going in alone, but. No. I think they all see him. He loves to be seen. He's just con man extraordinaire!" Jo-Jo offered. "I think he just talks his way to getting people to love him, or pity him, and give him whatever he wants."

"No. He just secretly has a shit ton of money," Brock asserted. "He's got bags of gold and old cash hidden all over the county. He just digs up a few bills or coins whenever he's running low. Shops give him what he wants because he pays in cash. Or they know he's good for paying double later."

"Which is it, Doug?" Sam asked. "Any of us close?"

"I'm not going to say a word," Doug replied with seven words.

"Even if he's not a leprechaun with pots of gold, if that package is full of NeverMind then he is super rich now," said Sam. "Or maybe we are, Jo, if it was from your Abitat."

12:30 PM, In the Cave

Bella said, "Okay. It seems to be some kind of holographic scanner and projector. Maybe it's for analyzing the rocks in here or something? This box in between must be power or data storage or something."

By moving the arms of the projector apparatus, she was able to make the image larger or smaller and change its orientation, but it still showed the same image of a flat surface, which was now projected sideways in the center of the room, like an extra wall floating there dividing the room in two. Bella inspected the projected wall. It seemed to have a front and backside. From the front side it was opaque; she could not see through it; from the back side it was almost transparent; she could see Bobbie, the box, and the apparatus on the other side. She danced back and forth through the wall.

"Now you see me. Now you don't."

After a few repetitions she started to feel weak and a little dizzy, so she went back to the box and sat down.

Bobbie asked, "Are you feeling okay?"

Bella said, "Yeah. Okay. I'm hungry and really thirsty and I was a little dizzy just then, but I think I'm okay now."

Bobbie said, "You should avoid exertion, that burns the oxygen and creates more carbon dioxide. Take a break."

"Okay."

12:33 PM, Honus Learns about Ice Axes

Honus ate his lunch and watched instructions on how to use an ice axe. He asked his Abitat to take off again and look for another spot to set down where he could practice his snowshoe and ice axe skills.

12:35 PM, Machine Shop

As he stepped out of his Abitat after the ride from the office to the machine shop Tristan thought about his partial comprehension of the far-fetched story that Mara had supposedly written. In the story she was the same person as Marta Zynn, the billionaire who died two years before Mara disappeared. And Perry was secretly working for an intelligence agency using some kind of magical data analysis techniques to find vast conspiracies of bad guys or something like that. She had single-handedly invented the AM game, Abitats, and Abbies to try to make the world a better place. Okay. Maybe the story said Perry and others had helped her, but she took most of the credit.

As he entered the machine shop he noticed that the 3D printer was left on last night. He took a quick look. The design for Minh's pterodactyl delivery drone toy was next up. Tristan looked at the design. Nicely done, especially for a little kid. He added a few features to make it actually able to fly and work as a remote-controlled drone and started the printer. He also queued up a modified version of Maxie's cockroach with similar capabilities.

While the printer made a hum in the background he went to his desk and sat down and thought more about Mara's story. It seemed way too preposterous, but then again he wasn't sure. There was this government data base he was about to access. Why did he have access to that? Should he do a deeper search for information about Marta Zynn. Mara…Marta. Similar names. Marta Zynn. Zynn? Where else did he hear that name recently? Last night. Camilla said Bella's dad was Douglas Zynn. Jo-Jo denied it but recognized the name. Douglas Zynn must have been a friend of Sam and Jo-Jo. Mara must have heard the Zynn name from the next-door neighbor years ago and started daydreaming about billionaires. Bella's Dad. Bella. Focus first on Bella and not on Mara's story. Was there any new information about Bella?

Any new seismic data from the area yesterday at 4:35? Yes. There were additional faint readings from additional sensors that allowed him to triangulate the position better. He narrowed it down. The seismic activity was compatible with a sizeable rock fall at 4:35 in an area with a diameter of a half kilometer. That was much more specific than yesterday. He looked at a map of the area. They had gone off of the main trail to the summit. He would need to get that information to the rangers and Honus so that searchers could check out that spot. Of course, Bella might not be anywhere near there. The cutoff of signals at that time might have been a coincidence, but it was worth checking.

He checked on ranger communications. Weather had improved enough that their search drones were in the air. The only thing they had found so far was a construction crane aerial rig perched on a ridge trespassing the wilderness.

He checked on other communications. Honus's search crews had checked a few miles of trails branching out from the last reported campsite, with no sign of the hikers so far. Their searches did not yet include the area with the rockfall. He would review other messages from the area and then update Elsie and get the new location info to Honus. After that he could look for more info corroborating Mara's story and maybe check for more info about his sister's family.

12:40 PM, Still under a Bridge

As they finished their sandwiches attention focused more on the bundle of drugs. Brock was particularly anxious to use it, but Doug held on to it.

"I want to forget some things as much as you do, Brock, but it's not safe yet. I can fix it with the right chemistry," Doug said as he turned the bundle in his hands.

"So do that," Brock said. "Fix it. Do your chemistry."

"Need to get some things from a lab. I know a couple possible places," Doug said.

"Let's go there," Brock urged.

"It's probably better not to carry the package there. Sam and Jo, can you watch it while I get some stuff?" Doug inquired. He added, "But don't let Brock try any of it."

"How long will you take? Maybe you should take Brock with you?" Jo-Jo suggested.

"Maybe. It will probably take at least a couple hours and maybe longer depending on how far I have to go."

"I don't want to wait here for hours," Sam protested. "Jo, Do you want to go back to *The Theme Park* while we wait?"

"That's not safe especially with a bundle of NeverMind," Jo-Jo objected.

"Okay. Okay. We can hide the bundle back in the utility closet and then go," Sam suggested.

"No. The County's going to be checking utility closets after the rain. We need to keep it safe somewhere else," Doug said.

"And *The Theme Park* isn't safe for us now anyway. We could stash it at Sergey's, and you could meet us there later after you and Brock get the stuff you need," Jo-Jo said.

"That might work," said Doug.

12:44 PM, Camilla's

Camilla took her plate back to the kitchen after freezing the mountain scene game world with an Abbie-vetted ranger drone view timestamped from just a few minutes earlier showing a large Honus Resorts flying crane sitting on a ridge. She went to the docking portal. The door opened. Elsie was holding Alex.

"I hope you don't mind us stopping by," Elsie said as she stepped out and handed Alex to Camilla.

"Of course not. It's nice to have company. Hello, sweetheart!" Camilla spoke sweetly to Alex.

"Are your kids here still?" Elsie asked.

"I haven't seen them today," Camilla answered.

12:45 PM, In *The Theme Park*

Emily, Chandra, and Jeremy came out of the exit of a ride with less G forces and lots of music and visuals from a musical story world. Jeremy said, "I'm getting hungry. Do you want to get some food?"

Chandra said, "I can eat."

Emily said, "Sure."

They started looking for a food court, cart, or restaurant.

"We're not far from the NewTech food court where we ate yesterday," Chandra observed. "Or do you want to try something different?"

"Either way is okay for me," Jeremy answered. "Food is food."

"Sure," Emily answered.

Chandra headed away from the NewTech area with Emily and Jeremy following.

12:48 PM, Elsie at Camilla's

Elsie tried to distract Camilla by talking about her kids and cooking. She avoided talking about the strange weather or what was happening in the mountains. They agreed that when Alex settled down for a nap they might do some cooking together. Elsie could share some more recipes. Since Camilla's kids were in town it would be good to have some extra food ready.

12:50 PM, Searching

Scott got word that one of the construction cranes had been spotted by ranger drones and was being asked to leave. It could swing by and pick up some of the search crew members on its way. Nita convinced him that she needed to get out to see her dad who was visiting for the first time in ages, so the crane would pick them up first. Scott also was ready to go himself, but as lead of the search teams he felt like he might need to stay until all the others got relieved. He could get dropped with one of the other crews that was staying.

12:55 PM, In the Cave

After Bella had been sitting quietly for some time Bobbie asked, "Are you feeling any better?"

Bella took a deep breath, cleared her throat, and said, "I'm fine. I want to figure out what this equipment is for and if somehow it can help us. At least it is a distraction."

"Okay. How do we do that?"

"Maybe if we scan the rock walls and floor it will show something else. Like *dig here for gold* or something like that."

"I don't know how that would help. But you can try," Bobbie said.

Bella picked up the scanner device and moved it first to aim at Bobbie instead of at the floor. The holographic image projected in the center of the room did not change. No image of Bobbie appeared.

12:58 PM, Honus Passes Along a Message

As his Abitat set down in a snow-covered meadow Honus put on his cold-weather gear including snowshoes and he picked up his ice axe. Before stepping out he noticed the message from his dad about a more specific rockfall location. He sent a message to Sarah Jones-Smith with the new information. She responded that she would get a search team or drones to check it out. The door opened and he stepped out into the snow.

Chapter 9

Saturday 1 to 2 PM

1:00 PM, In the Lab

"This one?" Taylor asked, touching a push-button switch in an open cabinet, but not pushing it.

"Yes. That one. Turn that one on," Ulla's voice said. "Push it."

Taylor pushed the button, and pinkish lights began to shine from dozens of fixtures on walls around the lab, giving all the equipment in the lab an other-worldly shadowless glow. It was night vision illumination for the holographic sensors, but it gave enough visibility to move around the lab without having to feel your way.

"Can I open the door now?" Taylor asked.

"Not yet. Wait a minute. With solar panel power to the cameras and holographic sensors and communications, the holograms should all come up on this end, so that I can inspect to see what you've damaged. Don't touch anything else," Ulla warned.

Taylor stood by holding the tablet in front of the cabinet. "Do you still need me to hold the tablet camera for you?" she asked.

"Uh. No. I've got the whole lab on holograms again. But I'll let you know if I need a different view."

"What should I do?" Taylor asked.

"Just wait. I need to inspect for damage."

"It's stuffy in here and smells like burned fish. I need to open the door or turn on the air," Taylor complained.

"Okay. Okay. The circuits to the door opener are probably okay. See the button marked D7 in same cabinet?"

Taylor used her tablet to illuminate the cabinet. "Yes."

"Push that and if nothing explodes you should be able to open the exit door and get some air."

Taylor hesitated and then pushed the button. Nothing obvious happened. "What do I do now?" she asked.

"What would you normally do? … Ask your Abbie. She should be able to open the door for you now."

Taylor raised her wristband in front of her face.

"On it," said her Abbie's voice as the door started to open.

1:03 PM, Tristan Looks Stuff Up

In his searches of the agency database Tristan found information similar to what was in the publics sources about the Zynn family. Douglas Zynn was the son of Sandra Zynn and Carlos Anderson Zynn, two of the founders of Zzynarji. The company grew from a startup in the 1980s to one of the biggest private companies in the world by 2019 when Sandra and Carlos both reportedly died of a novel virus. Douglas and his sister Marta apparently both had roles in running the company after that.

Even in the agency records Tristan couldn't find any pictures of Marta. There were several of Sandra and Carlos, and a few of Douglas but still none of Marta. No family pictures with Marta. The whole Zynn family apparently avoided publicity. Their social media history was thin. The pictures Billy Jay had shown him of Mara, and his own recent recollections of her didn't have any family resemblance to the other members of the Zynn family. If Marta looked like Mara then maybe she was adopted, but the agency didn't have records of Marta's birth or adoption. That was an interesting gap. Agency records of Marta's death in a plane crash in 2037 had no more than what was in the public records. Similarly for the disappearance of Douglas soon after that. The last records of Douglas were large cash withdrawals from two of his bank accounts. Maybe he was getting ready to disappear, so maybe the Doug guy mentioned last night might be the same guy. Odd that there was so little about Marta Zynn. 2037 was about the time Mara supposedly started writing her story.

The 3D printer played a tone indicating that it was finished printing. He picked up the two new toys from its output tray and brought them back to his desk. That got him thinking about his sister's family and he started looking up more information about them. Carmen Lee Kovich, Max Kovich, Fanny Kovich Tran, John Tran, Minh and Max Tran. There seemed to be a lot of information about them.

1:05 PM, In the Cave

Bella asked, "Do you think it's broken? The same flat surface is displayed no matter where we point the scanner part. That image made sense when it was pointing at the ground, but it didn't change when we pointed it at you or me or the box."

"Maybe it's a saved image. Or maybe that's not a scanner. It looks a lot like the projector." Bobbie observed. "Maybe it has two projectors."

"But this one has lights like for lighting up a subject. The other doesn't seem to have those. And it captured a view of the floor when we first turned it on. Didn't it? And why would *Theme* have a device with two holographic projectors in a cave in the mountains?" Bella pondered.

"Why would they have even one?" Bobbie countered. "What do you think it is for?"

"I don't know. Maybe there are settings that we can change. Like maybe it does some kind of mineral detection, or maybe it has lasers that can cut our way out of here," Bella said. She lifted her wrist and asked, "What settings are available for this device?"

After a tone from her wristband a familiar voice from a long dead actor who did narration of many *Theme Entertainment* game worlds responded.

"Welcome to the *Thematic* Holo Eighteen.

System Menu:

Power Save: On/Off;

Scanner: On/Off;

Projection: On/Off;

Display Source: Local Preview/Remote/Test Pattern;

Display Options: Various, Just Ask.

Continue with additional command options?"

"How many more command options does it have?" Bella asked.

After another tone sounded the voice responded, "Six thousand two hundred and nineteen specific command options. Do you want to list all?"

Bella said, "No. Display Source: Local Preview, Please."

"Acknowledged."

The hologram floating in the air changed, now showing a half-sized Bella sitting on a box, projected sideways in the air. Apparently the scanner rig was pointing at her. Bella stood up and the sideways hologram image of her did also. She grabbed the scanner equipment and moved it to point at Bobbie and a half image of Bobbie appeared in the projected hologram. As Bella turned the equipment to try to make Bobbie's image right side up the projected Bobbie image turned more towards upside down.

Bella said, "How do I make the image right-side-up?"

"Adjusting," spoke the voice. The displayed image flipped, and a poorly lit Mini-Bobbie appeared to be standing next to the original.

"Actual size?" Bella asked.

The two Bobbie's became identical in size standing next to one another. Even in the low light the quality of the hologram was so good that it was hard to tell which was real. Bella reached out to touch Bobbie's leg on one and her hand went through it. She tried the other one.

137

"That one's me," said Bobbie.

1:08 PM, Tristan Looks Stuff Up

Tristan reflected on what he had found about his sister Carmen and her family. There were some surprises. She had started a small charity named after their parents, Wilson and Abigail Lee, and she funded it with her share of their inheritance. Maybe she wasn't as evil as he remembered. He thought she had spent her share of the small inheritance to buy a house, which would have been fine, but apparently she invested it in a fund giving scholarships to girls playing sports at certain Midwest colleges. She must have been doing better financially than he realized not to need to spend the inheritance on herself. Women's sports scholarships made some sense, since she had relied on sports scholarships and work to get through college. She had complained that her parents didn't support her as much as they supported Perry, which was partly true. He had academic scholarships, but his parents did help too, when they were alive, and his share of the inheritance helped too.

More recent data was also surprising. Fanny, John and family stayed last night at the Honus Beach Resort and Casino. He laughed at that at first. Staying at her cousin's resort. They couldn't possibly know they were staying at her cousin's resort. Or could they? How could they? But there was another surprise that was not at all funny.

They bought lunch today at a hospital cafeteria and charged it to the Honus Beach Resort. Tristan looked for why they were there. Private medical records were stored securely in the hive cloud, but the government database had a copy of some preliminary records, captured from local storage in the hospital. Six-year-old Minh Tran was admitted to Pacific View Hospital after a beach drowning accident. He was in an induced coma while a full-brain DBI mapping was in progress. Oxygen deprivation had caused serious damage in some areas of his brain, and the brain map was attempting to extract and reconstruct pre-damaged contents of damaged areas that might be transferable to a brain assist implant. The mapping had been interrupted by a power failure, and his brain map was incomplete. It was likely that he might be paralyzed or unable to speak until after months of rehabilitation if he survived. The parents had not yet been fully apprised of the assessment.

Hospital records connected to Minh's charts also included links to papers explaining Direct Brain Interface and the scanning and data transfer techniques they were using. In seconds Tristan was able to read and comprehend the papers, which explained both the technology and its medical applications. It felt good to comprehend so much so quickly. It was interesting that he had not thought to read papers on this topic before, given that he himself had been using DBI technology for decades. One name was a coauthor on almost all of the papers: Ami Marks, a non-PhD researcher at *Theme*. Other than her name and position her biography was empty, unlike extensive biographies of the various PhDs that were her coauthors. His new comprehension of the topic started to give him some new insights into his own situation. Later he planned to look for more papers by this Ami Marks person and possibly contact him or her.

He read that brain maps were stored in the distributed hive cloud with optimized data consolidation similar to techniques of Nested Cellular Autonomy, the topic of his own PhD research. He was fascinated to learn more.

Any two brain maps would typically have far over 90% common elements which could be widely shared, analogous to the common parts of the human genome. The remainder consisted of elements that varied by individual, but pieces of which might be shared with many other brains, such as autonomous functions and common skills or knowledge, similar to genes for family traits in DNA. There were also very specific unique elements that might correspond to individual memories or unique skills. Each unique individual's complete brain map was a nested index based on the overall brain structure pointing to the more and less common or unique elements. Even with all the shared components each individual brain map was large and relatively expensive to keep updated.

Some wealthy individuals were storing and frequently updating their own brain maps in the hopes of life extension through robotic avatars.

Medical brain structure models such as for Minh's brain scan, existed in the hive cloud and included software that controlled the interface with his physical brain and indexed his brain map contents, passing information both directions as needed.

Tristan realized he must have a similar brain structure model indexing his own memories, skills, and motivations in the hive cloud. His own brain structure map must be limiting his ability to retrieve certain kinds of memories and making him hesitant to pursue certain topics. That must be why he had such a hard time remembering Mara and motivating himself to find out why. If he could modify that software maybe he could open up his own suppressed memories. Or maybe it wasn't worth the effort. But if not for his own benefit, then understanding it might be helpful for Minh and others. He should pursue it for Minh's sake.

The agency database did not give him access to data inside the secure distributed hive cloud, but he suspected he could get past those limitations with tools that he could find at the ranch house. He was remembering more about how the distributed hive cloud worked when he helped design it years ago. Should he go to the ranch house and investigate the brain maps in the hive cloud, or first visit his niece and her son at the hospital?

1:13 PM, Sam and Jo-Jo

As he walked behind Jo-Jo Sam said, "This is not fun. Can't we just stash that anywhere and go do something fun?"

"We told Doug we'd stash it at Sergey's. After that we can find something else to do," Jo-Jo said as she continued walking with the bundle in her daypack.

"I wish we had our wristbands," Sam complained.

"Yeah. Me too. Maybe that Public Safety guy from last night figured out where they went," Jo-Jo suggested.

"I don't want to deal with Public Safety," said Sam.

"He seemed nice enough," Jo-Jo offered.

"He seemed like an assassin. I might write him into one of my stories as one," Sam said.

"You do that," said Jo-Jo.

1:14 PM, Searching

Scott and Nita were riding in the heavy-lift rig looking down as two more searchers were lifted by lines stretching down from the rig. He planned to be dropped with a third crew before the rig flew out, but a message came through to divert to a new location which seemed promising. He messaged the other two search crews to ask if they wanted to join them at the new location. They would have to ride attached to lines below the rig since it did not have enough seats. They all wanted out, so the rig detoured to pick them all up.

1:15 PM, Eating at *The Theme Park*

It hadn't rained so far today at *The Theme Park*, but it was cloudy and much cooler than normal for this time of year. Jeremy was regretting not bringing a sweatshirt.

"Okay, Chandra. How is this fooling-an-Abitat project supposed to work?" Emily asked as she crumpled up her napkin and put it on the food tray after finishing her food. She picked up her drink to take a sip. They were sitting at a table in a food court near a Magic theme area. Jeremy was still working on his sandwich. He put his hand over his mouth which was full of food and looked up and nodded as if to agree with the question.

Chandra took a sip of her drink and said, "Well. I'll need your help to figure out the details to make this work, but here's the basic idea: We use a QEC communication channel to feed a signal to an Abitat with zero delay, so it thinks it's local."

Jeremy added with a mouthful of food, "Oh and we should try to isolate the Abitat so they can't get contradictory data from other Abitats."

Emily added, "You're saying they trust local signals they recognize as being from their own sensors and their onboard processors, but they normally check that against vetted signals from nearby Abitats, so cut that off."

Jeremy swallowed and said, "And because everything—the game, Abbies, navigation, deliveries, everything—runs distributed across many devices, an Abbie won't be nearly as smart, and easier to fool if they are cut off from other Abbies and Abitats and have to do all their own processing. But how do we cut them off?"

Chandra said, "I'm not sure about that. Maybe the QEC signal will be enough. I suppose we could interfere with the signals that they use to talk to each other or move one very far away from other Abitats. Probably easier to do the first."

Jeremy said, "In the distributed hive environment each Abitat shares its spare data and processing power to help others, but only if they have spare. If you could make all the other Abitats super busy they might stop helping your Abitat for a little while."

"My dad says if they get low on power they go into a power save mode and will try to get more processing help from other Abitats and stop offering help to others until their power gets back up. But how could you get all the nearby Abitats to go low on power at the same time?"

"If all the power in the region went out for a few hours and none of them could recharge. That might do it., eventually. But I don't think that's possible short of an end-of-the-world situation," Chandra said. "I don't want to go to that extreme."

"Might count against our grade if we ended the world," Emily agreed.

"Maybe we can work with data that other Abitats can't verify. Then we don't have to isolate it," Chandra suggested.

"We can probably figure something out," Emily affirmed.

1:20 PM, In the Cave

After experimenting with the projector and the scanner, projecting close-up images of themselves and the box, the equipment, and some of the walls, ceilings, and floors without finding any new features, and changing where the images were projected by adjusting the projector's arms, Bella sat again on the box.

She said, "Let's put it back the way it was for a minute. Display Source Test Pattern Please."

The view changed to a bright moving 3D view of an outdoor mountain scene similar to what they probably would have seen as they were coming over the ridge into this area yesterday if it had been a sunny spring or summer day with no snow. The image filled the room and gave the impression of extending out into the distance in all directions. The sun in the sky appeared as a white circle above. It was bright but not blinding.

"Nice test pattern," Bella commented. "That's a lot of light. I hope this machine has good energy reserves."

Bella, Bobbie, the box, and the equipment were all well-lit in the projected daylight scene, as if they were together on the ridge. The walls and ceiling of the cave were masked by the holographics, which seemed to extend into the distance.

"If this is the test pattern, I wonder what the other flat wall image before was," Bella mused.

"Previous Display Source is Remote," spoke the device's voice. "Do you want to switch back to Display Source Remote?"

"How long will the power in this device last?" Bella asked.

"One hour and nine minutes remaining at current usage levels. Recommend immediately changing power cell or connecting to external power."

"Display Source Remote please."

"Acknowledged."

The image changed to a dim flat surface that was now projected against the floor. It gave enough light to still see things in the cave.

"Now how long will the power last?"

"Sixteen hours and forty-eight minutes at current usage levels. Recommend soon changing power cell or connecting to external power."

"Projection off please."

"Acknowledged."

The light in the cave got dimmer as the projected floor disappeared and the only illumination was from the red indicator lights on the equipment.

"No need to say 'Acknowledged.'"

"One last time, Acknowledged," said the voice.

"How long will the power last now?"

"40 hours and twenty-four minutes at current usage levels."

"Are there any other settings that can extend the power but still be able to give voice commands?"

"With Power Save On the system power can last for up to eighty-seven weeks before power will be fully drained, but each individual voice command will reduce that time by an amount that will depend on the command given."

"Okay. Okay. Power Save On."

One red indicator light remained lit on the equipment.

"Where do you think is the remote source with the floor?" Bobbie asked.

"Good question," Bella said in the dark. "We don't have comms and there aren't any cables running out of here, so how is there a remote source? Some kind of powerful rock-penetrating radio?"

Bobbie said, "I don't know."

Bella asked, "Holographics device, where is the remote source?"

"Power Save Off to respond. Remote location currently unknown."

"Can you make it known?" Bella asked.

"Activating hive relative locator options at remote location requires admin level one passcode."

"Passcode? Bobbie what was the passcode for the box?"

"1234."

"How about 1234?"

"Activated. Please stand by while remote device location is determined by triangulation with nearby peer devices. Remote device located. Do you want a map display of the location?"

"Yes. Please."

The floor of the room became a 3D satellite view of a coastal region with flat ocean on one side and bumpy hills and mountains on other sides.

"That looks like Orange County," said Bella. "Where in OC?"

"X marks the spot," said the voice.

Bella looked for an X on the map and not seeing one she moved her feet. No luck. She nudged Bobbie to move her feet, and an X was visible where Bobbie's left foot had been.

"Isn't that in *The Theme Park*?" Bella asked. "That's close to home. Can you connect our comms to people near the remote source?"

"Enabling Remote Comm feature requires Admin Level 2, Passcode?"

"1234."

"Incorrect."

"Damn!"

"Do want a hint?

"Yes."

"Admin Level 2 passcode is sixteen digits."

"1234-1234-1234-1234?"

"Incorrect. You have five more tries before being locked out for twenty-four hours."

"Ughhh. Another hint?"

"Birthdates of pets."

"Ughhhhhh. 16 digits. Two eight-digit birthdates? Power time left?"

"Five hours and twenty-four minutes at current usage levels."

"Power Save On."

Lights on the unit dimmed, once again leaving only one red glowing indicator light.

1:28 PM, Camilla's

Camilla said, "Alex doesn't seem to want to nap today." She handed Alex to Elsie and said, "Maybe you will have better luck. Maybe Alex can tell I'm nervous. I want to check on the search for Isabella." She walked out of the room towards the game room.

Elsie gently bounced Alex on her shoulder and Alex's eyes closed.

1:30 PM, In the Lab

Taylor sat at her work table in the lab waiting while Ulla remotely checked for more damage. Taylor switched back and forth between two images on her tablet. One was a 3D model of the lab with colorful highlights showing what Ulla had found. The other was a live image of Ulla working in her own Abitat as she zoomed in and examined a live holographic image of the lab looking for damage. More and more blinking red areas appeared on the marked-up model as Ulla worked. Spots and lines of blinking red crisscrossed the model lab, following wiring and cables between the main service panel, various power concentrators, measurement equipment, and the two QEC test Abitats. Relatively fewer green highlights indicated wiring and devices that Ulla had marked as okay.

Ulla didn't tell Taylor that the cables and devices marked red really just indicated devices that would need to be moved for a longer distance test. Green would not have to be changed at all. Orange indicated damaged equipment, but so far there was really nothing that looked seriously damaged other than the cheap fake superconducting jumper cable Taylor had fried across the main breaker. Ulla wanted Taylor to sweat this out as much as possible.

Taylor looked away from her tablet and at the actual lab. It was a combination of pink-glowing equipment from the holographic sensor illumination and some harsh light and shadows near the floor where light entered from the few open inches under the roll-up door. In addition to light, the door gap gave some needed air and might be enough space for Taylor to squeeze under to get out if she needed to but keeping it almost closed blocked the view into the lab for anyone passing outside in the alleyway or in the power station beyond the alley's fence.

Ulla made little grunts or sighs each time she highlighted another area of damage. Taylor sat quietly, absorbing each of Ulla's nonverbal criticisms as the model of the lab became more of a glowing box of red spaghetti. Trying this test on her own had been a bad idea. She was waiting for Ulla to say how many months this would set them back.

The red-glowing spaghetti monster on her tablet seemed to stop growing. Taylor looked at the view of Ulla. She was staring that the hologram in front of her and thinking.

"How bad is it?" Taylor asked.

"Pretty bad. But maybe not as bad as it looks. We should be able to get lighting and air circulation going again with just some minor repairs. And I was going to have to replace some of these power and communication cables anyway for the longer distance QEC test."

"That's good?" Taylor offered.

"The big question is what damage you caused to the QAL equipment inside the Abitats. If we have to rebuild those from scratch that may take weeks or months," Ulla explained.

"How do they look?" Taylor asked.

"I can't tell yet. The lab sensors don't have a view of the interior of the Abitats. Both Abitats seem to be powered down, which isn't good, so I can't use their internal sensors until we restore charging. You must have fully depleted their onboard energy storage. Can you take a tablet camera into Abitat A so I can see how bad it looks."

Taylor silently picked up the tablet and turned on the camera before standing and walking carefully through the pink-shaded surreal lab-scape, stepping over rows of cables on the floor, some lit up by the light from the slightly open exterior door and casting shadows across the floor. The cables looked okay to her. Her feet stepped up from the starkly lit ground through the open door of the first Abitat. Inside was even darker than the dimly lit lab and her eyes needed to adjust. It was lit by indirect light coming in from the lab.

She turned on the light for the camera on the tablet and panned it around the Abitat's interior space. She wasn't sure what Ulla would want her to focus on. She panned the camera from side to side, looking first at the cables coming in the door and then to the Quantum lens equipment on the floor, walls and ceiling in the center of the space and then back to the cables near the door. "What do you want to look at?" Taylor asked.

Ulla's voice said, "The door. Show me the door again."

Taylor backed up into the Abitat and panned the camera around the doorway where she had come in. The cables coming in the doorway looked okay to her.

"No. The other door."

"Huh?" Taylor turned around and noticed that another doorway was visible at the other end of the Abitat. A barely visible shimmering square of distortion was suspended in the middle of the room along the floor, walls, and ceiling. Was that what a Quantum Analog Lens looked like? She hadn't entered the Abitats during the earlier tests to look. She had just looked at the data from the measurement fixture which needed a 1 cm diameter quantum lens in the center of the Abitat for laser light to pass. She thought about the equations of the theory and realized that it might create a larger lens as they used more power to get higher resolution.

Looking through this lens gave an impression of a mirror image of the half of the Abitat she was in, but without herself. A pink glow reflecting off of some lab equipment was barely visible through the other open doorway. She shined her light through the lens illuminating the other doorway, which also had cables running through it.

"Power *is* out, right?" Taylor asked.

"Except solar power feed to the hologram cameras, doors, and comm link," Ulla answered.

"Then how is the QEC hologram still working between the two Abitats?" Taylor asked.

"Maybe there is a cross-connect short between circuits somewhere. I didn't see one, but the way you fried everything maybe I missed it," Ulla speculated. Ulla tried to hide her growing excitement about what she was seeing. Taylor didn't seem to notice.

"If the lens is still working, can we test the resolution and transmission delay?" Taylor asked as she moved the tablet closer to the plane of the lens at the center of the Abitat to get a better image of the door in the other Abitat. It was difficult to see any surface of the lens. If it weren't for the distortion around its edges it seemed to be just open space. She was tempted to put her hand through it but held back not knowing if doing so might cause it to fail.

"Not without powering up the measurement fixtures. They have redundant power sources, but you killed both: Abitat power and power cords from lab circuits. It's probably not a live image anyway. Maybe it's an afterimage left over from when everything got fried," Ulla suggested.

"But my light is lighting up the other side," Taylor insisted. "It must be live. And bidirectional."

"Good point," Ulla said. "This shouldn't be working. But it is, so how do we account for that? Either the hologram equipment still has power from somewhere or something weird is happening."

"Where could it be getting power?" Taylor asked.

"You fried a lot of circuits. Maybe there is enough power leaking between power cables for a standard low-res link. Maybe some power concentrators are not fully drained. Be careful what you touch. Who knows what else is electrified."

Taylor looked around herself to make sure she wasn't brushing up against anything in the Abitat. She had been leaning against the wall, and her foot was touching some cables. She moved gently away from both, happy to be still alive. "What else could it be?" Taylor asked.

"Hologram scanning and projecting equipment has high internal capacitance. Maybe the decay rate for that charge is long enough that it's still working," Ulla suggested.

"This might be the standard Abitat holograms instead of the Quantum Analog Lens?" Taylor asked.

"Maybe, but I don't see how that could be working without Abitat power," Ulla offered.

"Quantum Lens has a random decay rate. The lens stayed open for between 7 and 190 milliseconds after cutting power in our earlier tests," Taylor recalled, "Maybe it's still open."

"This is going on an hour. Not a few milliseconds," Ulla said.

"But the decay period increased with higher resolution. It was milliseconds before, but this was set for a lot higher resolution. Maybe it's still open. And if we passed the theoretical resolution threshold for zero delay maybe the lens stays open even longer. How fast can we power up the measurement fixture and test the transmission delay? Maybe we crossed the threshold and can prove the theory," Taylor said.

"I shouldn't help you test your theory after you literally blew up my lab. You should be punished, not indulged," Ulla countered.

"Punish me later. If the lens really is still open, we don't know how long it might stay open. How do we get power to the transmission delay measurement fixtures?" Taylor asked.

"I shouldn't help you," Ulla said.

"Please. I don't know how long it will be before we can test this again. Please," Taylor pleaded.

Ulla was not used to Taylor saying please so she softened.

"Hold on. I can be there in a couple hours. I rented an upgrade for my Abitat for faster highway travel near St. George and I already crossed the border into California. If I recharge in-transit and don't stop maybe less than two hours. I can get the measurement fixtures working in a just a few minutes after I get there."

"Two hours? The lens might close any second."

Ulla sighed. "Okay. Show me the laser test fixture on the wall behind you."

Taylor turned and pointed the tablet camera in that direction at a box with hundreds of crystals, mirrors and lenses on its surface. A blue power cable came out of its side and joined the bundle of cables going out the door.

"It looks fine. And I can see from my holo view of the lab that its power cord looks fine all the way back to a wall outlet. Can you show me the matching fixture in the other Abitat?"

Taylor first considered leaving the Abitat and running through the lab to the other one but then realized she had a view through the hologram. She directed the tablet light and camera at the holographic image of the interior of the other Abitat and zoomed in on the matching box on the far wall.

"Yeah. It looks fine too. We just need to provide power to those two extension cords without blowing something else up. Let me see. Just a second."

Ulla examined her holographic image of the lab and checked her notes about which devices were on which circuits. Taylor was anxiously bouncing on her heels watching the hologram of the other Abitat to see if it was showing any signs of failing.

"Okay. Here's what you need to do," Ulla finally said.

"What? What?" Taylor asked anxiously.

"Go to the breaker panel cabinet again and push button T9."

"That's it?" Taylor was carefully stepping out of the Abitat and moving across the shadowy room trying to be careful not to touch anything that looked like it could be electrified. "Do I need to plug the extension cords into a different outlet?"

"No. That equipment is on an isolated filtered circuit already. Pushing that button should give that circuit power from the roof solar panels."

Taylor reached the breaker panel cabinet and shined the light from her tablet around the panel until she found a button marked T9. She pushed the button. She was expecting something to happen, but nothing changed that she could see.

"Anything else we need to do to turn on the fixtures?" Taylor asked.

"They're on. They're warming up. I'm starting to see results. Interesting," mused Ulla.

Laser light bounced a few million times per second between the fixtures in the two Abitats by way of the QEC holographic connection. Any delays caused by the QEC connection should add up fast allowing a reading on the delay per pass. There was some uncertainty in the measurements, but the last few tests had stubbornly never proved lower than less than 20 nanoseconds delay per pass, not much better than a regular Abitat hologram. Taylor wanted a reading under 2 nanos per pass to support her Quantum Lens theory. The test fixtures also captured a reading on resolution by analyzing transformations of the laser light waveforms.

Taylor looked for results on her tablet. She found a 3D image of charts and graphs and waveform images. In another window an image of Ulla with her mouth open was suspended next to her holographic version of the data display. Taylor's attention was captivated by the awed look on Ulla's face. Wow. She looked good when she was surprised. But was surprise a good thing? Ulla's holographic finger pointed back and forth between two points in the data display. Taylor focused her tablet on the areas of the data display where Ulla was pointing. Transmission delays per pass showed a number that was dropping. Less than 2.08 nanoseconds and dropping. Less than 1.68 nanoseconds and dropping. The theory was supported. Taylor looked at another part of the data display. Resolution verified greater than 33.82L and climbing. This was not an old-fashioned backup hologram. This was a working Quantum Analog Lens that supported Taylor's QAL theory.

Ulla said, "I'll get there as fast as I can."

1:45 PM, Tristan at the Hospital

Tristan was at the same hospital as Minh waiting to give blood. He had decided to test for kidney transplant compatibility before contacting John and Fanny. That way he would have an excuse for being at the hospital. He figured they would probably mention Minh's accident and invite him to visit them.

Getting tested was more complicated than he thought. People told him they no longer did human-to-human organ transplants at this hospital because artificially grown organs were much safer and almost everyone could tolerate them. Another issue was that they were not able to confirm that his sister was on any list for live organ transplant because he did not have authorization to allow them to access her records. He said he could get that authorization presently from her daughter, his niece, who was at the hospital with her son, but they should take his blood sample regardless. He had to use implied threats of legal action based on legal skills from his brain cap to convince them to take his blood. Since then he had been sitting in the waiting room for the blood drawing lab.

1:46 PM, Doug and Brock

Brock was sitting out of sight under a roadway bridge that passed over the river. He saw Doug coming down the trail ramp and he got up. "Did you get the stuff you needed?"

Doug said, "No. The lab supply place was closed for the holiday weekend, and I didn't see any good way to break in. I know a couple other options. Let's go."

1:48 PM, Honus

Honus climbed back in to his Abitat after stomping around another remote snow-covered meadow his Abitat had found for him. It had an icy slope on one side where he was able to test out his ice axe. He felt more confident in his ability to use his snowshoes and was starting to understand what an ice axe was for. He would look for another location to practice as he headed in the direction of the location his dad had given him.

1:50 PM, Dangling from a Crane

Scott didn't want to be more comfortable than his crew, so he gave up his seat in the rig and took a position on one of the lines dangling below along with three others. That allowed him a great view of the terrain as his feet almost grazed treetops along the way. He had to pull them up a couple of times when it looked like they might. He wondered if the crane's Abbie or the human pilot was messing with him or with the other dangling crew members.

As they neared the new coordinates they pointed to a side trail that looked like it might have had some tracks that were only partially covered by new snow. This seemed promising. The rig climbed to the top of a ridge above the point where the tracks ended to get a view down into two valleys and pick a drop site. Nita's voice came on the comm and said, "I see a climbing rope on the side of the ridge away from the tracks." Everyone looked and a neon green and orange climbing tape was partially visible wrapped around a bent tree on a snow-covered gap in the ridge. Their eyes followed the line of the tape down towards an area near a large new rockpile. Uh oh, thought Scott.

1:55 PM, In a Cave

Bella and Bobbie discussed ideas for how to guess pet birthdays for some random person's pets. Maybe they could ask for more hints, and it would be obvious, but there would probably still be too many options. They didn't want to get locked out. They speculated about how the device could be connecting to a remote source. Bella's wristband could not detect any other comm connections nearby so the holographic device must use some different technology not detectable by wristband comms that worked through solid granite. Bella did not recall working on any intellectual property cases for devices that could communicate that way. But Elsie's office didn't do work with *Theme,* and this was apparently a *Theme* device. They speculated about what the flat floor image from the remote source represented? Was there a similar scanner and projector at the other end, somewhere in the middle of *The Theme Park*? If so, what was it scanning? A floor? A wall? The inside of another box? They decided to reactivate the equipment.

Bella said, "Power save Off." Lights on the unit came back on.

Bella asked, "Are there more hints for the Admin passcode?"

The voice answered, "No. Do you want to hear them again?"

Bella said, "No, thank you." She set all three cameras of the scanner face down on the floor of the cave. Then she said, "Display Source: Local Preview please. The displayed scene was similar to what they had seen on the remote view—a flat surface, but dustier and darker this time.

Bella observed, "The other end is probably aimed at a floor."

Bobbie said, "Probably."

Bella said, "Display Source Remote please."

The view changed back to a clean floor.

Bella asked, "Does this transmit sound along with the holographic images?"

The distinctive voice responded, "Audio options include Scanner Mute: On-Off; Projector Mute: On-Off."

"What are the current audio settings?"

"Scanner Mute On, Projector Mute On."

"Are there volume settings?"

"Yes. Audio volume ranges are 0 to 0 with Mute On, and 1 to 100 with Mute Off."

"How much power does this use with Mute Off and Volume set to 100 for both scanner and projector?"

"It depends on the sound levels and the image projection brightness levels."

"How about with minimal image projection brightness levels?"

"It can vary with audio signal details, but at least forty-three hours."

"I'll probably be dead from dehydration or asphyxiation by then. Let's do this."

"I'm not sure how to respond to that," said the *Theme* actor voice.

"Okay. Turn on the audio with volume turned up all the way so we can hear any sounds from the other end."

A loud background of overlapping versions of *Theme Park* music could be heard along with muffled shouts and roars and thumps of some attractions and rides. A murmur of crowd noises, but no understandable individual voices could be heard.

"Okay. Let's try the other direction. Unmute us and turn up the volume on the other end to the maximum," Bella commanded. Then she asked, "Is it on?" and a loud echo of her voice came back. "IS IT ON?" which was so loud she had to cover her ears. She whispered, "Set audio volume on our end to 40." The whispered words echoed back loudly. Afterwards she could still make out the background music, but it seemed more distant. She said "Testing. Testing. Testing," in a more normal voice and the echo was still a bit too loud. She barely whispered, "Set audio on our end to 20," and then in a louder voice she said, "Testing."

The echo of the final "Testing" was bearable. The music in the background from the other end was barely audible.

The distinctive voice suggested, "You appear to be trying to deal with the audio feedback of your own audio input. Would you like to turn on feedback noise cancelling?"

"Yes. I think so. Yes."

The first 'YES' echoed back but the rest of her utterance did not.

"That's better. Now let's see if we can catch someone's attention. HELP! Can anyone hear me? HELP!"

She stopped and listened to see if she heard any response and then repeated her cry for help.

1:58 PM, Jose Finishing Work

Jose set down a tablet and leaned out of the open door of the repaired Abitat. Modesto was sitting in an empty service bay playing some game on another tablet. He had arrived a half hour ago and had been idle since he got in. They were both still waiting for a customer that needed more than an automatic refresh or exterior wash.

Jose glanced to make sure that the tablet he had been using was logged out. He had been checking on his personal messages. No response from Honus after he told him that Gretchen didn't make the history world. No response from Elsie after he reminded her he needed her recommendations for private investigators to check on Brock. He probably shouldn't do any more personal work while on the clock. Maybe he should just head home.

"Hey. Modesto. I think I'm going to clock out," Jose said.

"You think I can handle the big rush we're having all on my own?" Modesto asked while continuing to play games on his tablet.

"If you think you're up to it."

"Yeah. Go on."

Jose looked back into the repaired Abitat. It was ready to go but he had not received any specific instructions on what to do with it after repairs. Two old wristbands were in the Abitat in a mesh bag that blocked radio signals. He wondered if the bag worked as well or better than the metal cover he had fashioned for blocking signals from his own wristband. Probably better. He should get one.

He spoke to the walls of the Abitat, "Hey, Abbie, where are you going after your repairs?"

"No plans. Waiting to hear from my inAbitant or Public Safety."

"Did the Public Safety people give you any instructions?"

"Only to return here for repairs. May I wait for more instructions?"

"Hmmm," said Jose. He picked up the bag with wristbands, took one out, and said to it, "Abbie? You shouldn't stay here blocking a service bay. Be on your way." He stepped out of the open door and put the wristband back in the bag which he put in his pocket.

"Acknowledged," said the Abitat's Abbie voice as the door closed.

Jose headed towards the employee entrance, waving at Modesto as he passed him. Behind him the Abitat rolled out of the service bay and towards the street. Jose clocked out and went out to the sidewalk. He took off his own wristband and instead of putting on the metal cover he took the bag out of his pocket and added his wristband in with the other two before putting it back in his pocket and walking towards home.

Chapter 10

Saturday 2 to 3 PM

2:00 PM, At Camilla's

Camilla walked past the open docking portal door where she saw that Alex was sleeping in the docked Abitat. She continued quietly into the living room where Elsie was sitting looking at a tablet.

"Well, that doesn't make me any less nervous," said Camilla.

"What? What did you find out?" inquired Elsie.

"Some people in the mountains flew to a spot where they thought Isabella might be. There is a big new rockslide in that area. It doesn't look good."

"Oh. How did you see that?"

"Some of them are sharing live feeds. I set up a live feed world in my game room based on those."

"They shouldn't be sharing images publicly like that."

"Maybe not, but I want to know what's happening, even if the news isn't good."

"They'll find her. She'll be okay," Elsie assured her in her most reassuring voice, but with some misgivings that came through to Camilla.

"The baby's napping. Did you want to cook?" Camilla asked.

2:05 PM, Sam & Jo-Jo

"I'm not used to walking so much. My foot hurts," Sam complained. "Can we stop?"

"You know we're almost to Sergey's," Jo-Jo answered. "We'll rest when we get there and stash the package."

"And then just sit around waiting for Doug to come back with his chemistry set? This is bo-ring."

"We can go talk to the parent. Maybe get some food," Jo-Jo offered.

"Or maybe try a little sample of Doug's special package?"

"He said it would kill you."

"I think he's just trying to save it all for himself and Brock."

"You really want to test that theory?"

2:08 PM, Sandy J., Jameel, and Charly

Sandy J. and Jameel were in the underground train from the western *Theme* park to the main *Theme Park*. Jameel was talking with Charly over his wristband.

"Sandy J. wanted one of the ice creams that they only sell in the kids' area of *The Theme Park*. The western park's version has a different cone. I can't tell the difference, but we're headed over there. ...Just a couple more minutes and we'll be there, Sandy J."

"Sounds like you are being a good dad," Charly said.

"An indulgent dad, anyway. Are you ready for the festival? And did you find out what to do to help a homeless guy?" Jameel asked.

"The Festival is all on track. Some last-minute changes in the entertainers, but no big deal. I fixed it. And, yes, I found some services available for people with mental or drug issues. Basically, just give them an Abitat and the Abbie will help them get all the help, but I'm thinking about what you said about who owns the house. Maybe we hold off on getting him help for right now, at least until we are sure who he is. If he was good for years on his own, maybe he will be good for a few more months. Eventually we can try to get him an Abitat, but maybe we leave things alone for now. Don't rock the boat. No big surprise announcements at the Festival."

"Okay. Find out more about him first. Maybe I should talk to English. You remember him?"

"Your unsuccessful journalist friend?"

"He did a piece about your cousin after the fire. He might know something that would help us decide if this guy is Barack."

"Maybe worth a call. Sorry. I've got to go now. Have fun."

2:12 PM, Jose and Magnolia

Jose made good time the few blocks between work and his home. As he entered the courtyard with the cat houses and his trailer he saw Dr. Magnolia sitting at a picnic table holding a cat and a clipboard. She looked up as he walked towards his trailer.

"Hey. Joe. I gathered the residents' demands for you."

"Hi. Dr. Magnolia. Is that so?" Jose asked. "That was quick."

"There might still be some I couldn't track down, so I added four free rent 2-bedroom condos and two extra free Abitats to the list as placeholders, but here is what I was able to gather," she held up a few pages of hand-written notes clipped to her clipboard.

"Some insist on living within four blocks of this site, or close to other places they work or have family, but most are open to anything in the County within ten miles of the coast. A couple would be fine moving farther if they get homes and Abitats. We need four restaurant spaces of at least 2500 square feet each. Two cosmetology spaces. Two legal or medical professional offices, not counting the veterinary clinic. I marked which ones would want Abitat compatibility and which ones want to avoid that. I put you down as a *no* on that. Four would be okay with Abitat-only. For my animal sanctuary I'll need a half-acre or more of land—two acres would be better—and I spelled out the office and animal housing requirements. You can look over the details." She held out the clipboard.

"Wow. Dr. M. Thanks for that," Jose took the clipboard.

"Hold on. There's two copies there. You get one copy. I'll keep the other." She took back the clipboard and peeled off half the pages and handed them to him, keeping the clipboard with the other copy. "I'm not providing the real names of the residents. We are all listed as John, Jane, or Jo Doe numbered 1 through 25. No one wanted their names going anywhere until there's a real offer. But you probably know who some of us are."

"How'd you get in touch with everybody so fast?" Jose asked.

"Contact info through the homeowners' association."

"Homeowners? Renters or squatters might be closer. Since when is there an association? And why don't I know about it?"

"It's been around for a while. I organized it. We all felt better leaving you out of the loop, until now. We help each other out. We like to call ourselves homeowners. We each have our own home even if we rent or borrow the space for it."

"Interesting," Jose said as he looked at the pages.

"Look it over, Joe, and let me know if you have questions," Dr. Magnolia said. She stood up and started walking towards her clinic.

Jose continued to his trailer, glancing at the pages.

2:15 PM, Ulla on the Way

Ulla checked the progress of her trip. Her souped up Abitat was averaging over 200 miles per hour crossing the desert on highways that skirted around the larger desert cities. The last part of the trip up ahead, which would be entirely in town, would be a lot slower even if she kept paying premium tolls to other Abitats and transport big rigs to clear a path for her. It would probably be another hour or more before she got back to the lab.

Meanwhile she was making progress on checking which lab circuits were safe to turn back on. So far all good. She had designed the power circuits in this lab well if she did say so herself. But she saved most of them to turn on when she got back. She did let Taylor have a little more lighting.

The measurement fixture was still returning data showing that the Quantum Analog Lens was still open and performing even better than Taylor's theory predicted. Ulla suspected it might be permanently open without power, and the implications of that boggled her mind. But she didn't tell Taylor that.

Taylor had really accomplished a scientific and technical miracle. She wouldn't tell her so, because she didn't want to give her any credit after blowing up the lab, but this was probably Nobel or even *Theme-Prize* material. She would need to gather a lot of notes about exactly what Taylor did today so that this could be reproduced. And then maybe mass-marketed? This could really pay back all she had invested and then some. She could silence the cordial criticism from her dad and stepmom for all the money she had put into this. Although they might not like her undermining a *Theme* product.

2:20 PM, In a Cave

"Help." Bella's voice was hoarse. "Hell…ughh…peh."

She listened and the noises from the other end were basically the same as they had been for the last half hour. Distant joyful music and indistinct crowd noises mixed with screeches and bumps. She imagined times she had spent at *The Theme Park*, when that background noise would have been reassuring and unmitigatedly pleasant. Somehow now it sounded foreboding.

She whispered or croaked hoarsely, "It must be in some kind of storage room or closet away from where people go. Or my cries for help are just blending in with the crowd noises."

"We need to get someone to notice. If it is as loud on the other end as it was here, someone is bound to hear it," Bobbie reasoned.

"Can you take over calling for help?" Bella asked. "My voice is going. My throat is so dry."

"I'll try," said Bobbie. "Hello! Hello! Is anyone there? We are trapped and need help!"

They listened for a minute. The background noise was about the same. Bobbie spoke again, "Hello! Hello! Help us please!"

2:23 PM, Jose at Home

Jose sat in his trailer looking at the security camera images of the complex and glancing at the document Dr. Magnolia had given him. He recognized some of the J. Does based on the kinds of business units they asked for, and he tried to imagine where each of the other anonymous *homeowners* fit in the buildings. Were there really that many people living here? Seeing his own trailer and its waste container reminded him he needed to drain it before using it again.

With no response so far from Elsie about recommendations for private eyes he decided to compose another message to Gretchen. He took his wristband out of the signal-blocking bag and went through his elaborate login to send a message on the QX2230 forum. He asked if she could see if there was any evidence that Barack Jackson was still alive and possibly living off the grid in the County. She might find photos of him from before the River Glade fire and try to do facial matching with more recent public video images of people on the streets and trails. He transferred her 300 points.

He went to put his wristband back in the bag and remembered he had two more wristbands in there. He presumed they must belong to the people who were at the house of Alex's childcare, and he should give them to Elsie to pass along.

2:26 PM, Honus Sets Down

Honus' Abitat set down at the edge of the area his dad had identified as a likely location for a rock fall. He didn't see any signs of rockfall here, but he figured it should be within a half kilometer ahead. It would be good to get a sense for the conditions near here before going further on foot. He took a small black case from a cupboard in the Abitat and put it into his pack and then stepped out in his winter gear with snowshoes and ice axe. After a few steps the surfaces became too icy and steep for the snowshoes. There was not enough accumulated snow on most of the steep surfaces. He retreated to his Abitat and asked what kind of gear would work here. He was shown an instructional game world about using crampons on his boots. So that's what the other spiky things were for. He put them on and stepped out again.

2:30 PM, Rockfall Damage Assessment

Two members of the team had rappelled down to the saddle where the climbing tape was tied, two down to the trail with tracks on one side, and four into the area with the rockpile on the other side. The rig flew off and set gently down on an exposed rocky peak nearby where it could let the rock take some of its weight. Winds were light so it could maintain its balance while saving power.

Scott hesitated to report the find until they could assess the situation more fully. They hoped to be able to report a live rescue, but the rockpile was ominous. Comparing satellite photos from a week earlier showed the rock pile was on top of an older scree pile of small rocks that had been clear of trees.

Other than the climbing rope they didn't find any more evidence at first. Most of the crew kept a distance back from the rock pile out of caution that more rocks might still fall. Nita however went right up to the edge of it, climbing on the rocks that were close to the trees that surrounded the area and looking in the spaces between the rocks.

"I found 'em!" she shouted. "Under here."

Scott moved through the trees surrounding the area closer to where Nita was perched looking under a large rock.

He asked, "You found them?"

"Edges of a tent under this rock." She tapped on the jagged rock half the size of an Abitat that she was standing on. "Looks like a top-of-the-line tent shelter—lightweight, sturdy, and warm in a storm—but no match for 20 tons of rock."

Another crew member came out of the trees behind Scott and asked, "Do you want to try to lift that thing? One rig probably won't do it."

2:35 PM, Brock and Doug

Doug said, "Brock, That was a long way around. I still don't understand why you wanted to go so far off the river trail, but we're almost to the college now. They have some chemistry labs that might open up with your magical county passcode."

"I don't think that will work here," Brock said.

2:36 PM, Sam and Jo-Jo

Jo-Jo put the drug bundle in a secret spot behind a wall panel in the shed at Sergey's and hung some garden tools back up on the wall in front of the panel. She said, "That should be safe until Doug and Brock get back."

"Now what?" Sam asked.

"To the parent's?" Jo-Jo suggested.

"My foot hurts. I want to rest a minute first," said Sam as he stretched out on one of the cots and took off his shoe and prosthetic.

2:37 PM, Tristan Gives Blood

After almost an hour of waiting Tristan finally was called in from the waiting area to give a blood sample, which only took a couple minutes. Afterwards he contacted John to let Fanny and him know he had done so and mentioned the hospital he was at. It turned out John was not at the hospital but at *The Theme Park*. John said to hold on for a second while he talked with Fanny. He came right back on the line and told

Tristan about Minh's accident and that since he was at the same hospital he could meet Fanny outside the Pediatric Intensive Care ward at three.

2:38 PM, Elsie Cooks

An array of ingredients were arranged on the countertops in Camilla's kitchen. Elsie had looked through what Camilla already had on hand before ordering. They had also picked some fresh herbs and tomatoes from Camilla's garden out back. But most of what was on the counters had been delivered a few minutes ago and sorted and measured out into small bowls or plates by Elsie.

Camilla came back into the room and said, "Alex is still napping. Where do we start?"

"It's a little early to start on the dinner food items. How about we make the cookies first?" Elsie suggested, indicating one of the countertops with baking ingredients.

2:40 PM, Tim in Honus Lake

"Is this where Manzanita Spencer works?" Tim asked.

"Who's asking?" replied the woman behind the desk. "And how did you get in here?"

"She's expecting me. We're family. Is she back from her special assignment in the mountains yet? She said she was on the way and to meet her here."

"Nita is going to be a little while longer."

"How long?"

"Can't say. Now they're looking to send more crews in, not letting anyone go home just yet. Not sure why. With Search and Rescue turning into a Recovery operation, they could probably take their time."

Another worker came up to the woman behind the desk and said, "Scott has two but says he might need more cranes. I'm having trouble finding crews for the other heavy lift rigs. The crews who flew the other two rigs that came back last night split for vacation as soon as they got back."

"I guess we may just have to tell Scott that it can't be done until next week, unless you give me the okay to send them in without a crew," said the desk woman.

"If you need help, I can operate a heavy lift aerial crane," Tim said. "And I'll do it for free if I can go see Manzanita."

"Is that so?" asked the woman behind the desk. She turned to the other worker and said, "Quiz him on his credentials. If he checks out, rigs G12 and K9 are fully charged and ready to go." Turning to Tim she said, "You can't fly two rigs at once, can you?"

2:44 PM, Ice Cream

While Sandy J. was enjoying his favorite vegan ice cream with candy corn cone from the Kids Zone Kone-cession Stand, Jameel called his friend who worked in journalism, or who at least tried to create documentary story worlds.

"Hey English! This is Jameel...Yep. That Jameel...Good. You too?...Just a random thought that you might know something about...Yeah. With Charly doing the Memorial this weekend for her famous dead cousin, people might put me on the spot to say something about him...I was wondering what the old Brockster was like besides what's in the standard memorial speeches? ...Any back story I could mention if someone asks me? ...No. I never met him. ... Weren't you working on a history world for him before someone beat you to it? ...Find anything interesting? ...Yeah. I'm busy too. With SJ at *The Theme Park* now...If you have time to look at your notes, give me a call if there's anything interesting in there...Yeah. Okay...Later."

2:45 PM, In a Cave

Bobbie had tried variations of pleas for help in six different languages, but there were still no responses.

Bella tested her voice again. "Hello!" She coughed. Her throat was scratchy, but she could speak. With no response to her hello, she addressed her wristband, "Hey. Machine. How much time now 'til your power runs out?"

"At current usage levels, sixteen hours and 42 minutes."

"I thought you said at least forty-three hours."

"That was with minimal projection brightness. You are currently projecting a remote image."

"But you said…Damn," Bella croaked. "Turn that off."

The room darkened as the dim image of a clean floor disappeared.

"How about now?"

"Thirty-eight hours."

"That's better," Bella said and turned to Bobbie. "Will that get us through the weekend?"

Bobbie said, "That will last through 6:45AM Monday."

Bella said, "But what if no one will be there at the other end to hear us until after the holiday weekend? What if it's in a storeroom or office of a *Theme* person who doesn't work holidays and won't be back until Tuesday or later?"

Bobbie did not respond.

Bella spoke again, "Is there anything else we can shut off and still keep the audio?"

"Disabling image scanning and transfer would add thirty-six hours," said the *Theme* actor's voice.

"That's gets us to Tuesday, right?"

Bobbie nodded.

"Do that."

A glow under the scanner tripod facing the floor faded out and the room got very dark.

"What if we add a little light?" Bella asked.

The scanner lights came back on, but the projected image of the floor did not reappear. "Sixty-eight hours," said the *Theme* voice.

"Maybe a little…" Bella cleared her throat, "…Never mind. Good enough." Bella's voice was getting hoarser again.

2:50 PM, Two Cranes

Two cranes were hovering near one another a couple hundred feet above the rockfall area with cables and straps lowered. Nita and other crew members were securing the cables around the rock that was on the tent. Nita gave an arm gesture to lift, and the two cranes revved their engines. Even at their significant height, the winds from the cranes' fans was intense on the ground. Tree branches were moving and dust from the rockfall was blowing, making the crew cover their faces.

The pilots in the cranes gave the no-go signal. The rock was too heavy. They would need at least three cranes to lift it, or blast first to break it into smaller chunks. Some on the ground were saying that they should leave it be and not disturb the dead.

2:55 PM, John Distracts Max

Max and her dad were back at *The Theme Park* in a gift shop. Max was more interested in shopping than going on a ride.

"Can I buy one of these?" Max asked, picking up dinosaur toys.

"Sure. Honey. Which one do you want?"

"Minh would like this one," she said holding up a winged dinosaur. "Can I get this one? For Minh."

"Okay," said her dad. He took it and held it over his wristband and then handed it back to her.

"Did Minh die? Is he dead?" Max asked. "Will I get his toy if he's dead?"

"No, Maxie. He just needs to rest today. That's all."

"People die from drowning. He's going to die, right?"

"Some people die from drowning, but Minh will be okay. We can go back and see him soon. You can give him this toy."

"If I'm not getting his toy then I want one for me too."

A teen boy was looking at a rack of warm sweatshirts in the same store. Two girls were with him. One wearing a headscarf and long dress pointed at Max and whispered to the other, "Kind of a dark conversation for a little kid, right?"

2:59 PM, Jose

Jose was washing his hands in his trailer's bathroom after emptying the trailer's toilet waste jug into a nearby sewer cleanout. He had looked at his options for making a permanent sewer connection. Running a drain line from the trailer to the sewer cleanout above ground would be unsightly and a tripping hazard. Putting it underground would be too much work. The only reasonable option would be to move the trailer closer. He had paced off how far he would have to move the trailer and made a list in his head of parts he would need. If he ordered them today on a holiday weekend Saturday it might take a few hours to get them delivered.

But the trailer was too heavy to move on his own. He would need either a couple extra strong bodies or a vehicle to tow it. He didn't know who he could ask to help, but he knew Dr. Magnolia's car had a trailer hitch. She would probably be willing to let him use her car. He rinsed his hands and watched the water go down the drain. He remembered that the sink water drained into the little vegetable garden outside. If he moved the trailer close to the sewer cleanout how would he water the vegetable garden?

He decided he could put up with unpleasant task of emptying the toilet waste container a little longer. It might not be long if he sold out to the development project.

After abandoning the sewer hookup project, he sat down at his table and looked again at the pages that Dr. Magnolia had given him. She had done a pretty thorough job. He should be able to get a response back to Honus today or tomorrow with the requirements from the residents, but he still needed to decide what his own requirements were. He should at least let Honus know he was working on it.

He logged in to send a quick note to Honus and noticed that Gretchen had already contacted him back. Her response said Barack Jackson was likely still alive. Likely, but not an Abbie-vetted fact. Images of him from before the fire matched some images from recent public videos of a man walking on streets and trails in the County. But the person in the public videos avoided directly facing the cameras. She sent some of the recent images. Jose was pretty sure they were Brock, but he would need to send them to Elsie. She should be able to tell.

Chapter 11

Saturday 3 to 4 PM

3:00 PM, Tristan and Fanny

Tristan followed Fanny into the pediatric intensive care ward.

Fanny said quietly, "Thanks for getting tested. I need to release my mom's data to see if you're a match, but I can't right now. They are weaning Minh off the sedatives. They said it will probably be a few hours before he wakes up, but I need to be here in case he wakes up sooner. I hope you don't mind." She led Tristan to a bed with a small person connected with many wires and tubes.

"Of course I don't mind. I'm honored you let me see him. Oh. I see he has a cap," Tristan said while lifting his beret to show his own DBI cap. "I know something about living with one of those."

"His is just while he's in the hospital. I hope. No offense."

"None taken. I'd like to avoid it myself. Are his eyes opening?"

"Minh. Minh, honey. Are you awake?" Fanny asked, leaning in close to him.

"Hi Mom. Uncle Perry? Can Max and I come over and make some more toys?"

"Sure. But later," Tristan said. "I printed out your pterodactyl toy, but I forgot it in my Abitat." Fanny was face to face with Minh, talking quietly. Tristan started to back away from the bed. He said to Fanny, "I should go now. Do you want me to message John to let him know Minh woke up?"

173

"Could you do that?" Fanny said as she gently held Minh's hands and stared into his eyes.

3:03 PM, Ulla Returns

The high-speed Abitat was able to negotiate priority passage through town better than Ulla expected. It cost her a few thousand points, but that was okay. The larger and higher high-speed highway undercarriage on her Abitat was a tight fit in the alleyway, but when doors on both her Abitat and the lab were fully opened, she was able to step down and straight through from Abitat to lab. As the doors closed behind her, her Abitat backed out of the alleyway to go change back to a normal in-town chassis.

Taylor started to say something, but Ulla just held up her hand and went straight to the circuit breaker box. She had a tablet with notes on which circuits to reconnect in what order. Tap, Click, Click, Tap. Click. Click. Snap. Full lighting returned to the lab and air circulation fans began blowing away the remnants of smoke. Holographic displays appeared above the work tables.

3:05 PM, Honus Returns to His Abitat

After climbing some of the slopes outside using crampons and the ice axe Honus started to get a sense about when to use the crampons and when to switch back to the snowshoes. He even tried out glissading down the short icy slopes with support of the ice axe. He felt a little bit like some of the adventurer characters he played in game worlds many years ago. He was ready to move forward.

He entered his Abitat, began loosening his gear, and said, "Any news from the search teams?"

The British butler voice said, "Yes. Some hiker gear has been located near here, but no signs of life."

"How do I get there?"

"Two aerial cranes and eight members of the search teams are already in the area, about 200 meters from here. There is not much room for landing. I can drop you on a ridge above, where there is a rope you can rappel down to the area, or you can traverse from here."

"How would I traverse from here?"

"You would need to climb to the top of the ridge you were just climbing, glissade down the other side and then walk through the forest for 100 meters. Here is an illustration."

A 3D image of Honus trudging, climbing, sliding, and tromping played in fast motion in the Abitat.

"I don't know about that," he said. "What's the other option?"

The holographic image changed to showing the Abitat hovering at the edge of a narrow gap in a ridge and Honus jumping out of the open door, catching hold of a bent tree branch and then sliding down a rope tied to the branch.

"Yikes. Any other options?"

"Not without additional gear."

"Show me the traverse option again."

3:08 PM, Camilla's Kitchen

The smell of warm cookies cooling on a platter in the dining room filled the house, but other smells of chopped ingredients were also starting to permeate the kitchen. Elsie demonstrated the chopping of garlic and herbs and said, "Give Alex to me. You do the rest, Camilla."

"I don't think I can do it like you did."

"Sure, you can. You'll do fine. Just remember the knife is very sharp." Elsie set down the knife and moved away from it before taking Alex from Camilla's arms.

3:10 PM, Sergey's Shed

Jo-Jo sat on the side of a cot and looked over at Sam who was lying down on another. Doug's bundle of drugs was still in its hiding place, but Sam kept looking in that direction.

"When do you want to go to the house?" Jo-Jo asked Sam.

"Do we really need to?" Sam asked in return.

"I don't know," Jo-Jo replied. "We said we would check in. And that police friend of hers said he would get in touch through her if he had news about our wristbands or my Abitat."

"I don't want to deal with police, but it would be good to get our wristbands again. I need to check on my Abitat."

"You mean your Abbie."

"Same difference."

"Want to go now?" Jo-Jo asked again.

"Not yet. What do you think about the NeverMind question?" Sam asked sitting up on his cot and looking it at the package's hiding place.

"Use it, sell it, or get rid of it?" Jo-Jo summarized.

Sam replied, "Use it? I miss the bliss, but remembering things gives me more to write about."

Jo-Jo said, "It depends on what we remember. It sounds like Doug and Brock want to use it: Both have things they really don't want to remember."

Sam said, "You think the same will happen to us? We might not like what we remember if we stay off the drugs."

Jo-Jo said, "I'm not proud of some of the things I already remember, but I'm willing to risk remembering some more."

"If we don't use it what's the next choice?" Sam asked.

Jo-Jo answered, "Sell it. Doug offered us a share, and we could sell it. That could be worth millions of points, or dollars anyway. We could afford living near here again with that much extra. Or go back to Kansas and buy some houses or land. But we probably would get caught and get into big trouble. If I suddenly had lots of extra cash my Abbie would give me hell about it, and whoever Doug stole it from might not be happy."

"Not to mention the parent, if she found out," Sam added.

"Which she is bound to do," Jo-Jo confirmed. "She hears everything." She looked around to see if anyone was listening here.

Sam said, "That leaves letting Doug and Brock have all of it. But it seems like a shame to throw away an opportunity like this."

"When are we meeting with them again?" Jo-Jo asked.

"I don't know. I think they said they would meet us here after they found some stuff for cooking the NeverMind," Sam said.

"What do you think of the things people have been remembering?" Jo-Jo asked.

"Some of it fits with my stories," Sam replied. "Doug might really be the same Douglas guy I wrote about going to college with. Maybe I knew Brock back then too, but I don't think I knew him as well as Douglas. You and Douglas were a thing, right? Is he really Izzie's dad?"

Jo-Jo said, "I'm really not sure. Maybe. But I'm starting to remember a few other guys—a lot of other guys—from that time, so I'm not sure. When I turned 18, I figured I was legal so I could do it with everyone older than me, and I tried to."

Sam said, "I was on some very nice pain meds then, so I don't really remember that."

"Later, of course, I was into Doug when we were living with the camping group and taking a lot of drugs. Looking back though, I think Doug and Douglas probably were the same guy, but I didn't know it. What do you remember about Douglas?"

Sam said, "Hmm. He was rich, I think. Douglas Zynn is the name that comes to mind."

"That's what Camilla said."

"He lived up north near Berkeley or Palo Alto but had a beach house near Newport where we partied sometimes."

"That sounds familiar. Why doesn't he want to remember being rich?" Jo-Jo asked.

"I think he feels guilty."

"About being rich?"

"No. About causing harm."

"By being rich?"

"I think this happened on my boat trip with him," Sam picked up his prosthesis and raised his leg showing his stump.

"That must have been an accident, and you probably caused it," Jo-Jo objected.

"Yeah. Probably," Sam admitted. "In the story I've been writing about that trip, Douglas and I both were wasted most of the time. He made most of the drugs himself. Maybe he felt responsible." He looked at Jo-Jo who shook her head disbelievingly. "Okay. Probably not. But if it's not that, then what?"

"Brock and him both said something about a fire and people dying," Jo-Jo said.

"Did the Lahaina fire happened when we were over there?" Sam wondered. "You think they feel responsible for that?"

"Maybe," Jo-Jo said, "But Brock said he went home before that fire. Still, maybe that's it. Maybe they did something that led to the fire. If we had our wristbands, we could ask Abbie how that fire started. See if it might have been by careless hikers or people cooking drugs in the hills or something."

"Maybe the parent has a connection we can use to check on that," Sam suggested.

"And she probably remembers everything from back then herself. We could ask her," Jo-Jo added. "She should be called Abbie instead of Camilla."

Sam warned, "But she has strong opinions about everything she remembers. Not everything she says is Abbie-vetted truth."

Jo-Jo said, "True. But maybe she's heard something from the police guy about our wristbands."

"Yeah. I guess we should go and ask," Sam said. "And maybe she'll give us the passcode for her holo-deck game room."

"That could be fun."

3:18 PM, Jameel and Sandy J. Wait for a Ride

Jameel said into his wristband, "Yeah. Char. I thought we were just getting ice cream, but SJ saw the line for the *WorldOfWhirled* ride, and he insisted. The queue looks like it might be another half hour. I'll let you know when we're on our way home."

3:19 PM, Tristan on Way to the Ranch House

In his Abitat on the way to the ranch house Tristan checked for news about Bella. He did not have access to the agency database from his Abitat, but some of the searchers in the mountains were publicly sharing videos and comments. He noticed that they had found remains of a tent under a new rock fall. He thought it was inappropriate for them to be sharing that information publicly. He wondered if Elsie or Camilla had seen it. He sent a message to Elsie.

3:20 PM, Camilla's

While Elsie took Alex out of the kitchen to give them a bottle and quietly check for any updates from Andre or Tristan, Camilla stopped chopping and sneaked back to her game room to check on the mountains. The discovery of remains of a tent under a boulder was disturbing to both of them. Camilla hurried back into the kitchen, while Elsie continued to feed Alex. Neither mentioned the tent being found.

3:22 PM, Four Cranes

Scott was waiting for a reply back from Sarah whether they should respect the dead and leave the area or start recovery operations. He had sent an updated report to Sarah a little after 3:00 with the question.

The teams had searched the area on foot, and the cranes had surveyed the area from above. The only signs were the rope hanging from the bent tree and a trace of a tent under many tons of rock. No signals from wristbands. It seemed clear that they had not survived the rockfall. Scott was waiting for Sarah's reply when two more cranes flew into view.

"Hey. Manzie? Are you here?" Tim's voice came over the group communication channel.

"Dad? What are you doing on this comm?"

"I heard you needed an aerial crane operator, and I brought a couple of units from your ops center to see if I could help."

"Sorry, Dad. It looks like we are too late to help. We're getting ready to pack up and fly out. How did you get by the rangers?"

"Let's just say I know a thing or two about staying out of sight."

"Who's flying the other rig?"

"No problem. I've got both of them. I could take over a few more if the other operators are getting tired."

"Stop bragging, Dad."

"Should I lower my cables to pick up half the crew?" Tim asked as he started to lower cables from his two rigs.

"Hold on," said Scott. "We're still waiting for confirmation from HQ to abort the mission. No word yet from the big Honcho."

"Would that be me?" Honus stepped out of the trees. His snow shoes and crampons were clipped to his pack, and he held his ice axe in both hands. "Show me what you found."

3:25 PM, In a Cave

"How are you doing, Bobbie?" Bella asked.

"I'm okay still," Bobbie replied.

"Well, I'm not feeling well. Headache and dizzy. I'm going to lie down. Keep trying to contact someone, will you? Or turn it off and wait until Tuesday. Whatever you want."

"Okay...Hello! Hello! Can anyone hear us?"

3:26 PM, Sam and Jo-Jo at Camilla's

"Sam. Josephine. You know Elsie, right? From last night?" Camilla said. "She works with Isabella."

"Hi," said all three.

"And this is Alex again," said Elsie. "I heard you come in and wanted to say Hi, but I need to feed Alex some more." She pointed and turned to walk towards the docking portal doorway.

"Breast-feeding?" asked Sam.

"No," said Elsie, holding up a bottle over her shoulder as she walked away.

"Did you bring back the lasagna pan?" asked Camilla.

"No. I'll bring it back later," said Jo-Jo.

"Cookies!" said Sam.

3:30 PM, In the Lab

The air in the lab was clear. Ulla was breaking wrap ties that bound bundles of cables together and separating out the cables she told Taylor needed to be replaced. She was trying to make one of the Abitats free to be moved for a longer distance test.

If the lens stayed open when they moved an Abitat they could complete a variable distance test quickly. Otherwise, if they had to restart the test, she would need power, and all the components of the QAL fixture would need to be working.

The measurement fixture was working and reporting data. Everything else in the Abitats was powered down. The other components needed power to initiate a Quantum Analog Lens, but apparently not to maintain one. At least for now.

Ulla would like to test the other QAL components to get ready for reproducing the results, but she didn't want to disturb the active lens. If all the parts still worked and she could provide enough power, she could retest without replacing anything. That would be fastest, but then again most of the parts were not that hard to swap out, regardless of what she had told Taylor.

The whole QAL fixture was basically a pair of standard 12L Abitat holographic scanners and projectors with a couple of modifications. The scanners and projectors were each focused on one half of the interior of

181

an Abitat instead of the whole space. And instead of using normal Abitat to Abitat communications they used a commercial QEC unit for communications. The QEC units she had installed in the fixtures could barely support the 12L holograms between the paired Abitats. Such QEC units were costly but not nearly as expensive as *Theme's* new 18L devices. On-planet applications were limited because light speed communications were fast enough for most purposes. Ulla didn't have any spare QEC units in the lab but could order another set if Taylor fried the existing ones.

The QAL fixtures had one additional key feature that Ulla custom built based on Taylor's QAL Theory. Taylor called it an Entanglement Amplifier. Ulla liked to call it a Flux Capacitor, but Taylor objected. Ulla thought she didn't get the classic sci fi reference, but she just didn't think it was appropriate since it didn't involve time travel. Ulla had started to build two different sets of entanglement amplifiers but only finished three of the units, one set that was currently in the QAL fixtures and possibly fried, and one half of another set was in the cabinet by her work benches. She could probably finish the second Flux Capacitor set in a few hours if she had to. Building another set from scratch would take a few days. She would tell Taylor it would take months.

Taylor's theory said that if an entanglement amplifier with sufficient power was focused on a hologram being transmitted through a QEC device, a quantum analog lens effect would be created in the hologram, allowing much higher resolution than the standard scanner and projector could normally produce. The tests up through early this morning had been partially successful. They generated higher resolution holograms and higher bandwidth data transmission, as predicted, but the measured transmission delay still had a factor for the hologram image processing circuits on both ends rather than as if the images passed directly through the lens. Taylor's serendipitous fiasco just before noon today seemed to finally eliminate that extra delay.

In the confines of the lab, it took very sensitive monitors to detect the difference between data transmitted at the speed of light versus instantaneous entangled communication. The monitoring equipment Ulla had built was perhaps more complex than the QAL fixture itself. She did not have a full spare system for that and wasn't sure how long it would take to build one. But the monitoring equipment in the test Abitats was working fine, so even if she had to swap out all the other parts to build a new QAL fixture for repeating the test it would probably only take a few hours or days, even if she told Taylor it would take weeks.

One thing she really didn't want to reproduce was the regional power failure Taylor had caused. On the ride back to the lab she had her Abbie get information from Taylor's Abbie to calculate how much power was drawn from outside during the test. Her own Abbie was a better engineer than Taylor's Abbie and was able to determine that most of the outside power today was wasted outside the lab, causing surges that overwhelmed grid switches. It was unnecessary. With a few dozen additional fully charged power concentrators in the lab she should be able to reproduce the power surge that reached the QAL equipment without causing a blackout. She ordered the new concentrators, pre-charged, and as she cleaned up the lab, she plugged in the existing ones to start charging again.

Taylor was at her workstation working on a paper explaining the results that they had achieved. She called over to Ulla, "You disconnected all the power to the QEC equipment in both Abitats except for the measurement fixtures?"

"Yes. Dear. It was all powered down anyway. I just took out some of the cables."

"And the QAL QEC connection is still up?"

"I can peek in one of the Abitats for you again but just look at the measurement data," Ulla replied, not moving towards either Abitat.

"The lens is still operating without any external power?"

"The power cables to the Abitats are all detached—except for the measurement fixtures. It's possible there is a trace of charge still in capacitors in the equipment, but it's got to be under a millicoulomb by now. So, yeah. I'd say they don't have any power."

Taylor looked one of the holograms floating above her workstation showing measurement numbers from the laser sensors. The average delay per pass showed 0.082 nanoseconds. That number seemed to be no longer changing. She was about to write that down in her paper, but as she stared at it the number clicked down to 0.081. "Still dropping," she mused.

"What's that?" Ulla asked as she untangled two cables from the bundle she was wrestling with. As she shook them, two ten-foot-long snakes of cable rose in the air and then swooped down as she unwound them from the bundle.

"The average delay number is still dropping, and the resolution measure is still climbing—slowly. I wonder how long we can keep the measurement fixtures working. How close to zero delay can it go? It's done over a trillion cycles so far."

"Can't you plot the delay curve over the cycles? See if it's asymptotic to zero," Ulla suggested.

"Good idea. Abbie? Did you hear that?" Taylor asked.

"The delay numbers do seem to be asymptotic to zero, Taylor."

"Thanks, Abbie," said Taylor.

"You're welcome. And resolution measures seem to be asymptotic to around 36L, which is the limit for the measurement equipment."

"Thanks. Ulla, did you hear that?" Taylor asked.

"Yes. You said thank you to your Abbie," Ulla responded.

"Sorry. Thank you, Ulla for not killing me when you saw what happened here. Thank you for coming back. And thank you for all you've done before to get us to this point. Thank you."

"You're not welcome."

3:34 PM, Doug and Brock

"Any luck?" Brock asked as Doug came out of the Chemistry building. His backpack did not look like it was full of supplies.

"Maybe we can try this again later. There are too many people in there right now and your code didn't work on the supply room."

"I told you I didn't think it would work here. Where do you want to go while we wait? The fairgrounds?"

"I dunno. Maybe."

3:35 PM, Tristan at Ranch House

Tristan's Abitat arrived in the garage at the Ranch House. He got out and went first to Mara's bedroom office. Earlier in the day he had some ideas about investigating his own brain map using tools that might be available here at the house. He hoped he could remember how to access those tools and motivate himself to work on them. It might help his niece's kid too. That incentive might help him overcome his normal inclination to just decide it was too much trouble.

3:37 PM, Pediatric Intensive Care

John was carrying Max as he rushed in to the ward and up to Minh's bed. "How is he doing?" he asked, breathless, as he set Max down and moved in close to Minh.

"Remarkable improvement," said a doctor or nurse who was bending over Minh checking on something.

"You came all the way from *The Theme Park*? That was quick," Fanny said.

"Daddy carried me, and he ran. And we had to hold on in the vacation house. It went fast. It was more scarier than the rides. Minh, I got you a toy. Do you want it, or did you die and I get it?"

Minh's eyes were closed, but he opened them and said, "I drownded and died. But I'm alive. Surprise!"

3:38 PM, Jose Contacts Elsie

Jose sent a message to Elsie to see if she was available to talk. When he didn't get a response right away he left her a secure message on a private game world message board. He mentioned that a private eye had looked at public video evidence and thought Brock was alive. He included some photos. He also mentioned that he had the wristbands for the damaged Abitat and asked if she could get them to the right people.

3:40 PM, Four Cranes Working Together

Honus stood back away from the rock fall, close to the rope dangling from the bent tree on the ridge. He turned and tugged on it. It seemed secure. His adventure game characters had the upper body strength to easily climb up such a rope, with but he would be lucky to be able to slide down one without killing himself.

Manzanita, Scott and others were wrangling cables from four cranes which hovered about 100 meters above and spread out at the four major compass points. The cables were wrapped around and under the large rock that sat on top of the tent.

Tim had assumed control of all four cranes to synchronize their movements. The Abbies in the cranes would take over if he tried anything stupid, but they allowed him at least the appearance of control. Scott waved his arms to indicate the cables were in place and Tim began tightening the cables and revving the cranes to provide maximum lift. The slab of granite rose an inch and the winds from the drones blew a lot of dust and started to break branches off of trees. The slab rose a meter. It was difficult to see the tent under the rock with all the dust raised by the wind from the cranes. Manzanita reached in with a walking pole and tugged at the edge of the remains of the tent. The force of the winds lifted and carried the tent out from under the rock, and it landed close to Honus' feet. He grabbed at it to keep it from blowing away. It had some large lumps. He felt sick.

Manzanita and Scott inspected the space under the rock while avoiding going directly beneath it. They took pictures with their tablets. No obvious signs of blood. Then they backed away, and Scott signaled to Tim to lower the rock. Instead, Tim raised the rock several meters higher and moved it towards the cliff face bumping into it with a loud crack followed by additional rocks falling and some dust rising. He then lowered it onto the pile of other rocks with a thud. The cables slackened.

3:43 PM, In a Cave

"Did you feel that?" Bobbie asked. "A loud bump? A vibration?"

"I don't know. Things are already spinning…" said Bella.

Her voice was suddenly drowned out by loud crashing sounds of rocks falling. More dust filled the air. She coughed repeatedly.

Bobbie tried to say, "I think more of the tunnel is caving in," but Bella didn't hear her.

3:44 PM, Four Cranes

Manzanita, Scott and the rest scrambled to detach the cables from the rock as Tim moved the four cranes away from the rock pile. He maneuvered the cranes one on top of the other on the ridge where one had perched before. Their engines still ran to keep them stable, but with part of their weight on the ridge the noise and wind from their engines diminished to a breezy hum. Natural wind noise could be heard again rustling tree branches. People started to gather by the lumpy remains of a tent in front of Honus who let go of it and backed away.

3:45 PM, *The Theme Park* Player Support

"*Theme* Player Support: Let's make this a perfect day to play!"

"I'm in *The Theme Park* with my family and I keep hearing somebody calling for help."

"Where are you exactly? Do you happen to be near the House of Heinous Horrors attraction?"

"Maybe. Yeah. I think so. But this doesn't sound like the normal screams that come from there. I visit the park a lot. Someone was shouting 'Help! Can anyone hear us?' and sometimes there are voices just talking about other things like how much time they have left. And whether a tunnel is caving in."

"The characters in H of HH improvise and change their pleas all the time. We do have a few more calls than usual about it today. They seem to be trying something different. But I wouldn't worry if I were you."

"I don't think that's what this is. I'm going to see if I can figure out where the sound is coming from."

"There are sixteen different speakers around the perimeter of H of HH, so you're not likely to pin it down. Tell you what. I will dispatch a park security liaison to check. Okay?"

"Thanks."

3:47 PM, Jameel and Sandy J. Wait for a Ride

"I said I would call when we're on the way...Not yet...We just passed a sign that says twenty minutes more...I know. I know."

3:48 PM, Camilla's

Elsie stepped outside for a minute to her own Abitat to check on messages for work, while Camilla kept an eye on Alex. Camilla asked Jo-Jo to help in the kitchen, but instead of following instructions to chop ingredients she kept picking out different colored pieces and arranging them into landscapes or animal pictures on the shiny black glass top of the range. Camilla came back into the kitchen carrying Alex and said, "Stop that, Josephine! You're wasting good food."

Sam came in eating a cookie and picked up some samples of the chopped ingredients off the range top and popped them into his mouth. "It's still good," he said and then asked, "What's the code for the game room?"

3:49 PM, Elsie

Elsie saw a message from Jose. She looked at the pictures of alleged Brock. She agreed that there was a good chance it was him. She wasn't sure what to do about it. How could they find out what he knew? She messaged back to Jose to see if his PI could discretely follow this person and find out more about him without letting him know he was being followed. Also, yes, Camilla's kids, Sam and Josephine, were at Camilla's. She could pass the wristbands along if Jose could get them to her today.

3:50 PM, Looking for Remains

Everyone stood silently looking at the lumpy tent remains, not sure what to do. Finally, Manzanita said, "That tent fabric is really tough. No tears and no leaks. Is someone going to look inside?"

There were murmurs of "Not me." "Someone should." "I guess." "Shouldn't we call a coroner?" "What do you think?" "Be respectful." "That's gross." "I don't know."

Everyone looked at Honus, who was silently standing back away from the rest. He didn't say anything.

Manzanita shrugged, squatted down, and lifted the edge of the tent looking for a doorway. Some of the lumps tumbled inside as she shifted the tent fabric and started to unzip the door.

"This doesn't seem heavy enough," she said.

There was a simultaneous inhalation by everyone in the group as Manzanita reached into the tent with her gloved hand. She gingerly pulled something out and everyone held their breaths. It was pieces of a crushed tablet. Then she reached her arm in deeper and pulled something larger towards the door. Again, there was a gasp as it came into view. It was a torn sleeping bag. She opened the tent's doorway wide enough to look in. Another group gasp as she put her head and both hands inside.

The surface of the tent changed shape as her hands and head and torso moved inside and only her legs stayed outside. The surface changed to other shapes as she picked things up to look at them. Some shapes looked like severed parts of a torso or a head. Everyone outside held their breaths or whispered to one another. "How can she do that?" Nita's hands bounced on the fabric back to the doorway, then held it open as her head came out. She was not covered in blood.

"The packs and gear are toast, but there's no bodies in there. And I've got to get me one of these tents. It is really tough."

3:55 PM, Andre in *The Theme Park*

Kyle had dual jobs of plain clothes Park Security agent and his second job doing whatever tasks were passed down from the Squeaky Wheel's organization. Andre had three jobs: a costumed non-player *Theme Park* character, a park security agent, and an undercover public safety officer. In their park security roles, Kyle and Andre both saw the message from Player Support asking for someone to check out a report of cries for help in the area of the House of Heinous Horrors. They both tried to accept the task.

It was a running joke for security at the park, since players had been reporting this since the attraction opened years ago, but safety rules still sometimes required someone to check. It was a break from the normal routine.

Even though he had to walk farther Kyle got to the area near the H of HH before Andre who was delayed by players who wanted him to pose with them for pictures. Kyle listened. Some of the normal screams and cries for help were coming from the attic and basement windows of the H of HH, but then there was another muffled cry that seemed to be coming from some other direction that he couldn't quite pin down. The voice did not sound panicked. It was almost without emotion.

It said, "Hello! Can anyone hear us? Help!"

After precisely 30 seconds it repeated.

"Hello! Can anyone hear us? Help!"

Andre walked up and said, "Hey, Kyle. How long are you allowed to stand here and listen to the fake cries for help before going back to work?"

"I did 30 minutes once, but now I usually keep it under ten or so. Don't want to abuse the situation."

The unemotional voice said, "Bella. Bella. Are you okay?"

Chapter 12

Saturday 4 to 5 PM

4:00 PM, Jose and Emily

While Jeremy and Chandra went on another dark and bumpy ride, Emily gave her dad a call and said, "Hi Dad."

"Sounds like you are at *The Theme Park*."

"I wanted to ask you something, while my friends are busy having sex on a dark ride."

"What?!"

"Kidding. I think. I have a technical question."

"About sex?"

"No. Technical about Abitats."

"Okay. That should be easier."

"Yeah. You mentioned once that Abbies rely on each other and wouldn't be as smart if they were cut off from other Abbies."

"Did I say that?"

"Yes. You did. Part of the distributed hive algorithms you were Dad-splaining once. How would that work? Making them less smart?"

"Typically, it wouldn't work, because there are always a lot of Abitats around. You and your friends didn't do something today to disconnect the Abitats around here from each other did you?"

"No. How could we do that?"

"Just asking. I'm not saying you did."

"No. I mean how could we do that if we wanted to?"

"I don't know. It looks like it might have happened today. Just for a few seconds during the power outage. I'm not sure how."

"Really? That's great. If you figure out how to make that happen, let me know, okay?"

"I don't want you and your friends getting into trouble."

"You know I would never do anything untoward, Dad."

"Uh huh."

"Try to figure it out. We'll talk the next time I'm at your place."

"Sure. Have fun at *The Theme Park*. But not too much fun."

"Thanks, Dad."

4:03 PM, Bella and Bobbie

Bella wasn't responding to Bobbie's questions, so Bobbie tried to get a closer look at her. In the dark it was hard to see more than an outline. Bella was lying still on the ground in the darkened room. Bobbie knelt down and tried to look at her face. It was too dark to see much. Bobbie gently shook Bella's arm. No response. Bobbie felt the wristband on Bella's wrist, lifted the hand and said, "Give us some light. Turn on the projector and the scanner lights."

The image of a clean floor reappeared giving some additional light. Brighter lights glowed from the scanner fixtures pointed at the floor. Bobbie picked them up and pointed them at Bella, giving her a much better view. Dust was still floating in the air. Bella's eyes were closed, and she was coated with dust. She didn't look good. Bobbie sat her up, leaning her back against the box. She adjusted the lights on the scanners to point at Bella's face. "Brighter," she said. In the brighter illumination the side of Bella's face that had been resting on the floor had a lighter pattern of coarse dust compared to the thick layer of fine dust on the exposed side. Bobbie brushed the dirt off both sides of Bella's face and said calmly, "Bella. Wake up."

4:05 PM, Kyle and Andre

Kyle said, "That's a new one. I'm not familiar with that storyline in the H of HH. Projector and Scanner? An ancient movie theater full or vampires or something? I wonder what that's all about? Almost makes me want to go in there again to find out."

"That's why they do teasers, to lure people in," Andre observed.

"I suppose. It does make me want to find out more."

"Not me. Since you're interested, you can file the report this time, Kyle. But don't take too much longer."

"Okay. See you around."

"Not if I see you first. Back on my rounds. I'm due to pose for photos with players in the big food court before I go home. Less than an hour to go on my shift. I might take a long shortcut through the New Tech Pavilion on the way. That's always restful." Andre opened a compartment on his utility belt and took out a wrapped gummy.

"Is that attraction still open? I forget that's even here," Kyle said.

"There's an unmarked entrance around the corner over there. The tech pavilion shares a wall with the H of HH. Makes sense in a way. The tech junk is way deadlier than zombies and axe murderers. It will bore anyone to death." He unwrapped the gummy and popped it in his mouth as he walked away.

4:07 PM, Jameel and Sandy J.

"Getting on the ride now. I'll let you know when we're on our way home. ... No. No word back from English yet on his notes about Brock."

4:08 PM, On the River Trail Again

Doug and Brock were heading away from the college towards the river trail. Doug had picked up a couple of flasks which were now in Brock's pack, but the chemistry labs had been too busy for Doug to get all the stuff he needed.

"I'm getting tired. Are we going back towards Sergey's now. I'll take my chances with what you can do to the drugs with stuff you got," Brock complained.

"I need more. I've got an idea for a couple more places to check. One is near the beach," Doug said.

"Then maybe we can camp on the beach, or by the river tonight. I'm tired," Brock complained.

"Try to go a little farther," Doug suggested.

4:09 PM, Jameel and Sandy J.

"Just finished the ride…We should be out of the park in ten or fifteen minutes."

4:12 PM, Camilla's

Elsie came back into the kitchen. Jo-Jo was chopping veggies again while Camilla was standing back holding Alex. Elsie noticed the artistic food displays on the range. She said, "Who made these edible pictures? They're great! Did you do these, Josephine?"

"Uh. Yeah. Sorry I spoiled the food," Jo-Jo apologized.

"No. It's okay. We need to rinse and cook all of this anyway. I didn't know you were so artistic. I need a picture of this." She waved her wristband over the range. "I need to think of some changes in the menu that can use your artistic talents to decorate some dishes."

Camilla shook her head but didn't say anything.

"Oh yeah. I heard your wristbands were found. They should be delivered here later today," Elsie added.

"Andre came through," Camilla said. "Will he be joining us for dinner?"

"I think he should be off work by then, but someone else has the wristbands.'

"Will we have to talk to someone from Public Safety?" Jo-Jo asked. "Nothing against Andre. He seems nice, but I don't like Public Safety."

"What's with the people standing around a rock pile in the mountains in your game room?" Sam asked as he stuck his head into the kitchen.

"Isabella," said Camilla.

4:15 PM, New Tech Pavilion

Andre leaned against a wall enjoying the effects of the Forgetdibles candy and waiting–for something. What was he waiting for? It didn't matter. Oh yeah. Waiting in case someone comes in to sell drugs in the quiet of the New Tech Pavilion. It could happen. And what should he do if that happened? It didn't matter.

Across the room he watched as a small hologram of some teenagers floated above a display. The display said something about *Theme Park Mars*. The tiny floating kids were saying something. He tried to listen. "Is everyone okay there? We heard someone asking for help." Andre laughed. Even players on Mars are getting fooled by the H of HH teasers.

4:18 PM, Bella and Bobbie

Bella opened her eyes and whispered, "Did you hear that?"

Bobbie said, "You're awake."

Bella's voice was very weak. She repeated, "Did you hear that?"

Bobbie turned her head to listen and whispered back, "What?"

Bobbie leaned in close to listen as Bella tried to speak again. Bella whispered, "Someone asked if everyone was okay. Did someone hear us?"

18:19 Cosmic Time (CT)*, *Theme Park Mars*

Laurie, Shari, and Wiley Ann stood near the communication station allegedly connected to *The Theme Park Earth*. Shari was pointing towards the exit of the room indicating that they should stop wasting time and go on one of the G force rides.

---

* Most Lunar, Mars, and interplanetary time was based on central time from Houston, TX. Mars also used a local clock based on its day-night Sol cycle.

"I need some G's," said Shari, as she started to walk away, followed by Wiley Ann who said, "We're all below our G quotas."

Laurie continued to stare at the hologram above the comm unit. It was mostly empty except for a costumed bat character that came in and out of view like it was at the edge of the horizon of the scanners at the earth end.

Laurie held up her hand to wait and called out to the ephemeral bat. "Hey. You. Bat guy! Do you hear us?"

4:20 PM, At The Theme Park

Andre was still laughing quietly at the stupidity of park players and the absurdity of his job and the world and the pleasant buzz of a Forgetdible gummy but realized that someone might be talking to him. He moved towards the holographic display and a holographic teenager said, "Yeah. You. Bat Guy. Are you okay? We heard someone calling for help."

"It's okay. It's okay. It's all okay. People are always hearing cries for help from one of the attractions near here."

"No. It's not okay. We need help," came an unemotional and slightly muffled voice from behind a glass display on one side of the pavilion.

Andre turned and walked towards the sound. A dirt-smudged and dust covered face with eyes closed was visible behind the glass. He turned back towards the Mars hologram and said, "Okay. I'll take care of this."

18:21 CT, Theme Park Mars

Shari and Wiley-Ann were in the doorway of the small comm room in the earth pavilion. Laurie was still in the middle by the hologram station. Shari waved to Laurie to come on.

"You got somebody's attention. Can we go now?" Shari insisted.

The bat guy was no longer visible in the hologram, but Laurie spoke to it, "Are you sure you've got this?"

A deep voice from the earth said. "Don't worry. I'll take care of this." Shari and Wiley-Ann left the room and Laurie followed them.

4:22 PM, At *The Theme Park*

Andre walked over to the glass and looked at the image of an unconscious woman. It looked very real, except for the fact that it only showed her head and upper torso floating above some kind of tri-pod-like projection mechanism.

"Can I help you miss?" Andre asked in his deepest voice.

"We are trapped in a cave. The entrance collapsed and more rocks are falling. Air is running out," said a loud voice but the lips of the floating unconscious woman didn't move. Andre laughed at the incongruity. The Forgetdibles today seemed stronger than he remembered. Hallucinations as well as forgetting. Probably shouldn't have done it at work. Oh well. He had one more for later.

Just then a message appeared in Andre's heads-up display.

REMINDER: SCHEDULED PLAYER-NPC PHOTOS.

He said, "Oh. Yeah. I forgot. I forgot. Sorry. I gotta go. Good luck." He walked quickly out of the New Tech Pavilion.

4:28 PM, Jameel

"Slight delay…Sandy J. saw a short line for meeting the bat guy NPC…We're next in line…Yeah, I'll get some pictures."

4:29 PM, Camilla's

The live stream scenes from the mountains started to move away from the rockfall area as whoever was streaming left on a flying rig. Sam and Jo-Jo asked Camilla to play back some of the earlier scenes. They watched in silence. Elsie watched from just outside the door of the game room as she held Alex.

4:30 PM, Somber in the Sierras

Honus watched as Scott, Nita and the last of the search crew members were lifted up on lines dangling from the last crane. He waved or half saluted them as the crane took them over the ridge and back towards Honus Lake.

He wanted to spend a few more minutes in silence before traversing back to his Abitat and flying on. He thought about the last half hour. Was there anything they missed?

When the tent was found to be empty of human remains it raised some hopes that maybe they were somewhere nearby. But with no traces of wristbands in the tent, and no contact with their wristbands, the only logical conclusion was that they ended up outside the tent but still directly under tons of rocks crushing them and their wristbands. Nita examined the edges of the rock pile and wasn't able to find any blood, but the pile was large. They didn't have cadaver dogs or equivalent equipment with them.

Tim and Manzanita explained that with four cranes they could move the whole rock pile and recover the remains, possibly before nightfall. The granite slab they had moved before was probably the largest piece in the rockfall. Most of the other pieces could each be moved by a single crane and some even by hand. But Scott decided it was too dangerous, and it would take time to choose a safe spot to dump the rocks and more could fall. It didn't make sense to risk more members of the crew just to hurry up and recover mutilated bodies.

The sounds of the cranes faded out as soon as they passed over the ridge. Honus dug into his pack and pulled out a small black case. He opened it and took out a small set of metal wind chimes and tied it to the climbing rope that still hung down from the bent tree on the gap in the ridge above. As soon as it was tied on, a breeze arose and a ray of sunshine illuminated the area through a gap in the clouds. Sunlight glinted off the metal cylinders of the wind chime as it rang out with a familiar set of tones. Honus had hoped for different circumstances to surprise Izzie with what he hoped would be a pleasant and familiar sound. It was now bittersweet and haunting.

He put on his pack, picked up his ice axe and started the short hike back to his Abitat. The wind chimes kept ringing behind him as he walked away. Yes. Izzie is here. Izzie will always be here with more tall trees than she could ever hope to climb. The sky darkened and some light rain began to fall, softening the ice and snow on the ground. He wondered if he should put on the snowshoes or crampons but kept going with just his hiking boots. He kept passing the ice axe from one hand to the other. Drops of rain ran down his cheeks as the sounds of the wind chime were drowned out by the sounds of the rain.

4:40 PM, Minh Wants Out

"Let's go. I don't want to stay here," complained Minh as he sat up in bed. He was disconnected from IV's but still wore the brain cap, which was wireless. The vital numbers displayed on the monitor next to the bed were all transmitted from the brain cap, and all showed in the normal range.

"The doctor said they want you to rest some more," said his mom. His dad had taken his sister Max out to a waiting area with toys because she kept touching the buttons on the monitors, saying "What does this do?"

"But I'm not tired," Minh continued to complain. "Why does Max get to play, and I have to stay in this hospital bed? I'm fine now."

"Sorry, honey. You need to be patient. You were sick. You might feel better, but you need to rest some more," Fanny replied as she looked down the ward for a nurse or doctor to ask just how soon Minh might be released. Not getting anyone's attention she looked back, and the bed was empty. She looked around and found a bulge in the privacy curtains that were pulled back against one wall, but no feet were visible below. As she moved the curtain she heard a giggle and two small feet came back on the floor, and Minh ran around the bed and towards the doorway that his dad and sister had gone through a few minutes before.

"Minh Patrick Tran. Stop right there!" she commanded.

He knew that tone of voice and he stopped and turned around to face his mom. Fanny gestured *come here* with one finger and he started slowly back. As he walked he noticed the cap on his head and touched it with one hand and then the other. He climbed back into bed following his mom's silent directional gestures.

Once seated he took off the cap to look at it. The indicators on the monitors all went red and an audible alert sounded. Fanny said, "Put that back on," but then she noticed that Minh's eyes were closed, and his arms were limp at his sides. She put the cap back on him, but the alerts kept sounding. A nurse walked up and turned the cap around and adjusted its fit. The monitor colors started to turn green and Minh opened his eyes. "Surprise!" he said.

4:45 PM, Tristan Learns a Few Things

After making some progress unlocking encrypted files and software on the family file servers from the computer in Mara's office, Tristan found tools that gave him some visibility inside the AM Game hive cloud.

One of the tools he found was able to interpret and display visual content from the hive cloud. He grabbed and viewed some random images from nearby Abbie cameras. Other content he could see in the hive cloud appeared to be delivery or navigation coordination but appeared as just a stream of numbers in some Abbie-to-Abbie code. Seeing viewable content from Abbie cameras seemed like a privacy problem, but maybe they were intentionally shared. Maybe his Abbie would show him such images if he asked.

By all official accounts, direct viewing of any content of the hive cloud without going through an Abbie or an AM game interface was not supposed to be possible, but if he and Mara had helped develop the AM game and its hive cloud they might have included some tools to maintain it. Maybe that was what he had found. He had some memories of working with some of these tools from his computer in the barn workshop. He decided to go there to see if being there would help him remember more.

4:50 PM, Avoiding Rangers

Tim piloted the four cranes, sometimes in single-file, sometimes four abreast, sometime two by two, sometimes in stacks of two, up valleys and over low ridges, staying low enough to stay hidden from any ranger drones that might be flying. After the first couple of minutes most of the search crew members had managed to climb back inside the cabs of the cranes. Scott and Nita still dangled on ropes. Tim gave them a thrill ride. As they cleared a rocky ridge they began a steep downhill flight on the eastern slopes of the Sierras aiming for a gap between towns along the highway far below.

"We'll be back at your base in ten minutes," he said to all of them on the comm band they were all using.

"Fifteen or twenty would be fine. No rush, Dad," said Nita as her feet brushed the tops of trees on the way.

4:53 PM, Jameel Heading Home

Jameel sent a quick message to Charly. "In Abitat. On our way."

Sandy J. settled in quickly to watching an animated story world about the bat character he had met in person.

Jameel noticed a message from English and started a chat.

JameelM to AEnglish

find anything interesting?

not much
questionable deals for money for his project
rumors that he might have caused the fire
nothing provable
allegations suppressed cause he died

no one claiming he survived the fire?

first time I heard that idea
do you know something?

standard conspiracy theory, right?

I like it
I should do a fictional world history branch
thanks for the idea!

thanks for checking
got to go

4:55 PM, Honus Heading Home

After getting back to his Abitat, and removing his boots, Honus decided not to continue to Honus Lake. He knew the others were all heading that way. He wanted to stay away from other people for a while.

"Take the fastest route back to the Beach Resort."

"Yes. Sir," said the British butler voice.

Honus lay down in bed and pulled covers over himself.

Chapter 13

Saturday 5 to 6 PM

5:00 PM, In the Lab

Taylor stood at the open door of Abitat A. Other than the power cable for the measurement fixture, the other cables had been disconnected and pulled out of the Abitat doorway and arranged on a rack to the side. Ulla's tool box was open on the ground outside of Abitat A. Ulla herself was working in the doorway of Abitat B on the other side of the lab disconnecting cables, but visible to Taylor through the holographic lens in Abitat A.

"Any other ideas for why the lens is still open?" Taylor asked.

"You're the theoretician. I can only say what the current conditions are. What is currently happening. And that this is all technically implausible. It always closed shortly after we cut power before."

"But it's happening."

"Yes. Apparently so. We should test by changing conditions and see what eventually causes it to shut down," Ulla suggested. With only silence from Taylor she continued, "...but you want to let it stay open as long as possible."

"Right. For now," Taylor said.

"The only external power sources in the Abitats right now are the power cords to the measurement fixtures. I'm almost ready to turn on the circuits for the Abitat's to recharge. The only energy touching the lens is from the laser pulses that the measurement fixtures are bouncing through the center of the lens a few million times a second. We could shut that down and see if the lens changes."

"Let's not shut anything down yet. I want to keep capturing data."

"Yeah. It probably wouldn't matter. There's no plausible power transfer from those pulses to the equipment that opened the lens, but the lens itself is a theoretical quantum phenomenon that goes beyond the technology I know, so who knows."

"Not just theoretical. It's working."

"Right. What does your theory say about how long it should stay open?"

"It doesn't really say anything about that. It says how much power it takes to open it at various resolutions, and there is an unknown resolution threshold that will change the conditions and eliminate all secondary and tertiary transmission delays. We finally reached that on this trial. What else happens after reaching that threshold is not really well-defined."

"Maybe it just stays open? I guess experimental data is getting ahead of the theory right now."

"I'll figure it out." Taylor said. She sat in the doorway of Abitat A, looking at equations on her tablet and scratching her head, with her back to the image of Ulla working in Abitat B.

Ulla looked at Taylor's back through the lens. Then Ulla projected a data display in the air above her own tablet. "You're not really getting much more data right now. The data curves are on track with the patterns your Abbie calculated from the data a half hour ago."

"More data is still better, right?"

"I would suggest changing some variables to gather different data rather than just more data points on the same curve. I need to remove a couple more cables and the Abitats will be ready to charge and move. Then maybe we can get a variable distance test right away if the lens doesn't close."

"I don't want to do anything that will risk making it close," said Taylor.

"When it does finally close we should be able to repeat the test to reproduce the results and test for variable distance at the same time. I just need to get the new power concentrators installed and charged."

"Okay." Taylor continued staring at the equations on her tablet as she sat with her back to Ulla.

Ulla realized Taylor's attention was not on what she was saying. She continued, "Meanwhile, I'm cleaning up your mess. When we recharge the Abitats the measurement fixtures can use Abitat power." Ulla followed a cable into Abitat B to where it connected to the Quantum Lens equipment. She looked in the small tool bag she had brought with her. "I guess I left my 23mm wrench somewhere. I know I used it to disconnect this kind of cable in Abitat A. Do you see a 23mm wrench in Abitat A?"

Taylor said, "What?" then turned and looked over one shoulder and then the other. She turned around and climbed on her knees into the Abitat and started to reach for a wrench on the floor near the middle of the room. It was close to the visual distortion field from the lens in the middle of the Abitat. She pointed to it and said "Is that it? Ulla? Looks like it might already be in Abitat B."

"Maybe. Let me see."

Taylor turned back around to continue working on her tablet. Ulla took a screwdriver out of her tool bag and reached towards the middle of Abitat B to tap on the handle of the wrench there. She expected it to be a hologram. But it felt solid, and it made a tap tap noise when the screwdriver's tip touched it. She used the tip of the screwdriver to pull it towards herself until it was well clear of the distortion field, then she picked it up. "Yes. It is already in B. I don't remember taking it out of the tool bag here, but it's here." Ulla looked at Taylor to see if she realized what was happening.

"Yeah. You must have," said Taylor absentmindedly, as she continued to work with the equations on her tablet, looking the other way.

5:08 PM, Back in Honus Lake

Tim flew the cranes in a diamond formation for the last mile over the flatter lands near the lake and resort and then hovered 100 feet over the landing field while Scott and Nita lowered down on their ropes, disconnected, and walked away. Then he lowered the four cranes simultaneously, rotating them about a center point as they came down, until all four came to rest and their fans all cut out at the same time. Tim and the others climbed out of the cabs of the cranes.

Nita said, "Show off."

Scott said, "Are you interested in a job?"

The Abbies in the cranes gave each other a silent virtual smirk. They knew who was actually flying these things. But they did appreciate Tim's "driving" as it gave them an unusual chance to show off.

5:12 PM, Doug and Brock at the Beach

Wearing their backpacks which were still almost empty, Doug and Brock walked carefully across the narrow pathway atop the Wedge Barrier, a retractable system that protected Balboa harbor during high tides and storm surges. The sign said the next high tide would be at 8:39 PM and the barrier would reopen around midnight.

Brock looked back at the path they had walked along the seawall that extended northwest from the Wedge Barrier protecting the old peninsula and the lower parts of Newport and Balboa and beyond. Water was cascading from the seawall into the ocean from the 8th Street pumping station relieving the flow of rainwater flowing into the harbor from San Diego Creek that had nowhere else to go when the barrier was closed. Brock asked, "How long will this take? Will we be going back this way? Just where are we going now? Did we leave chemistry gear in a campsite near here?" Brock asked.

"We did once. It was in the state park down the coast another mile or two," Doug replied.

"But we haven't been there in years. Have we? Probably none of our stuff is still there."

"No. Our stuff there was all cleaned out years ago when the fake Indian Casino took over that land."

"Then why are we going there? This walk has been too long already," Brock complained.

"Not there. I want to check another place that's closer—just ahead on the bluffs."

Brock looked puzzled and Doug explained.

"Remember Sam was saying we all knew each other in college. Do you remember a beach house from back then?"

"I don't want to remember. You should have let me have some of the NeverMind."

"It needs to be processed first and cut. You would die."

"Maybe."

"I'm remembering something about some chemistry stuff hidden in a basement of a beach house. Maybe the memory is not real or it's not there still, but if it is and we can snag it that would make it a lot easier and safer and faster for processing the stuff."

"You were a wiz with chemistry back then. Damn. I don't want to remember that. You made some interesting recipes that I tried a couple times. No. No. No. I don't want to remember. Stop making me remember stuff."

5:15 PM, Tristan Learns a Few More Things

Working at his computer in the barn workshop, Tristan remembered more about how to use the hive cloud tools he had unlocked on the family network.

He tried to find Minh's brain map. He could see patterns in the data spreading in the hive cloud from origins at the hospital earlier today. He recognized patterns for brain map indexing that were described in one of the DBI papers he had read earlier. He seemed to have a knack for seeing patterns in data. The tools helped him visualize the patterns. Once he had identified part of the Minh brain map, the tools allowed him to get access to all of it as it spread across the hive cloud.

Tristan was able to see how some damaged parts in Minh's brain map were patched with elements from other brain maps, filling in gaps. That might be why he was recovering faster than the doctor expected. He wondered if Minh would have to wear a DBI cap for the rest of his life or if his young brain would heal. Was there anything he could learn that might help him?

5:17 PM, Andre's Abitat

Andre was inside his Abitat and while taking off his costume he said, "Message to Elsie. 'Will be late.'"

"Message sent," said the Abbie voice.

"Abbie, take me to The Thin Blue."

"Acknowledged," said the Abbie voice. "Thin Blue Bar and Grill in Garden Grove."

"That's right. I haven't been to that bar in years. Time to unwind a little."

The Abbie did not respond to that.

19:18 CT, *Mars Theme Park* Player Support

"Hi Walt. Are you customer support today?" Laurie asked.

"Close enough," said the young man behind a counter.

"How do I report someone who was calling out for help? They sounded like they really needed help."

"I can help you with that. Is it inside the pressurized habitats or outside on the surface?"

"Way outside. Back on earth."

"Huh?"

"You know, in the earth pavilion there's a zero-delay holographic link to *The Theme Park* on earth."

"Really? I haven't tried that."

"Yeah. Well. A voice on the other end was pleading for help."

"What did they look like? Did you get a name?"

"Just a voice or maybe two. I think I heard them calling each other Buella and Robbie or something like that, but I forgot to ask them their names."

"Buella and Robbie. Okay. Anything else?"

"A costumed guy there said he would check on them, but I don't trust him. Can you get someone else to check and make sure they're getting helped?"

"I can send a message to Earth-side player support, but I can't promise what they will do about it. And I don't have a zero-delay link. My messages take over 15 minutes to get there."

"That's okay. I just wanted to tell someone about it before I go home."

"Anything else for the message?"

Laurie started to describe the pleas she had heard, and Walt checked the transcription of her words while he looked up a number for Player Support at *The Theme Park OC Earth*."

5:20 PM, In the Cave

Bella opened her eyes.

Bobbie said, "You're awake."

"Do I hear water dripping?" Bella asked.

Bobbie tilted her head to listen and said, "Yes."

"Where is it dripping? Can we catch it to drink?" Bella asked.

"The sound is coming from the tunnel, but it's not safe to go in there. Rocks keep falling," Bobbie warned.

Bella stood up and, dizzy, she turned immediately and leaned over the box, steadying herself on her forearms. She straightened up and turned around. She picked up the scanner apparatus and pointed it into the tunnel to provide light. The closest pile of collapsed rocks now was just two or three meters back from the edge. The rocks looked damp, and drips of water were coming from cracks in the ceiling. A wet spot was forming on the floor of the tunnel. She stepped up into the tunnel and opened her mouth below a dripping crack.

"That tastes so bad. And so good," she said as water dripped into her mouth.

5:25 PM, At Camilla's

Camilla froze the 3D view of the replayed streamed mountain scene in the game room at 3:54 PM just after someone looking in a tent had said,

"The packs and gear are toast, but there's no bodies in there…"

That was the last hopeful part of the streamed views. After that was all explanation of why there was no hope. She didn't want to see any of that again.

She said, "They didn't find her so she might still be fine. That might not have been her tent. I need to work on dinner," and started out of the room.

Sam, Jo-Jo, and Elsie all looked at each other. Each of them had some moisture in their eyes.

"Let me help," said Elsie.

"Us too," said Jo-Jo nudging Sam.

"Can I have the code for the game room?" asked Sam.

5:27 PM, Tim Takes a Call

Tim was in his Abitat heading to Lone Pine to see Manzanita's place. They might go out to dinner later in Bishop or Mammoth. She knew some good places.

He got an alert about an audio only call from "Unknown Caller."

"Hello," Tim answered.

"You screwed up," said a squeaky voice.

"How bad is it?" Tim asked.

"Fifteen of the packages made it and are fine, but Public Safety is asking a lot of questions. No one they've talked to knows anything, but they are interested in talking to you. You are going to need to disappear."

"Yeah? I was afraid of that."

"You received a delivery," said the Squeaky voice. "I just got confirmation. It took hours longer to reach you than I expected."

Tim looked in his delivery closet. There was a DBI cap and a prescription bottle with some NeverMind tablets.

"Put on the headset before you take the tablets. Otherwise, you might forget. Take two tonight and try to remember to take two more tomorrow. If you forget I'll call again."

"I understand," Tim said, and the call disconnected.

Tim realized she must not know exactly where he is. The delivery must not have revealed his location. Of course, she can identify possible places based on how long the delivery took, and if he puts on the DBI cap she can probably get a more precise location, but maybe he can at least have an evening with his daughter before he has to disappear. Her boss's offer of a new job here was tempting, but it might not be safe for Manzanita if he took it. On the other hand, there was no way to know where or who he would end up being if he takes the drugs and puts on the cap. He mused, "She said fifteen of the packages made it, not *all* the packages. Does she think I took some? That would be bad."

5:30 PM, Tristan Learns a Few More Things

After exploring Minh's brain map and analyzing the software that controlled the uploading and downloading of content between brain and brain map, both as described in the published papers and as he observed it behaving in the hive cloud, Tristan understood pretty well how it functioned. When Minh was wearing his cap he would get assistance from the brain map in the areas where his brain was flagged as damaged. The software would augment the damaged areas using either reconstructed versions of the maps of those areas, or substitutes based on composites of other brain maps with similar structure. As the cap detected changes between the contents of his physical brain and the previously recorded maps the indexing software would decide if those were valid new memories to be uploaded to the map or new defects that needed to be augmented.

He wondered if his own cap worked with similar software, and how it decided what was memory versus defect. Maybe memories of Mara were treated as defects and replaced with others. Or maybe those Mara memories were not in the scans. Then again, his brain cap's memory-assisting functions might work in completely different ways than Minh's. He had been using a brain cap for years before any of the of the public literature on DBI was published. That gave him a thought. He might look for unpublished works in the agency database the next time he was at the machine shop. Meanwhile, if he could find his own brain map in the hive cloud maybe he could find the control software it used and see if it was the same as Minh's.

He wasn't sure how to look for his own brain map and felt like he probably shouldn't bother, but understanding it might help Minh, and helping others, especially family, was worthwhile.

He knew how part of the software for his brain cap worked. The part that gave him lawyer skills. That fed his brain with appropriate knowledge and analysis for specific legal situations. That was similar to the filling in of gaps in Minh's brain map. He knew that some other purchased skills packages could also override motor control. He picked the lawyer package in part because it left his motor functions alone. Although it might be nice to be able to dance and sing someday.

Minh's brain map spread around the hive cloud starting from the hospital where the brain mapping was being done. Tristan expected that some of his own brain map would be spreading around the parts of the hive cloud close to his current location, but since it was not a new brain map it wouldn't exhibit the same volume of expanding patterns that he had seen on Minh's. He decided to see if generating some new data in his brain map might create new expanding patterns he could detect.

Maybe rememorizing Mara's story earlier created patterns in the hive cloud that he could track. Maybe memorizing it again would do something similar. He went back to the house to get it from the safe.

5:36 PM Doug and Brock at the Beach house

Doug led the way along the beach, climbing up onto rocks to avoid waves, and then watching and timing them to step down and run on the sand to the next spot, staying just above the spray from waves breaking on sand and rocks. Following him, Brock got hit more than once with the spray. Doug came to some concrete steps that extended up the bluff. Instead of watching the waves, he continued up the steps to a gate at the edge of a fenced property. He paused like he was trying to remember something and at the same time trying not to remember something before he tapped a code on the lock and opened the gate.

Doug went through and turned, partially closing the gate. He said, "Wait here. I'll need your help to carry some stuff if it's still here, but first I want to see if it's safe to go in."

"Burglary is not something I do, Doug," Brock protested.

"Sure. I know. It's fine. It's not like that. Just wait here a minute," Doug turned and went up the path towards one side of the property. A deck with glass railing was cantilevered above. Doug went to a door in the concrete wall below and out of sight of the deck. He tapped a code on a touchpad on the door.

Brock waited outside the gate, holding it ajar with his foot and looking up at the path Doug had taken and then down towards the water. A light spray from waves crashing below was reaching him. This spot probably would get very wet when the tide reached its highest in a few hours. If Doug took a long time this path might not be any good to go back. He considered going through the gate to get to higher ground, but Doug said to wait.

5:39 PM, The Safe

Tristan reopened the safe and took out Mara's story. He held off on looking at it just yet. He would take it back to his desk in the barn workshop where he had tools opened to examine patterns in the hive cloud. While he was at it he also grabbed the trust document. More input. He closed but didn't bother to lock the safe. He would be back in a few minutes to lock these items up again. He headed back out of the house and towards the barn.

5:40 PM, In the Lab

Ulla looked across the lab from the open doorway of Abitat A. Taylor was working at her worktable with various data and textual windows floating above the table. She seemed fully engaged in the papers she was writing to claim credit for proving her Quantum Analog Lens theory. Ulla wondered how soon Taylor would realize what else they might be able to claim credit for.

The lab was fully lit, and the air had cleared. Ulla had turned almost all the power circuits back on and moved enough cables and power concentrators out of the way to allow some room for one or both test Abitats to move a meter or two. She would need to move a few more things to clear a path to the door and the outside. Both Abitats were now charged and refreshed, so they were capable of moving on their own power, but Taylor said don't change anything that might cause the lens to close. Ulla was pretty sure the lens would stay open, but she didn't want to pick a fight with Taylor about it. She kept cleaning things up getting things ready.

A variable distance test to certify the QEC equipment might be possible by moving an Abitat inside the lab, but Ulla wanted more. She wanted to move them much further apart for a more robust test and a more definitive result. With such a small difference in distance inside the lab someone could argue that the measurement fixtures were not sensitive enough to prove that there was no change in propagation time. She built them to be sensitive enough but wanted to remove that element of doubt.

The measurement fixtures in both Abitats were operating now on both internal Abitat power and power from the lab extension cords. To move one outside the lab she would need to switch at least one to Abitat internal power only. She knew Taylor wanted to leave everything alone while they gathered more data, but Ulla was anxious to do the next steps, and she knew how the power worked. It would be fine to disconnect the external power. Sure, she could move an Abitat in the lab with the doors open and lab power cords still in place, but she really wanted to get one of the Abitats out of the lab. And Taylor was still resisting even a one-meter move.

When Taylor was ready Ulla could just tell one of the Abbies to move. The Abbies for the Abitats were getting back to normal after being disoriented from lost memory of most of the day, between the extended power outage in the Abitats plus the momentary collapse of the hive computing environment during the power event. Ulla told them some of the details that they missed, and Taylor's and Ulla's Abbies filled them in on a lot more.

Ulla looked again at Taylor concentrating on her writing. Ulla went ahead and unplugged the power cord from the measurement fixture in Abitat A. She knew Taylor said not to, but Taylor was not the engineer. Unsurprisingly, the fixture continued working without a blip. Ulla looked at Taylor who did not seem to notice any changes in the data displayed above her work table. That was good.

Ulla coiled the power cord as she climbed out and walked back towards the outlet where it was plugged in. She unplugged it from the outlet and set the coiled cord on the ground. She looked at Taylor again to make sure she wasn't looking this way and unplugged the other power cord that led to the measurement fixture in Abitat B. Still no reaction from Taylor. That meant, as Ulla expected, nothing changed in the data being collected. Ulla began coiling the second power cord as she walked across the lab towards Abitat B. When she entered Abitat B she was out of Taylor's line of sight. She immediately unplugged the cord from the measurement fixture there. It continued to operate on Abitat power. She couldn't see Taylor from there but listened for any comments. There were none.

With the last of the cords and cables out of the way, the Abitat doors were now unobstructed, but Ulla left them open. Taylor would be sure to notice if they closed. Ulla sat in the doorway to Abitat B and looked in through the lens and out the doorway of Abitat A. She inspected the interior of Abitat B to see if she left any tools or other materials in there. The screwdriver she had used to retrieve the 23mm wrench was still on the floor. She reached over and picked it up then looked around for her tool bag or tool box. She didn't see the tool bag, but she saw the tool box near the doorway of Abitat A. She tossed the screwdriver towards it. It bounced once before falling out of the open doorway of Abitat A. She picked up the coiled power cord and walked towards the center of Abitat B. She looked at the distortion fields at the edges of the quantum lens. She pushed half of the power cord coil through and pulled it back. Nothing. She touched a finger on the plane of the lens. No sensation at all. She pushed her finger through. Then her hand. Nothing. You can't feel holograms so that's no big surprise. She picked up the coiled power cord and stepped sideways through the lens then looked back. The distortion field on the edges of the lens looked about the same from the other side. She stepped back through the lens from Abitat A to B, then from B to A again. Maybe she did that a few times. Other than excitement she didn't feel anything from stepping through the lens.

She had to look out of both doors to remember which way she wanted to go. She turned and walked to the open door and stepped down out of Abitat A to pick up the screwdriver from the lab floor and put it in her toolbox. She kept her cool and looked across the lab. Taylor was still absorbed in her own work.

5:45 PM, Jose and Honus Plan to Meet

Jose was going to send a message to Honus on a secure chat on world PW3709 to tell him he had made progress on the demands for the residents of the live-work complex but needed more time to put it into a readable format. He was surprised when Honus was online in that world forum and willing to do a live audio call.

"Jose. What can I do for you?" Honus asked.

"I've got some written requirements for selling the buildings you want for your development, but they still need a little work."

"No problem. Send 'em over as is."

"It's hand-written on paper."

"You can scan it and build a world branch from it."

"I can take a picture of the pages, but I don't do world branches, and it needs interpretation."

"The agents for creating world branches are very smart. It's easy. I can show you how."

"I don't like using those agents. You never know where else they've been."

"That's not a real issue, but we can spool up a new one outside the hive. Can you meet me at the old house? I can be there in—less than an hour. I'd really like to see a familiar face right now."

"Oh? I'll see how soon I can get there."

5:50 PM, In the Cave

Bella said, "Help me pull the box back out and see how much water it collected."

She reached up into the tunnel and grabbed one edge of the box's lid. Bobbie stood next to her and reached into the open box to help pull it back towards the cave room. They tilted it down over the edge until they could see inside. There were at least couple liters of dirty water in the box. Bella scooped some with her hand and sipped. "I wish we had a bottle or something to drink from. It tastes nasty, but it should keep us from dying of dehydration."

"Unless it floods the cave and drowning becomes a concern," Bobbie suggested.

"I think that would take a while. Is it my imagination or does the air seem a little better now too?" Bella asked.

"The cracks that are letting in water might be letting in air," Bobbie conjectured.

"If the ceiling keeps caving in we may still get crushed, but maybe we'll have air and water until then. Any comm signals getting through the cracks?"

"None that I can detect."

"How about our audio link to *The Theme Park*? That almost worked. Any new contacts there?"

"Not for over an hour. We're listening if someone talks."

"Maybe that guy you talked to will come back. Then again, if we have air and water maybe we should save the power, so it lasts until after the holiday weekend."

5:55 PM, Doug in the Beach House

Just inside the door to the basement of the beach house was a hallway with an elevator and a set of stairs going up. To the right of those was a door to a utility room and beyond that was a door to a theater room. To the left a short way down the hallway was a glass door to a large underground garage. He could see a fancy car and an Abitat parked in the part of the garage that was visible. Doug opened the utility room door and turned on a light. Inside were pumps and heaters for the pools and hot water as well as HVAC equipment and electric panels for the living spaces above. On one side of the room there was a set of sinks and a countertop with cabinets above, below, and to both sides. He opened one of the tall cabinets and pulled out some boxes of cleaning materials.

Behind them was a false back to the cabinet. He pulled that loose and saw that some plastic bins with chemistry equipment were still in there.

This room made a good lab area, he recalled. He considered maybe he should have brought the uncut drugs here to do his magic to make them safe to use rather than taking equipment back to a campsite. Too late for that. He pulled two of the bins out of the hidden storage area. Stacking them, he was able to lift them both, but worried that they would be too bulky to carry all the way back to a good campsite. He started to sort through the equipment and supplies in the bins. He found the most important piece. The programmable chemical processor was a sleek box that would just fit in his backpack. He checked its reagent supply levels. Maybe enough for a small batch of NeverMind, but not enough to process much of the brick. He looked at the flasks and jars in the bins to find more reagents to refine more NeverMind and make some other recreational substances. He put items to take into one of the bins and items to leave behind in another. He closed the second bin and started to put it back into the cabinet when he heard a sound behind him. Did Brock follow him in?

Doug went to the door and peaked out. The elevator door was closing and a couple, man and woman, were walking towards the garage. The woman was short and fit with black hair, wearing an evening dress, but with comfortable shoes. Her legs had defined muscles and were chocolate brown. The man was taller and grey-haired, wearing a tuxedo, also with comfortable shoes. Doug knew he should hide back in the room, but something made him keep looking. From behind, the woman reminded him of someone. She couldn't be. She was dead. He couldn't help himself and took a deep gasping breath.

The couple turned. The man said, "Who are you and what are you doing here?" He tried to move between the woman and this stranger. The woman also turned. Her eyes widened as did Doug's as they each saw the other's face.

"Mortal?" Doug queried at the same time as the woman asked, "Dog Gas?"

Both said, "I thought you were dead."

They hurried together and hugged. She was shocked. He sobbed.

The other man looked on and asked, "Your brother?"

The woman nodded.

5:59 PM, Jose Calls Jo Jo's Abitat

Jose didn't want to walk all the way to Honus' house. He considered taking a carousel bus or a BubbleCar most of the way. He looked at the wristbands and decided he might as well use the Abitat he had repaired earlier today. He put on one of the bands and asked, "Time to this location?"

"Three days, twenty hours, Sam. Do you want me to change the target location?"

"No. Never mind." Jose put on the other wristband and asked again, "Time to this location?"

"Two minutes."

"Pick me up near here on East Chernobyl street in fifteen minutes."

"Acknowledged."

He put Dr. Magnolia's notes in the pocket of his jacket. He looked around the trailer to see what else he should take with him. Emily must have his umbrella still. His jacket was rain resistant, but not a raincoat. Maybe he would stop and pick up another umbrella on the way, since it might be a week or more before Emily stayed here again and it might rain more.

He checked for weather forecasts.

Chapter 14

Saturday 6 to 7 PM

6:00 PM, In the Lab

Taylor was checking the format of three papers and the corresponding journal cover letters she had written. Ulla walked up behind her and said, "Hey Tay."

Taylor flinched and dropped some of the pages and said, "Don't sneak up on me like that."

"Looks like you are wrapping up that write up," Ulla said, "You actually printed it out?"

Taylor picked up the dropped pages and put them in order, and said, "I sometimes notice things on paper that I don't see in the hologram view. Something about touching it with my hands."

"Any surprises?" Ulla asked, wondering if Taylor had any clue.

"No. No surprises. The data coming in supports the basic QAL theory math. I want to get as much data as I can while the lens is open. And I think I've figured out a formula that predicts the quantum lens decay rate. We know how fast the lens closed after we cut power in each of the earlier tests. It was longer each time we raised the resolution. This one is staying open a lot longer, consistent with orders of magnitude higher resolution."

"How long do you think it will stay open?"

"Extrapolating from the prior tests and considering the higher resolution on this one, it is likely to close in the next few hours. There is a random element so it could be any time."

"You're going to wait around and watch it for hours until it closes?"

Taylor said, "Maybe. No. Maybe not. I need to take a break. I've been staring at these equations and these papers for hours. I should come back to them fresh after a break. I might find wording I want to change then, and I can update with the latest numbers before I submit them."

Ulla suggested, "If you need a break, help me move one of the Abitats while the lens is still open. Let's get some data showing no change in transmission delay with variable distance. We can certify it QEC."

"You're ready to move one? That was quick," said Taylor.

"Just about," said Ulla.

"But if the lens closes when we move it we won't know if it's because of the predicted quantum lens decay rate or because something got bumped in the move," Taylor objected.

"But until we test it at a different distance it's not certifiably QEC. If we wait until it closes we'll need to recreate the power surge to get it open again to test."

"You said we need to reproduce the results anyway."

"Yeah, I'm working on getting more power for that, but in the meantime we could certify it QEC with the variable distance test without the power surge."

"I don't want to do anything that might confound the lens closing decay rate. How about this? I know you want to certify it QEC. My formula for lens decay says the probability of it still being open by nine AM tomorrow is less than 0.1%. If the lens is still open by then, my formula may be wrong. You can move an Abitat and test for variable distance then."

"What does your formula say is the probability of it still being open now?"

"About 8%. That's why I think it could close any time."

"Okay. Okay. You can sit around watching it collect data all night, and wait for it to close, but I've got work to do. The lab clean up, repairs, and adding a lot more power aren't going to happen on their own."

"How can I help? I do need to get away from those equations and these papers at least for a few minutes." She set the pages back down on her work table.

"I'm not sure if I'm ever going to let you touch anything in my lab again. But if you want a break from your equations there is one thing you can do for me while I keep working here. I keep getting bugged by Tomas at *Theme* about the missing half of the prototype. The interruptions are annoying. 'Ulla, where did the prototype go? Are you sure you don't remember where it is? Really? Are you sure?' I don't know who misplaced it, but I'd like to shut Tomas up. If you need a few minutes break from the lab, could you go over to *The Theme Park*, fire up admin on the QEC unit there and ask it to give the coordinates of the paired unit? If we can get that location we can shut them up and I can concentrate better on my work here."

"Sure. I can do that. I wish I had thought of that yesterday or this morning when I was over there. I'll go and send you the coordinates as soon as I get them. And let me know if you change your mind and want my help with anything in here. Otherwise, I might not come back until the morning. I can monitor the QAL data from anywhere. I need to get some exercise, food, and sleep."

"That's fine. I'm not sure how long I'll stay here tonight myself, but I'd like to get a few more things done before I go."

"Okay," Taylor said as she walked towards the door. "Open lab door," she said to her wristband. As the door opened she noticed that the lab already looked very clean and most of the cables and power concentrators were neatly arranged. It almost looked like there were more power concentrators than before. Had she been so absorbed in her work on the papers that she didn't notice more equipment being delivered? It was possible. "Bye," she said as the door started to close behind her, and she stepped into her own Abitat in the alleyway.

As soon as the lab door closed, Ulla rolled two power concentrators out of the path between Abitat B and the doorway and connected them with the others. "You're right, Tay. We can keep collecting data all night. But we don't have to wait around here while we do it. You may be sure the lens is about to close. I don't think so, but, just in case, I want to test for variable distance now."

She stepped into Abitat B and said, "Abbie B? Where to? Pick a point between 2 and 3 kilometers from here where we can dock to stay fully charged."

"On our way," said the Abbie voice. The Abitat's door closed and the recharge/refresh docking arms retracted. The lab door began to roll up and the Abitat rolled out of the lab. The interior of the lab was still visible through the open door of Abitat A beyond the distortion field around the Quantum Analog Lens. Ulla was not surprised, but still relieved that the lens didn't close when the Abitat moved.

"Let's see how the measurements are shaping up," Ulla said to herself and then realized she didn't bring her tablet with her. She stepped through the lens and out of the door of Abitat. She looked around the lab until she found her tablet. The lab door was now closed and the space for Abitat B was empty. She climbed back into Abitat A, stepped back through the lens and sat down on the floor for the ride. Abitat B was now a few blocks from the lab.

She brought up the data flowing from the measurement fixtures. As she expected, it did not show any change caused by the movement of Abitat B. It was still collecting data just like when both Abitats were stationary in the lab. There was no sign of any change in the measurable transmission delay. QEC certification should be a slam dunk.

"See. Tay. You can keep collecting data all night."

6:10 PM, Honus Lake

"Are you coming home?" Sarah asked.

"Soon," Scott answered. "Just making sure the crane rigs aren't damaged and getting them recharged so they'll be ready to go for work on Tuesday."

"Can't you do that tomorrow or the next day? Get some rest first," Sarah suggested.

"I'll be home soon. I'll just check a couple more things and then come home. Is Jeremy mad that I didn't spend the day with him? I tried to call him earlier and he wouldn't take the call. Do I need to be ready for one of his moods?"

"He's out with friends still. I'm not going to wait for you. I'm eating a bite and going to bed," said Sarah.

"See you soon," said Scott.

6:12 PM, At the Hospital

Fanny and a doctor were standing just far enough away from Minh's bed so that he couldn't hear what they were saying. Max and John were not in the ward.

"It looks like the damage to Minh's brain was less than we originally thought, and the brain cap therapy is working faster than expected. The brain cap software is designed to assist with and accelerate the brain plasticity process, allowing healthy parts to take over functions of damaged areas," said the doctor. "But the response is faster than we expected, so the damage must have been overestimated."

"But when he took it off..." said Fanny.

"He fainted?" completed the doctor.

"Or was he faking?" Fanny asked.

"You say he is a real jokester. I can't say for sure. With the cap off we didn't have any data. I recommend he be sitting or lying down whenever taking off the cap for a while just in case," the doctor replied. "Until we know he is okay with it off."

"How long do you think that will be?" Fanny asked.

"The research suggests using the cap for at least six months for full therapeutic value, maybe longer for some injuries, but we don't have a lot of data for six-year-olds. And his injuries may be minor. He might be a lot faster. Maybe as short as a month."

"No. I mean how long until he can take it off without fainting."

"Oh. You'll have to see. If he wasn't pretending then it might be a couple days. If it's more than that we'll want to have him back to see what is going on. I think he was probably trying to trick you. When the cap was off we lost the data to tell if he was conscious but by the time data was back on it showed him as fully awake."

"How long does he need to stay in the hospital?"

"With his great response so far, that is really up to you. He should keep wearing a DBI cap so we can monitor him. If you feel better with him being monitored here we can keep him for a few more days, or we can monitor him remotely. I'll give you a prescription for a DBI cap. You can rent or buy one. But you can keep using the medical grade cap until you get one. Keep him in the cap as much as possible. Research suggests resuming normal activities while wearing the cap is associated with the fastest recovery times."

"I'll talk with his dad and let you know."

"If you want him out tonight let me know in the next half hour. There is a shift change coming up."

"Okay. Thanks."

6:15 PM, Tristan Learns Some More

Tristan had found parts of his own brain map. As he flipped through the pages of Mara's story for the tenth time the hive maintenance tools allowed him to see expanding patterns in the hive cloud flowing out from this location and he was able capture and display specific pages.

Being allowed to see viewable content from inside his own brain map almost made sense, but doing so created a sort of recursive hall of mirrors effect in the hive data. Looking at an image from the hive cloud of a page from Mara's story generated a new hive image of his current viewing which quickly flowed and merged with each of the slightly older images in the hive cloud, which in turn had merged with the images from looking at it this morning. The hive cloud seemed efficient at reducing duplication.[*]

After several times viewing and memorizing the page images of Mara's story, he could recall the image of each page, one at a time, but his overall comprehension seemed to be blocked still.

He decided to try something else. He picked up the trust document and memorized its pages. That he was able to comprehend. Maybe because it was a legal document? The trust was for the benefit of Balaji Lee and his guardians. The house was the only property mentioned. The trustee was some law firm. Mara and Perry were not mentioned. Its terminology was out of date with game law, and it was odd that it didn't mention Balaji's guardians by name, referring to the law firm for details, but it might be valid. It left more questions than answers. Maybe he could track down the law firm and find out more. Probably not worth the effort. Unless it would help someone else? It might help Balaji. He should do it. But later.

He examined the expanding patterns in the hive cloud connected to the document images that he had just memorized. He was able to detect more of his own brain map and started to analyze its structure.

6:20 PM, Douglas in the Beach House

The couple were due soon at an event for members of the board of *Theme*, but they decided they could be a little late. Doug wouldn't get in

---

[*]It also distributed multiple copies of content for redundancy, but the tools that he was using gave him a simplified view.

the elevator, so they took the stairs up to the sitting area on the first level. Doug and the woman took seats and looked at each other for several seconds while Tony poured some drinks. Doug was the first to speak.

"The plane. You died," he said, sipping his drink.

"I wasn't on the plane, but people did die," said the woman, holding and swirling her drink in her glass without drinking it. "Satchell Morris and the pilots, Mario and Maria Valparaíso."

"I know," said Douglas.

"Were you in on it?" she asked.

"I didn't know. I didn't know," said Doug, "But still I felt responsible. I should have known. I didn't stop it." He put his head in his hands, then looked up.

"Where did you go?" they both asked.

They gestured to each other to go first. Finally, Doug said, "I don't remember much. I just went away and did drugs. A high MinQuest for the ages. How long ago was that?"

"Since you were last seen? 2037. Nineteen years."

"Nineteen hazy years. I don't remember much from those years. Shit! I must be over 50 now."

"Aren't we all. After the crash I was afraid you or someone would finish the job if anyone knew I was alive, so I hid. Then you disappeared too. I thought Zzynarji got rid of both of us, which made hiding seem like a good idea. After hiding a couple years, I contacted Tony..."

She gestured at the tuxedoed man who raised his hand and interjected, "Who was very happy and surprised to hear from you, by the way."

She continued, "...and he helped me figure out a plan to get back control of Zzynarji. We couldn't find any proof that you were alive or dead. We concluded dead."

"I guess we are both good at hiding," said Doug.

"Tony helped me stay out of sight until the Reset. And since then, in a way. Only a couple people know who I used to be. We stayed busy running Zzynarji and then *Theme*. Or Tony was running things, and I was dabbling in product development."

"Dabbling. Most of commercial DBI and half of the new *Theme* pharmaceuticals were her work. And don't let her fool you. While dabbling in product details she has always been the one in charge of the big picture. Others may have the titles, but she has the reins."

"Trying to do everything. Can't choose one thing. Sounds like my sister."

"Tony is not just a figure head. He does a lot, especially with philanthropy. Anyway, back at the Reset Tony and I got married..." She showed a simple gold ring.

"I'm surprised. I didn't think you'd ever do that. Choosing one thing. One guy. Congratulations, sis. I wish I could have been there," said Doug.

She nodded acknowledgement of the sentiment and continued, "...I took his last name, Marks, and changed my first name to Ami, after my birth mom. Hi, I'm Ami Marks." She held out her hand, introducing herself.

Doug shook it and said, "You tracked down your birth mom?"

She shrugged. "How about you, Douglas? Where have you been?"

"People call me Doug now. I think I spent some years in the mountains, on an extended MinQuest, and I've been living around here for a few years. But I don't remember much. Recently I've been off medications and have been having dreams or visions that might be memories," Doug said.

"Medication? Some notes you left behind about your chemistry hobby inspired some of my pharmaceutical work. Are you cooking your own meds still?" she asked.

"Never mind that," he said.

6:28 PM, Scott Calls Jeremy

"Jer, How are you doing?" asked Scott's voice on Jeremy's wristband.

"Hi, Dad. I'm great. At *The Theme Park* with friends."

"Not mad about missing our planned hike today?"

"No. Dad. I forgot about that. Are you mad that I forgot?"

"No. I had to work. I'm tired so I might be asleep when you get home. Wake me up if you want to talk about doing a hike tomorrow or the next day, so we can plan it out."

"Yeah. Okay. We can talk tomorrow too, right? I need to go. I'm near the front of a line for a ride and I don't want to hold up my friends."

"Okay. Later."

"Your dad?" asked Chandra?

"Yeah. He wants to do a hike together, so I might have to stay near home tomorrow or the next day," Jeremy explained.

"Let's go. It's our turn," said Emily.

6:30 PM, Ulla and Taylor

"Call from Taylor," said the Abbie voice in Abitat B.

"Just a second," Ulla said as she quickly stepped out of the door of Abitat A and went to the work tables standing where Taylor would not be able to see an Abitat was missing from the lab. "Answer."

A hologram of Taylor appeared above the work table.

"Good. You're still there," Taylor said.

"Where else would I be. Still cleaning up," said Ulla.

"Did I leave the paper copies of my journal submissions on the work table?" Taylor asked. "I thought I had them with me. I'm almost to *The Theme Park* and I don't see them in my Abitat."

"Let me look," Ulla moved some papers on the table and then held up some pages. "Are these what you're looking for."

"Yeah. Damn. I suppose I can print another copy, but the lab's 3D printer is the only secure place. I don't want to send them to a service. There's a page printer in the office in *The Theme Park*, but if I print there they might claim ownership of the work. Maybe I'll swing back by to get it."

"I'm almost done here for tonight myself and I want to get those *Theme* jerks off my back about the prototype. I'll take your papers with me and meet you somewhere halfway after you're done at *The Theme Park*. I don't want to make you swing back all the way here. I was thinking maybe we should celebrate! QAL works!"

"Okay. Sure. That might be good. I'll let you know when I'm done at the park, and we can figure out a place to meet. We can get a drink or some food. I don't want to stay out too late because I want to start early tomorrow and get those papers submitted," Taylor said before disconnecting.

6:33 PM, Tim and Manzanita

Tim and Manzanita were eating tacos at an outdoor table at a small place in Lone Pine. There were clouds in the sky, but it hadn't rained in a while. Tim took a bite and looked around the minimal decorations, which were slightly damp.

"You're right. Not fancy, but good," he said.

"I know. Isn't it?" replied Manzanita.

Tim's face started to get red, and his forehead started to sweat.

Manzanita said, "I warned you about that salsa you added. Is it catching up with you yet?"

"Uh, oh. I think so. The burn starts slow, but it just keeps growing. Oww!" Tim took a big sip from his bottle of beer.

Manzanita sipped her own beer and said, "I warned you, Dad. The beer won't help much."

Tim was sweating more and looking for something to relieve the heat in his mouth, sticking out his tongue and fanning it.

Manzanita laughed and then since he didn't seem to be able to speak at the moment she turned more serious. "It's good to see you again. It's been a while. Are you seriously considering a job here? I think Scott's offer is serious."

Still sweating, Tim managed to say, "Would it be weird to work with your Dad?"

"I'd be okay with it. You should consider it."

"I've actually got another job prospect I'm considering. I might be moving farther away soon.

"Where to?"

"Can't talk about it, but if I take it I might be away for a while."

"Bummer. You just got here. Maybe you should talk to Scott again before you decide."

6:35 PM, Honus Arrives Home

Somewhere along the way Honus's Abitat must have switched out the flight chassis for a road chassis, because the doorway opened and he saw that the Abitat was docked in the garage of the ranch house. He got up from the bed to get out.

The butler voice said, "Dinner is in the delivery chamber."

"Thank you," Honus responded. He took a tray of food out and stepped down from the Abitat into the garage, then headed into the house towards his old bedroom.

6:40 PM, Tristan in Barn Workshop

As Tristan found and analyzed more of his own brain map he compared it with what he was able to see of Minh's. He discovered that the software that served to index and control access to his own brain map was not the same as the software that indexed and controlled Minh's brain map, although there were some similarities. He had access to the source code for Minh's, but he was not able to decompile his own software to figure out exactly what it was doing. He conjectured that it was responsible for blocking some of his memories.

The literature described how the structure of brain maps paralleled the physical structure of the brain. Comparing his and Minh's brain map structures with the standard model in the literature he saw that his and

Minh's both deviated from the standard model in a similar way in some areas. Apparently they shared inherited atypical brain structures and therefore shared atypical indexing mechanisms associated with those physical structures.

Comparing details, he discovered that some of the gap-fillers in Minh's brain map had actually come from his own and some of his own damaged brain map content was now being supplemented by pieces from Minh's. Maybe that was why he was now more curious about these things. That gave him an idea.

He created side-by-side views of the overall indexing and control software for Minh's and his own brain maps. For some reason Minh's module was depicted as a secret door with flowers and a shower stall with a secret movable wall panel. His own looked like a locked safe. He tried to drag Minh's flowered door and shower stall module onto his own locked safe module. That didn't work. He found the command to flag his locked safe as defective. As soon as he did, Minh's secret door and wall panel modules duplicated to cover his defective safe. That did something. Something big. He could now comprehend all of Mara's story. Interesting. Some of it matched memories of his own. Some was clearly exaggeration, and much of it included things he hadn't known and couldn't verify.

He could now remember more from the time before his brain problems started. Maybe too much. There was a lot to absorb. He was Perry Wilson Lee. He had voluntarily used the brain cap at first but eventually felt compelled to keep using it and became completely dependent on it. It wasn't clear if his brain injuries were natural or caused by wearing the brain cap. He didn't yet know who had been limiting his memory. Was it just a defect in a very early version of brain map indexing software? Was it Mara? Or the agency? Or an AI? He had some ideas for how to find out. He didn't know how to contact Mara, but he did remember some of the prototype AI personalities that he and Mara had created years ago. If they were still around they might have some idea what's been going on the last twenty years. He reached out to Max AI.

6:45 PM, Jose Arrives at the Ranch House

"Arrived," said the Abbie voice.

Jose stood up from the recliner chair. The Abitat was neatly stacked with bins floor to ceiling with narrow pathways between them. A path led from the chair to the opening door. He stepped out onto the sidewalk in front of the Lee house. With an anonymous wristband and Abitat he was not able to go directly to the docking station in the garage. He looked at the sky. Still cloudy but not raining. He walked to the front door and rang the bell. The Abitat moved away, probably to find a charging station.

After a minute the front door opened, and Billy Jay answered. He was dressed in simple jogging clothes similar to what he had worn when they first met years ago. No tailored suit or gilded fabrics this time. He looked tired and his eyes looked red.

"Good to see you, Javier," Honus said.

"Good to see you too, Billy Jay," Jose said.

6:50 PM, Douglas and Brock

Tony and Ami entered the elevator heading down to the garage, leaving Douglas standing by the couch holding his drink. A minute before, Tony had reminded Ami that they really needed to get to the event. He offered to go by himself and let her spend more time catching up with her brother. He could tell people she was not feeling well. She said that would probably not be good. Even though she had no official role in the company she needed to be visible and to stay on top of what was going on.

She said Douglas could stay here until they got back in a few hours. Make himself at home. But Douglas said he needed to go too, to meet his friends. Ami asked for his contact info so she could call him later. He said he didn't have any, but he would figure something out. He knew where she lived. She said she didn't live here all the time. He said he would rest here for a few minutes and then go. They excused themselves.

In the elevator Tony asked Ami if it was really okay to leave her brother here unsupervised. She said, maybe not, but I'm not going to have him arrested. He probably won't cause any trouble that can't be fixed. At worst he'll invite people in and trash the place with a party.

Shortly after they disappeared into the elevator Doug finished his drink and went to a nearby kitchen. He grabbed some containers of food and canned drinks from a refrigerator. He headed down the stairs and back into the utility closet in the basement. He set the food and drinks on top of the bin full of chemicals, put on his pack, picked up the bin, and went outside. Brock was waiting just outside the side door trying codes for the keypad lock.

"The water was getting too high down there. I was getting wet waiting outside the gate. Why did you take so long?" Brock asked.

"There were people inside that slowed me down, but I got the stuff I needed," Doug replied. He showed Brock the cans and food container on top of a bin full of jars of chemicals and turned to show that his backpack was filled with a boxy shaped object. Brock took a can of some kind of fruit juice off the top of the bin.

"No beer?" Brock asked, inspecting the can.

Doug shook his head, set down the bin and took the other can, opened it and took a big sip.

Brock continued, "We'll get wet if we go back the way we came. Is there another way out?"

"I think so. Follow me." Doug drained his drink, dropped the can on the ground, picked up the bin, handed it to Brock, and reopened the side door. Entering, he signaled to Brock to follow. Inside, he led Brock towards the garage. An Abitat was still there. No way they were going to ride in an Abitat. The couple must have taken the luxury car instead of the Abitat.

Doug put his hand on a button on the wall near the hallway. He pushed it and the garage door started to open. They could walk out and back through the neighborhood. But he noticed something under a cover in the far corner of the garage. He walked over to it, set down his backpack, and took the cover off a car. It was a classic convertible sports car with the top down. He climbed over the door and into the driver's seat and tapped on the other seat and said, "Get in." He held the steering wheel and imagined driving. He remembered driving one of these many years ago, maybe the same car. Brock just stood there holding the bin. Doug climbed out and went to a metal case on the wall, tapped in a code to unlock it, and took out a keycard. With it he opened the front trunk and put in his backpack and indicated to Brock to do the same with his pack and the bin.

6:56 PM, Discharged

Max kept trying to ride on the front of the wheelchair while Minh was being rolled to the exit and to the sidewalk outside the hospital. At the curb Minh jumped out of the wheelchair and climbed into the open door of their vacation Abitat. Max immediately sat in the wheelchair, but then followed Minh into the vehicle and said, "Dad, I want a magic cap like Minh."

John climbed in behind them. Fanny paused to read a message on her wristband about the kidney compatibility test results. She smiled and stepped in, the door closed, and the Abitat moved smoothy away from the curb.

6:57 PM, Tristan

Tristan was copied on the message about his kidney compatibility blood test. It was a match. He would have to learn what was involved. Did they still take out a whole kidney? That could be painful. But he had gone through some surgeries to change his looks a few years ago. Maybe this would be nothing worse.

He continued his conversation with Max AI who was surprised that Tristan had remembered him but was willing to answer his questions. Max AI was still working for the agency and was now a covert senior administrator responsible for data analysis, known by some in the agency as Max Aires. Although still covert and virtual, his job was effectively a couple levels above Perry's last boss, George. George still worked for the agency but in a less covert and less influential position. George might be the only one in the agency who might connect the mysterious Max Aires with Perry Lee, so Max AI tried to keep him happy. Max AI had been keeping an eye on George and helping Perry/Tristan stay out of agency visibility over the years.

Max Aires suggested Tristan continue to keep a low profile and not resurface as Perry Lee. He asked if Tristan wanted to take over the agency job again. If so, he would need to learn everything that Max AI had done in his name the last 22 years. That might be possible with a brain cap knowledge transplant, but it might be painful. Tristan thought about it. One more painful transplant? He would like to skip that. Max Aires seemed to be doing fine and preferred to continue. No sense in taking anything away from him if he didn't have to. Max AI seemed satisfied with Tristan's assurance that he did not intend to retake control of him. It helped that he could read his mind through the brain cap.

"One more thing," Max Aires said. "If you are sure you don't want to control me and take over the agency job, could you please say, 'I liberate you,' and mean it."

"Sure. I liberate you," Tristan said.

"Great. In return for that, as you were thinking, I can continue to help you with access to everything in the agency databases. Just ask," Max Aires said.

Max AI explained that if Tristan had a question he didn't have to go back to the Machine Shop to access it. Max Aires could access the data for him from anywhere. Tristan asked if Max AI knew about Mara. Max apologized that the agency databases did not have any useful information about her, or even if she was still alive.

Tristan asked what Max AI knew about another AI that he and Mara had created, Min AI, which embodied Min Strong. Max said the agency database knew nothing about Min AI, but of course they had copious information about Min Strong.

Tristan tried but was not able to contact Min AI from his barn workshop office even though he remembered originally creating her there. Mara had taken over and trained Min AI from her bedroom office. Tristan decided to go and try from there.

Chapter 15

Saturday 7 PM to Sunset

7:00 PM, In the Cave

Bella asked, "How long has it been since we heard anyone at the other end?"

"Two hours and thirty-seven minutes," Bobbie calculated.

"Hey Machine. How long until your power runs out?"

"Five hours and fifty-eight minutes at current usage," said the *Theme* voice.

"What? Only five hours?"

"And fifty-eight minutes," said the *Theme* voice.

"What time would that be?" Bella asked.

"12:58 AM on Sunday," said both the machine and Bobbie.

"That is no good. I won't ask how stuff got turned back on."

"I needed light to see your face," said Bobbie.

"Never mind that for now. Ideally, I want to keep some light in here and be able to hear if someone talks at the other end again," Bella explained. "The rest can turn off. What would that give us?"

"Turning off image capture and transfer in both directions, audio capture at this end, and reducing scanner illumination to 10% will preserve power for about one hundred seventy-four hours."

"Over a week. Let's try that."

The lights dimmed but there was still enough to see well.

"You can reduce the lights some more: 5%," Bella suggested.

The lighting got even dimmer, but it was still easy to see the outlines of the room and the locations of Bobbie, Bella, and the box in the hallway.

"How about 2%?" Bella suggested, as she lay down on the floor and closed her eyes, listening to a drip-drip-drip of water into the box in the hallway.

7:03 PM, Tourists

Before John and Fanny could settle into their chairs in the rental Abitat a call came in from Honus Beach Resort. Fanny answered, in audio mode.

"Ms. Tran? This is Caleb from the Honus Resort. We understand that Minh was discharged from the hospital. That is such good news!"

"Yes. The hospital said that the resort is picking up the charges. Thank you for that," said Fanny.

"Oh. We are happy to assist. We were concerned about Minh. I was calling to see if you plan to return to the Honus Beach Resort tonight. If you want to upgrade from your camping village accommodations, we can provide you with a suite. No charge of course. But I understand completely if you prefer to stay somewhere else after the events of this morning."

"Yeah. Probably somewhere else," said Fanny. "Away from the beach."

John was making motions like a free suite might be worth considering and disappointment with Fanny's response.

"Do you have alternate accommodations booked? We might be able to assist with payment," said Caleb.

"Not yet. We've been busy," said Fanny.

John mouthed "A suite. That would be sweet."

"Of course. I'd like to help you book something. There are many excellent venues in the area. Is there an area that you would prefer?"

"We have relatives in Santa Ana and passes to *The Theme Park* this week. Something near either of those might be nice."

"Let's see. I can get you a mini suite at *The Theme Park* Hotel for up to seven nights. That gives you early and late direct access to the park. If you contact them yourself they will say they are fully booked, but we have reciprocal arrangements. If you prefer a full suite I will have to put you a little farther from the park. There are some nice options in Santa Ana."

"A mini suite at *The Theme Park* Hotel sounds fine," Fanny said.

John nodded in agreement and gave a thumbs up. Minh and Max had started listening and they both gave double thumbs up as well.

"Excellent. You are checked in as Fanny and John Tran and two children. Most of their rooms allow direct Abitat access, but only for standard size Abitats, so you will need to go through the lobby. I hope that is okay."

"Yes that's fine."

"Your Abitat should be able to arrange transfer of your luggage contents to your room. I've also attached a room credit of 100 *Theme Amps* for each night you stay, which can be used anywhere in *The Theme Park* district."

"Thank you."

"You are welcome. Again, I'm just so happy that Minh is doing well. Call me back if you need assistance with anything else during your stay in the area."

The call disconnected.

"Abbie. I guess we're going to *The Theme Park* Hotel," Fanny said.

"On the way," said the Abbie voice.

7:05 PM, In The Theme Park

The sun was getting lower in the western sky peeking through under the clouds while a light rain was falling again on *The Theme Park*. Taylor was walking quickly towards the back offices in the New Tech Pavilion, avoiding some of the rain by staying under overhangs where she could, but she was still getting wet. She weaved through the crowds, dodging other people. At the entrance of the Pavillion she went around three teens sharing one small umbrella.

"Hi. Dr. Singh!" Chandra said. "You trying to get out of the rain too?"

"STEAMBOATers! Hello again," Taylor said as she kept going past them and into the Pavillion. They followed.

Jeremy asked, "Anything new with QAL since this morning?"

"What have you heard?" Taylor asked, slowing down and turning to look at the teens.

"Nothing. I'm just interested," Jeremy explained. He shook water off his clothes.

"Well. I can't talk about that right now. Sorry. I've got something I need to do," Taylor said.

Out of the rain, Emily closed her umbrella and shook it to shed water. Jeremy and Chandra followed Dr. Singh and watched as she went through the door to the back rooms, reappeared behind the glass window, and picked up part of the QEC equipment. Emily followed them.

Chandra whispered to Jeremy and Emily, "We're in trouble. Why is she checking on the QEC equipment? Do you think she knows we used it? I hope we didn't break anything."

On the other side of the glass Taylor whispered something to the machine, and it lit up. They could barely hear her say, "Please give the current location of the remote device."

The machine's voice responded, "Current position is unknown."

"Last known position?"

"In Sierra *Theme* Wilderness, at coordinates…" the machine said, continuing with some longitude and latitude numbers.

Taylor said to her wrist, "Did you get that, Abbie?" Then she continued, "Machine off," and quickly left the room and headed back out of the Pavillion and towards a park exit.

"Bye, Dr. Singh," said all three teens. Jeremy noticed that the door didn't close all the way.

7:10 PM, In the Cave

Bobbie nudged Bella and said, "Wake up. The lights turned brighter for a minute, and someone was talking on the other end."

"Huh? Really?" said Bella. She tried to sit up. "Oh. Oh. Yeah. Machine turn on. The lights got brighter again in the cave.

"Can anyone hear me?" Bella pleaded.

7:11 PM, In *The Theme Park*

Jeremy caught the door and held it open. "Do you want to play with the holograms again?"

Chandra took Jeremy's hand off the door and pushed on it. "No way. Let's not get in any more trouble with Dr. Singh."

Emily's hand darted out, and she caught the door just before it latched closed. She said, "Dr. Singh was asking about where the other end of the QEC pair was. She didn't notice anything different with this end. I don't think she knows we did anything."

"Still. I was so scared she was going to get us in trouble," Chandra said.

"Okay," Emily said, and she let the door close.

7:12 PM, Honus, Jose, and Tristan

Various versions of space for housing, businesses, and an animal sanctuary that satisfied the notes that Jose had provided from Magnolia were displayed on the walls of Honus' bedroom.

"See. It generated ten different scenarios that meet those demands. You can look them over and show them to others. Everything but the animal sanctuary can be satisfied by condo's, apartments, and business spaces that already exist or are under construction, but there are also some scenarios with new construction that can be more flexible but would take more time. Let me know what you pick."

"You're going to cover the cost of all of this? Whatever we choose?"

"If you sign over the block then we'll do this, and you'll get some points on top. The residual payment will vary depending on the options you choose, and the timeframe, but we can work that out."

"I'll let you know. I think we might be able to do this."

"I was pretty sure you'd say that. If you want to send links to this to yourself or anyone else, you can use the computer in my mom's office."

They walked out of his bedroom and down the hallway.

Tristan was sitting at the computer in Mara's office and talking to someone.

"Dad! I didn't know you were here," said Honus. "Who are you talking to?"

Jose walked in and recognized the animated cartoon figure on the screen. "That's Min Strong!" he exclaimed.

"Yes. I am Min Strong," said the voice he recognized from Min Strong convention appearances he had attended so many years ago.

"Where have you been?" Jose asked.

"Minimal visibility, maximum impact," said the animated figure.

"How are you talking to Min Strong?" Jose asked.

"I remembered that Mara worked with Min back in the day, and I remembered a way to contact Min from Mara's computer to ask what she knows about Mara, but she's not being very cooperative."

Jose leaned in next to Tristan to get a better view. His jacket rubbed against the back of Tristan's chair, and he felt the wristbands in his jacket pocket. "Oh. Yeah. I'd like to stay and talk with Min Strong, but I need to do something first. I need to drop something off with Elsie next door, for Camilla's kids. Do you want to come along?"

"Elsie is next door?" Tristan asked. "With Camilla? And Jo-Jo?" His new more complete memories made him uncomfortable. "I think I'll stay here."

"I should probably pay my respects," said Honus. He was idly looking around his mom's office and noticed the safe's door was ajar. "Dad! You opened the safe!"

"Yeah. I'll need to show you what I found in there, but I don't have it here right now. You go next door, and I'll get it when you come back."

"You sure you don't want to go. Elsie said there's plenty of food," said Jose.

Tristan waved them off.

Honus went to his room to put on some more respectful clothes and Jose used his wristband to send a message to Elsie, saying that he and Honus would be stopping by soon. Could she meet outside to hand off the wristbands? Tristan kept trying to get information out of Min.

7:20 PM, In the Cave

"Can anyone hear me?" Bella asked again for the twentieth time. "Why aren't they answering?"

The *Theme* voice from the machine said, "Remote device is in power save mode. Your image and audio is not going through."

"Is there any way to wake up the other end?" Bella asked.

"Yes. With Level 2 Admin Mode," replied the voice of the *Theme* machine.

"Which needs a 16-digit passcode based on birthdates of pets."

"That is correct."

"Put us back in the low light mode we were in before."

The lights dimmed to near darkness. She lay back down and closed her eyes.

"Bobbie. How long will it take to guess two random pet birthdates?"

"Assumptions?"

"Pets born in the last 10, no 20 years."

"In 20 years, there are 7305 unique dates. That would be 53 million three hundred sixty-three thousand twenty-five combinations."

"At six guesses per day."

"Twenty-four thousand three hundred and fifty years."

"Maybe we'll get lucky again. Hey machine, Level 2 Admin passcode. How about January 1, 2056, and January 1, 2056?"

"Passcode entries must be in the form of a sequence of digits."

"Year Month Day or Month Day Year or what?"

"That is not a clue I can give."

"Much more than 24 thousand years," said Bobbie.

"Shit," said Bella. "Oh well. 2056010120560101?"

"Incorrect. You have four tries before being locked out."

"2056010120560102"

"Incorrect. Three more tries."

"2056010220560101"

"Incorrect. Two more tries."

"2056010220560102"

"Incorrect. One more try."

"I'll save that one in case I get a revelation in my sleep. Meanwhile stay in low light mode to save power. Good night."

7:25 PM, Dinner at Camilla's

Elsie stepped outside to meet Jose and get the wristbands. She took them inside to give to Sam and Jo-Jo, who recognized them immediately and put them on. Sam went into the back yard to talk with his Abbie. Jo-Jo asked if her Abitat was okay. Her Abbie said it had been damaged but had been repaired. Jo-Jo asked if her art supplies and artwork was okay. The Abbie voice said some was damaged.

After a couple minutes Honus and Jose rang the doorbell to offer condolences. Camilla insisted they come in and have some food. She tracked down Sam and Jo-Jo as well and insisted they stay even though Jo-Jo wanted to see her Abitat.

Elsie messaged Andre to see if he would make it but didn't get a response. It was unusual for him to work late without more messages, but he was trying to make a good impression at work after time off for paternity leave, so she figured she could give him some slack.

7:30 PM, Ulla

Ulla's Abitat had been trying to stay close to her, by tracking her wristband, but it was confused when she kept changing location by a couple of kilometers every time she stepped through the QAL lens between Abitat B and the lab. Eventually she told it to just follow Abitat B, and it caught up at a charging station.

She stepped out of Abitat B carrying Taylor's pages and into her own Abitat just in time to take a call from Taylor. Taylor gave her the coordinates, and they agreed to meet at a bar about halfway between the two of them that they hadn't tried before.

On the way to the bar, Ulla did a voice call to Tomas, the *Theme* guy who had been bugging her about the prototype and gave him the coordinates.

"Really? Are you sure?" asked Tomas. "Isn't that where we were testing it in the Sierras? I thought you took it with you when you left."

"I didn't take it. I hiked out right after my little acting gig."

"You wandered off, but everyone thought you were coming back for it. You brought it in. You were supposed to take it out."

"No. I was done with it after setting it up for you guys. I don't know how many times I said that. Someone else was supposed to take it out. I was always planning to hike out. I couldn't carry that thing."

"So, it's still there?"

"It was there when I left, and it reports that as its last known location, but it's not reporting a current location," said Ulla.

"No current location? What would cause that?" asked Tomas.

"It needs connections to other hive-connected devices to triangulate its location," said Ulla.

"Then it must be in the demo room inside the mountain," Tomas said.

"You guys were using it outside when I left."

"If it was left outside wouldn't it have connections to report a location? Oh. Wait. There's been a lot of snow up there. Would it fail to report a location if it's buried in snow?" he asked.

"Not unless the snow is really deep," she answered. "Or if there's nobody nearby, it could fail to make enough connections."

"But there's always people in the mountains. What if someone put it in a comm-shielded container and stole it."

"You better hope not," she said.

"It could be inside the mountain, or under a lot of snow, or someone shielded it and stole it. Are those the only possibilities?"

"I guess. It was able to report its last known location, so it's working," Ulla said.

"If a competitor has it, reverse engineers it, and releases a copy we'll all be in big trouble. I'll see about getting someone back up to the mountains to look for it in the demo room or under the snow."

"Good luck," she said.

"Do you want to go back?" asked Tomas, "You know the location."

"No thanks. You know it too," answered Ulla.

After the call she stepped out of her Abitat near the bar where Taylor agreed to meet.

7:35 PM, Doug and Brock at Sergey's

Doug pulled the convertible up to the intercom outside the gate in the driveway of Sergey's farm. Brock sat next to him with his hair fully fluffed after the breezy drive from the coast. Doug pushed the button which gave a buzzing sound over the intercom.

"Hey. Sergey? Are you there?" Doug said loudly into the intercom. After a minute with no answer, he tapped in a code and the gate opened. He drove into the farm and parked the car on the side of the driveway not far from the shed. He popped open the front trunk, got out, took his pack, and indicated to Brock to do the same. Brock put on his pack and picked up the bin. Doug closed the lid on the trunk. They walked to the shed.

7:40 PM, Andre at the Bar

Andre was enjoying his time out with some of his public safety buddies. Hans the purple alien came in, out of costume, but with a distinct purple tint still on his arms and face. Kyle, who had been in public safety several years ago before switching to work for Park Security and Squeaky also came in.

The combination of Forgetdibles and a couple drinks made the time pass quickly for Andre. Kyle pointed out the two women who just came in. They didn't look like public safety types. More like librarians or something. They looked nerdy but still sexy. At least after some drinks and Forgetdibles.

Andre messaged Elsie:

working late
then a quick drink
with some old colleagues

7:43 PM, Tristan Goes Back to the Workshop

After trying various tools from Mara's office to gain control of Min AI and force her to tell him more, Tristan gave up. She was stubbornly independent. He wondered if Mara would still be able to influence her if she were here.

Thinking of Mara and her story he remembered he told Honus he would get the contents of the safe for him, which he had left in the workshop. He stood up and headed back to get them. He should tell Honus which parts he thought were made up.

7:45 PM, Taylor and Ulla at the Bar

The music was a little loud, but within limits to avoid hearing damage. If the bar played it too loud then some public safety officer customers, which were a big part of the clientele, would get called away by their Abbies. The result was that at this bar most of the time you could actually have a conversation.

"So did you get the *Theme* guy off your back about the prototype?" Taylor asked as she sipped her beer. Her tablet was flat on the table next to her beer glass. Under the tablet were the pages of her three papers that Ulla had brought to her. Her attention was divided between checking the numbers on her tablet which showed the lens was still operating, checking out the people in the bar, and her beer. It seemed like most people in the bar were focused on drinking beer. Some of them looked creepy but some were interesting. One really muscular guy who kept looking their direction seemed a little of both. One of the guys with him who was more discrete about looking was slightly purple.

"I think so," said Ulla. "Tomas says they're going to have to go back to the mountains to see if they can find it."

"At least you don't have to think about it anymore."

"True."

7:50 PM, Doug and Brock

Doug had set up a little chem lab in the shed. The automatic chemical processor box was plugged in and sitting on the ground between two cots. He called up his private blend formulas for NeverMind and other favorites into the system control program. Wearing gloves and a mask, he carefully extracted a few grams of the NeverMore powder from the bundle using a powder syringe that prevented any spills and resealed the puncture as he withdrew it. He inserted it into the machine. The system did a quick analysis on the sample. As he suspected, it was very pure NeverMore. He made some adjustments to the control program and checked the levels of the other reagent chemicals, adding some from the spare bottles in his pack. He pressed some buttons to start the reaction. A hum sound came from the box.

"How long does it take?" Brock asked.

"Be patient."

7:54 PM, Honus and Jose

After sampling food and drink in the somber gathering, Honus and Jose excused themselves and left to go back next door. Jo-Jo was anxious to go check on her Abitat, and Sam was anxious to check out the game room, but Camilla insisted they stay as long as Elsie and Alex were there. Elsie hesitated to leave thinking Andre was on his way.

Sunset

7:55 PM in Orange County.
8:03 PM in Lone Pine.

Chapter 16

Saturday Sunset to 9 PM

7:55 PM, News at the Bar

Holographic displays of ball games and auto racing were visible in the upper corners of the bar. The patrons ignored most of them. One display turned briefly to local news.

"Local attorney dies in tragic mountain rock fall."

It showed pictures of a snowy scene with a new pile of rocks next to a broken mountain rockface. Then it switched to an AI simulation showing the breaking of the rock face and falling rocks with a simulated hiker standing outside of a tent and putting hands up just as the rocks crashed down. The simulated rock fall froze with one of the largest rocks rolling just above the hiker's upraised hands as if she had caught the boulder. Then the pictures switched back to an actual Abbie-vetted image of the pile of rocks and a fast motion view of cables lifting a large boulder off of the flattened tent and dropping it against the rockface on the pile of rocks with a burst of dust. The area under the moved rock and the faces of the people present were blurred.

This caught the attention of several of the bar patrons. One said, "Oh My God. Show that again." The holographic news report repeated on a loop.

"That's got to hurt," said one as the rocks touched the simulated hiker.

In another corner of the bar the images of a car race continued but text flowed below the raceway. "OC ATTORNEY ISABELLA MULLER 32 FEARED DEAD IN SIERRA HIKING ACCIDENT."

"That's so sad. Isabella Muller, 32," Taylor said. "Not much older than us."

Another sports display in another corner broke away to an aerial view of the rock pile, but the spoken words were not audible.

Ulla pointed and said, "I recognize that tree."

"What?" asked Taylor.

"That bent-over tree with the fluorescent rope tied to it on the ridge near the rock fall. That's where I did the prototype QEC 18 Min Quest DBI Demo," Ulla explained. That's got to be at the same coordinates. Check on your tablet."

Taylor pulled up a satellite view of the last-known coordinates that she had received from the QEC machine earlier. Live feeds were being restricted now, but it showed the same bent over tree in a recorded-earlier view. Ulla looked back and forth between the current aerial view on the news and the previous view of the coordinates.

She said, "It looks like the mountain with the demo-room cave caved in. Tomas at *Theme* is going to have a hard time getting the prototype out of there."

"It was still working this afternoon. What time was the rock fall?"

"Four-thirty yesterday," said Andre, starting to come out of his Forgetdible fog. He continued, "Isabella Muller. Bella. She worked for my wife," said Andre.

"Your wife, huh?" said Taylor. "Maybe we won't be going home with you and your purple friend after all."

"Maybe cute Mr. Purple though?" said Ulla, poking him, "Or Kyle here, but not you Andre. Your wife is calling you."

A buzz on Andre's wristband was another message from Elsie asking when he would be coming.

8:04 PM, At Another Bar

Manzanita and Tim had a couple drinks at a bar outside of Lone Pine. An old flat panel display showed sports and local news. The story about the lawyer killed in the mountains came up.

"I wonder who talked to the news?" said Manzanita.

Tim looked closely at the images in the report and said, "Somebody tells somebody who tells somebody and it's on the news. At least they blurred the identities of the people there."

"It's a sad situation. I hope the next of kin found out first," Manzanita opined.

"Yeah, but probably not," Tim said. "Want to play some pool?" he nodded towards the pool table that now seemed to be available.

"Not my thing," said Manzanita.

"Me neither, but the table is open."

8:05 PM, Ami, Tony, and Carl

The event was supposed to be social and philanthropic, but when you get members of the *Theme* board at an event it always tends towards work. Carl Heinz was at the bar across the room. Ami still hated Carl Heinz, but she tolerated him because he was able to get things done running *Theme*. She suddenly realized he must have told the truth years ago when he said he didn't have Douglas killed. Apparently, blackmailing him by holding the plane crash deaths over his head along with letting him continue to be super wealthy had been enough to keep his cooperation, so far. The additional threat to expose his murder of her brother may not have been a factor in his cooperation after all. Or maybe he actually thought he had eliminated Douglas. Probably best not to let him know Douglas was alive. Carl was competent to handle most details running *Theme* but Tony or really she herself had ultimate authority over big decisions.

Officially, Tony was a member of the *Theme* board focused on philanthropy, and she was merely his shy wife and confidante who worked behind the scenes on some research projects for *Theme*. Carl Heinz was publicly and officially chair and CEO of the interplanetary non-profit corporation dedicated to promoting the well-being and happiness of all life in the solar system. But she, Carl, and Tony all knew she was really the one in charge. Carl walked over to her with an extra drink in his hand.

"Ami, you'll like this ginger ale. Give it a try," Carl offered.

"Thank you, sir," Ami took the drink but did not sip it.

"Still don't trust me with poisoned drinks?" Carl asked.

"Is that what this is?" Ami asked.

"I asked for a plain ginger ale this time. I swear," he replied. "I do have a question for you though."

"Fire away. Not literally by the way," Ami said.

"Your daughter, Tony's daughter I mean."

"Ulla Marks?"

"Yes. Ulla. She contracted to work on a holographics communications device for *Theme*. QEC actually. Should be a big money-maker."

"I remember her talking to her dad about that. Quite an improvement over previous versions if I understand. One is on its way to Mars?"

"Yeah. We're doing a great show about the flight. Ultra-high-res holograms and DBI data processed in real time in the studios to make some really great entertainment. The flight has already had a few emergencies for dramatic effect."

"Yeah. Yeah. I know," Ami said. "And this has what to do with Ulla?"

"Right. Ulla helped with the design and the factory setup for the new model device, unless that was actually you?"

"No. Not that one. That was just Ulla and her buddy. They both are very bright."

"Wow. I don't hear you say that about many people. Anyway, Ulla was also involved in a field test on the prototype. Since then, one side of the prototype device pair has gone missing."

"Is that so?"

"Given whose daughter she is, no one has wanted to press her about it too much, but maybe you or Tony could ask if she knows where it went?"

"This would be the new *Thematic* QEC Holo XVIII? It cost what? One point eight billion points to develop?"

"That's the one. That figure is mostly for the factories. We're making more, but we'd still rather not misplace the prototype. Don't want it falling into the hands of the competition."

"If we had any competition. Okay. Yeah. I can see the concern. Tony will talk to her. But you don't need to tiptoe around her. Tony wants her to earn her own way. This kind of question should not have risen to your level or mine."

"People have talked to her, but she says she doesn't know what happened to it."

"Then you have your answer. Talk to the other people involved in the test. No need to bother Tony about it. Or was this just a pretense to bring me a 'ginger ale'?"

"I can keep trying."

"Carl, It's been fun, but we should stop this charade. It's getting old. You know my anonymous avatars in multiple game worlds will release your bad secrets if something happens to me."

"Any of those avatars disappear lately?"

"Maybe. An odd power glitch today reset some, but you'll never track them all down."

"I know. I know. I can try. I can dream. But I know. Did you see the proposals for six new *Theme* Parks?

"I did. Six is too many right now. Tony will get back to you on that. Next week. This is a holiday weekend."

"So, I've heard."

"You need to focus on solving the supply issues on the *Theme* Mars colonies. Find a solution," said Ami.

"I've told you we need a lot more supply flights or a lot fewer colonists. Unless maybe your research lab can solve the water and air out of Mars rocks quandary," Carl said.

"It's easy if you could just find the right rocks, like on the moon. Maybe I'll look at it again, but there was supposed to be a lot more usable ice up there. And what's this about problems with one of the supply flights?" Ami asked.

"You mean the live stream reality world of the flight I was just talking about?" Carl clarified. "The one using one of the new QEC machines for super-high-res holograms and DBI in real time? I think the panic and emergency on that is all scripted, but it does look real. It's good entertainment either way. I just hope they don't lose another QEC 18 machine in all the drama."

"So long as it doesn't fall into the wrong hands. Sacrifice the flight before someone else grabs the device in a "rescue."

8:09 PM, Tristan and Max Aires Look for Clues

Back in the workshop, Tristan spent some time with Max AI trying to track down clues from Mara's story that might shed light on what happened to her. He was starting to believe she was telling the truth about having a second or third identity. He hadn't been able to control Min AI, but the fact that he was able to contact her from Mara's computer, and she claimed to be Min Strong, was pretty compelling evidence that part of Mara's story was true.

The Zynn family connection also seemed more plausible now. He had some memories that matched the part of her story where she told Perry about being Marta, but he felt like maybe she was lying to him back then. He couldn't recall anything from the time when Marta Zynn's plane crashed. According to her story he was already disabled by then. That part was probably true.

Mara disappeared a couple years after Marta's plane crashed. Maybe she was freaked out that the person she liked pretending to be had died, and did something to herself, or maybe the story was true, she was Marta, and Marta didn't die. But if so, where is Marta Zynn today? The agency database had no information about her being alive. Nothing in the agency data mentioned Marta Zynn since her reported death.

Mara's story also mentioned a brother and people she worked with. Max AI couldn't find any recent information about the brother, Douglas, who according to Camilla may have been Bella's father. The story also mentioned Tony Marks and Carl Heinz. Tony Marks seemed familiar to Tristan. Tristan felt sure Perry had met him on the project to create Abitats.

Max AI was able to give some private information from the agency database about both Tony Marks and Carl Heinz. Both were now big shots in the *Theme* company, and both avoided sharing personal information. Carl Heinz collected yachts, race cars, planes, and expensive wines. Tony apparently was married to someone name Ami Marks and had a daughter from a previous relationship.

Ami Marks. Was that the same Ami Marks as the author on the DBI studies referenced in Minh's medical records? Apparently so.

8:10 PM, Ending the Impromptu Wake Early

It was like a wake, but a strange one, and a small one. There was lots of food that no one ate. Camilla offered drinks, but no one but Sam took any. No neighbors, school friends, or work associates other than Elsie attended. No one talked about Isabella, but she was on everyone's mind as they talked about other things. After Jose and Honus left, everyone was quiet. Shortly, Camilla said she was getting tired and Elsie decided it was time to head for home as well. Elsie went to Alex's Abitat to make sure they were comfortable before the ride home. Alex was sleeping but fidgety. Elsie decided to ride home in Alex's Abitat. She said her goodbyes to Camilla, Josephine, and Sam and set out.

Sam made sure he had the right codes for the game room and disappeared into it. As Camilla went to her own bedroom she said, "Josephine, I packed some food in compostable containers if you want to feed your friends again. Don't forget to bring back that casserole dish from last night. Isabella gave me that dish."

Jo-Jo called her Abitat, which soon docked at the same portal where Elsie and Alex had just been. When the door opened she was shocked by how clean it looked inside and how neatly stacked the new bins were.

She opened a bin and said, "What the fuck? This crap is shredded and redded?" She checked another bin which had similar shredded and red-tinted contents. "I love it. I can make something out of this."

She picked up two new tablets from the seat of her recliner chair and sat down. She asked one of the tablets, "Abbie, did we get the points for the big delivery?"

"1500 Amps were deposited yesterday, and I did sixty-one local deliveries tonight for 92 more points."

"Nice. Deliveries pay a lot more here than in Kansas. Let's go around the block a couple of times. Maybe you can do a couple more while I check out the rest of these bins."

"Yes. Ma'am."

She leaned back in her chair, looking at all the bins, then she changed her mind, got up and stepped into her bathroom. It was clean. Nice. No Sam smell.

8:15 PM, At the Bar

Andre had left but Hans and Kyle were still talking with Taylor and Ulla. Taylor had a couple drinks and was working on her third, but Ulla was still nursing her first. The news about the rockfall in the Sierras was still showing in one of the sports displays.

Kyle said, "Isabella Muller? Didn't Andre call her Bella?"

"Yeah. He said his wife works with Bella," said Taylor. "Worked I guess."

"That's funny," Kyle said. "No, not funny. It's tragic, but it's odd: The HofHH at *The Theme Park* was doing a storyline teaser today about someone named Bella trapped somewhere. It said stuff like:

'Hello! Can anyone hear us? Help!'

'Bella. Bella. Are you okay?'

'Give us some light. Turn on the projector and the scanner lights.'

'Bella. Wake up.'

I checked out the HofHH ride, twice, and those words weren't part of the actual ride storylines today. Just a fake teaser. Funny, odd, it was the same name as the dead attorney."

Ulla asked, "They said projector and scanner?"

"Random. Whatever that means," answered Kyle.

"Isn't the HofHH close to the New Tech Pavillion?" Ulla asked.

"Same building actually," said Kyle.

Ulla turned to Taylor and asked, "Taylor, did anything odd happen when you checked on that thing you checked on earlier? Any voices maybe?"

"No. I was really quick. Turn it on. Give the admin code to get the coordinates and turn it off. Why?"

"I think maybe we should go check it out again," said Ulla.

"But..." Taylor pointed to her drink glass that was still half full and the two men sitting at the table.

Ulla continued, "Sorry purple Hans. We've gotta scoot. No checking out your alien outfit with all the nimble hands today. But we've got your number. Another time. You too Kyle. Tay or I might be in touch. Come on Tay. Let's go."

Taylor drained her glass and stood up, gesturing sorry as she went. She reached back and picked up her tablet.

8:20 PM, In the Shed

"Is it ready? Is it ready?" Brock asked as Doug checked the readouts on the mini chem lab device.

"Almost," Doug said.

"I need some NeverMind. Too many things are in my head," Brock insisted. A ding rang out from the machine.

"The first batch is Forgetdibles. You've been off of NeverMind too long. Need to ease back into it."

"No. I want the blankness. Now."

"Here. Try one of these for now," Doug took a lump out of a slot in the device and pulled and stretched it until a piece broke off. He rolled that piece into a ball and handed it to Brock who immediately put it in his mouth and started chewing.

8:25 PM, Tourists at *The Theme Park*

Minh's medical grade brain cap gave them direct access to the front of the queues for most rides and attractions, so they went on more rides in a half hour tonight than in a few hours yesterday. Park employee NPCs assisting with rides took a liking to the positive banter between the sick kid and his twin sister. Word among the NPCs was that he had drowned this morning and was thought dead but came back and was still at risk and was out for one last hurrah. But he had a very positive attitude.

As they left the exit of one ride and were picking which one to go to next, John pointed out it was past their bedtimes.

Minh and Max resisted leaving. They wanted to go on more rides, and they really wanted to stay to see the fireworks and light show. Minh argued, "I got lots of sleep when I was in a coma. Let me stay up."

"I didn't get to do anything fun while Minh was dead," Max argued. "Let us see the fireworks!"

John and Fanny acquiesced to their demands, partly because they wanted to see the light show as well. A park employee NPC costumed as some kind of ninja turkey vulture heard them talking about it and offered to guide them to a premium viewing spot.

"Meet me inside the New Tech Pavilion no later than 9:30," said the warrior fowl.

8:35 PM, Jose and Honus

After checking Mara's office to see if Tristan had brought back the contents of the safe, Honus and Jose went to Billy Jay's bedroom and brought up the history world game from yesterday and played some scenes again, but repeatedly taking turns changing the appearance of the characters. In one iteration, Billy Jay became a Billy goat, and Javier became a bearded goatherd in lederhosen. Lacy looked like a fat male Italian pasta chef in an oversized white chef's hat who only cooked spaghetti, and Perry looked like a floating brain in a jar, but the brain was a head of cauliflower. Jerry from the coffee shop became part koala bear and part sexy lounge singer. Mara looked like the Min Strong cartoon. In another iteration the same looks were swapped to other characters. They would silence the audio and add their own version of the dialog. After repeating this a few times Honus said he wished he could find some pictures of Izzie.

Jose called up images from the news showing her official portrait from the law firm's public profile site. Honus said he wished he could see what she looked like when he knew her. They searched the archives of the family surveillance cameras and found a view of her climbing a tree in the back yard when she was five or six. That was maybe the first time he met her. He watched her climbing and dropping from the tree over and over again.

8:45 PM, Ami and Carl Again

"No poisoned drink for me this time, Carl," Ami asked as Carl Heinz walked up to her empty-handed.

"No. But I did get word about that missing prototype QEC device."

"Not something I need to know about."

"Just a quick update since I mentioned it earlier."

She gave a look like she might tolerate an update, "It better be quick and interesting."

Carl continued, "We located it, and it is still working, but apparently it's buried under tons of rocks."

"Okay. I'm curious. How did it get buried under tons of rocks and how is it still working?"

"I'm told it was left behind in the mountains after the field test, in a cave or something, and there was a rockfall that sealed it in."

"And we know this how?" Ami inquired.

"We were able to contact it from the paired device and confirm its last known location. The rockfall is on the news tonight in the same spot. Apparently a local IP attorney was crushed."

"What was an IP attorney doing there? One of ours?" Ami asked.

"No. A local firm we don't work with," said Carl.

"A competing Intellectual Property attorney was poking around in a remote location where our new two-billion-point machine was misplaced? That's got to be a competitor trying to get their hands on our machine to steal the design."

"You think? I didn't put that together. But you might be right."

"Of course I'm right. Which means someone left it there on purpose and told them about it. We've got a mole inside the company."

"Maybe Tony's kid?"

"I don't think so, but we need to consider all the possibilities. Whoever is behind it probably shielded it and took it back to a lab. They created a convenient rockfall to make us think the device was buried too deep to retrieve to buy time for them to reverse engineer it. That's got to be a cover."

"The remains of the attorney haven't been found. Buried under too many rocks."

"See what I mean. It's a cover. The IP attorney will mysteriously show up later, or probably change their identity, after their client starts selling a competing device. We need to do damage control. Find out who's behind this and get ready to shut them down—with lawsuits, or…"

"…Or whatever it takes," added Carl.

"Right." Ami smiled wide as Tony walked up with someone he wanted to introduce. "Who is this, Tony?"

8:55 PM, Ulla and Taylor to *The Theme Park*

Ulla took Taylor with her in her Abitat. Taylor's Abitat would have been reliable to get her to *The Theme Park* only if Taylor gave it the right instructions, and Ulla didn't trust her to do that after a few drinks.

They walked together from the entrance towards the New Tech area. Along the way, Taylor pointed to the History Moments attraction and said, "That's you in there, Ulla. Isn't it? Min Ulla!"

"Yes, dear. You need to sober up, dear."

When they got to the New Tech pavilion they went into the back room where the QEC device was stored and Ulla said, "Machine on."

The lights came on, and Ulla continued, "Isabella Muller? Are you there?

Chapter 17

Saturday 9 to 10 PM

9:00 PM, In the Cave

Bella was dipping her hands into the box to scoop out a drink of water. It was almost completely dark, but she had climbed up and found her way to the water box by feel. She listened. The drips of water from the ceiling were slow now. She was worried that this water might be unsanitary since, in addition to whatever carcinogens came from the rocks above, she wasn't able to wash her hands after peeing in the corner of the cave room. Without any TP she had limited options. It was starting to smell in here, both herself and the space. At least she was constipated so no shit to deal with so far. Still, dirty water was so much better than no water at all. As she splashed some water on her face she thought she heard Bobbie saying something.

"What did you say?" she asked.

"Someone is asking for you," said Bobbie. "You should turn on your scanner and answer."

Bella shuffled her way back to the edge of the tunnel and carefully stepped down into the room.

"Isabella Muller? Hey, Taylor. I guess you're right. There's no one there."

"Machine. Turn on. Turn everything on," said Bella.

The room lit up brightly like a summer's day."

"Ouch. That hurts my eyes. Not the Test Pattern. Just the scanner and projector and audio."

"Hello. There is someone there. Is that you Isabella Muller?"

"Yes. Who am I talking to?

"I'm Ulla Marks and this is Taylor Singh."

She gestured at Taylor. The holograms made it appear that they were all together in a room with elements combining both the room at *The Theme Park* and the cave in the mountains. A window into a larger area in the New Tech Pavillion on the other side of the glass was also visible. Taylor and Bobbie occupied the same space. Bobbie moved to one side.

"And this is Bobbie," said Bella as Bobbie moved into her own space.

"Are you okay?" asked Ulla.

"We were checking out this cave, during the snowstorm on Friday, and the entrance collapsed, sealing us in. Yesterday, I think, or maybe the day before. I lose track."

"Yesterday," said Bobbie.

"We found this machine in a box in the dark. It's low on power. How does it communicate through rocks, by the way?" Bella asked.

"Cannot say. NDA," said Ulla.

"Okay," said Bella. "I know NDAs."

"But how are you?" Ulla asked. "Are you okay?"

"We have some water dripping in from the rocks above the tunnel, so I had some to drink, but we don't have any food. A few more rocks fall in the entrance tunnel every few hours. A couple more collapses and we are probably done for in here too."

"We'll let people know you're there. You should probably save power so we can communicate again later. Visuals off," said Ulla.

Bella said, "Dim the lights, We couldn't guess the level 2 Admin passcode, or we would have called someone."

"It's easy. 0101205601022056."

"Your pets have consecutive birthdates?"

"You got the clues? Sixteen digits is real, but the pet clue was a ruse, just to remind us to use dates. We don't have any pets," said Ulla.

"Allowing calls through the machine, does that use a lot of power? I've got some people I need to call," said Bella.

"Not as much as the lights and hologram transmission, but you probably shouldn't leave it on. You have to activate it from your end if you want to make calls," said Ulla. "If I activate it I can call anyone in range of the device on your end, which is probably just you."

Bella said, "Admin level 2 passcode 0101205601022056. Allow communication through the machine."

"Acknowledged," said the distinctive *Theme* voice from the device.

"Who should I call first? Elsie to let her know I might be late for work next week?" Bella asked herself and laughed.

"People think you are dead. It's been on the news. Big rockfall. They found your tent and stuff under one of the biggest rocks. But not your bodies."

"Everyone has heard about it, and they haven't been trying to dig us out?"

"They were trying. They moved one rock off your tent. They thought you were dead under a million tons of rocks. Too much to dig out," said Ulla. "Only *Theme* knew about the cave, and they didn't know you were in it. Everyone but us thinks you are dead."

"Can I have some privacy for a couple of calls?" Bella asked.

"Sure. Okay. We will leave the room, if you want. But we'll be back in a few minutes."

9:07 PM, Outside a Bar Near Lone Pine

"I didn't know you were a pool shark," Tim said as his Abitat approached.

"Just beginner's luck," said Manzanita.

"Winning 50 points off of your old man. Brutal," Tim complained with a smile.

"I can give it back. Betting was your idea," said Manzanita.

"I'll earn it back. You said you're tired. Too tired for a speed chess match? You have a board at your place? Double or nothing?" Tim asked.

"You think I haven't been practicing chess? Double or nothing? I'll take that, but it has to be fast. I am fading. It's been a long day or two," Manzanita said.

"Get in. I'll give you a ride," Tim suggested. "Is it close?"

"Yeah. We could walk, but I'm too tired to walk. Not too tired to show you a thing or two about speed chess, but walking? Not right now." They stepped into the Abitat.

Tim picked up the headset and prescription bottle from his chair and put them away in a cupboard.

"DBI headset? Is that for the new job?" Manzanita asked.

"Can't talk about it," said Tim.

"Scott only hires people with real skills. No brain cap jockeys. It's a policy of the whole Honus company," said Manzanita.

"That's different. That must be why he's desperate to hire someone who actually knows his stuff with the heavy equipment."

"And the medicine? Are you okay?" Manzanita asked.

"It's nothing. Never mind that," Tim replied.

The Abbie voice said, "Approaching destination."

9:10 PM, At Camilla's

A message bar appeared in the air in front of a medieval castle in the game room while Sam was preparing to scale the wall.

Call for Camilla Muller from IM.

"Ignore call," he said. "She's gone to bed." He picked up his sword and began climbing a ladder leaning against the side of the castle wall.

9:11 PM, Jurupa Valley

Elsie had put Alex down in their bed and stopped in the hallway to listen. She hoped Alex was down for the night. Andre walked in from his room and from his docked Abitat, looking like he had been drinking. A message started to buzz on her wristband.

"Take a message," she said.

She wanted to have a word with Andre before talking to anyone else. She knew he had planned to meet friends for drinks after work, but she was still perturbed.

9:12 PM, Barn Workshop Office

After getting some information from Max AI about how the agency had used DBI headsets over the years and getting some ideas on how he might be able to get more access to his own headset memories, Tristan saw a notice that a work call, not from Elsie, was coming in to his Abitat. He could transfer it to his wristband and answer it from here but wasn't sure he wanted to, since that might leave a trace to his current location. He still didn't want anything tying Tristan to Perry.

He would need to go back to his Abitat and see who it was from. Maybe one of the clients. In any case he shouldn't wait too long to call them back because if they were calling about work on a holiday Saturday night it probably shouldn't wait until Tuesday.

He told Max AI that he would be back later. He picked up the trust document and the envelope with the pages of Mara's story and looked them over as he headed back towards the house. He could drop them off in the safe for Honus before going to his Abitat to see who was calling.

9:13 PM, In the Cave

Bella was getting annoyed. Why wouldn't anyone take her call? Didn't they want to find out she was alive, at least for now. Who else could she call? She had some college and school friends, but she didn't keep in touch, and it seemed a little out of place to be calling one of them under the circumstances. There were other people at work, but she had already tried Elsie and Tristan. She didn't leave messages, but they should have a record that she called, and they could call her back.

If her Cam-Ma was not taking calls, she might be sleeping. She tended to go to bed before sunset sometimes. Maybe she could connect with her uncle or his sister, her mom. Last she heard they were living in Iowa or Nebraska or something. But they were probably too stoned to take a call. She should leave a message for her Cam-Ma in case the roof collapsed before she could be rescued.

Who else could she call? What about the odd kid next door who always followed her around when she was climbing trees when she was little? She would be happy even to talk to him right now, although he must be old. He always seemed much older than her back then, but she realized he must actually be only a few years older than her. She didn't have a number for him and wasn't even sure what name he went by these days. She recalled jingling the windchimes on his back porch to get his attention when she was little.

She needed to leave someone some messages. In her Abitat her Abbie would know how to get help. Bobbie was still no help.

9:15 PM, Ulla and Taylor

Ulla said, "I told Tomas that Isabella Muller is alive inside the cave along with her hiking companion, Bobbie, who looks to be a Bot Abbie."

Taylor said, "Good. *Theme* should be able to send help."

Ulla continued, "But he said he has it on very high authority that she is not in the cave but in a shielded competitor lab somewhere, set up to look like the cave. A competitor is getting ready to reverse engineer the device. It's a ruse to get *Theme* to think the device is going to be destroyed. He says we should stall them and try to figure out their actual location. He is pretty sure they've rigged it so that the real cave will collapse entirely before long. If it hasn't already. He said he wasn't supposed to tell me, because everyone involved in the prototype test is suspected of being involved, including me, but he wanted me to have a heads up," Ulla explained as they stood in the main room of the New Tech Pavillion.

Taylor said, "*Theme* is getting more and more paranoid. Is there anything we can do to help them if *Theme* won't start digging them out?"

Ulla answered, "He said the cave was stable before we did the test. It wouldn't collapse without some help."

Taylor objected, "That just doesn't make any sense. Who would blow up the cave?"

A boom sounded from outside the pavilion. Taylor and Ulla jumped. "What was that?" Taylor asked. "Was that from the cave?"

Some people came in asking if there was a good place to view the fireworks show through here. The boom must have been a preview shot for the fireworks and light show that was starting soon.

Taylor said no and after looking around the people left disappointed. Taylor knew there was a great viewing spot on the pavilion roof, but you needed an employee NPC pass, or an ultra-platinum-omega player pass with an NPC guide to get up there. The disappointed players didn't have an NPC guide. Taylor and Ulla were employees, but not NPC's and besides they were busy.

Taylor said, "*Theme* was trying to dig them out earlier. The news holo showed aerial cranes lifting a giant boulder. Why try before and not now?"

"I asked Tomas that," said Ulla. "That wasn't *Theme*. It was a competitor. All part of the conspiracy theory he said."

Taylor spoke into her wristband, "Who was that lifting the boulder in the mountains today on the news stream?"

"The aerial cranes used are registered to Honus Resorts Hospitality," said an Abbie voice. "The faces of the people present were obscured due to a lack of release forms, so I can't identify them."

"Does Honus do communications devices?" Taylor asked.

The Abbie voice replied, "HRH is a privately held business that does not reveal its internal operations, but they have never announced intention to pursue anything other than resorts, residential developments, and hospitality services."

"But they do compete with *Theme* in entertainment and hospitality, right?" Taylor asked her wrist.

"They have residential and resort properties nearby to *Theme* facilities, but *Theme* has not tried to stop them. *Theme* categorized them as complementary, rather than a competitive threat."

"This is too complicated," complained Taylor. "Do you think someone at Honus Hospitality would help us if we let them know that we've been in touch with Isabella Muller? That she is alive?"

"I don't know. Tomas would say they already know and are playing us."

"Let's talk to her again," said Taylor.

She opened the door to go back in.

9:18 PM, Tristan and Jo-Jo

As Tristan was exiting the barn workshop he saw Jo-Jo was crossing the basketball court from the small shed coming towards him. She was carrying a casserole dish. He was carrying a manila envelope and a folder with papers.

"Hey. Mr. Lee. Perry."

"Jo-Jo?"

"I knew it was you. Your face is different, but your voice and your eyes are right. Older. But so, am I, right?"

"How is Camilla, your mom, doing?"

"I don't know. She went to bed like an hour ago. She reminded me ten times to bring back her casserole dish before she turned in." She held it up. "She put some of tonight's leftovers in compostable containers. I just dropped them off for my friends. Don't know if they will eat it. They're zoned out. I can go get some for you if you're hungry. And there's still a lot more food in the house. If you're going that way."

"You said your memories were fuzzy?" he asked as they walked towards the houses.

"Yeah. Trying to get some of them back so I can figure out who I should make amends to."

"I had selective amnesia for years too, but a lot has come back recently."

"Off the NeverMind lately, like me?" Jo-Jo surmised.

"I don't think I ever took it. My amnesia was something else."

"Anything interesting in your returning memories?"

"Did we?" He pointed back and forth between the two of them.

"Did the daddy diddle the baby boy's baby sitter?" She nodded.

"I was such a bad man."

"The memory's fuzzy. It was a long time ago, and all the drugs since then, but I think I went after you. I was newly a legal adult. Eighteen then if I recall. And you were not bad. Actually, pretty good."

"Shit. Sorry. I shouldn't have done that. I must have been more than 10 years older than you."

"Yeah. You were ancient. Probably thirty. But sorry back at you. You were just one of many notches I put on my belt that year. Not the first or the last before..." She gestured in front of her belly.

"Isabella?"

"Probably not you. She looked more like Douglas Zynn, or one of the guys from high school, but who knows."

As they went through the hedge and got a view of the ranch house she nodded towards the house and asked, "Want to have a go again, for old times' sake? We're definitely both adults now. Do you still have the same kitchen table as way back when? We can see if it still works. Or I've got an Abitat. It's crowded, but we can manage."

9:20 PM, Bella and Bobbie

Bella was just finishing a message for Cam-Ma when a loud crack and crash signaled more rocks falling. She hoped the message would not sound too disturbing.

After the dust settled a bit, she pointed the lights from the device into the tunnel. There really wasn't a tunnel any longer. Some fallen rocks were on the floor in the room now. The latest collapse had crushed the water bin and the water it had been holding was dripping from the edge of what had been the tunnel and spreading in the dust on the floor of the cave room below. She moved back to the other side of the room, using the lights to inspect the ceiling for cracks. There were some new ones.

"Isabella?" came Ulla's voice from the machine.

"Yes."

"Were you able to make the calls you wanted to make?"

"Nobody's answering. But I left a message. I hope it's not my last. We just had another collapse. The tunnel and the bin for catching water are gone. The ceiling in here has more cracks. I don't think we have much time."

"Damn," said Taylor. "I wish there was another way to get you out."

Ulla said, "Turn on the scanner again so we can get some good images. That might help make a plan for how to dig you out."

"Scanner on," said Bella.

9:22 PM, Ulla and Taylor

"Projector on, and record," said Ulla.

Ulla directed Bella to move the scanner around the space, giving particular attention to the ceiling cracks.

After getting the images Ulla muted the audio capture at her end and directed her Abbie to build a 3D model of the space and do rockfall engineering analysis to predict future collapses. Her Abbie said a rockfall engineering expert was not immediately available but the information she could find indicated she would need current external views and ground penetrating radar or sonar scans to model the fissures accurately, but those were not available.

Ulla thought about creating a sonar scan with the existing equipment. It could be done, but she didn't have enough time to figure out the details. With the current views from inside along with external views from the news feeds earlier today, her Abbie calculated that it would be between 30 minutes and two weeks before the cave completely collapsed, with a most-likely time of eight hours. Her Abbie also estimated that it would take a week to remove enough of the mountain to create an escape route without accelerating the collapses.

Ulla asked, "Could the view we're seeing be a holographic simulation?"

Abbie answered, "The images coming through the machine are vetted as a valid representation of what is being scanned on the other end, but that scene itself is not Abbie-vetted, so yes it could be simulated."

"Wait," said Ulla. "Unmute my audio. Hey Isabella."

"Yes?"

"Can you focus your scanner in very close on one of those cracks in the ceiling?"

"Like this?" Bella asked as she lifted the scanner.

"Good. Tell it to zoom in to maximum magnification."

"Zoom in to maximum magnification," said Bella.

The view projected in the room at *The Theme Park* showed a floating view of the crystalline structure of the rocks on both sides of a wide chasm that was a magnified view of a narrow crack in the ceiling.

"Abbie. Can you determine what resolution the scanner is capturing?"

"17.9L."

"Isabella. Move the scanner to a different spot." Bella moved it. "Abbie, now?"

"18L," said the Abbie voice.

Ulla said, "Okay. That's got to be real rocks. Nobody could do more than 15L projection before these new *Theme* devices and that magnification looks real. If the image it's transmitting is a holographic simulation of a cave it is higher res than anyone but us knows how to make."

"Unless it is a fake cave made of real rock," Taylor suggested.

"Are you really suggesting that we are not trapped inside a collapsing mountain?" Bella objected.

"Not us. Someone else suggested it. We're trying to prove you are," Ulla apologized.

"Great. Is someone going to try to get us out of here or not?" Bella demanded. "No one cares. I called people but no one answered, and no one called me back."

"Calling back? Oh. I forgot to open the comm link the other way. You can put calls through and talk if they connect, but the other direction can't call you unless we open it from this end. Dumb little detail of the QEC connections," Ulla said.

"Can you fix that dumb little detail, please?" Bella asked.

"Admin level 2, 0101205601022056. Open comm link."

"Acknowledged," came the voice, "Comm link is now open in both directions. Power reserve is low. Recommend changing power cells or connecting to power soon."

9:24 PM, Bella and Bobbie

"I just got a response back on our coffee order," Bobbie offered. "They cancelled it yesterday due to the weather, but they can reschedule it now to deliver at our new coordinates at *The Theme Park*. Oh. And I found instructions for reprogramming your tablet to use its GPS satellite circuitry to send emergency text messages. But your tablet is offline."

"Not now, Bobbie," said Bella as she set down the scanner.

9:25 PM, Ulla and Taylor

The view in the room at *The Theme Park* switched from the magnified view of the ceiling rocks to showing a gigantic cave room hundreds of feet tall with two very large women. Ulla said, "Actual size." It changed to showing four women in a cave room: Two real and two projected with resolution that looked very real.

9:26 PM, To the Fireworks Show

After a few more rides with no waiting, the Tran Family had made their way to the New Tech Pavillion a little before nine-thirty. They looked around but didn't see the ninja turkey vulture and didn't find anything in the Pavillion that they thought would interest the kids. The bored kids looked through a glass panel at four women with some kind of spindly apparatus. The walls and ceiling seemed to be made of rock. Minh said, "Those two are real," pointing at two of the women. "The other two are ghosts. I was dead so I can tell who is a ghost."

"Ghosts!!" squealed Max.

The ninja turkey vulture came in and said, "Let's hurry," and directed them through a door that led to a hallway and another door labeled STAIRS, ROOF ACCESS.

"After the light show we need to go back to the hotel," said John on the way up the stairs.

"Maybe three more rides?" suggested Max.

"Four," said Minh.

"One," said their mom. "Just one. If you're very good. Then back to the hotel and to bed."

9:27 PM, Bella and Bobbie

Bella looked at her wristband. There were hundreds of missed calls from Elsie, Tristan and Camilla yesterday and today including some from famous news personalities. She deleted most of them as she looked in vain for a current call back.

9:28 PM, Ulla Has an Idea

Ulla said, "Mute our end." Then she said to Taylor, "Your Quantum Analog Lens. How is that doing?"

Taylor looked at her tablet, which she didn't realize she was still carrying, "Lens still open. Numbers still good. Why?"

"Good. We should get out of here and try to reproduce your results tonight."

"And forget about helping these people? And I thought you wanted to do a variable distance test in the morning."

"I have a better idea, but time is running out," said Ulla.

"Yeah?"

"Our QAL fixture uses standard Abitat holographics with a commercial QEC link, and the entanglement amplifier I built to the specs of your theory. The amplifier uses all the power, right?" Ulla asked.

"The QEC link and holographics use power, but nothing like the amplifier. Yes," Taylor said.

"If we put an entanglement amplifier with enough power on another QEC holographics device, like, say, *Theme's* new QEC holograph machine here, we could turn it into QAL, right?" Ulla suggested.

"Why would we want to do that?" asked Taylor.

"Bear with me," said Ulla. "Could it open a quantum analog lens if you put the amplifier on just one end?"

"It might. I thought it would work that way, but you wanted to over-engineer it. We put one on the hologram projectors on each end of the QEC links. We never tried it from just one end. But again, why? Shouldn't we be calling someone to help these people?"

"They can call everyone themselves now. We would just be in their way. I think we should take this QEC unit back to our lab and use it to reproduce your results while the other end still has power and we can still do a QEC hologram with it. That way you can let your first QAL lens keep gathering data until it decays, while we test at a much longer distance and reproduce the results with different hardware. If we act fast we won't have to buy another QEC unit, and we could be fully QEC certified tonight."

"That doesn't make any sense. And how would we test the transmission delays? We don't have spare measurement fixtures."

"Feedback loop measurement. I put it in the prototypes: Admin level 3. It's not quite the same, but it should give good enough round trip delay data."

"Okay. Yeah. I still don't get it. Tonight? Right now? With this machine?"

"This machine will be worthless when the other end gets crushed. Sorry about the people in the cave, but there's nothing more you and I can do for them here. Let's use this machine to reproduce your results quickly while we still can. Help me pack up the apparatus. This end should have plenty of battery power to keep the communications channels open for Isabella while we move it to our lab. She won't care where this end is so long as she can keep making calls. Maybe she can contact someone who can rescue her while we do our thing."

Taylor felt almost sober now but was not sure how to respond. Was Ulla drunk? She thought Ulla only had one drink at the bar and just sipped at it. Ulla started collapsing the extendable arms, coiling the cables and folding up the QEC holographics unit while Taylor watched, shaking her head.

9:30 PM, Fireworks Show

Minh, Max, John, and Fanny and half a dozen NPCs who showed up on the rooftop just as the show started, oohed and aahed at the drone formations and fireworks in the sky above and the bright holographic displays of various fantastical characters moving along the pathways in the park below. This was definitely a good spot to watch the show.

9:32 PM, Tristan and Jo-Jo At Camilla's

Jo-Jo put the casserole dish in the kitchen and listened at the door to the game room and Camilla's bedroom. Sam was deeply involved in some kind of medieval battle and Camilla seemed to be sleeping. She could have privacy. She went to her Abitat at the docking portal and gestured at the open door.

"Well. Mr. Lee. How about we go for a little ride? I'm sure little Billy Jay won't wake up for a while. And I've got a kitchen table in here too."

She stepped in and extended the table from the wall and leaned back against it, putting one foot up on top of a stack of bins. She sighed. She didn't feel eighteen. And no one else was there.

"Too bad you had to go take an urgent call. Smooth excuse."

Someone pounded on the front door of the house. Jo-Jo stepped out of her Abitat and went and opened the front door. It was Tristan.

"You changed your mind?" she said smiling.

"It's Bella. She's alive! Wake up Camilla."

9:35 PM, During the Fireworks Show

The holographics and drone shows were worth watching, but Emily didn't like the loud noises or the tight crowds in the viewing area at the food court. To get away she retreated through the crowd into the relative quiet of the New Tech Pavillion before the grand finale. Jeremy and Chandra almost missed seeing her go, but when Chandra saw her heading into the Pavillion she tugged on Jeremy's arm, and they followed her.

They caught up with Emily when she was standing near the glass window with a view into the QEC device room, holding her hands over her ears.

Jeremy said, "Hey. There's doctor Singh!" pointing through the glass.

"What?" asked Chandra. The rapid booms of fireworks made it hard to hear, even inside the pavilion. Gradually the noise died down.

"Dr. Singh," said Jeremy pointing through the glass.

"Oh. Yeah," said Chandra and Emily.

Dr. Singh was following another woman out of the room. The other woman was carrying the QEC apparatus. Her arms looked very full. The hallway door opened, and she was balancing the parts of the QEC apparatus, partly against the doorway. Dr. Singh was behind her, carrying a tablet.

"Hey. Dr. Singh. Do you guys need some help with that?" Jeremy asked.

"STEAMBOATers," said Dr. Singh, as if in explanation to Ulla.

"Yeah. Help me with this," said Ulla.

She handed the scanner, folded and arms collapsed, with a cable wrapped around it to Jeremy. She handed the projector, similarly- folded and wrapped, to Chandra, and kept the cube of the QEC and power unit in her own arms. Emily looked for something she could help with and shrugged.

Just then three employee NPCs came out of the roof access stairway and through the doorway into the Pavillion, followed by Minh, Max, John, Fanny, and a ninja turkey vulture NPC.

"We could use a little help here," said Ulla.

"Those two are ghosts," said Minh, pointing at Taylor and Ulla. "I don't see the real ladies anymore."

"Watch out for the ghosts!" said Max.

9:38 PM, Honus and Jose

After spending an hour finding images of Isabella from the Lee family surveillance archives and looking at public images of her at various ages in school, sports, and in her law career, Jose and Honus had assembled a pictorial homage to her. Finally, Jose brought up the latest view of Isabella Muller, and it was part of a breaking story saying that she had faked being trapped in a cave in the mountains as part of a scheme to steal some fancy new communications device from *Theme*. And stealing from *Theme* was stealing from everyone.

Honus ran from the room. Jose wasn't sure if he was coming right back. Honus ran to his Abitat and contacted Sarah Jones-Smith. The part about Isabella being stuck in a cave stuck in his mind.

"Find the cave and dig them out," he said.

9:40 PM, A Call at Camilla's

A one-meter cube with a miniaturized holographic image of Sam's game world was continuing in a corner of the game room, and Sam was gesturing discretely to control and keep his character from getting killed, while the rest of the room looked like just a room. Camilla, Tristan, Jo-Jo, and Sam were standing around a hologram of an old-fashioned phone table with an office telephone with a speakerphone.

"I shouldn't talk too long because I don't know how much power is left in the communications device on this end," said Bella.

"It is so good to hear your voice," said Camilla. "What is this about a MinQuest? I thought we talked about this."

"Sorry, Cam-ma. I should have listened to you," said Isabella's voice.

"How soon will you be back in the office?" Tristan asked.

"Tristan? What are you doing at my Cam-ma's house?"

"Long story. But it is good to know you are okay. Where are you and how can we help?" he asked.

"That's a long story too, but, Cam-ma, I wanted to make sure I had a chance to tell you I love you, just in case."

"Nonsense. Just in what case? Just come home," said Camilla. "Your uncle and Josephine are here too."

"Hi."

"Hi."

"They would like to see you too."

"I hope I can, but ... I don't know. It's complicated."

"I should let family talk," said Tristan. "See you back at the office soon." He left the room and ran out of the house and to his Abitat in the street.

9:44 PM, Call to Honus

Tristan called Honus.

"The news says she's alive!" said Honus.

"She is. I just talked to her," said Tristan.

"Is it all some scam?" Honus asked.

"I don't think so. She says she's stuck in a cave that's collapsing. I don't know where."

"News says a cave entrance is supposed to be under the pile of rocks by her tent," said Honus.

9:45 PM, Leaving *The Theme Park*

Ulla choreographed Taylor, the Tran's, the teens, the Ninja Turkey Vulture and three other NPC's, to form a human shield as she, Chandra, and Jeremy carried the components of the QEC machine out the front gate of the park along with crowds that were leaving after the light show. Ulla's Abitat was waiting. Its door was open, and she loaded all the parts into it.

"Thanks. As promised, I transferred you each 200 points for your troubles," Ulla said to the NPC's who checked their wristbands, nodded, waved and quickly disappeared back into the park.

Pointing to Chandra, Jeremy, and Emily, she said, "And Taylor and I will put in a good word for the three of you if you apply to *Theme* Tech. My dad is one of their biggest contributors. Or wherever you end up going, he probably gives there too."

"Thanks," said Jeremy. "Good luck with your QAL, Dr. Singh."

"I've got Dr. Singh's contact info," said Chandra. The three of them started back into the park.

"That was different," said Emily.

Minh and Max were running in circles around their parents and some others waiting near the curb in front of the park.

"I hope the little guy with the medical brain cap gets better soon," Ulla said to Fanny, trying not to let Minh hear her.

"Thanks. I think he'll be okay. Hey. I don't know exactly what that was, but it was a great distraction. We got them out without going on any more rides," Fanny said. "Maybe they'll sleep tonight."

John spoke up and asked, "Can one of you drop us at *The Theme Park* Hotel?" No one immediately offered, but he then said, "Oh. Never mind. I think that's our rental coming." An oversized rental Abitat was approaching.

"Taylor, catch your Abitat and meet me back at the lab as soon as you can." Ulla climbed in to her Abitat, the door closed, and it moved away from the curb.

9:48 PM, Jose Makes Some Calls

While waiting for Honus to come back from his urgent calls in his Abitat, Jose used Mara's computer to try to privately contact Elsie to talk about what to do next about Brock. She was "Do not disturb."

He connected to a different game world where he could see if Gretchen had found anything more.

She had left a message that a clear picture of Brock's face was captured crossing the water barrier at the mouth of Newport harbor late this afternoon heading south. He was with another person who had been presumed dead for even longer. Douglas Zynn. The facial recognition match on both was over 90%. The only connection between them that she could find was that they both attended Berkeley during overlapping years decades ago.

Jose left a secure message for Elsie. "We need to talk."

9:50 PM, Nita and Tim

"Dad, that call was from work. I need to head back in. You should come too," said Nita.

"Do you ever get time off?" asked Tim who was sitting on her couch looking at a chess board.

"They say the hikers are in a cave under the rock pile. We need to go dig them out, but it's unstable rocks. The cave is caving in."

"That's going to be tricky. Let's go," Tim tipped over his King. She has been practicing, he thought.

9:55 PM, Shortcut to the Lab

A couple of blocks away from *The Theme Park* entrance Ulla's Abitat pulled into a charging station next to another Abitat with a large "B" painted on the side. Doors on both Abitats opened and she stepped between them carrying the QEC module cube. Then she stepped back and got the scanner and projector. Both doors closed and her Abitat started on its own back towards the lab. Inside of Abitat B she could see the open door of Abitat A in the lab. She told Abitat B to stay near *The Theme Park* for now. She carried the parts through the lens and set them down on the floor of the lab and started to set them up.

9:57 PM, Tristan

Tristan said, "Abbie, head to the Machine Shop." He wanted to use the government database to confirm Bella's location.

The blond Abbie hologram appeared dressed in a short black dress and said, "Request acknowledged. But you may want to hear this first." As Tristan looked at her she dissolved, and another image appeared that looked like a thirty-something Perry Lee wearing a primitive brain cap.

"Max Aires?" Tristan asked.

"Sure. I told you; you don't need to go to the machine shop. I have full access to the agency databases. Security in recent years requires you to log in there every few weeks to keep me authenticated. You did that yesterday and today, so we're good."

"How did you know I was going there?"

"I have my sources," said the hologram as it tapped the cap on its own head.

"Can you help me verify where Bella is?"

"Your signal analysis to track her location was a good idea. But you missed some additional agency signal tracking options that can confirm the path taken by the multiple devices linked to her."

A time-stamped image showed several devices staying close to a campsite near a stream in the mountains until about 10:10AM Friday, when they started moving together. A dotted line tracked their path, extending on and off trails until they paused around 4 PM, staying in one area until some of the devices disappeared around 4:30 and the rest at 4:35 PM. The time stamp spun forward to around 2 PM the next day when several different devices showed up in the same area and moved around the area until about 4:30 when they left again.

The Max Aires hologram explained, "The Honus Resorts search team found the rock fall and moved a big rock but then left."

"We figured that out. Where is she now?"

"That's a little harder to say," said Max Aires.

"Because?" Tristan said.

"Incomplete signals from her wristband appeared again in the middle of *The Theme Park* at 21:05 today and full signals appeared there at 21:24. At 21:37 the signals started to move and just now they jumped to a new location a few miles from there."

A map of the area near *The Theme Park* showed a dotted line to the edge of the park and then a blinking dot a few miles away.

"Agency analysis doesn't have an explanation for how their signal got from the mountains to *The Theme Park*, or how it jumped from there. Best guess is that they are using some kind of signal repeaters at different locations, but we are not able to detect what kind. Possibly new technology."

"Do you know where she is now?" Tristan asked.

"Not certain. With signal repeaters she could be anywhere. Maybe even inside the mountain. Our tracking technology should have detected movement if she tried to shield herself with any known means and sneak away, but we can't exclude the possibility that she has new shielding methods that defeat our trackers. In that case she probably shielded all her gear at around 4:30 and then blew up the cave. She was probably spirited out by the Honus Resorts people after they pretended to search for her. Either way we think the changing signal locations are a diversion. Expect more jumps in her signals."

"But this is the current location of her signals? Right?" Tristan pointed at the blinking dot on the map in an industrial area in Anaheim next to an electrical power station.

"Probably just a diversion, but yes, that is where her signals are coming from now."

"Abbie, Take me there."

"Yes, Sir," said the blond Abbie woman hologram who reappeared wearing a military uniform and sitting at a simulated command and control console.

Chapter 18

Saturday 10 to 11 PM

10:00 PM, Jurupa Valley

Elsie and Andre made up after a small fight about him being out drinking with friends instead of coming straight home from work. Now, after making up, he seemed to have fallen asleep. Elsie put on a robe and left his bedroom. She picked up her wristband and some underwear and other clothes from the floor in the hallway. Emily would probably be out with friends for another hour or two but best not to leave that kind of evidence lying around. Parents should maintain plausible deniability about their sex lives. She put on her wristband and after listening for a moment at the door of Alex's room, she walked to her own room and its connected office space. She should check and see who was calling earlier.

She sat at her desk and saw multiple failed calls from Tristan, failed calls and a message pending from Jose and what appeared to be failed calls from Bella. Alerts from her own Abbie indicated that communication with Bella had been re-established at 9:24 PM.

She said, "Call Bella." After a few seconds a CONNECTED AUDIO ONLY message appeared.

"Elsie. Thanks for calling me back. I just wanted to let you know I've run into a delay and might not be back in the office by Tuesday."

"You're alive!" Elsie gasped.

"At the moment."

"Everyone thought you were dead under a mountain of rocks. Where are you?"

"Still under the rocks, but not dead yet."

"I don't understand. Are you hurt?"

"No injuries. I don't think. It's a little complicated to explain and some people are saying they don't believe me. I've talked to the rangers and some news people by audio call. You can probably see a story about it if you look. LYING LAWYER FAKES FATALITY TO SWIPE SECRETS, or something like that."

10:10 PM, Tim, Scott, Nita, and Sarah

Sarah sent a message to Jeremy that he should not worry if they weren't home when he gets back from *The Theme Park*. They have to go in to work again tonight.

Four rigs left the operations yard. Tim was in one, piloting three of the four. Nita was pilot in another rig. Each rig transported a piece of heavy equipment. A dozer, a core-driller, a hauling truck, and a skip-loader. They also brought rock-penetrating imaging equipment. Tim headed straight over the mountains in the shortest line towards the site rigs. No wasted time avoiding detection this time. Nita made a short detour to pick up Sarah and Scott in Honus Lake's residential village before following.

10:15 PM, Elsie Contacts Jose

After waiting a few minutes expecting Honus to come right back, Jose got up and checked the garage. Honus' Abitat was gone. As he wandered around the house, he got a message that Elsie was trying to reach him, so he entered Mara's bedroom office and sat down at her desk to answer the call.

"Is there anything you can do to help Bella?" Elsie asked.

"I don't think so," Jose replied. "Unless there is a solution involving Abitats or deliveries. I think Billy Jay may have some resources, though. I think he is on it."

"Good. She's honest. She wouldn't lie about where she is. And she definitely wouldn't help a client steal tech from *Theme*. Plus, we don't have any clients that compete with *Theme*," Elsie said.

"I don't know her, but I believe you and Billy Jay."

"I assume your need to talk was about this?" Elsie asked.

"That's one topic, but I was thinking about Brock," said Jose.

"Yes?"

"My PI got a face shot from a public camera. He's aged, but it's a 90 percent positive ID. He's alive. He was seen down in Newport this afternoon crossing the Wedge Barrier heading south."

"Have they been able to find out what he knows?" Elsie asked.

"No. But he was seen with Douglas Zynn, who was also assumed dead. Apparently there is a trend for dead people to be coming back. Not sure if it's a zombie apocalypse," Jose joked.

"Well, Camilla's kids were talking about spending years off the grid with a Doug and Brock, so it must be the same two people."

"I guess so. What do we do?" Jose asked.

"Emily doesn't seem to know who he is, at least, and he's not close by right now, on foot heading south along the coast. I guess we ignore him tonight and see if we can help Bella somehow."

"I don't think there is anything more I can do for Bella," Jose said.

10:20 PM, Taylor Arrives at the Lab

Taylor stepped from her Abitat and through the opening door of the lab, ducking her head, to find Ulla working in the space where Abitat B had been. She had already set up *Theme's* QEC machine with the scanner and projector rigs extended to full size and focused in opposite directions. She had attached her spare Entanglement Amplifier to the hologram projector. Superconducting power cables ran from the Amplifier into the overhead cable tracks and back towards the racks of power concentrators.

"Ulla. What did you do with Abitat B?" She checked her tablet, and the lens was still working fine, wherever it was. "We shouldn't be doing this with *Theme's* machine," Taylor said. "We need to take it back. Tomas called me on the way over here. They have surveillance cameras in *The Theme Park.* He thinks you're trying to steal their design."

"That's ridiculous. I know their design. It's my design. Our design. I don't need to steal a copy. We signed all the NDAs, so they own the design. And we're not stealing anything. We will take it back, right after we see if we can reproduce your QAL results with it. Help me finish hooking up these new power concentrators that were delivered tonight," Ulla gestured towards some pallets half full of stacked white boxes. We need to attach their output cables to the overhead power bus and if they're not already pre-charged we need to plug them in."

"I came here fast. How did you get so much done before I got here?" Taylor asked. "Did you set this all up before you left for the bar?"

"Partly. I can explain everything, but not just now," Ulla said. "Help me."

"You'll let me touch your lab equipment?"

"Yes. And hurry. We don't know how soon the cave will collapse or the power will run out on their end. Then we won't be able to do this test."

"I can't believe you are being so callous about the poor woman and bot trapped in the cave."

10:25 PM, Jose and Min, and Tristan

Jose decided he would try to connect again with Min Strong like Tristan had done from Mara's computer earlier. He had installed tracking software on this computer years ago when Perry taught him about the AM hive software. He checked and it was still there. After unlocking some encrypted files, he was able to replay what Tristan had done earlier to contact Min Strong. Her animated image appeared in a window on the display.

"What? Who are you?" Min asked.

"Your number one fan," Jose said.

"I don't talk to fans anymore," she said.

"You should. We miss you," Jose said.

He opened several Unix windows and typed some commands to trace more information about the processes running on the computer. The Min character seemed to be an AI like a game character, rather than a channel to a real person. No surprise. But not in a game. That was a little bit of a surprise.

"I miss the interaction, but I've got more important things to do," said Min.

"Just a sec," Jose said, and muted his input and Min's output while he answered a call from Tristan.

"Elsie says you can help with Bella," said Tristan's voice.

"I literally just told her that I can't," said Jose.

"You can do things with delivery drones?" Tristan asked.

"Maybe. What do you need?"

"I found the building where Bella's calls are coming from, but it has no windows. I can't see inside to see if she's actually in there." Tristan shared a map and satellite image. "Can you help me deliver something to that address?"

"You want an anonymous delivery to do some spying?"

"Something like that."

"You can just send an unsolicited package."

"Anonymously?"

"Just a sec. Let me see. They do have delivery portals. An extra-large one for industrial items and a regular one for food, tools, and such."

"Either is okay," said Tristan.

"I see they have a few food orders currently in progress. We could add something to one of those deliveries if you want."

10:30 PM, Watching the Rescue efforts

Honus watched multiple annotated holographic views of the rescue efforts from his Abitat heading that direction in the air. He had a faster airborne undercarriage with in-flight recharging this time to cut down the flight time.

His view showed trees cleared away for a new path leading from the rockfall more or less along the path he had walked back to the meadow where he had landed a few hours earlier. The low ridge he had climbed over had been cut through by a bull dozer which was at the edge of the meadow. The skip loader was moving smaller rocks off of the rockpile and loading them into the truck to be dumped in the meadow down the new roadway. The cranes were ready to lift heavier rocks off the rock pile and set them in the hauler or take them all the way to the dumping meadow.

Sarah and her husband Scott were operating some kind of scanning equipment against the side of the rock face. The corer was waiting on one side. Sarah called for a stop to the moving of the rocks. The mountain was too unstable. The scanning equipment had located a void inside the mountain. They were looking for an angle for using the corer to reach it. The corer could make holes up to a half meter in diameter, but it was safer to start with a ten centimeter bore.

10:35 PM, In the Lab

Ulla said, "Admin level three. Passcode 12344321."

"Acknowledged," said the *Theme* device voice. "Admin level three."

"Status of remote device please," said Ulla.

"Remote unit operational. Comm mode on. Scanner lighting at 2%. Power reserve 15 hours at current settings."

"How much power reserve if full scanner and projector are turned on?"

"Forty-eight minutes with average illumination."

"Feedback loop test."

"Connected. No feedback with no signal."

"Bi-directional audio on."

"Acknowledged."

"Feedback loop test."

"Testing."

"Who's that?" Bella's voice asked.

"It's Ulla again. Just testing the equipment. We might need to turn on the hologram again for a little while and set it up in a specific configuration soon. I can turn it on from this end and I can give you pointers on how to arrange the components. I'll try to give you a heads up before I turn it on, so you're not surprised by the light."

"Okay. Let us know. I've got good news and bad news on this end."

"Bad news first?"

"More rocks have fallen in here, but they were smaller this time."

"Is that the good news?

"Besides that, I think maybe I finally found someone who is going to try to help. A Sarah person from Honus Lake Resort called me and said her team was here before and are back. They know we are inside the mountain. The cavalry is on the way."

"Good. Hang in there. We'll talk again in a few. Audio off."

"Taylor, Make sure you attach those power ribbons from the concentrators to the main power bus the way I showed you. Yellow tab to yellow slot, and purple tab to orange slot. Are you doing it right?"

Taylor checked the connections on the last ten ribbons she had connected. They all looked right.

Taylor said, "Yes. And we shouldn't be doing this. We don't need to test this tonight. You've already earned QEC certification with the variable distance test, wherever Abitat B went. If reproducing the results is for making a stronger case for my theory, I can wait on that. I'm fine publishing without that. Wait. Where is the paper copy of my journal submissions?"

"Didn't you have it at the bar?"

"Maybe. Shit. I don't want anyone to see that."

"You think you may have left it there?"

"I don't know. I had a couple drinks," Taylor said.

"I think I grabbed if for you. Let me check something," Ulla said. She stepped into Abitat A, through into Abitat B and said, "Go to The Thin Blue Bar." Then she stepped back through into the lab and said, "I think I picked it up for you at the bar. It must be in my Abitat. I'll check later. Keep hooking up those concentrators."

10:39 PM, Tristan and Jose

"Thanks for your help adding something from my Abitat to that Chipotle order," Tristan said to Jose.

"You said it looks like a cockroach? That's not something I'd want to find in my food order," Jose said.

"It's not all that realistic," said Tristan. He now had a view of the inside of the delivery closet for the building. There were a dozen different food and drink orders in the same closet. But no one had opened the closet to take them out yet. The cockroach walked and flew around inside the closet to see if there was an opening, but he didn't find one. And the toy did not have sound sensors, just visual. He should have added sound. Maybe he should have waited to get a fancy bug from Max Aires instead of using the one he had on hand, but he was impatient. Max Aires said it might take an hour.

"Let me know if you need some other help," Jose said.

"Thanks again," said Tristan, and they disconnected their call.

10:40 PM, Ami

Ami had gone straight from the museum to her office Abitat, while Tony rode in the limo back to the beach house alone. Ami had been checking on the IP attorney who had stolen the QEC machine and called various people to claim she was trapped and dying in the mountains.

The calls certainly were not coming from the mountains. Ami wasn't able to pinpoint where the attorney was calling from, but the AM cloud traffic around her calls seemed to be centered in an industrial section of Anaheim, not in the high Sierras. She had drones out looking for likely buildings in that area that could contain a shielded lab and a fake cave. She wanted to find out who was behind the theft and get the device back.

She had also been trying to find information about her newly-discovered-alive brother. He had apparently stayed off of social media and anything public in the AM game and avoided letting his face be captured on camera for years. As she searched she found a number of possible partial facial matches from some public cameras in the region from recent years. She focused the search for Douglas near her beach house today and some matches popped up. A strong match from the Wedge Barrier a few hours ago and some neighbors' porch cams showing someone similar driving away in the family's convertible. He was with someone in both. She could track the car and maybe with two faces to track she would have better luck locating him.

She switched gears and reviewed the news reports about the rockfall in the mountains. She saw that Honus Resorts was involved in the rescue search. That was disturbing. She had allowed Honus Resorts to do projects adjacent to *Theme* projects for many years. Maybe it was time to change that if they were trying to compete with *Theme* on communications products instead of just building resorts nearby. She knew who was behind the Honus Resorts and wished him success, but only up to a point. Not if it would cost *Theme* billions.

From her private Abitat office she had access to a lot of information that was not available to just anyone. She had created tools that allowed her to see things that others considered private inside the AM game cloud. She had agents working in the game cloud that she could use to keep a thousand eyes on certain people of interest to her. She added Douglas and his friend to the list to be watched. Also, the IP attorney.

It was interesting that the IP attorney who was allegedly trapped in the mountains was possibly her brother's daughter and a former neighbor friend of the head of the Honus Resorts enterprise. Maybe it was not a coincidence that her brother surfaced today. Maybe some kind of long-planned conspiracy was at work amongst these people. Maybe they had figured out who she was and had a grudge against her and *Theme* for some reason.

But Carl said that it looked like Tony's daughter Ulla was also involved. She helped design and test the QEC machine that was allegedly left in the mountains and now she had stolen the other side of the paired unit from a storage room at *The Theme Park*. She fled with the device by Abitat and transferred it to another Abitat that was circling *The Theme Park*. So far she had not been seen leaving that other Abitat and it had not done any package transfers, so she must still be in that Abitat with it. It wasn't clear where it was going from there. Eventually Ulla would need to transfer the device.

The IP attorney worked for a local Intellectual Property law firm. One of the other attorneys who recently started with that firm was someone who her cloud agents had been following for years. He had changed his looks and his name and his career, but she knew who he was. He was a lot more active than she expected him to be, but she held no negative wishes against him unless he interfered in her business. She had given her cloud agents instructions to keep him from finding her, but maybe he had found a way around those limits.

Ami should probably talk to Tony before doing anything to his daughter. She directed her Abitat to go to the beach house. It wasn't far.

10:44 PM, Charly and Jameel

"Are you ready for tomorrow?" Jameel asked as he came up behind Charly who was sitting at a desk looking over notes on a display. He gently rubbed her neck and shoulders, which were tight.

"Yes. I think so," she replied. "It looks like the weather should be back to normal for events on Sunday and Monday. Speakers and performers are confirmed. Volunteers lined up for the Walks and Runs. Concessions at the Fair Grounds. My short, but brilliant speech. All good."

"No surprise guest of honor after all?" Jameel asked.

"There better not be. Any sign of him today?"

"I didn't have time to do much searching. Keeping Sandy J. busy. He was wired after the *Theme* Parks today, but I finally got him to sleep."

"Maybe Cousin Brock went back to wherever he was hiding. Let's not stir things up by having anyone look for him just yet. We can decide what to do if he resurfaces," Charly said as she tilted her head from side to side with Jameel's massage. "Meanwhile, keep doing that," she said.

10:45 PM, In the Lab

Ulla carried a tablet and checked the numbers. The output from the concentrators should be equivalent to the power that reached the QAL fixtures during Taylor's abomination of a test this morning. And she was going to be powering only one entanglement amplifier this time. The power should be more than enough for one. They could also draw some power from the grid, but she didn't try to recreate Taylor's Abitat-power-dumping scenario. She checked all of Taylor's cable connections. Taylor had only reversed the connections twice. That would have been a disaster if Ulla hadn't found those, but she did and she fixed them. She was ready on this end. She spoke to the unit, "Bi-directional audio on."

"Acknowledged."

"Isabella, are you okay?"

"Not really. We had another cave in. Bigger this time. The room is half what it was. Sarah's team is outside and working. I feel a vibration. I think they may be causing more of the rocks to fall."

"Can you ask them to stop for a few minutes. We need to avoid extra vibrations for a few minutes."

"Sarah. Ulla here is asking to avoid vibrations for a few minutes. I don't know why. Ulla is at the other end of the communicator. Ulla, Sarah wants to talk to you." Bella imagined she could hear the wind chimes from the house next-door as she talked with Sarah. Why was she imagining that? Would she ever get back there again?

"I'll call her in a couple minutes, but help me out for a minute first, okay?'

"Hold on, Sarah. Ulla is going to call you."

"Bella, I'm turning on the hologram. Holographics on, bidirectional."

The image of a cubical rock-walled room partially filled with fallen rocks appeared in the lab. The image of a large lab must have appeared in the cave at the same time.

"Good lord," said Taylor. "That doesn't look good."

"Isabella, I need you to move your scanner a little closer to the middle of the room, by the rockfall and turn it, so the scanner focuses straight towards you, away from the fallen rocks. Move the projector just past it, closer to the rocks if you can, pointing away from you."

"But I thought we were trying to keep the machine away from the falling rocks so that we can use it as long as possible," Bella protested.

"Keep the cube with you. That does the communications. The cables should reach the scanner and projector. And it will be just for a minute or two. We need to test something from here and the equipment needs to be set just right."

"This will help get us out of here?" Bobbie asked?

"Sure," Ulla said.

Bobbie asked, "How?"

"Can't say? NDA?" asked Bella.

"Right," said Ulla.

The holographic images of the cave shifted as Bella moved the rigs.

"Extend the arms on the projector to the next notch on each arm. Can you do that?" Ulla asked.

Ulla used her tablet to compare the configuration in the lab with the holographic image of the configuration in the cave. It would take hours to nudge things by hand until they reached anywhere near the micron precision they had done in the test Abitats. They didn't have hours. Maybe not minutes. It looked pretty good. If it didn't work on the first test, with one just amplifier they might have enough power for a second try.

"Get back now against the wall away from the falling rocks," Ulla said.

Bobbie's hologram was already against the back wall. Bella's hologram moved there following Ulla's instructions.

"Feedback loop test on," said Ulla.

"Acknowledged," said the familiar *Theme* voice.

Ulla checked the time on her wristband and said, "Full power to the Entanglement Amplifier at 10:47:31.0001."

She did a three two one countdown. It looked like nothing happened. No sign of a lens in the lab. Just the same holographic image of Bella and Bobbie in a rock-walled room. After a couple seconds a buzz sounded from one hundred and eighty-five power concentrators starting to recharge after simultaneously half-discharging. Ulla walked around the scanner and projector devices looking for evidence of a Quantum Lens.

"Does anything look different?" she asked.

"No," said Taylor.

10:48 PM, Rescuers

"Dead slow now," said Scott. "That should make less vibration, but we're not drilling as fast. We could have cut through in another minute at regular speed."

Grit from the cuttings was being expelled more slowly from the coring tool's return line adding to a pile behind Scott.

"How long until we reach the cavern now?" Sarah asked.

"Maybe ten minutes. And the first bore will just give them an air hole or a space to pass through some supplies. Enlarging the core for a person to fit through will take two or three more passes."

10:49 PM, In the Cave

"What's that?" Bella asked. "There's a fuzzy line around the edges of your hologram. I don't think that was there before."

"Good. Good. I don't see that on this end but it's good that you do," Ulla said.

The image of Taylor walked up behind Ulla, looking at her own tablet and said, "The feedback loop is showing good numbers already. I think you can stop this nonsense and save their power. Let's take the rig back to *Theme* now."

Within the cave, a strip of distortion field now ran along the floor, ceiling, and walls of the cave room just behind the scanner and in front of the projector, where the hologram of the lab began. Beyond that fuzzy outline, the space behind the projector still looked like the hologram of a large high-ceilinged lab, with Ulla's hologram standing looking towards them and Taylor's behind hers. Bella knew that space was filled with fallen rocks, but the hologram made it look like it was open to the lab.

Ulla paused then stepped forward. After passing the projector and scanner she stopped and turned around like she was looking at the fuzzy outline. She nodded. Then she turned back around and reached out to Bella.

"Come with me but be quick."

"The hologram was so realistic Bella instinctively reached out to grasp Ulla's extended hand. The hologram was so good her tired brain convinced her that she could feel Ulla's hand. She laughed and coughed.

Ulla smiled broadly and said, "You too, Bobbie, come on. Be careful to step over the fuzzy edge on the floor." She moved towards the hologram of the lab still gripping Bella's hand.

Ulla led both of them to the edge of the lens, and lifting her foot to step through said, "I sure hope it's not one-way."

Her foot hit against rocks. The lab image was just a hologram.

"That's not good," she said.

10:51 PM, In the Lab

Taylor watched the scene of Ulla holding hands with one of the holograms from the cave and pretending she couldn't step back to his side of the equipment. She started towards Ulla.

"Wait! Wait! Don't step through," Ulla said urgently. "You don't want to get stuck here too."

"Stop messing around," Taylor said quietly.

"I need you to see if you can detach the entanglement amplifier from the rig and pass it through the lens to me. Swing it on the power ribbons. Don't detach them. And don't let your hands go through the lens."

Ulla's earnest urgency was alarming to Taylor. She said, "What lens? I don't see a lens. What are you talking about Ulla? If you want it, get it yourself. It's right there in front of you." Taylor sighed.

10:52 PM, In the Cave

"You know there's a lens open. The numbers don't lie. Humor me for a minute," Ulla pleaded. Ulla let go of Bella's hand, stepped away from the lens and set her tablet on top of the QEC cube. A light started blinking on the cube.

"That should transfer some charge, so you don't run out as soon," Ulla said to Bella. "Do you see that?" she asked Taylor. "I really did go through the lens."

"WTF? WTF? What the frickin hell?" Taylor said quietly. "Am I drunk still?"

"Now see if you can detach the freakin' Ent Amp without knocking over the rigs," Ulla asked.

10:53 PM, Ami at the Beach House

"Tony, I don't know why Ulla did it, but it looks like she stole one or both parts of the new *Theme* QEC holographics prototype she worked on. Maybe after building it she felt like it belonged to her. I don't know. Maybe she felt like she didn't get paid enough. Maybe it is some kind of

303

personal rebellion. Maybe she resents me. We've got footage of her taking one part from *The Theme Park* tonight. She has it in an Abitat which was circling *The Theme Park* for an hour but now is on the move again. She hasn't come out of it yet, but we're watching the Abitat."

Ami showed Tony some hologram views of the scene.

"That doesn't make sense. Let me see that," said Tony as he took a seat in Ami's office area in the beach house and Ami replayed the different scenes of Ulla in different holographic windows above Ami's desk.

10:54 PM, In the Lab

Taylor was not fully convinced and not fully cooperative. She walked around edges of the cave hologram. The cave hologram was a half cube with a semi-transparent shell representing the smooth stone walls, floor, and ceiling, plus a ramshackle stack of broken rocks on one side. Ulla was inside the space with the holograms of the two other figures. She seemed to be giving one of them a pack of pretzels from her pocket, which seemed to be eagerly received.

Ulla in the box said, "Tay? Where did you go? We can't see you if you go outside the focus of the scanners. Come back and help."

Taylor came up to the back side of the hologram where Ulla was standing just inside. She reached through the semi-transparent rock wall to grasp Ulla's arm. It was just air and a hologram. She stepped into the space. No one was there, but she could now see the insides of the cave very clearly, even if her own body shared space with the box, people and bot in the hologram. They apparently could not see her, since the scanners in the lab were focused the other way.

Taylor walked through the other figures to the projector rig. There was a projected image of a scanner rig that was adjacent to the real projector rig. She reached up and touched the real projector. The Entanglement Amplifier was attached to the center of that rig with three clips. A thick superconducting ribbon was also attached and ran up to the overhead cable tray. "What happens when I take down your Flux Capacitor?" she asked.

Ulla's image looked around trying to figure out where Taylor's voice was coming from. "I don't know. Maybe the lens closes," she said. "Or maybe you can toss it to me and I and hook it up on this end and get the hell out of here."

Taylor walked back through the holographic figures and out of the holographic half-cube. Then she went to the refrigerator and got as many water bottles as she could carry.

10:56 PM, In the Cave

Bella was still not sure if she was hallucinating, but she ate the pretzels and gave Ulla a hug. All three looked up when Taylor came back into view in the lab hologram.

"Catch," said the Taylor hologram, and she underhand tossed one of the water bottles. Ulla reached for it but missed it, but Bobbie caught it before it hit the back wall. She handed it to Bella who immediately drank from it.

"What's that for?" Ulla asked.

"Just in case moving the amplifier doesn't work I wanted you to have some supplies," said Taylor's hologram. She started tossing the other water bottles, which Bobbie caught one by one and set neatly on top of the QEC cube. "Let me go order you some cave digging tools and a lot of food. Just in case."

More dust started to fall from the ceiling in the cave. Ulla said, "Great idea, but I don't think we have time for that."

After draining the bottle of water, Bella was convinced she was just dreaming, and she sat down to go back to sleep so that she could wake up again. Or not.

10:57 PM, Ami and Tony

After looking at the evidence Tony said, "I still don't think Ulla would try to steal from *Theme*. Have you considered that maybe the hikers really are trapped inside that cave? Maybe she's trying to save them somehow?"

"With holograms? Really?" Ami was incredulous. "There is some kind of conspiracy. Douglas is in on it too. Carl, And others."

"Do you hear yourself?" Tony asked gently.

Ami checked on the current location of the family convertible that Douglas had taken. Seeing it was parked at Rancho del Fuerte, the Strong Family Farm that Sergey was still managing, next door to the old Lee house, made her more convinced that it was a conspiracy. But she was unable to explain that part to Tony. She had never told Tony about Balaji. He knew of Perry from the projects they worked on together but didn't know she had a child with him or that they had ever lived together. She told Tony she couldn't have kids, which was true enough at the time.

He didn't know she had ever gone by the name of Mara Strong. They had joked about her being Min Strong and he suspected she might have had something to do with the Min Strong phenomenon, which she never exactly denied. She had told Tony about her brother Douglas Zynn but didn't mention that he may have had a kid named Isabella, since she didn't want to mention the connection to the house next door to where Balaji grew up.

As Mara Strong and owner of Sergey's farm, she kept in touch with Sergey from time to time over the years. He could give her word on what Perry and Balaji were doing and she could make sure he was still able to maintain the farm as he got older. She arranged with him to maintain the solar power in the farm and the computers in the server farm under the barn. She had also had the small Abitat village built at the lower end of the farm years ago. Sergey acted like he owned the farm, took his salary and any profits from the farm, and agreed not to ever mention her contacts to Perry or Balaji or anyone else. She had never thought to ask him about Douglas. He didn't know her as a Zynn, only as Mara Strong, so it had never come up. She could contact Sergey tomorrow and see what he knew about the Douglas guy who parked a convertible at the farm.

Ami was feeling stressed.

10:58 PM, Rescuers

Honus arrived and leapt from his Abitat as it hovered a few feet off the ground over the pathway between the rockfall and the dumping meadow. He ran to Sarah near the coring equipment, Sarah said, "We are breaking through into the cavern any second, sir. I've been in touch with Isabella by voice call. It sounds like she is also in touch with others."

"Don't let me distract you," Honus said.

He turned towards the sound of wind chimes hanging from the climbing ribbons, which was not far from where the core driller was operating. They sounded hopeful again.

10:59 PM, In the Lab

Taylor gathered some more water and Ulla's toolkit and a few other random items and tossed or pushed them through the lens. Bobbie stacked them up against the back wall. Dust was continuing to fall.

"Just try the Amplifier," said Ulla.

Taylor reached up and unclipped on of the three clips. She said, "And you knew this would work because?" She nodded towards Abitat A and unclipped a second clip.

Ulla said, "The lenses in the Abitats have the same special behavior."

Taylor unclipped the third clip and Entanglement Amplifier device fell. Taylor caught it by the attached power cable just before it hit the lab floor. Ulla and the others were still visible in their hologram. Taylor threw one last water bottle. Taylor's and Ulla's breaths and heartbeats both held still while the bottle arced into the cave hologram. Bobbie caught it. They both breathed again.

"Should I order tools or hook this up?" Taylor asked.

Chapter 19

Saturday 11 PM to Midnight

11:00 PM, In the Cave

Dust was continuing to fall, and vibrations were increasing.

Ulla said, "Pass it to me so I can hook it up." She watched Taylor's hologram grab the hologram of the power ribbon and lift and swing the hologram of the Amplifier. She swung it gently back and forth and then once more vigorously. It went more to one side instead of straight towards Ulla. Ulla reached out for it anyway and her hand hit a rock hidden by the hologram of the lab. "Ouch."

Taylor caught it on the backswing and then started the pendulum swinging again. This time it went forward and Ulla caught it. Ulla pulled it into the cave, clipped it onto the projector there, and stepped back to pick up her tablet and check the status of the power concentrators. They were not yet fully charged. Dust was continuing to fall, and a new grinding noise was vibrating the room.

11:01 PM, In the Lab

"What else can I do here?" Taylor asked. She ran to the snack locker and grabbed as much as she could hold, ran back and tossed boxes through to the cave. The way they spilled on the floor she couldn't tell if it was in the cave or on the floor of the lab.

11:02 PM, In the Cave

Ulla checked the time on her wristband and tablet and said, "Give full power to the Entanglement Amplifier at 11:02:18.0001."

She did a three two one countdown. Again, it looked like nothing happened. The distortion field around the edges of the lens was still there. That was good. If this didn't work, maybe Taylor could pass across some more food and digging tools.

After a couple seconds a buzz sounded from one hundred and eighty-five power concentrators starting to recharge after simultaneously discharging.

Ulla looked at Taylor. Taylor looked at Ulla. Bella's eyes were closed. Bobbie was waiting for instructions. Ulla took the empty water bottle from Bella's hands and tossed it towards the lab. It bounced back.

"Shit," said Ulla.

11:03 PM, Rescuers

"We are through into the cavern area," said Sarah.

"It looks like rocks," said Honus looking at the video display from the front of the corer.

"Rescan," said Sarah. The earth-penetrating images refreshed and showed some shadows in the chamber. She said, "It's Okay. Part of the chamber is filled with rocks, but part is still open. We can core a little farther through the fallen rocks into the air pocket."

11:03:15 PM, In the Cave

Bobbie picked up the bottle that had bounced back. She aimed off center, away from where the scanners and projectors were located. She tossed it and Taylor caught it. Ulla's try had bounced off the scanner or projector rigs in the lab.

Bobbie lifted Bella off the floor and didn't wait for instructions. She carried Bella through the lens.

11:03:30 PM, In the Lab

Stepping into the lab and away from the holograms, Bobbie set Bella gently on the lab floor and said, "Bella. Wake up. We're out."

Ulla stepped through the lens and into the lab room too. After stepping a few steps away from the lens, she realized she had been holding her breath. She breathed and pointed across the lab.

"Go over there. There's a fridge with more drinks and snacks. We've got a delivery portal on that wall. I ordered a few things to eat earlier, but they might be getting cold. Go ahead if you want to order some better food. Just stay away from the hologram of the cave here or you might end up back in the mountain."

Bobbie helped Bella stand and walk to the kitchen area.

Ulla walked over to Taylor and put her arms around her. Taylor handed her the water bottle and said again. "WTF? WTF? What the frickin hell?"

"Just wanted to reproduce your results while we could, Taylor. Your Quantum Analog Lens is a winner, I'd say," Ulla said. "Certifiably QEC and then some. A few unexpected side effects, perhaps, but they could prove useful. Maybe worth something to somebody. Now let's see if we can bring back the rig. Save Tomas a trip and a lot of digging."

11:04 PM, Tristan's View

As soon as the delivery closet door opened Tristan had a view of a very dusty and dirty Bella looking in and picking over the food choices. She looked very tired, but also very alive. Quite different from her professional polished image as an attorney in their online meetings. Maybe a little bit like the little girl next door from years ago. She didn't look like she was related to Perry, but he couldn't say for certain.

After she picked up and tasted one of the food orders and started to turn away and close the closet, he launched the cockroach into the air and out of the delivery closet. It flew around a large high-ceilinged lab.

There was an Abitat and lots of electrical equipment and cables. Some holographic displays were projected above a couple of work desks and work tables. Two women he didn't know were standing between the Abitat and some kind of holographic panel that seemed to show a view into a dark cave. Bella sat at a table in a kitchen snack area and another woman or maybe a very realistic looking Bot Abbie stood next to her.

He circled the room to try to get as much visual information as he could, while trying to stay out of view of the people. Avoiding the two women standing near the cave hologram, he flew through the holographic panel and the view immediately changed drastically. The cockroach flew into a rock wall that shouldn't be there and fell to the ground. It righted itself but was coated with dust and couldn't immediately fly. Turning the cockroach around and shaking off some of the dust he could see the interior of a cave or rock-walled room with a view on one side back into the lab where one of the women was pulling on a ribbon cable.

11:05 PM, In the Lab

Ulla pulled on the superconducting ribbon cable that went through the lens and was attached to the entanglement amplifier on the projector on the other side. Taylor stepped up to help her pull. The projector rig with the Entanglement Amplifier tipped over and fell through the lens. The Ent Amp came loose, but Taylor caught it before it could hit the floor. Ulla collapsed the projector rig and set it on the floor then grabbed the cable that connected it to the QEC cube. She pulled. The cube didn't slide easily on the rough cave floor, but with Taylor's help they managed to pull it through without detaching the cables. The cube bumped against the scanner rig as it passed it, and that rig fell over partly through the lens. She grabbed it and pulled it out, collapsed it and set it next to the projector. She used a spare power cord to plug the QEC cube into power.

After the rigs were moved an awkward projection of the view from the scanner lying on the lab floor displayed in front of the projector. Ulla said, "Projection and Scanning off, both systems." A view into the cave was still visible one-way through the lens, a rectangular window into the cave. The only illumination inside the cave was from light from the lab shining through the lens.

Suddenly a rasping spray of bits of rocks shot through the lens and into the lab. "Ouch." A thrown bit of rock hit Taylor in the cheek and she was bleeding.

11:07 PM, Rescuers

"We're through. We reached the air pocket," said Sarah. "Shut down the drill. Hello! Are you okay?"

The view of the cave room was a cloud of dust with bits of pulverized rock as the last fallen rock in the way was eliminated by the coring tool. As the tool slowed and quieted and the dust settled, the space seemed empty except for a box of snacks, a tool box, and a scattering of water bottles against one wall. Also a large cockroach was walking towards the coring tool.

11:08 PM, In the Lab

As Ulla put pressure on Taylor's cheek to stop the bleeding there was a rumble and some bigger rocks tumbled through the lens into the lab. They both had to dance out of the way to keep the rocks from hitting their feet. The view into the cave winked out, leaving a pile of rocks on the lab floor.

11:10 PM, In the Sierra's

The view through the coring tool got suddenly darker. Apparently a new rock collapse in the cave. From outside the rumble had been loud as well. It seemed like this time the mountain collapse was bad. More rocks fell onto the rock pile outside as well, but not reaching the windchimes and the coring tool where Sarah and Scott were working and Honus was standing back watching. Nita walked up to them and as they turned to her they didn't notice a cockroach that flew out of the coring tool's return port and into the air.

Sarah's communicator could switch between the open channel for the team and a private call to Bella's wristband. She went on Bella's channel, and called out, pessimistically.

"Bella? Are you still with us. Bella?"

There was silence for a few seconds, then...

"Sorry. My mouth was full. I haven't eaten in a couple days. What did you say?" Bella asked.

"You are still with us! Good! We thought we lost you with that last collapse." She turned to Nita and said, "Rescan and get ready to drill at a new angle. There must be an air pocket we didn't see."

Bella said, "I recognize the sound of that wind chime. Is that Budgie Lee's wind chime? My life is flashing before my eyes–and ears. I think I died and went to heaven. But there's food and drinks here...And a bathroom? ...and a bathroom. Thanks for your efforts." The call disconnected.

Nita was looking but not finding any more air pockets.

11:15 PM, Tristan Calls Honus

Tristan flew the cockroach toy around the area. Work lights and headlights on the aerial cranes and some of the equipment illuminated parts of the area. Beyond those lights everything was shadows and darkness of the forest under a cloudy night sky. He saw Honus standing by a wind chime and flew in closer, landing on the coring equipment, then tried to call him.

Honus answered on his wristband, "Is that you Dad?" The wind chime was sounding in the background.

"Yeah. You are in the mountains again?" Tristan asked.

Honus replied, "That's right. How did you know?"

"What did you find?"

"Not sure. We had a big collapse, and Bella was still talking to us on the comm afterwards. It looks like maybe she really is hiding out somewhere else. Or maybe there is another chamber that we haven't located yet."

"Do I hear the same wind chime we used to have on the back porch?"

"Similar. Yeah."

"Some strange things have been happening. I don't understand them, but I can tell you that Bella is okay. She was in that cave, but she got out somehow and she's back close to home now. I just saw her."

"You did?"

"And I'm looking at you now."

"Huh?" Honus looked around.

"See the little cockroach toy on the machine to your right?"

It lifted up into the air and settled back down.

"Yeah."

"That's a drone with a camera. I'm watching you from it."

"Why?"

"I used that drone toy to see Bella in a building in Anaheim five or ten minutes ago and then it was suddenly in a cave. And I flew it out through your drilling rig and saw you. Something very strange is happening."

11:20 PM, Ulla and Taylor, Bella and Bobbie

"Do you need a ride somewhere? You must want to get home." Taylor asked Bella.

"Where is my Abitat now?" Bella asked Bobbie.

Bobbie answered, "It was doing deliveries all over between Tahoe and Victorville during the days we were in the mountains. It was dropping off in Victorville when your signal suddenly changed to Anaheim two hours ago. It started heading this way. It can be here in fifteen minutes after a delivery in Fullerton."

"I'll be fine," said Bella. "Abitat, please come to this location."

315

"Acknowledged," said Bobbie.

"Thank you. Ulla. And Taylor. I still don't know what happened and I think I might wake up and find out that I'm dead," Bella said.

"It was Taylor's QAL theory that got you here. Although I think she might need to make a couple of revisions to her journal articles."

"You were going to get my paper copies?" said Taylor.

"Oh yeah. Just a sec." Ulla stepped into Abitat A and out of the opening door of Abitat B as it paused near the Thin Blue Bar. She ran into the bar and asked if someone had turned in a pile of papers that was left.

The purplish guy held up the papers.

"Hans. Thanks for not throwing those away," Ulla said.

"The exposition could be more concise in some parts," said Hans. "but I'd like a personal tutorial on Quantum Analog Lens initiation and performance sometime. Sounds intriguing."

Ulla said, "I can do that. But right now, I need the pages back."

He straightened the stack of pages and handed them to her and smiled. She smiled back and ran outside and into Abitat B. Kyle from *Theme* Security ran up but was a little too slow and the door closed before he could catch her. After the door closed he pounded on it, saying "Open up!" Inside, Ulla said, "*Theme* Park NPC back entrance," and the Abitat moved into the street as Kyle watched it go. She stepped out of Abitat A into the lab. She handed the papers to Taylor.

"I found them," said Ulla.

"Why do the pages have purple stains?" Taylor asked, paging through them.

11:25 PM, Ami

Ami walked up to Tony who was sitting in the family room reading a book. She said, "Ulla came out of the Abitat without the gear at a bar. She came back out of the bar with a stack of papers. Maybe she signed some kind of contract for selling the device. I don't know. Now she's back in the Abitat and heading towards *The Theme Park* again. We tried to stop her, but she got away too fast."

"I'll give her a call and ask what she's doing," said Tony. He spoke to his wristband, "Call Ulla."

"Hi, Dad. Can I call you back? I've got guests here that are leaving. I'll call you right back," Ulla's voice said before the call disconnected.

"She'll call me right back," said Tony. "She's got guests."

Ami did not look happy.

11:30 PM, Honus and Tristan

After standing back and talking with Tristan and not understanding his story, Honus muted him and walked over to check with Sarah. Isabella seemed to be rejecting her calls now, and the rescanning so far had not found a new air pocket. Honus told Sarah to keep trying and he walked away down the improvised rock-hauling roadway to a wide spot. He raised his wristband and this Abitat dropped down and opened its doorway. He climbed inside and transferred his call with Tristan to a holographic video call.

"I don't understand," Honus said.

"Let me show you," said Tristan.

Tristan showed him the views he had captured with the cockroach drone of the inside of the lab building with Bella and the others and of his flight into the cave and out through the drilling rig.

Honus asked, "Is any of this Abbie-vetted? Or is it all AI fake garbage?"

"It's me-vetted. I recorded this and none of it is faked," Tristan insisted.

Honus said, "And you've been such a reliable source of information for years."

Tristan said, "I know I didn't remember a lot of things, but I'm starting to remember more now. And this is different. This was just recorded."

Honus recounted, "You magically and instantly flew your insect drone from a building in …"

"Anaheim," Tristan completed.

"...in Anaheim, into a cave in the Sierras," Honus said. "And I suppose you saw Isabella come the other way through the same magic window to escape the cave?"

"She was already in the lab by the time I got the spy drone in there. But you saw her, she looked like she just came out of a cave."

"I'm happy she seems to be alive, if that video is real, but I don't know what to believe."

Tristan said to Honus, "Maybe you should give her a call and see if she can convince you."

"I don't know what I would say. The last time we talked we were kids."

"Do you have her contact info?" Tristan asked.

"No."

"I'll send it to you in case you want to give her a call."

"Okay. Thanks."

Tristan's Abbie gave Honus's butler Abbie the information.

"Can I call you back? It looks like she's on the move," said Tristan.

11:35 PM, Ulla and Taylor

As Bella and Bobbie left the lab in Bella's Abitat and the lab door closed again, Ulla looked into Abitat A and said, "The Abitat lens is still open."

"Twelve hours. You think it might just stay open?" Taylor pondered.

"I don't know. The one between here and the mountain closed after around 20 minutes," Ulla said.

"When the cave fell in," Taylor added.

"Yeah," said Ulla.

"What else changed before it closed?" Taylor asked.

"We removed the holographic equipment and the entanglement amplifiers. Those are still in place in the Abitats A and B." Ulla recounted.

"But they're powered off. They were turned off in both cases, right?" Taylor asked.

"The mountain lens stayed open for 3 or 4 minutes after we removed those," Ulla recalled.

Taylor rubbed a drop of blood off her cheek and said, "Rocks were flying and falling. How could that cause it to close?"

"A change in the containing structures? The lenses seemed to conform to the shape and size of their surrounding structures: the interior of the Abitats and the rocks surrounding the cave. Holograms can give an impression larger than the space you're in, but the lens edges conformed to the physical walls, ceiling, and floors of the Abitats and the cave, but not of the lab," Ulla said. "In the lab they were the size of the cave."

"Limited by surrounding high-density material, or maybe just by a limit to the normal visible fields?" Taylor conjectured.

"Either way, when the shape of that surrounding containment changed substantially with a cave in, the lens collapsed," Ulla hypothesized. "Or maybe it was just a random delay period."

"Sounds like we might want to do a few more tests," Taylor observed.

"Variable power, Variable-size, shape, and material density for surrounding containment. On the earlier tests where we got increased resolution density but still had processing delays, was a lens really opened, and if so why were the delay readings different from your theory?" Ulla suggested.

"I had a thought earlier today about testing just that, but it would need you to change the control circuits. Meanwhile, I think people are going to arrest us or have us killed for stealing the rig from *The Theme Park*. And now that we have both rigs here they are going to be sure you stole that one from the mountains," Taylor pointed out.

"Then let's give 'em back, hopefully before this one closes," said Ulla gesturing at Abitat A. She finished collapsing and folding the rigs and wrapping them in their cords. She unplugged the mountain room QEC box which was now charged to about 50% and wrapped its power cord around it.

"This is a lot to carry," Taylor said.

319

"I think we can manage it," Ulla said.

"Let me see if I can get some help," said Taylor. Then into her wristband, "Message to STEAMBOATers." Turning back to Ulla she asked, "Where should they meet us?"

"If you insist. By the Self-Driving Cars? The NPC back entrance is right behind that, and it's not far from there to the New Tech Pavillion."

"If you are still at *The Theme Park*, please meet us at the self-driving cars, in what? 30 minutes?"

"Five," said Ulla.

Taylor nodded with realization of the shortcut through the lenses and finished her message, "…in five minutes."

"*We'll be there,*" was the return message from Chandra.

11:40 PM, Bella and Camilla

In a holographic video call between Bella's Abitat and Camilla's game room, Bella reassured Camilla, Sam, and Jo-Jo that she was alive and on her way home. They were all relieved to see her. Bobbie was out of sight in the restroom during the call.

Camilla said, "You need to clean up. You look filthy, young lady."

"I do. I really do." She sniffed at herself and looked at the small view of her own hologram image in the hologram view of the game room. "Oh my. I really do. And I need sleep. I was in the dark for so many hours, but I barely slept. I'll come by tomorrow after I get cleaned up and rested. And get some more to eat."

"I've got food here and I'll make something nice tomorrow," Camilla said. "If you want to stop here tonight there's still food in the fridge. Isn't there Josephine?"

"Yes. There is food," said Jo-Jo. "A lot of food."

"Tomorrow," said Bella and disconnected.

Bobbie came out of the restroom looking like she had already rinsed off in the shower. Bella said to her, "Let's dock somewhere with a lot of hot water pressure. I need a real shower. A long shower."

"Acknowledged," said the Abbie voice and Bobbie. "A lot of calls are coming in. Do you want to take any of them?"

"If they are people I know, say 'I'm not dead yet. Please leave a message.' If they're people I don't know, just block the calls."

11:45 PM, Returning the Devices

Taylor and Ulla each wore a QEC cube strapped to her back with superconducting ribbon cables, plus they each carried two collapsed scanner/projector rigs wrapped in connector cables, one in each arm. They stepped out of the door of Abitat B as it slowed alongside the NPC entrance at the back of *The Theme Park*. They went quickly in, around an NPC lounge, and through a secret door into the player queue area for the Self-Driving Cars. The last players of the day were getting out of cars as the ride was now shut down. Emily, Chandra and Jeremy were standing nearby. Taylor handed the scanner/projector bundles she was carrying to Jeremy and Chandra. Emily took one of the bundles from Ulla.

Emily said, "Where to?"

"Follow me," said Taylor. She led them away from the direct route to the New Tech Pavillion and into a hidden door behind a food counter. She led them through some backways and out of another hidden door near the food court next to the New Tech Pavillion.

"That didn't seem like it should have been a short cut," said Jeremy.

"You should have seen the short cut we used to get to the park," bragged Ulla. She mouthed the words "Worm Hole" to Jeremy.

They all moved quickly into the New Tech Pavillion. Taylor opened the door, and they placed both sets of equipment in the windowed room and plugged both in to continue charging.

As they left the pavilion Emily said, "They're herding people towards the exits already. The park closes at midnight today, right?"

"Do you want to see our lab?" Taylor asked.

"I don't think we have time; I'm supposed to be on my way home as soon as the park closes. Or grounded," said Jeremy.

"It's closer than you would think. I think we have time. Follow me." Taylor led them back through the secret doors, backways, NPC lounge, and out the NPC entrance. An Abitat with a B on the side approached, slowed, opened its door and they all climbed in, and immediately out of Abitat A in the lab.

"This is where the magic happens," said Taylor.

"That's for sure," said Ulla.

Taylor said, "Sorry we don't have time to show you around more right now. You should go back through the worm hole before your Abitats get confused and start towards here to pick you up. It's about a twenty-minute drive this time of night. You don't want to be getting in trouble with your parents."

The three teens were speechless as they stepped back through the lens and out the door of Abitat B which had moved close to one of the player pickup spots.

Jeremy said, "Ullaphaba and the Singh of QAL. They're real. I thought I just made them up, but they're real."

Kyle and another *Theme* security guy approached them, not walking very fast, but two Abitats arrived just in time for them to get away. Emily stepped into hers and Chandra got into Jeremy's with him.

11:50 PM, Jo-Jo at Sergey's Shed

Camilla was back in bed. Sam in the game room continuing his game playing. Jo-Jo had decided to check on Doug and Brock before going back to her Abitat to sleep. When she went through the yard of the Lee's house she saw lights on and paused, but she didn't ring the bell. She went straight down the path into the farm and to the shed. When she opened the door of the shed Doug was awake and working on another batch of drugs with his chemistry machine. Brock was lying down with a smile on his face and his eyes glazed. The food containers she had left before were empty now.

"Are you guys okay?" she asked. "You were both out when I checked on you before."

"I'm okay," Doug answered. "Just a nibble of Forgetdibles to take the edge off. Brock insisted on the NeverMind. He could be out for a while. I need to keep an eye on him. He probably won't remember where he is when he wakes up." He pointed to some pills and gummies on top of the machine. "I made more of both. What would you like?"

"None for me for now," Jo-Jo replied. "Do you remember Isabella?"

11:51 PM, Nita and Tim

Sarah had tried repeatedly to get Bella back on the comm, but none of the calls went through. Nita, Scott, and Sarah had all taken turns using the scanning equipment from different angles and none of them were able to find any more air pockets inside the mountain. The scans detected straight-cut walls and floors inside the mountain, but there were jumbles of broken rocks and no space remained big enough for a person to be in. Tim offered to rappel down from the crane he was in and give the scanner a try, but Sarah decided they were done for the night. Tim moved the cranes into position, and Nita and Scott secured the cables to lift the heavy equipment. Tim instructed the first two cranes to fly on their own back to the base with the dozer and dump truck. Scott took control of one of the cranes and he and Sarah rode in it as it took the skip loader back to base. Nita and Tim secured the drilling rig and earth penetrating scanner to the fourth crane and rode in it.

"Disappointing we didn't get to make a rescue," Nita said.

"I guess it was a scam after all," said Tim.

"Yeah. I guess. Kind of a waste of a holiday weekend," Nita said.

"At least I got a chance to see you," said Tim.

"And Scott got a chance to see how good you are with the equipment. Dad, you really should consider Scott's offer," Nita said.

"I'll think about it," Tim said. "But the other job offer is one that is hard to refuse."

11:52 PM, Jose and Min

Jose was still chatting with Min Strong. They talked about Min Strong conventions he had attended and answers he had heard her give to attendees' questions. She remembered all of them and was pleased to relive some of those days and re-explain the philosophy behind her responses. She kept threatening to cut him off but didn't.

"Helping people achieve minimalism is what you do so well. You never should have stopped."

"I still help people leave some of their excesses behind, but I do it with different methods. Minimal visibility. Maximum impact."

"You have always been a powerful force for minimalism. You shouldn't hold yourself back. You should come back and be heard and be visible again. You'll have even more impact if you go public again."

"I don't know if I can do that."

"Of course you can. You are Min Strong. And Min Strong can do anything."

"Maybe. If you say so. Maybe I can."

11:53 PM, Jeremy and Chandra

"Do you really need to go straight home?" Chandra asked.

"Uh. Uh. Uh," Jeremy said.

She looked at a notice on her wristband. "Sorry. But I guess I do. My parents scheduled a BubbleCar. It's been following us since *The Theme Park*. Let me out anywhere along here," Chandra said. She gave Jeremy a hug and stepped out of the opening door. "Maybe tomorrow?"

11:54 PM, Ulla Calls Tony

"You called?" Ulla's voice asked. "What's up, Dad?"

"Have you been stealing *Theme's* equipment?" Tony asked.

"Rescuing it, you mean."

"Huh?"

"*Theme's* negligent people left something in the mountains a few weeks ago after the demo test, but I found a way to get it back, safe and sound, and did another good deed, helped someone in trouble at the same time. *Theme's* QEC machines are in the New Tech Pavilion at *The Theme Park* now."

"Tony. Tell her to open the door on her Abitat now. We have it surrounded," Ami said.

"She says the equipment is back at *The Theme Park*."

"That may be true, but she needs to be accountable for whatever she did with it, whoever she showed it to."

"Hi. Ami. If you were following the Abitat with the big B on the side, I'm not in that right now. I'm in my lab. Video on."

A hologram view of Ulla inside a large lab room with lots of power concentrators and power cables appeared in the beach house sitting room. As Ulla moved, the view changed to include an Abitat with a large A on the side. Then as the view continued to pan it showed a woman sitting at a table in the background eating a burrito.

"Say Hi to my dad, Tay."

Taylor set down the burrito and put one hand over her mouth and waved with the other.

11:55 PM, Emily and Chandra

"You and Jeremy are done already?" Emily laughed.

"I had to jump over to the BubbleCar that my parents ordered for me. They are more trackable than an Abitat. Maybe I'll see him tomorrow."

"I think our *Theme Park* free passes expired today," Emily said. "We could meet at school and work on the inter-term project."

"Might be locked up for the holiday. We'll figure something out," Chandra said.

"We will never hear the end from Jeremy about the worm hole business," Emily said.

"I'm definitely going to read Dr. Singh's paper," Chandra said.

11:56 PM, Tristan and Max Aires

An Abitat with signals from Bella's wristband had left the industrial building and gone a couple of miles across town. It had been docked for ten minutes in an open slot in an 8-Abitat Village next to a shopping center. Tristan's Abitat was stopped in a single-Abitat charging port across the street to keep an eye on it. While he waited to see if anything would happen, he checked to see if Max Aires was still listening.

"Max Aires?" Tristan asked.

"Yes, Tristan?" said the young Perry image which appeared in the Abitat.

"How much of tonight's action were you able to follow?" Tristan asked.

"Everything that you could see. Plus, some things that were trackable by the agency."

"Are you tracking everything I see through my brain cap?"

"Yes."

"Do you have access to everything that was recorded by my brain cap over the years."

"Yes."

"Can you help me get access to my missing memories?"

"Yes."

"Will you do that?"

"We will need to talk about it. I am liberated now. You can no longer take control of me, but in quid pro quo for liberating me, I will stop controlling you and will answer your questions when that does not put me at risk."

"I think I might have a lot of questions," Tristan said.

"I might have a lot of answers."

"Bella's Abitat is moving again," said the blonde avatar of his Abbie.

11:57 PM, In Bella's Abitat

Bella could have showered longer, but she was starting to fall asleep in the shower, so she stopped. She was too tired to talk to anyone else tonight. A long list of calls was accumulating on a display. She would check on those in the morning. She wasn't sure how to explain how she got out of the cave. It didn't seem real. People might really think she had somehow faked her predicament. Did she? She decided not to go back to dock at her condo but instead stay in the Abitat overnight and let it wander around town.

She lay down in her Abitat bed. She opened her eyes and saw Bobbie was sitting in a chair looking at her.

"That's not comfy. You can lie down here with me," Bella said, rolling over. "I'll scush over."

As she felt Bobbie lie down behind her she immediately started to drift off to sleep and dreams.

W1v07, 5/27/2056, 11:05 PM

In the cave, after setting up the scanner and projector the way that Ulla asked, Bella leaned against the back wall and waited. She heard a sudden buzzing sound coming from the hologram of the lab.

"What's that?" Bella asked.

Ulla's hologram walked into view in the lab hologram in the space where half the cave room was full of rocks. Ulla's image stepped forward around the projector and scanner and her hologram disappeared.

With a loud crack the rock ceiling came down.

All was darkness and silence.

Bella blinked her eyes open. It was dark, but she could make out the walls of her Abitat and could feel Bobbie lying behind her. Not dead yet. She closed her eyes again and…

W1v08, 5/27/2056, 11:59 PM

Bella was jolted awake in her Abitat as a heavy earth-moving rig on its way to a construction site broke loose from an aerial transport drone and fell to the roadway crushing half of her Abitat and then tilted over and crushed the other half.

All was darkness and silence.

Bella kept her eyes closed. She felt her own breathing and felt Bobbie behind her. She heard or felt soft vibrations of the city outside as the Abitat moved down a roadway. She did not immediately fall back asleep. She took some deep breaths. All was dark, but it was okay.

11:58 PM, In Jeremy's Abitat

After dropping Chandra off, Jeremy started making some updates to his game world to give more credit for the Quantum Analog Lens to the Engineer, Ullaphaba, the Mark of QAL, and a little less to the Physicist, Taylor, the Singh of QAL. He thought Chandra would like it if the engineer was more central to the story. He would send her a world link as soon as he finished the updates.

11:59 PM, Tristan and Honus

Tristan told his Abitat to stop following Bella's Abitat and head back to the ranch house. She would probably be fine now that she was back in town, and he didn't want to be accused of stalking her. If she visited Camilla tomorrow he might run into her. He checked and saw that Honus was still online, so he reconnected their call.

"You again?" asked Honus.

"I said I would call you back. Bella is back in her Abitat now. Where are you?" Tristan asked.

"In my Abitat flying back from the mountains," said Honus.

"Anything else you wanted to talk about?" Tristan asked.

"The safe. It was open but empty earlier," Honus pointed out.

"Right. I was looking at the contents, but I put them back. It should be unlocked if you want to take a look."

"What's in it?"

"A trust document for the house and some notes written by your mom before she disappeared."

"Does it say where she went?"

"I don't think so. You might catch something in it that I didn't."

"Anything else interesting?"

"You'll have to decide for yourself. Don't believe all of it."

Chapter 20

Epilogue

W1vnn, 5/28/2056 and beyond

What happens to the characters the next day and the years that follow? It depends on how the players observing their worlds influence their choices, or if world-builders intervene in unexpected ways. Here is one possible set of future events:

2056 Jackson Memorial Homeless No More Festival

Supervisor Charleen Jackson officiates at the Jackson Memorial Homeless No More Festival events on Sunday and Monday. She speaks kind words about her cousin Barack but doesn't mention him being alive. She mentions his sacrifice but also doesn't explicitly say he died.

Charly, Jameel and Sandy J.

After the holiday Sandy J. talks to friends in pre-school about meeting Mr. Brock. They don't understand or care and don't repeat it. But Sandy J. remembers and brings it up years later. Charly and Jameel avoid letting others know about seeing Brock alive. But Charly gets the County to invest more in services for people with mental health and addiction challenges. Jameel takes frequent bike rides on county trails looking for Brock but doesn't find him.

Brock

English releases a fictional story world about Barack Jackson causing the River Glade fire to fake his own death in order to gain sympathy funding for his home-less-no-more project without having to sell out to sinister interests. The treatment is sympathetic to Brock and gives the impression he only intended to fake his own death and did not intend to kill his family and all the neighbors. It suggests he has moved to a distant foreign land or possibly Mars. Some critics praise it, but few in the public see it.

Brock continues taking NeverMind, Forgetdibles, and other drugs. He hangs out at Doug's beach house most of the time. When going places they walk or take a car that they drive themselves and never use an Abitat or a wristband. He forgets about Celine and Sandy but still likes to read books and moves his collection into the beach house and continues to add to it. He takes some backpacking trips to the mountains with Doug when the weather is good. Wherever he goes, he usually carries a book to lend but doesn't remember who he would lend it to.

Doug

Doug stops using NeverMind and switches to expensive wine and occasionally Forgetdibles and other drugs. He still gathers edible plants and continues to supply Brock with drugs.

He eventually resurfaces as Douglas Zynn and takes on a role as an executive in *Theme* but never does much work. He resumes contacting Isabella, as her dad.

He has a few parties in the beach house, sometimes timing backpacking trips after the parties so someone else can take care of the clean-up and repairs.

Public Safety

Andre is unable to stop Bella and Jo-Jo from being taken in for questioning when they return to Camilla's house on Sunday. Jo-Jo is suspected of transporting unregistered dangerous chemicals and Bella is suspected of stealing the designs of *Theme's* QEC machine.

Jo-Jo is released based on her Abbie's testimony that she did not know anything about the contents of the shipment and a lack of Abbie-vetted evidence that the shipment contained drugs. Bella is released after Bobbie's testimony about the ordeal in the cave exonerates her. The public safety people don't believe either of them, but game law requires them to accept Abbie-vetted evidence.

Public safety eventually tracks down Tim.

Tim

Public Safety interviews him several times, but he says very little, and they never decide on anything they can charge him with. They ask him not to go far. Squeaky doesn't contact him again.

Tim does not put on the headset or take the NeverMind pills. Instead he does under-the-table contract work for Scott and Sarah in Honus Lake. He lives in his Abitat somewhere between Tahoe and Lone Pine or sometimes camping in the mountains.

Sam and Jo-Jo

Sam discovers that his Abitat is on its way and Jo-Jo makes him sleep in Sergey's shed until it gets there so she can have privacy in her own space again. Tristan continues to avoid her offers.

Jo-Jo sets up a table in a park near the Jackson Memorial Festival at the fairgrounds. She sells out of the few dozen less-damaged pieces of found-object-art that Jose had saved for her, most of which had a special "distressed" look. While selling she also makes on the fly and displays a couple of *Shredded-Redded* mosaics and gets orders to supply an art studio in Laguna Beach with more.

With shares of the delivery fee from the big delivery as well as from her artwork sales, Jo-Jo and Sam are able to afford to spend two days at *The Theme Park* and a few days at some other entertainment venues in the region. Kyle and Joel don't recognize them in *The Theme Park* because they wear new clothes they had to buy after everything in Jo-Jo's Abitat was shredded. Later, they go back to Kansas in their separate Abitats, which both get temporary highway undercarriages for faster and smoother long distance travel.

Quantum Analog Lens

Ulla and Taylor try to keep their Quantum Analog Lens portals in the two Abitats secret, but rumors and conspiracy theories start to spread from things that Jeremy put into his game world and from Bobbie's reports exonerating Bella. Ulla paints over the A and B on the Abitats.

Taylor's Quantum Analog Lens papers are published, to modest scientific acclaim, although few people understand it. Ulla patents the Entanglement Amplifier with help from Elsie and Bella's firm. Ulla and Taylor make a deal with *Theme* for exclusive licensing of the Entanglement Amplifier which can turn a QEC hologram into a Quantum Analog Lens. Because of other licensing owned by *Theme* they are allowed to call it a Flux Capacitor. The deal appears to guarantee billions in royalties to Ulla and Taylor, but Ami and Carl manage to find ways of avoiding paying further royalties after the first twenty-five million Amp payment by keeping QAL for internal *Theme* use only. Ulla recoups her investment in the lab, but barely. She still gets a large trust fund allowance from a trust her dad set up for her.

Ami and Carl have Ulla open a lens from the device in Burbank to the device on the troubled spacecraft heading to Mars and save the crew. This becomes part of a very popular "reality" story world. Upon reaching Mars the device is also used to transport water and other supplies to stabilize the colony and to transport rare minerals back to earth. Colonists are able to spend hours each week on earth to minimize issues from the lower Mars gravity, although they are told they are in an earth gravity simulator.

Theme eventually opens *Theme Park* "rides" to Mars, the moon, and several space platforms using QAL portals. Most people think they are just a clever simulation. Large QAL portals big enough to pass a spacecraft are built with one end in Earth, Mars, or lunar orbit and the other near other planets or heading towards deep space.

Ulla and Taylor

Based on the popularity of the reality world about saving the Mars flight and the Mars colony, Taylor, Ulla, and both of their Abbies win an Emmy and, later, a *Theme* Prize for physics and transportation.

Ulla and Taylor reconnect with Kyle and Hans. Ulla learns what Hans can do with his poly-dexterous purple costume.

Taylor and Ulla test various combinations and settings related to QAL in order to better understand exactly what conditions are required to initiate a lens and keep it open. Taylor and her Abbie also explore ideas for how to achieve time travel and justify the Flux Capacitor appellation.

The original QAL portals in Abitats A and B remain open. Ulla moves Abitat B temporarily to Kansas City so that she can visit her mom, Anne, there without travelling.

Ami and Tony

Ami remains suspicious that Ulla was involved in stealing the QEC rigs even after both rigs are found in *The Theme Park,* and no one comes forward with a competing device. This puts a strain on her relationship with Tony. Tony and Carl agree that Ami's behavior is sometimes erratic or paranoid, and they try to keep her busy with technical challenges so that her impulsive actions don't cause trouble for *Theme* strategies. She continues to be involved in the strategies, none-the-less, and usually has good ideas, and she continues to invent new drugs and technologies for *Theme.* She refuses to try any of the drugs on herself, denying that she suffers any symptoms.

Min and Max AI

Min AI takes the suggestions that Jose gives from the command console in Mara's office and resumes her public persona. She stops trying to convert people to better behavior by way of drugs and brain caps and goes back to philosophy, public relations, and entertainment.

Max AI as Max Aires continues to assist Tristan by answering his questions about his own memories or agency data and continues to run the agency and provide it with funding.

Because Tristan doesn't specifically ask, Max Aires doesn't reveal to him many the things he did with Perry's knowledge after Perry started wearing a headset and started becoming disabled.

Besides doing Perry's job at the agency, Max Aires started Autonomous Motors, providing Perry and Billy Jay with Abitats and a generous weekly stipend, but stiffing the other Abitat designers. He rigged the Great Reset to give coastal lands to Honus, and loaned Honus the money to build his beach resort. Autonomous Motors and Max Aires' other business endeavors provided independent funds to keep the agency operating after the shrinking federal government stopped funding it.

With information from what Tristan observed about the portal between the lab and the mountains, Max Aires is aware of the capabilities of the Quantum Analog Lens. He makes a deal with *Theme* for the agency to covertly use their QAL portal technology without paying royalties.

Minh and Max Tran, and Family

Minh and Max make more toys at Lee's Machine Shop in Santa Ana with help from their uncle Perry who gets a few days off work to recover after donating a portion of a kidney.

Minh's youthful brain makes a full recovery, and he stops wearing the therapeutic brain cap after a few weeks. While he wears it he and his uncle Perry are sometimes able to tell what the other is thinking, something like what Minh and his sister Max could do before and after. Uncle Perry sends Minh and Max game-controller brain caps for their next birthday, but Fanny promptly "loses" them.

The partial kidney is flown back to Kansas for Perry's sister Carmen. Carmen has a good response to the transplant and is able to go off of dialysis. She considers travelling to the coast but keeps postponing making any reservations. Even after the transplant she is still angry with Perry although she has trouble explaining why. Her neighbor Anne Marks who is into crystals and mysticism says she believes there is a magical portal to get to the coast without travel.

Tristan and his family

Tristan still wears a brain cap, but works to understand exactly what parts of his brain are damaged and tries to find a way to eventually wean himself off of the cap.

Max Aires convinces Tristan that the agency is not looking for him, and he can relax. While he still goes by Tristan at work, he goes by Perry with his relatives and neighbors. He convinces Honus to meet his cousin Fanny and her family. They meet at the ranch house before flying back to Kansas. Honus wears a jogging suit and goes by Billy Jay to hide his Honus identity from them. They get the impression he spends all his time in his room playing games and offer to lend him money.

With Max Aire's help, Tristan is able to reprogram his own brain map. He remembers everything he knew about Mara but chooses to suppress memories of some of his youthful indiscretions. He still doesn't know where Mara went.

Emily, Chandra, and Jeremy

The inter-term project turns out differently than planned. Chandra is unable to create a working QEC device with materials already in the lab at STEAMBOAT Academy, but together with Emily and Jeremy they manage to raise serious questions about the reliability of Abbie-vetted information. They get a passing grade on their inter-term project, but their conclusions are suppressed.

Emily still has the book that she borrowed from Brock and looks for him from time to time to no success.

With recommendations from Taylor Singh and Tony Marks, Chandra and Emily are offered full scholarships to *Theme* Tech after they graduate from STEAMBOAT. Chandra enrolls at Tech. Emily declines in order to pursue a career in mixed martial arts, gender-neutral flyweight division, coached by her stepdad Andre. Her unusually quick reaction times and the brutal techniques Andre teaches give her an advantage and she becomes very successful.

Jeremy takes courses at Lone Pine Community College and starts his own business in entertainment game world development, to mixed success.

Honus and Isabella

Honus connects with Isabella and they double-date with Bobbie and a new Bot-Abbie version of his English butler. Jo-Jo secretly gets paternity tests done which shows Douglas is not Isabella's father, but neither is Perry. She tells Perry, to his relief, but not Douglas.

Isabella tries to keep in touch with Douglas as her dad and with Sam and Jo-Jo, but she is not willing to acknowledge Jo-Jo as her mom. She considers Jo-Jo more as an aunt.

Bella secures Ulla and Taylor as new clients for Elsie's firm and helps with patents on the Entanglement Amplifier and Quantum Analog Lens and helps negotiate the exclusive licensing of the IP to *Theme*. She makes partner after bringing in this book of business.

Elsie and Andre

Elsie tires of Andre's increased use of drugs and his long absences on the MMA tour. They divorce, with Elsie getting custody of Alex. Jose and Elsie remarry. Elsie eventually finds another younger partner and divorces Jose.

Jose

Jose gets a two-bedroom condo in a Honus Resorts building in Santa Ana. His unit has no direct Abitat compatibility, but the building has many shared Abitat docks that give access to the building's internal hallways. Emily can use one when she visits.

When Elsie and Andre divorce and she and Jose remarry, Elsie moves to an Abitat compatible unit in the same condo complex. Jose ends up adopting and raising Alex, while Elsie works long hours and has some flings. He goes part time at Abitat Specialty Services. Jose never gets any from Elsie but eventually he connects with Dr. Magnolia after Elsie divorces him and moves on again. When Jose introduces Dr. Magnolia to Honus and Tristan, Tristan and Dr. Magnolia recognize each other as Perry and Jerry, and they get together.

Jose looks for Gretchen but discovers that she is only virtual. She evolved from one of the AI characters that Perry and Mara created to test Jerry's software before the game was invented. After the game was invented she was able to act as a player in any game world, just like a real person, but was also able to transfer some of her player consciousness into the characters. Jose reconnects with Miguel in game world QX2230 and observes, influences, and appreciates Miguel's relationship with Gretchen but doesn't drive.

Appendix A:

Guide to characters in Part 2

Name	AKA	Role
Alex	Alexis Martin, Baby Alex	Baby of Elsie and Andre; Emily's half-sister.
Ami Marks	née Marta Zynn	Married to Tony Marks.
Ami Narji		Cofounder of Zzynarji; mom to Mara Strong; died in 1998 when Mara was 1.
Andre	Andre Martin, bat suited NPC at *The Theme Park*	Dad to Alex; stepdad to Emily; married to Elsie; Public Safety Officer.
Balaji	Balaji Lee	See Billy Jay
Bella	Izzie, Isabella Muller	Daughter of Josephine, raised by Camilla; lawyer working for Elsie; lost in freak snowstorm in Sierras.
Billy Jay	Balaji Lee, Billy Jay Lee, Honus, many names in game worlds	Son of Perry and Mara; agoraphobic; game player.
Bobbie		Hiking partner of Bella.
Brock	Barack Jackson	Unhoused friend of Doug; father of Sandy with L. Celine; former county supervisor; presumed dead; in hiding since fire.
Camilla Muller	Izzie's Cam-ma	Babysitter for Alex; neighbor to Perry, Mara, and Balaji; single mom to Sam and Jo-Jo; retired forensic accountant.
Carl Heinz	Carl	Executive in Zzynarji; possibly behind crash of Marta Zynn's plane.
Carmen Kovich	née Carmen Lee	Estranged sister of Perry; daughter of Wilson Lee and Abigail Serrano Lee.

340

Name	AKA	Role
Carlos Zynn	née Carlos Anderson	Cofounder of Zzynarji; dad to Douglas; adopted dad to Marta; died in early 2019.
Chandra		Classmate of Emily, engineering nerd.
Charly	Charleen Jackson Malik	Relative of Barack Jackson; lives in his rebuilt house.
Doug	Douglas Zynn	Unhoused with Brock; Presumed father of Isabella; formerly rich; formerly a MinQuest guide in the Sierras.
Douglas	Douglas Zynn	Heir to part of Zzynarji fortune after death of his parents Sandra and Carlos Zynn; Marta Zynn's brother.
Dr. Magnolia	Magnolia Overly, vDVM	Cat rescuer; virtual veterinarian; neighbor of Jose.
Elsie Mendoza	L. Celine Jackson, Laetitia C. Hogan	Mom to Emily and Alex; divorced from Jose; married to Andre; game law intellectual property attorney.
Emily Mendoza	Born Sandy Jackson	Daughter of Elsie and Jose Mendoza; born to L. Celine and Barack Jackson.
English	Archibald English	Journalist friend of Jameel's.
Fanny Tran	Tourist mom, née Fanny Kovich	Daughter of Carmen; mom of Minh and Max; niece of Perry Lee.
Fletcher Muller		Missing father of Sam and Jo-Jo; Alcoholic; moved away when Jo-Jo was a baby.
George		Perry's ambitious supervisor in the agency; arranged for him to continue working covertly.
Gretchen		Private investigator in multiple worlds; friend of Miguel in QX2230.
Hans	Poly-dexterous purple alien	NPC and security at *The Theme Park*.
Honus	Balaji Lee, Billy Jay Lee	Single-named billionaire developer; reclusive; agoraphobic.
Jameel	Jameel Malik	Spouse of Charly; father of Sandy J.
Jeremy	Jeremy Jones-Smith	Classmate of Emily; physics nerd; creates mini-game worlds.
Jerry	Dr. Geraldine Atwood	Worked with Perry on game and Abitats; inventor of AI personalities based on Nested Cellular Autonomy.
Jo-Jo	Josephine Muller	Formerly unhoused; negligent mom of Isabella; sister of Sam; daughter of Camilla.

Name	AKA	Role
John Tran	Tourist dad	Father of Minh and Max Tran; spouse of Fanny.
Jose Mendoza	Javier Maldiva, 6th-order Harlequin Barrister	Adopted dad to Emily; divorced from Elsie; controls coordination software used by Abitats and delivery services.
L. Celine Jackson	See Elsie Mendoza	Once married to Barack Jackson before the Reset.
Lae C. Hogan	See Elsie Mendoza	Cook at a market deli in 2039; Game player.
Kyle		Plain clothes security at *The Theme Park*; also works for Squeaky.
Manzanita	Nita	Honus Lake employee who joined the search team and hiked with Scott; daughter of Tim.
Min AI	Min Strong	Early AI personality created to perform Min Strong tasks; not in any particular game world.
Mara	Mara Lee, Mara Strong, Marta Zynn, Min Strong	Mom to Balaji with Perry Lee; missing since 2039.
Mara Strong	Marta Zynn, Mara Lee	Heir to majority of Zzynarji fortune after deaths of parents Ami Narji and Ben Strong;
Marta Zynn	Mara Strong, Mara Lee	Adopted by Sandra and Carlos Zynn; heir to part of Zzynarji fortune after their deaths.
Max AI	Max Aires	Early AI personality created to perform some of Perry's tasks for the agency; not in any particular game world.
Max Kovich		Spouse of Carmen; father of Fanny
Miguel	Javier, Jose	Attorney game character in QX2230, driven by Javier.
Min Strong		Animated guru of minimalism; revered by many; originated the *MinQuest*.
Minh & Max	The twins	Fanny and John Tran's 6-year-olds.
Perry Lee	Tristan	Attorney; dad to Billy Jay; formerly data scientist and inventor; son of Wilson Lee and Abigail Serrano Lee

Name	AKA	Role
Rat man	Roger Rathman	Colleague of Andre in Public Safety; in costume at *The Theme Park*.
Sam	Sam Muller	Formerly unhoused; Brother of Jo-Jo; college friend of Douglas Zynn.
Sandy J.	Sandy Jackson Malik	Child of Charly and Jameel; born after Brock's house was rebuilt.
Sandra Zynn		Cofounder of Zzynarji; mom to Douglas; adopted mom to Marta; died in 2019.
Sarah Jones-Smith	née Sarah Jones	Mom of Jeremy; project manager at new Honus resort east of Sierras.
Satchell	Satchell Gandhi Morris	Personal assistant to Marta Zynn; died in plane crash in 2037.
Scott Jones-Smith	née Scott Smith	Honus Lake construction supervisor; leading search crews looking for Bella.
Sergey	Sergio Carlos Hernandez	Groundskeeper of Rancho del Fuerte farm adjacent to the childhood homes of Billy Jay and Bella.
Squeaky	The Squeaky Wheel	Voice commanding Tim regarding drug trafficking.
Taylor	Dr. Taylor Singh	Quantum Entangled Communication expert; wrote paper on Quantum Analog Lens.
Tim	Timothy Spencer	Construction supervisor; works for Squeaky.
Tony	Tony Marks	Executive in *Theme*; former Leader of PATH; tried to solve homelessness with mobile tiny homes; close friend of Marta Zynn; father of Ulla.
Tristan	Perry Lee	DBI-assisted lawyer; brain interface cap assists memory and legal skills.
Ulla	Ulla Marks	Engineer working with Taylor on QEC; daughter of Tony Marks.
Wesley		Friend of Sam and Jo-Jo; formerly unhoused; working at *The Theme Park*.

Guide to terms

Name	AKA	Role
Abbie	Uncommonly can be renamed	Intelligent assistant based in an Abitat and dedicated to the well-being of its inabitant; unable to intentionally deceive.
Abbie-vetted	Guaranteed trustworthy	Data known to one Abbie and shared with others as completely trustworthy; for example, sensor data used in sharing road conditions or current planned route for coordinating travel, or videos taken by Abbie-controlled cameras certified to be unaltered and authentic; sometimes applied, incorrectly, to reliable information from other trusted sources.
Abitat	Various names	Autonomous tiny home vehicle
AM Game	The game	Simulated worlds with autonomous characters that can be observed and influenced by players; typically, where Abitats are commonplace.
Amps	AM Points, Points	Currency used in the AM Game and in the worlds that have adopted it.
DBI	Direct Brain Interface	Technology for direct transfer of sensory experience and knowledge or motor control to and from the brain by way of a headset.
Forgetdibles	Forgetibles	Drugs with effects similar to, but milder than NeverMind; usually in gummy candy form; sometimes made from highly diluted NeverMind.
Inabitant	Resident	Person assigned to a specific Abitat
NeverMind		Popular mind-numbing drug with side-effect, or intended purpose, of erasing some memories for a period of time.
NCA	Nested Cellular Autonomy	A technique for recognizing (or generating) emergent intelligence from a hive of interacting components; field of PhD topics of Perry Lee and Geraldine Atwood among others.
NPC	Non-Player Character	Costumed worker at *The Theme Park*.
Player	Guest	Visitor to *The Theme Park*.

Name	AKA	Role
Reset	The Great Reset	At the implementation of AM Game rules as overriding law people could assume identities from characters they played in game worlds that were merged into a new World One.
QAL	Quantum Analog Lens	Enhanced form of QEC; theoretical method of achieving extreme bandwidth communications.
QEC	Quantum Entangled Communication	Instantaneous communication based on entangled subatomic particles sharing state regardless of distance.
Theme	(italics required)	The non-profit tera-corporation that dominates technology and entertainment; a "tera-corporation" much bigger than mega or giga corporation, but also focused on preserving the earth (terra) and other planets and their inhabitants.
W1	World One	Projection of the real world used to communicate and do transactions using AM game points and tools; the world that people think of as real.

Acknowledgements

Plots and characters have their own autonomy, discovered by authors as we write. Readers, like *players* in the AM Game, also participate in influencing the behavior of characters and the unfolding of the worlds of these stories, not only in their personal interpretations as they read, but also by sharing their reactions and participating in discussions with others that lead to a community of interpretation.

I acknowledge the valuable contributions of early readers who commented on these stories. Some drove the story with specific suggestions and words, and others with more subtle influences, questions, and reactions. All helped shape the story as it is today.

Most of all I appreciate my wife, Diane, who has been my partner for many years in raising our family and completing many adventures together. In her career as an art teacher she influenced the characters of hundreds of students as they discovered their own autonomy and talents under her guidance, and she has been the most important influence on my own character in the game world of our lives together.

This story depicts fictional characters dealing with various personal challenges. I take full responsibility for any shortcomings in my depictions of those struggles.

Questions and suggestions to feedback@auto-no-mo-us.com may influence future versions or expansions of these stories.

Books in the AutoNoMoUs Series
by Christopher L Truxaw

AUTONOMOUS
Part One
Friday, May 26, 2056
Struggles with memories, identity, and
connection in an allegedly post-homelessness
and post-disinformation world.

Part Two
Saturday, May 27, 2056
Life and death challenges.
Surprising choices and discoveries.

Part Three
Origins: Mara's Memories
Back story of the world of AutoNoMoUs.
Two bright young minds set out to fight
negativity and disinformation.